# OLIVIA

For The Love Of Money

## A True Story

**Written By:**

**Jerri L. Smith**

ISBN: 0-7596-5263-5 (E-book)
ISBN: 0-7596-5264-3 (Paperback)

This book is printed on acid free paper.

1stBooks - rev. 07/17/02

## Dedication

This work is dedicated to Al Baker, my loving mother Ms. Barbara L. Smith, Betty Looney, my brother and sisters and all of my relatives, for their encouragement, support and unconditional love.

Also dedicated to teenagers, runaways, drug users and addicts and ladies and children of the night who are lost and turned out. To the spinal cord injured. May you all be inspired.

Special thanks to my Lord and Savior Jesus Christ, Al Baker, my nieces Shakedra D. Easterwood and Erika N. Gibbs, my sister Linda (Sue) Richardson and son Benjamin (B.Rich) Richardson, Gayle Johnson of Kansas City and Kathy Hollaway of San Antonio, for their input, assistance and encouragement and to Heather at Kinko's in San Antonio, for her assistance and graphic skills.

She was just a small girl growing up in a house that overlooked the projects (low income housing) and was right next door to a bar or nightclub. Olivia was in a neighborhood that was, unknowingly, molding her and schooling her for streetlife. Olivia's mom, Sara, taught her right from wrong and good from bad, but somehow, Olivia was curious and even fascinated with things that had a dark side or that trouble could stem from.

Olivia was shapely, even as a young girl. Some of her relatives would sometimes tease her by calling her, "duck butt". Olivia had pretty white teeth and a beautiful wide smile that her adult relatives and her mom's friends referred to as a million dollar smile. Sara would just smile proudly and say, "that's a cheap smile". Olivia didn't know what that meant until she got older. She smiled all the time though. Olivia was a dancer too. Her mom enjoyed entertaining guest on Friday and Saturday nights. Sometimes she would pile Olivia and her other children into the car and go to one of her sisters' home or to a close friend's home to party. From the gatherings Sara had at her home or took her children to, Olivia and her siblings would sometimes watch the adults drink alcoholic beverages and party. Often times, one of the adults would have one of the children bring him or her a beer from the refrigerator. From time-to-time, one of the children would sneak a beer out the back door and share it with the other children. Olivia was always the first to be affected by the beer she drank. It made her sleepy, while the other children seemed to have more fun once the beer took affect. Frequently when the adults partied, Sara called her children into the living room where the party was and had them dance. While partying, the children taught the adults some of the latest dances. Sometimes the adults taught the children dances. Being that Olivia was the youngest of the seven children Sara had, she was coaxed into dancing most of all because everyone thought she was so cute and got a kick out of watching her dance. One dance in particular she did really well was The Dog. The Dog dance was a raunchy dance. It was seductive, provocative and everything a child Olivia's age shouldn't do, see or even know about, but Olivia knew that dance and all the moves: the slow grinding with her shapely body, right down to getting on her hands and knees, humping her ass like a bitch in heat and raising one of her legs while on her hands and knees, like a dog by a hydrant. Olivia did the dance so well, that when the adults got together to party, they wanted to watch her do it and would buy her candy, ice cream or give her coins if she did that dance for them. That really made her hump and grind harder when she did The Dog. She even got to the point where she would do the dance when there was no party and her only audience was her own image in a mirror or TV screen when the TV was turned off or when her shadow was visible on a wall or the ground when the sun shined.

*Jerri L. Smith*

Olivia always listened to music though. On weekends Sara partied at home or at someone else's home. Sometimes she went to a bar, which in that era was called a tavern. On weekdays when Sara didn't party, she still had the radio on and sometimes played records. At her house, the music that played in the building next door could be heard. You see, on the south side of Sara's house, a couple of doors down, was the barber-slash-record shop owned by the man Sara was buying their home from, but right next door, on the north side of Sara's house, was the tavern. The sound of music came out of the walls of the tavern it seemed. Often times, there was a live band playing inside the tavern. There was also another tavern a few doors north of Sara's house, so Olivia was surrounded by music and was exposed everyday to the glamour of partying, going to nightclubs and life in the fast lane. It was pretty-much an average day for her to see women going into the taverns all dressed up wearing high-heeled pumps with their tight-fitting dresses or skirts and red color on their lips. Men got out of their big, clean cars, going into the taverns wearing their suits and hats cocked to the side with the brim broke down in the front. As Olivia grew older, she became more and more attracted to the activities that went on in taverns. She and her siblings would sometimes hang out in the barber and record shop on weekends and would go into the tavern next door to their home during the daytime, to buy whole dill pickles or a hamburger cooked on the tavern's grill, which was alright with Sara. The owner of that tavern knew Sara and her children well, but Olivia and her siblings knew not to go into the tavern in the evenings or at nighttime. They weren't even allowed to be outside the front door of the tavern during those times. Being as close as they were to the tavern, Sara had rules for her children and did her best to keep them from any physical harm that could come to them from the goings on inside or outside the tavern, but the mental harm was done, especially to Olivia.

Olivia remembers some of the things that went on when she was three or four years old. One incident in particular she remembers is one Saturday morning after Sara had, apparently, been out all night. Into the house, up the stairs and into the bedroom where Olivia slept with her siblings, Sara came, took Olivia from her bed, quickly bathed her and got her dressed. Of course Olivia didn't ask any questions being the age she was. All she knew was that she had to be going somewhere special because Sara combed her hair and put on her one of her good dresses and fancy socks that she could only wear to church or some other special place. After getting Olivia all dolled up, down the stairs and out the door Sara carried her. She didn't even put shoes on Olivia's feet. She just put her in the back seat of the car and off they rode. About four blocks down the street from home, the car turned a corner and was parked. Olivia had been past the building the car was parked next to, a number of times, but had never been inside. The

2

building was another tavern. Sara got out of the car, took Olivia from the back seat and carried her into the building. It was kind of dark inside, but Olivia could see the few people who were sitting around, drinking alcoholic beverages and smoking cigarettes while listening to music that played on a low volume. Sara and her friend Jean (the driver of the car) started talking to the people in the tavern about Olivia dancing. Sara then put Olivia upon the dance floor (which was a stage to Olivia) and asked her, "are you gonna dance for mommy"? Olivia nodded her little head, indicating that she would, so Sara and Jean went over to the jukebox (music machine, to Olivia) and selected a song they knew Olivia liked or could dance really well to. Both Sara and Jean, then, went back to the dance floor. The music started to play and all Sara had to say was, "get it baby". Olivia knew that meant dance as well as she knew how to dance, so she started moving her feet and her little hips while snapping her fingers. The people in the tavern started clapping their hands, smiling, laughing and saying things to egg Olivia on. One person threw money on to the dance floor to her, then another threw money on to the dance floor. Auh! It was on then. Sara, close to the dance floor, shouted out, "Do The Dog baby". Auh man! Olivia grabbed her knees with her hands while squatting just a little bit and started grinding and humping her little ass. Then Sara shouted out, "walk that dog baby". Man, Olivia, smoothly, got down on her hands and knees and started crawling while she was still humping, stopping occasionally to raise one leg like a dog stopping to piss. That was what the adults referred to as walking The Dog, back then. The small crowd in the tavern went wild with cheers and applauds. They kept throwing money on to the dance floor too. As Olivia danced, she saw one-dollar bills being thrown on to the dance floor, along with coins. When the song ended, Sara and Jean took her and the money that was thrown to her, from the dance floor and hugged Olivia tightly. They resumed talking to the people in the tavern, while the people cooed Olivia, told her how cute she was and how well she danced. Sara and Jean took Olivia home soon after she finished dancing. "Oh boy", is how Olivia felt as she rode home all excited, just thinking about how the people in the tavern acted while she danced. She sat in the back seat of the car, thinking that she must have done a really good thing for the people in the tavern to throw money to her. Later on that day, she got to spend some of it at the candy store on the corner from their home and that was the beginning of her love of money.

Back in the era when Olivia was a small girl, Sara didn't have a lot of money since she didn't have a job. Her and Jean were such good friends and Jean didn't have a husband nor did she have children, that she became Sara's roommate. Jean worked at a hospital, so she was able to share the bills with Sara. It all worked out great. Olivia and her siblings couldn't have a lot of the things they wanted, but now that Sara had Jean's help, they always had what they needed.

Whenever Olivia would ask for money to buy candy or junk food, Sara and Jean would tell her they didn't have any money. Sometimes this was right before they left in Jean's car. When Sara and Jean returned, they had several sacks and boxes of food and other store-bought items. Olivia would help (as much as she could) bring the groceries into the house, but would sit on the porch afterwards and wonder how Sara and Jean could leave home with no money and come back with sacks and boxes of new things. She knew very little about banks or getting things on credit at that time, so she couldn't figure out what Sara and Jean had done. This was really puzzling to Olivia too, because she knew what it was like to have money and thought money was what it took to get what she wanted, so if there was some way she could get candy and other items from a store without having money, she wanted to know about it. After she grew older, she learned that Sara and Jean had a tab (credit) at the neighborhood grocery store, but until then, it was a mystery to her. She always remembered the time money was thrown to her when she danced in the tavern though and she remembered the times she got money from adults who partied with Sara and Jean. Olivia wanted mo' money, mo' money, mo' money. One day, she overheard from one of her siblings, that he or she was gonna take a soda pop bottle back to the store and get a refund for it. Olivia was about six years old by this time, but was smart for her age. Especially since she had six siblings older than she, whom she also learned from. She didn't know what the definition of refund was, but used common sense to figure it out. Returning bottles to the store was a great way to get money without doing something she would get in trouble for, so that became her hustle. She would go from yard-to-yard, through alleys and would even crawl into hedges, bushes or weeds if she thought she would find a refundable pop bottle. Sometimes she would accumulate a box full of bottles and would drag the box down the street to the store to cash the bottles in. Olivia's sisters and brother were too ashamed to help her when she had several bottles to return. Sara would say to them, "if you all don't help Olivia carry her bottles, don't ask for anything she buys". Of course the siblings would con Olivia (when Sara wasn't watching) to get some of the goods she brought back from the store. Even though Olivia was younger than the others, she was very smart and knew when her siblings were conning her, but she made sure they kept their end of the deal they made or she would tell Sara about it. Hustling for refundable pop bottles was an everyday thing for Olivia though, at first, but she was so thorough when she looked for them, that she soon realized she needed to wait a day or two after she cashed in a box full of them, before going on her next search.

As Olivia grew, she became more shapely and Boys began noticing her. She became more creative when she danced too. She would make up dance routines and enter neighborhood and school talent shows. She usually won first place too, but sometimes came in second. Now she was ready to go to teenage parties. As badly as she wanted to though, she wasn't allowed to go to those parties until she completed the sixth grade of elementary school. The first party she went to was at the recreation center right across the street from home. Olivia's brother and sisters had been going to parties there all along. It seemed like forever to her, but Olivia finally graduated from grade school and was able to go to a party at the rec (they called it) that summer before she started junior high school. That is where she met a boy who was a year or two older than she. The boy and Olivia danced together a few times, exchanged phone numbers and began courting. By the time the next school year started, it seemed every one of the seventh grade students, knew Olivia was going with (dating) this boy. Marcellis was very popular. He didn't go to the high school on the east side that Olivia went to. He went to high school on the west side of town, but he and Olivia were big news at both schools. Olivia even got into a fight with a girl in one of her classes, whom she believes was jealous of her dating Marcellis.

A couple of months into that school year, Sara and Jean bought another house. Olivia and her sister Yulonda, who was a grade ahead of Olivia, were transferred from the east side school, to the school on the west side of town that Marcellis went to. The house they moved from was bought by the man who owned the barber and record shop, whom Sara and Jean bought the house from. It was all good though. Olivia and her siblings were happy about moving to another home, but Olivia and Yulonda were a little anxious about going to the west side school where they hardly knew anyone. By the time they started the new school, they had made friends with some kids who lived on the same street they moved to and some neighborhood kids. They were still un-easy though, about the unknown at the new school.

Going to the new school was hell for Olivia at first because many of the students realized she was the girl Marcellis was dating and some of them whispered as they pointed at her, showing and telling other students who she was. You know the talk for teenagers. Someone else or others who were from the west side, must have been at the party where Olivia and Marcellis met, because they sure knew who Olivia was. While Olivia and Yulonda sat in the counselor's office getting enrolled the first day at the school, girls stopped and pointed as they looked through the office window. Come to find out, Marcellis was also going with a girl at the west side school, who was a grade ahead of him. The girl was in the ninth grade. Through that school year, the girl never said anything to Olivia, but her friends, her homies picked on Olivia. One of the friends even put her foot out to try and make Olivia fall in the school's hallway the time Olivia wore a cast on one of her legs and foot. Olivia stopped walking, starred at the girl and showed no fear. Finally, it all blew over. That girl and the others stopped harassing Olivia and Olivia's and Marcellis' relationship tapered off.

Olivia's second year at the west side school was a breeze. She tried out for and made co-captain of the majorette team and became really popular then, well known for how well she danced. She began dating Carlton who was a grade ahead of her. After dating him a short while, Olivia discovered he was and had been dating a girl in his class since their seventh grade school year. This girl was on the cheerleading squad, was shy and quiet, so Olivia never had any confrontation with her nor her friends. Olivia really liked Carlton though and thought he was so fine (good-lookin'), that she still dated him even though she found the rumors about how in love he and this girl were, to be true. Carlton, being older than Olivia, was a little bit more advanced than she, so Olivia's attraction for him was a lot about her being curious. Carlton would get her alone whenever he could, so he could get some kisses. His and Olivia's bodies would be close at times when he would feel on Olivia's plump ass and try and put his hand under her dress, between her legs. Olivia liked it too. Her breast weren't quite developed, but Carlton would still feel on the little bumps she had on her chest. Eventually, he wanted to go further. Even though Olivia liked what she felt thus far, time and time again, she said, "no". Having six siblings older than she, Olivia had a little knowledge about sex from listening to the stories her sisters told. During this time, three of her sisters each, had at least one child. Olivia's brother didn't talk about sex with or around her, but he would ask her to introduce him to her advanced girlfriends. Whenever Olivia and one of her friends she had introduced her brother to, would skip school and stayed at Olivia's home, Olivia's friend and brother would go upstairs to his bedroom and close the door. Olivia knew they were in the bedroom having sex. Her girlfriends who did this would, later, tell her about it, so Olivia had been educated, tempted and really close to doing it too. One night when Sara and Jean had gone to bed early, Olivia's three younger sisters than the two oldest ones, were sitting around the dining room table talking about who knows what and drinking beer with an older male friend of the family, who lived across the street. Olivia's siblings could still handle alcohol better than she could. She didn't like alcohol at all at that time. If she drank one beer, it made her sleepy, two beers caused her to lose her composure. Not only did she lose her composure when she drank alcohol, but she remembers seeing the drunkards who lived in the rooms over the corner store from the house she grew up in. She used to watch them from the hallway window upstairs in that house, as they stumbled and fell trying to get up the outdoors staircase, to get to their rooms. "It was very sad", said Olivia. She also remembers seeing her father on his deathbed the night before he died from alcoholism. She didn't like the way alcohol made her feel and had seen what it does to people, so she wasn't in to sitting around drinking with her sisters or anyone else. What she was in to at this time was boys. Carlton, in particular. That's why she met him outside while her sisters were socializing with Alex. Carlton had called on the phone earlier that evening and asked if he could come over. When he got there, the fun was on for Olivia. She and Carlton played around, talked, hugged, kissed and even did a little bumping and grinding. As things got heated up and x-rated, Carlton grabbed Olivia's hand and led her to the back yard where it was darker and no one could see what they were doing. Immediately, Carlton got Olivia to lay on the ground so he could lay on top of her and really get his freak on. It didn't take long for his penis to get hard neither. Olivia had no intentions of going all the way (you know, actually giving up the pussy), but this night, she was hotter than she had ever been. At this point, she had already let Carlton go further with her than he nor anyone else had gone before. Bumping and grinding on his hard penis felt so good, that Olivia didn't want to say no this time, not yet anyway, so she went with the flow. As she and Carlton were forcefully grinding their asses with Carlton lying on top of her, Olivia's virgin vagina slid up and down on Carlton's penis, giving him the impression that she wanted the penis inside of her. That's when Carlton raised up on to his knees, pulled Olivia's shorts and panties off and asked her to open her legs. Olivia told Carlton she was afraid. Carlton replied, "come on, I won't hurt you", so Olivia said, "okay" and opened her legs. Carlton pulled his pants and underwear down to his ankles and laid on top of Olivia with his hot penis on her vagina. As he tried to stick it in, Olivia said, "wait, it hurts". Carlton said, "Okay, I'll go slower". He then pushed a little bit of his penis inside Olivia's vagina and then a little bit more and started grinding (moving his ass) slowly. "If going slow is the way to keep intercourse from being painful the first time a girl has it, it wasn't working", thought Olivia. She tried to bare it and let Carlton continue, but what he was doing was too painful, so she asked him to stop and to get up. She didn't know if any sperm came out of his penis (not knowing that was called "getting a nutt" or "having had an orgasm"), but she didn't care if it didn't. She got up, put on her panties and shorts and told Carlton she was going in the house. Carlton didn't press the issue. He just said, "okay". After getting dressed, the both of them walked to the front of the house making sure no one saw them, kissed and hugged one another and agreed they would see one another at school the next day. Carlton left, Olivia brushed off the grass from her clothes and hair and went in the house. To play it all off, she went into the dining room and stood for a few minutes, watching her sisters play cards so they wouldn't get suspicious. Then she went upstairs and drew herself a bath. Olivia had never had a menstrual period before. She heard it said that a girl could not get pregnant if she had never had a period, so she knew she didn't have to worry about that. The funny thing she learned about the vagina that night, was that shortly after Carlton took his penis out of her vagina, the discomforting feeling she felt, went away. That was amazing to Olivia. She was cool with what had happened now that it was over. After bathing, she put on a clean nightgown and clean panties and went downstairs to socialize with her sisters. While sitting at the dining table acting as though nothing unusual happened that night, Olivia felt something strange. She casually got up (still acting inconspicuous) and went back upstairs to the bathroom. When she pulled down her panties, there was an unusual color of liquid in the crotch. Olivia instantly got nervous. Even though she had just taken a bath minutes ago, she felt the need to take another. After doing so, she went back downstairs and continued socializing when the same thing happened again. She wanted to panic, but had to remain secretive to hide what she had done. Back upstairs she went. This time, she yelled from the top of the stairs for her sister Yulonda to come there. Olivia didn't tell Yulonda where to come to because she was still trying to be discreet, but Yulonda found her in the bathroom and determined what the matter was. It turned out that Olivia's first intercourse experience, brung down her first menstrual period. Olivia was pretty excited about that. This to her meant she was going into womanhood. Afraid though, of what Sara might do if she found out what actually happened, Olivia swore Yulonda to secrecy by making her promise she wouldn't tell anyone and so Yulonda did. Olivia stopped dating Carlton soon after their ron de' vu. She was kind of afraid of him after the uncomfortable way he made her vagina feel. Even though she was excited about her period, she couldn't help but wonder if something was wrong with Carlton's penis or maybe he just did something the wrong way, with his penis. However, it physically changed her.

Olivia started growing up faster and faster after the episode with Carlton. She even started wearing tight-fitting clothing and makeup, which made boys notice her more than before. There was one boy in particular, who noticed Olivia and played around with her between classes and after school. That let Olivia know the boy liked her. Before long, She and Waylon started going together (dating). Olivia had lots of sex with Waylon. She and Waylon would skip school and have sex in her bedroom while Sara and Jean were at work and sometimes they had sex at Waylon's home while his mom was at work. The more sex Olivia had, the more noticeable she became (it seemed) and the hotter she got. Even older guys started noticing her. Olivia's brother Willie, who was six years older than she, had friends who came to their home and sometimes stayed late. Olivia and three of her sisters younger than Willie, often hung around and kicked it with Willie and his friends. For some reason though, one of Willie's friends named Alphonso, whom was called by his nickname, Hump, constantly flirted with Olivia. If he was only playing, Olivia took his words and actions seriously. Actually, the playing around was mutual. Olivia flirted with Hump as well. She would sit on his lap when no one was around and made his penis hard. Hump liked it and even encouraged Olivia to do it often. Olivia liked it too. It made her coochie (vagina) twitch and get hot. Before long, Hump was doing Olivia (having sex with her) on regular basis. Even in Sara's basement. Olivia would sneak Hump in from the side door that led to the basement stairs, while everyone else in the house was asleep. She and Hump had sex in a chair or on the kitchen floor at Hump's grandmother's house while his grandmother was asleep or had gone to bed. Hump lived with his grandmother. By this time, he and Willie had graduated from senior high school. Willie was at home some afternoons, so Olivia skipped school some days and spent the day with Hump while his grandmother was at work. She and Hump had sex two or three times before school was out those days she spent with him. Olivia had began tapering off her relationship with Waylon when she developed the crush on Hump. After all, Waylon was a year younger than her; while Hump was older than she and had way more experience and techniques with the girls, that Waylon knew nothing about. That alone, was attractive to Olivia. She was like a wild flower now. At this point, she was only fourteen or fifteen years old and had already had sex with three guys, including Hump. She didn't see anything wrong with that neither, even though she see's the wrong in it now. At that time, she was just having big fun. This was also the time when she started smoking weed (marijuana) too. Even though she didn't know it, smoking weed was an experience that was about to take her on a long journey she could never return from. She thought it was okay to smoke weed though, because Sara, Jean, her siblings and other relatives drank alcoholic beverages that she couldn't handle. Marijuana, she could handle or so she thought. She even thought it was okay to smoke weed because to her, it was just a form of entertainment just like alcohol. If it was okay to drink alcoholic beverages, it was okay to do drugs. At least that's the way she saw it.

Olivia's feelings for Hump grew stronger and stronger. She didn't expect she would fall in love with him, but she did. When she realized how deep she was feeling him, she discovered he was a player. Whorish if you will. Hump liked Olivia quite a bit, but Olivia was too young to go some of the places he frequented or wanted to take a girl to. She was too young for Hump to be out in the open with their relationship. Therefore, every time she turned around, she saw or heard of Hump with a different girl. She confronted him several times about one girl or another, but Hump would just say, "oh she's just a friend" or he would use Olivia's age as the reason someone else only accompanied him to a party or other affair. A few months later, Olivia got tired of the excuses and explanations Hump gave her and started hanging out with others she knew who got high, while trying to keep from tripping on Hump. There was nothing she could do to stop him from doing what he wanted to do and she couldn't change their age difference, so she just tried to occupy her mind and time, doing other things with other people.

Dating an older guy and smoking weed really made Olivia more advanced than girls her age should be. Feeling more grown up than she was, she often disobeyed Sara and was even caught skipping school a numerous number of times. Twice, she tripped out on weed after she had come home from hangin' out with older folk. Sara had to give her a cold shower and make her drink milk, to bring her down from the high she was on. That didn't stop her from smoking weed again though. The things she was doing even led her to a detention home for adolescents a few times. Sara kept her there for six or eight weeks one of the times she was sent there. You would think that would have scared her straight. After all, that was Sara's intentions, but it didn't. It seemed Olivia got more rebellious. However, she was determined to do what she wanted to do. Things she wasn't supposed to be doing. She was straight and did well through the last year of junior high school, her ninth grade year. She even made captain of the majorette team, which meant she had to stay in school and keep her grades up. Because of that and her being eager to go to the senior high school on the east side, she passed the ninth grade, but it was only by a hair. Olivia was very intelligent, book-wise, but she had a tendency to only do enough learning and applying herself, to pass a grade. That way she could use part of the time to bullshit and be fast.

After passing the ninth grade, during summer break before she would start senior high school, Olivia started kickin' it with a girl from the neighborhood, whom she met during her brief stay at the east side junior high school. Gloria lived with her parents and a few of her siblings, a couple of blocks from Sara's house. Sara's house was on the eleven hundred block, while Gloria's family lived on the ten hundred block, which was the block that ended the east side school district. Sara and her siblings, Jean, their friends and other relatives all attended the east side school, so it was a tradition that their children go to the same school. Olivia's four oldest siblings had already graduated from that school and the fifth and sixth siblings were now attending that school. Therefore, Sara arranged it so that Olivia could go to that school as well, even though they didn't reside in the area of that school district. It all worked out. Olivia and her friend Gloria were now reunited since they would, once again, be attending the same school. The two of them were born the same year, month and day.

Gloria was the youngest girl of the nine children her parents had. She had three older brothers and one younger than she. The second brother of the two eldest, was fine as wine to Olivia. Since summer break began, she had seen the brother a few times on the block his family lived on, but he never said anything more to her than hello or goodbye. He didn't hang around very long and always seemed to have things to do, places to go and people to see or something like that. He was always businesslike though. Too grown for Olivia, so she understood if she was just a kid to him. That didn't stop her from being fascinated with him. One evening though, when she was hangin' outside in front of Gloria's home, the brother, Troy, arrived and went in the house. A few minutes later, he came outside and was about to leave when he asked Gloria if she would ride with him to his apartment and stay there for a couple of hours while he made a run to take care of some business. Gloria agreed to do it and since Olivia was hangin' with her, she went along. As it was, Troy was dealing marijuana. He liked kickin' it too, smoking weed and drinking alcohol, so Olivia and Gloria had it going on while they were apartment sitting. Troy sat aside some weed for them and showed them different bottles of wine they could choose from, to have a drink of. Chillin' at his apartment was way cool. When he returned, he messed around the apartment for a few minutes and then took Olivia and Gloria home. To Olivia's surprise, Troy took Gloria home first. He started getting his flirt on a little bit while they were all at his apartment, but he couldn't really get off into it like he wanted to with Gloria there, so he took her home first and then got his mack on. Olivia had no idea Troy was interested in her, but she was glad he was. Apparently, he had been checking her out as well, the few times he saw her. The two of them talked along the way as Troy was taking Olivia home. Basically, he asked the usual questions a guy asks a girl when they first meet. Troy asked Olivia, "how old are you; are you dating someone; what time do you usually have to be home; what's your phone number". Back then, "what's your sign", was a popular question to ask, but Troy was too mature or too sophisticated or too cool to ask that. He was just smooth with his flirt, as he drove slowly to take Olivia home. Before getting her there, he pulled his car over to the curb down the street from Sara's house and leaned towards Olivia with his elbow resting on the armrest (pimp stool back then), as he talked to her. While leaning on the armrest, Troy brought his face closer to Olivia's, gradually testing her to see if she was going to shy away from him. Olivia just sat there looking into his eyes, so Troy made his move, kissed Olivia's lips and then backed off for a minute. Still looking into her eyes, since Olivia didn't resist the kiss he gave her, Troy kissed her again, only this time, he stuck his tongue in her mouth to add a little french to it. That was all good with Olivia. She responded by adding a little French in return. That told Troy what he wanted to know. He had action. Troy backed away after the second kiss as he looked pleased, but cool about it. Then he told Olivia to write down his phone number as he took the car out of park and proceeded to drive. Shortly after, Troy pulled his car over in front of Sara's house to let Olivia out of the car. He told her that he worked and gave her his work hours. "Call me", he said. Olivia told him she would as she opened the car door to get out. Troy stopped her before she could get out of the car and gave her another peck on the lips. Olivia then got out of the car and went in the house feeling like she was the shit because someone with Troy's looks and of his caliber was trying to get with her. She thought she had it going on. After all, Troy was about twenty-two years of age, had a job, his own apartment and a fairly new Cadillac. He had his shit together for a young adult. He was raised to be responsible, independent and to keep a job. Selling weed wasn't right, but Troy wanted a lot of things that he couldn't afford with just the salary his job paid him. Therefore, he did what he felt he had to do and got his hustle on. He was a fancy guy who wore suits most of the time, even when he was working, so he was fairly high maintenance. Troy was a cashier at the time. On the job, he wore suit pants, a dress shirt and a tie, but wore a long, white apron wrapped around his healthy, but sexy body. He had a cute ass too, that the apron strings tied above. He was a six-foot honey, but was also very intelligent.

Olivia called Troy on the telephone a couple of days later, just to say, "hi". She never wanted to seem desperate nor pushy with a guy, so she didn't call too soon or too much and she didn't keep him on the phone long when she called. After talking with him that day, she waited and called him again, two or three days later. The routine she made for herself was that she would wait two or three days after talking to Troy, before calling him again. That way, she wouldn't crowd him. After about a week or two of talking to Troy on the phone when she did, Olivia called him one evening not wanting anything in particular except to hear his voice and chat with him a few minutes, when Troy surprised her and asked her about visiting him. Knowing Olivia wasn't of age and couldn't just get away anytime she wanted to, Troy asked her to call him in the morning. Olivia kind of figured why he wanted her to call him then and she agreed she would. That night, she went to bed all excited about what the next day would bring. The following morning, she got out of bed all bright-eyed and bushy-tailed, ironed something cute to wear, fixed her hair in a fly ass (cool) do and sneaked into Sara's cologne after she took a bath. It was still summertime, so Olivia didn't have to go to school. She worked a summer job at a daycare center, but she could call in sick or give some other reason for her absence from work that day. When she called Troy on the phone after Sara and Jean left for work, Troy asked her if she would spend the day with him at his apartment. Olivia had a good idea he was gonna ask her to come to his apartment and she was prepared to go, so she told him she would. Troy told her he would pick her up around the corner from Sara's house. That way, no one on the block Olivia lived on, would see her leave in his big car. Olivia told Troy to give her time to get dressed and then come and get her. After she hung up the phone, she called the daycare and gave the person she talked with, some excuse she made up, which was cool because having the job was by choice, not something she had to do. The excuse was accepted and Olivia was on her way. She, then, met Troy where they agreed to meet and off they rode, straight to Troy's apartment. After getting there, Troy loosened his tie (which is something Olivia enjoyed watching him do) and sat down on one of the throw pillows that were placed on the floor, surrounding the round coffee table in the living room. Troy didn't have a sofa or chairs in the living room. His only furniture was a three-piece kitchenette set that sat in an area before the kitchen, the table he was seated at, a rectangular table his stereo sat on and a mattress and box-springs that sat on the floor in his bedroom. That's all. The apartment had wall-to-wall carpet, so it was pretty comfortable sitting on pillows on the floor. After joining Troy for a sit down, Troy opened a box he had under the table and rolled a joint of the weed in it. Firing the joint up, taking a couple of puffs and passing it back and forth to one another, Troy and Olivia sat there and got high while conversating with one another. After getting their buzz on, Troy put the joint in the ashtray, stood up and reached for Olivia's hand to help her up. "Come with me", he said. He then led Olivia to his bedroom. All confident, Troy took off his tie and then his shirt, while Olivia sat on the bed watching him. Olivia was unsure about how quickly to respond, so she waited for Troy to lead the way and he did. He was a lot of things, but shy wasn't one of them. Troy on his hands and knees crawled across the bed to where Olivia sat and began kissing her passionately. Olivia, then, responded by rubbing Troy's back and the hair on his head. Troy started unbuttoning Olivia's blouse and then her pants. Kissing her while doing so, he moved forward to lay Olivia down and laid himself down beside her. Still kissing her, Troy started caressing Olivia's small, but firm breast and massaging her crotch. Olivia was getting hot, so she started to grind her ass slowly, gradually opening her legs so that Troy could really get his feel on. Troy went a little further and put his hand down Olivia's unzipped pants. Olivia didn't mind at all. She responded by opening her legs wider. The invitation inspired Troy, so he stuck one of his fingers in Olivia's vagina and started fingering her in and out to jack her vagina off. Olivia, then, started grinding her ass vigorously and moaning by now. After her vagina was good and wet and Troy's penis was good and hard, Troy stopped, helped Olivia out of her blouse and pulled her pants and panties off as she laid on the bed. He then, stood up and took off his pants. Standing there naked with a hard-on, Troy got on the bed on his hands and knees and started kissing Olivia's lips and sucking her breast while rubbing her body and finger-fucking her. Then he climbed on top of her and gently stuck his penis inside Olivia's moist vagina. It was on then. They started off fuckin' nice and slow, but as their sex organs wrestled with one another, the fuckin' got real serious. Bumpin' and grinding vigorously with Olivia's legs high up in the air and parted like the red sea, Troy went all up in the pussy with gentle force until

13

his hot liquid squirted in Olivia's already wet vagina. This to Olivia was what making love was like. Of course Troy wasn't in love with her at the time, but the sex they had felt like he was. The two of them fucked for a while before Troy's penis erupted. It was wonderful, even magical to Olivia. The finale was kisses before the two of them fell asleep all hugged up together. When they awakened, they both took a shower, got dressed, Troy rolled another joint for them to smoke and then he took Olivia home. Letting her out of his car at the same place he picked her up at, Troy gave Olivia a kiss and told her to call him. Olivia replied, "okay", as she was closing the car door. Her face glowed as she walked home, replaying in her mind, the wonderful day she had. She wasn't sure where her relationship with Troy was going, but she wanted to see and be with him again. With the sex they had being as good as it was, Olivia was confident that Troy enjoyed her as much as she enjoyed him and wanted more of her as well.

Olivia matured quite a bit more after she started dating Troy. She still would only call him once every two or three days. Even though she felt like calling him several times a day, as a rule for herself, she didn't. When she did call him, sure enough, he would ask her to let him pick her up so she could spend the day with him at his apartment. Several weeks went by, that Olivia spent at least two days of each week at Troy's apartment. School was about to start now, when she would be a sophomore. She was really diggin' Troy now and wondered how she was gonna spend time with him when she went back to school. It worked out though because Troy wanted to continue seeing her too. When Olivia was back in school, she went home everyday when school was out and made an appearance. After doing so, she and her two older sisters who were still in school, had Sara's permission to go and hang out. Olivia and her sisters knew to be home by nine-thirty or ten pm, so Troy would let Olivia know the night before, to call him when she got home from school so he could pick her up at the usual place or at the store around the corner. It was all good except, the two of them didn't have time to play around and fall asleep together after a good fuckin. Because she soon got bored with school, Olivia started skipping school again. It wasn't everyday that she didn't go to school and when she didn't, she wasn't always with Troy. At least not at first. Olivia wasn't dating anyone except Troy, but she would skip school and hang out with other older folk who sat around getting high all day. Just kickin' it. Sometimes Troy had to work during the daytime, so Olivia couldn't be with him unless he had a later shift or he had the day off. Finally, Troy wanted more time with Olivia than the two of them had together in the evenings, so since Olivia was skipping school some days anyway, Troy suggested she spend the day with him. He was sweet. He never came straight out and asked Olivia to skip school, but Olivia loved the suggestion and agreed to do it. She knew that meant she had to skip school the next day, but she didn't mind.

She was game (all for) for spending a day with her man like she did before school started. After kickin' the suggestion around a little bit, Troy told Olivia he would pick her up in the morning, down the street from the school and so he did. When Olivia got to school that next morning, she entered the building through the front door and in the mix of the crowd of students, she slipped out the back exit of the building. She could see Troy's Cadillac parked down the street, so she hurried to it, got in the car and off they went to Troy's apartment. Upon arriving, Troy walked through the door loosening his tie as usual, sat down on the throw pillows and rolled a joint. As he and Olivia smoked the joint, Troy got a phone call and had to make a run. He told Olivia he would be right back and asked her if she would straighten up the apartment for him. Of course she said she would. Olivia was glad to do it because it made her feel like a housewife or that she and Troy lived together. This way, she could really play house (as she used to say when she was a kid). After Troy left the apartment, Olivia took her clothes off, put on his robe and started her housework. She was just about finished when he returned. Standing at the kitchen sink washing the dishes, Olivia was naked underneath the robe. She knew that sometime during the course of the day, there was gonna be some fuckin' going on so she wanted to be prepared when Troy got back. As soon as he walked into the kitchen and saw Olivia in his robe, he must have smelled the scent of a hot bitch or just knew there were no panties and bra underneath the robe, because he came up behind her as she stood at the sink. That's where the foreplay began. Troy started kissing the back of Olivia's neck, stuck his tongue in her ears, put his arms around her and started squeezing her breast gently. Olivia's nipples were already at attention from Troy kissing and sucking on her neck. As he stood there behind her, Olivia could feel his hard dick, so she started grinding her ass and sliding up and down against the dick. She wanted to feel it hard and make it throb. Troy was ready to go up in Olivia by this time. He turned her around and kissed her with his tongue all in her juicy mouth. He then reached down and grabbed Olivia's ass with both of his hands, picked her up and sat her upon the sink. The sink was too high for Troy's dick to reach Olivia's pussy, so Troy finger-fucked her. "Ooh, he had his finger all up in the pussy", said Olivia, so she rode it like it was a dick. Troy knew the dick was what Olivia really wanted and she was ready for it right then, so he lifted her from the sink. Her legs immediately wrapped around Troy's waist and her arms around his neck, as he carried her to the bedroom and laid her on the bed. Olivia laid there squirming, still grinding for Troy to bring the dick on. The foreplay was over, Olivia was ready to fuck and Troy could see that. He was ready too. That's why he hurried out of his clothes, climbed on top of Olivia and immediately stuck his dick in her. He and Olivia sweated and fucked like minks, for a while. Troy flipped Olivia over and got the pussy from behind, then he flipped her back over and worked the pussy from the front until it purred and the both of them reached their climax. With so much passion, the two of them huffed and puffed as sweat glistened on their bodies. Troy sealed the love they made, with a gentle kiss, he and Olivia held each other tightly and fell asleep. "Man, some sleep after a good fuckin' is the shit", thought Olivia. She and Troy slept for a couple of hours and laid there making pillow talk after they awakened. Troy was hungry (like men usually are after they get some pussy or get a nutt), so he asked Olivia to fix him something to eat. Again, Olivia was glad to do it. She could tell Troy was getting use to her being there and that was her mission. She showered first. Then she cooked a meal and sat down to eat with Troy to nourish her body as well. By this time, school was about to let out, so Olivia got dressed while Troy rolled a joint for them to smoke and couple for her to take with her. Then he got dressed, took Olivia a couple of blocks from home and let her out of his car. "Call me", he said, after giving Olivia a goodbye kiss. Olivia told him she would and closed the car door. Olivia walked home with a bigger smile on her face than the one she had the other times she had spent the day with Troy. She was so happy and was getting to the point where she didn't want to depart from him after a day like this one. Along the way home, all she could think about was how it would be if she and Troy lived together. She was mesmerized as she walked along replaying in her mind, everything that went on in the apartment that day. She felt she was on top of the world.

Olivia finally made it home, trying to play that "I just got out school" role. It didn't work though. Sara got a call from the school, informing her that Olivia didn't make any of her classes that day. Sara was furious. "Where have you been", she asked. "At school", Olivia replied. With it being a school day, Sara wouldn't ask that question unless she knew or suspected Olivia didn't go to school that day. Still, Olivia said that was where she had been because that was the likely answer to give Sara. The minute Olivia said that, Sara went off telling Olivia she was lying. With Olivia being the age she was and Sara being tired of whipping her for all the bad things she did when she was younger, Sara told Olivia she was grounded for one week, that she couldn't go anywhere after school nor on the weekend and she couldn't talk on the phone. "Get out of my face", Sara told Olivia. Feeling like she had fallen from the top of the world, Olivia did what Sara told her to do, went to her bedroom and chilled thinking about how she was gonna miss going to Troy's apartment in the evenings after school and talking to him on the phone. The day she had with him that day was worth it to her though, but she could hardly wait to go to school the next day, so she could call Troy and tell him what the deal was. Olivia chilled for a few days though, as far as going to see Troy and skipping school, but any chance she got, she would sneak and call Troy when Sara and Jean were in bed or away from home. She was only grounded for one week, but it seemed to Olivia that she had been grounded for two weeks. When her punishment ended, she didn't skip school for a couple of weeks, but she did spend some evenings with Troy when he didn't have to work. That was all good, but it wasn't enough for him nor Olivia. The two of them had gotten use to the time they had all day with one another and were craving it, so even though Sara would possibly find out, Olivia started cutting her classes again. Troy would pick her up in the mornings, down the street from the school, just as he did before. Sometimes Olivia didn't even go inside the school building. She and Troy hurried to his apartment, had wild sex and played house all day. Olivia got busted skipping school, time-and-time again and would be on punishment for longer periods of time each time she got busted. That is, the times Sara found out. Sometimes Olivia got away with it, but getting caught didn't stop her from doing it again. She was hooked on the fun she had when she was at Troy's apartment and by this time, was sure she had fallen in love with him. At this stage, she still tried to get her sneak on and skip school to be with Troy, but she really didn't care if she got busted.

Apparently, Troy was now feeling Olivia more as well, because he didn't want to stop seeing her anymore than she was able to stay away from him. By this time, Olivia was more experienced with sex, but there were still a lot of things she didn't know about. One Friday night, she and her three sisters closer to her in age, went to a party at one of the recreation centers in their old neighborhood. Even though it wasn't Troy's kind of party (with his age difference and all), Olivia told him she was going, hoping he would make an exception and come just to be with her. When she told him about it, to her surprise, Troy told her he might come. It wasn't a sure thing that he would, but Olivia was happy that he might. Friday night rolled around, Olivia and her sisters went to the party and Troy wasn't there when they arrived, but Olivia got her boogie on anyway and just kept an eye out for him. After being at the party for about an hour, Troy arrived, but he didn't come to stay and kick it. He wanted Olivia to leave with him and you know she wanted to go with him as well, so she talked with her sisters about it, whom agreed to cover for her, but she had to be back by the time the party was over. The party was over at midnight, so Olivia had plenty of time to spend with Troy since it was only about eight-thirty pm. She had never been with Troy past nine o' clock, so she was very excited. Of course Troy took her straight to his apartment. Exactly where Olivia wanted him to take her. She thought she knew what was getting ready to go down and was willing to receive it, but Troy had something more in mind. This night turned out to be a very special night for Olivia. She and Troy had done a lot of fuckin' since they started dating, but this night, Troy planned to take Olivia to another level. After arriving to his apartment and getting comfortable, Troy rolled a joint of weed and poured himself and Olivia a glass of wine as they chilled, sitting on the carpeted floor in the living room. This was the early seventies. For some reason, sitting on the floor while getting high, smoking weed was the thing to do. It was damn near like a fad, so it was cool. After getting their buzz on (getting high), Troy crawled over to Olivia. Face-to-face with her, he began tongue kissing her. He then went on to kissing her face gently with his soft lips and sucking her neck. Undressing her while doing so, Troy continued to suck Olivia's neck in a trail fashion that led to her breast. After getting the last article of her clothing off, Troy undressed himself while on his knees, as Olivia watched. Olivia was cool as she waited patiently. She just picked up the joint from the ashtray that sat on the floor next to her, lit it and sat there toking on the joint while waiting for Troy to get all of his clothes off. After his clothing were off, Troy, on his hands and knees, proceeded to kiss Olivia from her lips down to her breast, while slightly pushing towards her until she was lying on her back. Troy remained in the same position as he continued to kiss and nibble on Olivia's breast. Olivia responded by rubbing his body with her hands as she moaned and groaned. Suddenly, Olivia felt Troy kissing and licking her body, slowly moving down towards her navel. There he stayed for a minute. Olivia just laid there with her eyes closed, wondering how far down Troy would go. Troy was more aggressive than he had ever been with Olivia. As hot as her ass was right about then and as much as she was in to Troy, Olivia didn't care what he wanted to do with her, sexually. She was going wherever the flow took her. Before she knew it Troy was kissing her thighs, her pubic area and then used his tongue to go further. Olivia was amazed. She had never had this done to her before. She had kicked it with older people all her life, (being that she was the youngest of seven children and all), so she knew this was one of those grown up things that she was just getting to. She heard more times than a few from her older siblings, "stop acting silly", is what they sometimes told her whenever necessary. Therefore, Olivia knew how to flow with the big dawgs (grown-ups/older folk), even if she didn't know or wasn't sure what was really going on. What Troy was doing to her felt good to Olivia, so this was a wonderful experience she didn't need a verbal lesson on. As Troy continued to lick and suck her vagina, Olivia grinded her ass slowly until Troy raised her legs high in the air and really got busy. "Hey", Olivia thought (in a good way). When Troy's lips first touched her vagina, Olivia didn't know the purpose of him going there, but minutes, no, seconds later, she started to feel what his intentions were. Even the thought of what he was doing was turning her on, causing a sweet sensation in her vagina, kind of like that of a volcano when it's lava is making it's way to the top, right before it erupts, so Olivia opened wider and gave it up to Troy. When she was good and wet and Troy was good and hard, Troy moved his face from Olivia's vagina, laid on top of her and stuck his penis in. Again, the two of them fucked like minks. Olivia didn't know ecstasy like she thought she did, until this night. Troy made her feel like she had never felt. This experience taught her that ecstasy is not just a physical pleasure, it's mental pleasure also. Troy put something on her mind. She had never even talked about oral sex before, but somehow she knew it wasn't some rare or nasty thing. Not if the two people involved are clean and care for one another. Still, Olivia had a lot to learn. After she and Troy reached their climaxes, the two of them cuddled with one another and took a nap. "It was breath-taking", said Olivia. As she and Troy drifted off to sleep, scented candles burned and even Troy's bare apartment was romantically set for the mood, while love songs continued to play on the radio on a low volume. Olivia and Troy woke up around eleven o' clock, took a shower and got dressed. Then Troy took Olivia back to the recreation center. By this time, the party was over. Olivia hooked up with her sisters and went home as though she had been with them all night. She had sweet dreams that night as she slept. Before this night, she suspected she had fallen in love with Troy. Now she was convinced. Olivia felt Troy had love for her too. It was years later when she learned "just because a guy wants to make love, doesn't mean he loves you".

Troy was really careful about being too open with his and Olivia's relationship. Remembering, Olivia was only in the tenth grade of high school and Troy was six years older than she. At Troy's age, Olivia was jail-bait. Troy could've been arrested for having sex with her. That didn't stop him though. He had it all figured out, apparently. Olivia didn't know it yet, that dating Troy would change her entire life, in more ways than one. She didn't know much about love, except the way it made her feel, with all the emotions that came with it and how it seems to dominate ones thought. She didn't know how to control her emotions if that were possible nor did she know the rules of love, if there were any. Olivia didn't know the games some people play with love or the way some people use love as a tool to manipulate and have their way. All she knew was how she felt. As Troy realized the depth of those feelings, he began to ask things of Olivia. Apparently, a gentleman in his early thirties, who lived in the same apartment building Troy lived in, had questioned Troy about Olivia. The old man (to Olivia) was interested in her and even offered to pay Troy for a date with her. Troy didn't know how Olivia would feel about him bringing something like that to her or even getting with a guy for money, but he was game if it was gonna get him paid, so he brought the proposition to Olivia in a subtle way, but first he baited her and built up her ego. He started making remarks to Olivia, like, "your pussy is good enough to pay for" and "your pussy is so good and fat, you've got enough to share with others and still have a lot left for me". These are the kind of things he said the next couple or few times he and Olivia were together, before telling her about the old man's offer. Finally, Troy told Olivia she could make a lot of money by spending a little time with a man he knew.

When he brought the game to her, Olivia didn't know what to say or what to think, so she just sat there looking at him and listened. Olivia didn't know the man Troy was setting her up with or so she thought. Come to find out, the dirty old man who wanted to date her, was one of the janitors of the high school Olivia went to. The combination of the macking Troy did, the love he made to Olivia, the weed she was smoking, her love for Troy and her love for money, persuaded her to accept the old man's offer to pay for some of her pussy. Troy had everything arranged. He told Olivia the man was going to give him the money first and while she was in the man's apartment, he would be in his apartment waiting for her. Troy assured Olivia she was safe because the man knew he would beat him down if he did anything to hurt her. Olivia second guessed doing this and more than that, she second guessed Troy's part in it, wondering how he was gonna feel about her after she dates the man. Being naive as she was, her logic on the matter, was, "Troy had shown no signs of not wanting to be with me anymore and he is setting the date up, so it must not be anything wrong with doing this for the money". That's the way Olivia saw it. She felt Troy loved her and thought no one who loved her would have her do something wrong or something such as this, if it was wrong. She didn't know better. Olivia grew up without a father, so she didn't have a male figure there, to tell her how it is when a man loves a woman. No one told her the things a man will and won't do when he loves a woman. Olivia didn't have a male figure around, who knew about these things and genuinely loved and cared about her to steer her in the right direction when it concerned boys and men as well as other things. Her brother was a year younger than Troy, growing up without a father or male-figure too and winging how to be a man himself, so Olivia had to trust what she thought she knew and did what Troy asked her to do. She went to the man's apartment and got right down to business. The man had a really small dick compared to the ones Olivia was used to and he quickly got an orgasm, which was great for Olivia. She wanted to hurry and get it over with. Afterwards, she washed her pussy at the man's apartment and was back at Troy's apartment in no time. Troy seemed to be pleased about what she had done. He had gotten the pussy before Olivia sold some of it, plus he got some of the money she made, so he was straight. Troy was already holding the money and Olivia brought the pussy back to him, so he should've been pleased. Troy was a money-dog. Olivia didn't know it before, but thinking back on her time with him, Troy had no morals about some things when it was about money. He did give Olivia a little more than half of the money the man paid to be with her, he kept her supplied with weed and most importantly, he still wanted to be with her, so Olivia was cool with the deal. Troy knew better though, even though Olivia didn't. Remember, Olivia had men and women throw money to her while she danced when she was just a kid. To her, dating the old man for money was just another way of entertaining for money. That was the way she saw it. She was a few dollars richer too, so it was all good. Olivia stayed with Troy at his apartment for a while after the date that day. She took a shower and smoked a joint with him while she got dressed. Then Troy took her home. She still spent days and even some evenings with Troy, even when the old man didn't want a date. The man would let Troy know when he had money to date Olivia. Meanwhile, Troy continued to bring Olivia to his apartment and spent a lot of time with her. With all the time Olivia spent with Troy, along with all the things the two of them shared, somewhere along the way, Olivia was ridden of the desire she had for Hump. She had not been with Hump sexually, since she started having sex with Troy, but at first, she thought about him a lot. Hump didn't sweat Olivia being distant from him neither. At least not at first. Olivia was in to Hump so tough (before Troy came along), that he got too sure of himself and didn't think he would lose her, even if he wasn't with her for a while. He thought Olivia would be available for him to get with, whenever he got back to her. He didn't know she was dating Troy, so he didn't know he had already been bumped (replaced). One night, Olivia and her three sisters closer to her in age, went to a party and Hump was there. Olivia kicked it, dancing with anyone who asked her for a dance and didn't even trip on Hump. When the party was over, Olivia wanted to stop at the store Troy worked at, before she and her sisters went home. The store was about to close and there were only a couple or three customers other than Olivia and her sisters, so Olivia was able to talk to Troy for a few minutes. After doing so, she decided she was gonna hang around until Troy got off work, which was in a few minutes. Her sisters told her she couldn't stay because Sara was going to wonder why she didn't come home with them. Olivia didn't care. She wanted to be with Troy. As she and her sisters stood in front of the apartment building Troy lived in, which was right across the street from the store he worked at, Olivia's sisters pleaded with her, trying to talk some sense into her head, to get in the car so they could all go home. Determined to wait for Troy, Olivia didn't want to hear it. Coincidentally, Hump drove by and saw the girls, so he stops his car and gets out to see what was going on. It was strange to Olivia that Hump drove down that street; since there were at least ten other ways he could get to the side of town they all lived on. Maybe he knew about Olivia and Troy and Troy working at the store on that street. However, Olivia's sisters were talking over one another telling Hump what was going on, so Hump decides he's gonna help out. Since neither of them could convince Olivia to get in the car, Hump suddenly picks Olivia up, to try and put her in his car. Olivia wrestled with him until she broke loose from the hold he had on her, so Hump slapped her. By this time, Troy was off duty and walked up on the scene. Olivia ran to him, crying and telling him she wanted to stay with him. Her sisters told him what the deal was and the trouble Olivia would be in, so Troy talked to Olivia, told her to go with her sisters and that he would talk to her the next day. Of course Olivia did what Troy told her to do. She didn't get in Hump's car though. She rode with her sisters. The next day, Hump came to Sara's house early that morning to apologize to Olivia for slapping her, but Olivia didn't wanna hear it. She wasn't slow. She knew the real reason Hump got an early start and came to apologize, was about him smoothing things out with her to get back in good with her. If he didn't know before, he now knew there was something going on between Olivia and Troy. Once he knew Olivia was dating someone else, a guy he knew of who's older than he and of Troy's caliber, Hump wanted Olivia more than he did before. It didn't matter to Olivia though. She was already through (finished) with him. She made it official that day. Hump knew too, that Olivia wasn't really over him for slapping her, but because she was involved with Troy and apparently, was diggin' Troy quite a bit. He didn't like it neither, but he was cool about it. Olivia's brother was angry about Hump slapping her, but he and Hump didn't fall out over it. Olivia's brother did have a talk with Hump though, so Hump knew not to be pushy or put his hands on Olivia again. He tried daily, to get her back, but things had changed. It was over. Olivia only had eyes for Troy.

Some things had not changed though. Olivia continued to skip school some days and spent them with Troy. She also dated that old man for money whenever Troy arranged it. Everything was all good between Olivia and Troy, until the news Olivia got one fall day. Out of the blue, after dating Troy for months, almost one year, Troy told Olivia he was leaving town to go to college. That day seemed like the saddest day of Olivia's life. She asked, even begged Troy to take her with him, but he told her he couldn't. During that time, Olivia never gave it much thought about how much younger than Troy she was. Of course Troy could barely take care of himself without a hustle on the side and was probably going to be rooming with someone or others. Even if he wanted to take Olivia with him, she was too young to leave home in the same city, not to mention going to another state. However, Troy told her she couldn't go with him. Before he left, he made passionate love to Olivia and told her he didn't want her to be with another man while he was gone, not even for money. As fast as Olivia was, she was still naive and actually agreed to not date any men while Troy was away. Now that she had sex a numerous number of times and knew what affection was like from being intimate with someone, it was gonna be hard to refrain, but she was in love with Troy though, so she thought she would try.

Olivia tried to be about school (once again) and hang out with schoolmates. You know, stay out of trouble, be faithful to Troy, stay in school and not hang out with grown-ups whom she had to skip school to kick it with. No matter how dedicated she tried to be, Satan was putting all kinds of bad, but attractive things in her path. Olivia enjoyed best, hangin' out with older folk, but they were attracted to her for some reason. Both older men and women took to her. It seemed that every time she met an older person who liked having her around, that person and the folk they flocked with, were getting high on one drug or another, so Olivia indulged as well, which made her fit in even more so. Along the way, while hangin' out with an older guy who was just a friend, Olivia was introduced to an older woman who was about fourteen years older than she. The lady was very attractive and had a twelve-year-old daughter she was raising by herself. During the introduction though, the lady looked at Olivia lustfully and made remarks to the guy Olivia was with, about how cute Olivia was and even said things about Olivia's anatomy. Olivia smiled at the things the lady said, but didn't pay too much mind to the comments. She and the lady hit it off right away, so they, along with Chubby (the mutual friend who introduced them), sat around the lady's house, smoked weed and listened to music while they socialized. When Olivia and Chubby were leaving, the lady (Brenda was her name) told Olivia to not be a stranger. Olivia knew that meant "come back and visit with or without Chubby". A few days later, Olivia did just that, without Chubby. She figured Brenda probably had some weed to smoke and since she couldn't catch up with Chubby, she went to Brenda's house by herself. From Brenda's actions and the things she said when Olivia met her, Olivia figured she was attracted to girls or women, but Olivia was okay with that. She had an experience of her own, with a girl who was a neighbor and schoolmate, so what Brenda was about, was no trip. After a few visits, the two of them became really close. Brenda initiated the first kiss, the first embrace and the first sexual contact. Olivia wasn't sure of what classifies a woman as being a lesbian or being gay, but to her, she was neither. She was a love child. She enjoyed loving, being loved and affection. Yes, she was also a freak for sex, but Olivia craved and was weak for men. She wasn't aggressive with girls or women nor did she desire the female anatomy, but if a female wanted to make love to her, that was cool. If a woman could make her feel good sexually, Olivia was game for it. At first, when she had brief intimacy with her neighbor-slash-schoolmate, Olivia wasn't sure about her sexual gender. She was very much attracted to boys and men and had been since her eleventh birthday, but there was so much closeness with girls from sleeping and taking baths together and being able to say and act out feelings with a girlfriend that wasn't acceptable for her to do with boys, that she was confused about how she was supposed to be. However, being naive about many things actually had it's rewards at times because it played a big part in Olivia realizing it was boys and men who were the right sex for her to be with and what was right for her. When her neighbor she was experimenting with had a miscarriage, Olivia felt the girl was tainted. Finding the girl had, apparently, been sexually involved with a boy while she and Olivia were kickin' it, changed Olivia's feelings for her and other girls or women too. Without planning to do so, Olivia started capitalizing off women who wanted her, women who were extra nice to her because they wanted her. She didn't come on to women nor did she seek women to be involved with in no way that required her being intimate with them, but if a woman sought her out and brung it to her, it was on if it would be beneficial to her in ways other than sexually. Therefore, Olivia didn't feel as though she was a lesbian or gay. She only took advantage of opportunities that were beneficial to her sexually, but more so, financially. Besides, she fell deeply in love with Hump and now Troy since she eased away from her neighbor, so her true desires had already confirmed which sex she really wanted.

Olivia remembered Troy telling her he didn't want her to be with another man while he was away. Being with Brenda would give her the companionship she wanted and the affection she needed so she could give Troy what he wanted, her refraining from being with another man. That was the way Olivia rationalized the way she handled this. This was one of those times her being naive was not a good thing, but she didn't know better, so she moved in with Brenda and stayed with her the majority of her junior year of high school. Sara allowed it just as long as Olivia went to school everyday. Olivia and Brenda got along fine and had a pretty good relationship until a male friend of Brenda's came to town. John was a guy Brenda dated off and on for a couple or few years before he moved to one of the northern states. The way it was, John would stay at Brenda's house whenever he was in town. The relationship Brenda had with John was probably the same as the relationship Olivia had with Troy now that Troy was away at school. Of course Brenda didn't tell Olivia the real deal about her and John. She was a little bit more clever than that. One Friday evening, for some reason, Olivia and Brenda had an argument that resulted in Olivia leaving to get away and cool off. Olivia stayed the night at her Mom's house that night. On Saturday, the next morning, Olivia walked to Brenda's house, which was only a couple of blocks away. Upon arriving, she saw a Cadillac parked in front of Brenda's house, with a northern state's license plates on it. Olivia figured the car belonged to a man and wondered what the deal was that time of morning, but she didn't jump to any conclusions just yet. She wasn't gonna let that stop her from going where she called home, so she proceeded with her mission, went upon the porch of the house and knocked on the door. Brenda moved the curtain on the door's window and looked out to see who was knocking. Then she opened the door just enough to talk to Olivia. Olivia could see how Brenda was blocking the entrance of the doorway, as though she didn't want her to come in, so she just told her she wanted to talk to her, thinking Brenda would let her in. That's when Brenda told Olivia she had company. Olivia immediately got a lump in her throat because she knew right away, just as anyone else would have, that Brenda's visitor was there for intimate reasons. Olivia had figured as much when she first saw the car there, but still hoped the driver of the car was the next-door neighbor's visitor. She didn't trip though. She just turned, walked away and spent the rest of that day and night, thinking about how Brenda played her. Olivia also wondered if the argument she and Brenda had, was staged because Brenda knew John was coming to town. She didn't really have a problem with Brenda being with someone else, man or woman, because that kind of thing from a woman, didn't affect her in the way it would if it were from a man her feelings were involved with. She only wanted Brenda to be honest. Olivia didn't know before, but Brenda was bi-sexual. All that was still cool with Olivia, but she just thought she aught to know that Brenda had someone else and when that person comes, she had to go. Brenda was a jealous woman. She didn't want Olivia to be with anyone else, so Olivia expected the same thing in return and most of all, to not be locked out of the place she calls home, where all of her clothes and belongings are. "The nerve of her", thought Olivia. Brenda was the stud of hers and Olivia's relationship. You know, the masculine one, but she still dated men; John in particular. Anyway, the following day (Sunday), Olivia walked to Brenda's house once again, to settle things. The Cadillac that sat in front of the house the day before, was gone, so Olivia went up to the door and knocked. Brenda knew how angry Olivia was or must have been, so she opened the door and came out on to the porch instead of letting Olivia in. One word led to another, which turned into a fight, physically. Because Olivia was out of control, Brenda ran into the house, closed the door behind her and called the police. Olivia was still furious and out of control, so when the police arrived, they took her to jail. She wasn't of age to be arrested and charged as an adult, so the police let her call Sara to have Sara come and resolve the matter. Olivia was released to Sara's custody after Sara and Jean arrived and she went home with them. After giving it some thought, she decided she wasn't going back to Brenda's to stay nor did she want to have anything more to do with her. A couple of days later, after the anger had dissipated, Sara and Jean took her to Brenda's house to get her clothes and things and to also chaperon to keep the peace between the two of them and that was that. A couple of weeks later, Brenda called Olivia on the phone a few times and wanted to see her, but Olivia was still bitter because she resented going to jail, but also had not gotten over the way things went down when her clothes were at Brenda's house. She didn't wanna give Brenda the chance to take her there again. When she finally talked to Brenda on the phone and agreed to visit her when Brenda asked her to, Olivia never went. Sometimes Olivia had good intentions to visit Brenda, but the memory of the weekend Brenda locked her out of the house and had her arrested, kept her from going.

During Olivia's short stay with Brenda, Troy came home a couple of times and had been informed about Olivia living with and dating a woman. Troy didn't seem to care all that much. In fact, he was more concerned about Olivia giving him the money he needed to get back to school, for expenses he had or for whatever he was gonna spend it on. One of the times he came home and needed some money, Olivia confiscated and pawned a musical instrument her brother no longer played, just to give Troy some money. For many years and still today, folk call teenagers' feelings they have for someone, puppy love or say that they are infatuated. Olivia attest that whatever one chooses to call it, those feelings are very intense and just as strong of feelings, as those one experiences as an adult, so she relates to the intimate feelings any teen claims to have because she probably would have done anything for Troy in the name of love or to be with him. Troy had been away so many months, that it seemed his feelings for Olivia weren't as deep as they once were. Olivia thought he may have been a little angry and/or ashamed about her being with a woman too or maybe she was feeling a little guilty, so she wanted to do something that would make him want her the way he seemed to before. It didn't matter though. Troy didn't spend any time with her and left without saying goodbye. The next time he came to town, Olivia didn't even trip. Troy was distant by this time. Olivia could see how he might feel differently about her now, after what she did (be with a woman) and it seemed to her that Troy always wanted money from her, but didn't have time to spend with her while he was home. That's when she let go of what once was between them. It was over and in reality, it was over when Troy first left town. Olivia was born proud or so it seemed. She never wanted to push herself on anyone and was always eager to remove herself from being with or around anyone who made her feel she wasn't wanted or welcomed, which was seldom. Most people liked her and enjoyed kickin' it with her. Olivia was also very confident. She walked with her head up high and showed her confidence around anyone, in any situation. She didn't allow most things to worry her or make her feel uncomfortable, but if so, she never let anyone see her sweat. Therefore, when it seemed Troy was avoiding her or didn't want her around, Olivia stayed away. What she sensed was obvious too. As she stopped going to those places Troy frequented when he was in town and trying to contact him when he came to town, Troy didn't try and get with her neither and that was that.

Olivia didn't have any plans at this point in her life. She just hung out and got high as often as possible, with anyone she knew who wanted to kick it with her and then there was Lena. Lena was the neighbor and schoolmate Olivia played around with their eighth grade school year. That was after Olivia's first sexual experience with a boy and before she dated Waylon. Lena never stopped coming around though, but she didn't press Olivia to have a relationship with her. When Olivia dated Brenda, she could tell that Lena was affected emotionally by it because she had more of a relationship with Brenda than she had with her.

That's just the way things turned out. "It was nothing personal", said Olivia. Maybe things didn't get as far with Lena because Olivia was hurt and turned off after Lena told her she was pregnant and then had a miscarriage. That's when Olivia, casually, shied away from her. After Olivia broke up with Brenda, Lena started coming around even more. She would come to Olivia's home looking for her, almost daily. Sometimes Olivia would visit with her for whatever it was worth and would sometimes play Lena off when she didn't want to be bothered. Lena didn't stay away though. She had fallen in love and would do anything she could, for Olivia to be with her. She even gave Olivia money and bought her things. Olivia accepted everything Lena had to give too. I mean everything. She liked and cared for Lena, but she liked men much more. Just hangin' out with a male friend on a platonic level, was more fun to her, than being with a female. By this time, she had experienced drugs other than marijuana: opium, blonde and black hash, hash oil, angel dust, super cools and t.h.c. She had even snorted cocaine a few times. It seemed that every time she met someone or started hangin' around a different crowd, (usually older folk), she was introduced to a drug she had never before tried, so getting high had come to be all she really wanted to get with.

Olivia was always kickin' it: hanging out, going places, having fun and gettin' high. One of the times she was hangin' out, she went to this guy's house with whomever she was kickin' it with and was introduced to the man who lived there. Hank was his name. Hank was good-lookin', charming, funny and was a drug addict slash drug dealer. His choice of drugs was cocaine, p.c.p. and marijuana. It was like a party house at Hank's. Olivia thought, "damn, this is the place to be" and Hank took a likin' to her. He not only thought she was cool, but also cute, so the two of them hit it off as they sat and got high. Olivia started hangin' out at Hank's on regular basis as she and him started diggin' one another more and more. She didn't know a lot about him, but the more she hung around, she observed the way he was when he came from the bedroom he shut himself in for fifteen or twenty minutes at a time. He seemed so calm and cool, but still comical more than usual when he came from the bedroom. Sometimes he would sit with his legs crossed and talk with everyone with kind of a joy about himself. Finally, after she and Hank were really comfortable with one another, Olivia wanted to know why he was feeling as good as he was after coming from the bedroom. It was nothing new that Olivia had snorted cocaine before, but it was Hank who took her to a new drug-using level. He introduced Olivia to his way of doing his drugs of choice, main lining (shooting up). Hank was doing it and so were a lot of others who hung around or was in and out of Hank's house, so Olivia thought, "it can't be that bad". She don't know what brought it on one day in particular, but that was the day that she was unusually spontaneous and wanted to try something new. That day, she was riding around with Lena in Lena's new car and asked Lena to go by this friend of hers' house. Olivia was really just stopping by Hank's house to get a small bag of weed or a few joints, whatever she could get. Knowing herself the way she was back then, Olivia thought, I probably ran inside Hank's house, discovered he was gettin' busy, getting high, so I said, I want some. Hank didn't know if I was joking or not, so he just looked at me with this smile on his face. A look that asked, "are you serious, do you really wanna do this", said Olivia. In return, she looked at Hank with this, I mean it, I want some" look on her face, so Hank took her in the bedroom and obliged her. First he wrapped a belt around Olivia's arm after preparing a syringe and then he injected the dope that was in the syringe, into her vein. Olivia watched everything Hank did. After all, he was no medical doctor. Olivia exclaims, "don't try this boys and girls, it is very dangerous and habit-forming". The injection sent her flying high. She sat there in Hank's bedroom and chilled for about fifteen minutes until she saw that she was okay. She didn't know what to expect, so she wanted to sit there with Hank for a few minutes. That way, if she began to experience some difficulties, Hank would know what to do. After seeing she was going to be alright, Olivia had to get out of there because Lena was still sitting outside in the car waiting for her. Olivia didn't let Lena know a lot of things she did or of a lot of places she kicked it at. She didn't allow Lena to come inside most of the places she frequented that Lena knew about nor did she allow Lena to come looking for her at those places. When she got into Lena's car, she was feeling like being free and kickin' it, so she told Lena, "ride me til I sweat", and that's what Lena did. After turning a few corners, Olivia told Lena she wanted to drive. Olivia had never driven a car before, but the high she was on was making her feel she could do anything she wanted to do. Lena wanting to do whatever she could to please Olivia, was down with her driving, so she began telling Olivia about the functions of the car, the gears of the four speed Volkswagen, how and when to shift the gears and then she let her get behind the wheel. Lena showed Olivia the way to the freeway, Olivia got on it and drove that car like she owned it. That was the day she learned to drive, at the age of sixteen. From that day on, Lena let Olivia drive the car just about everyday, until Olivia got really good with it. Then Olivia began to drive the car without Lena being with her. Lena didn't mind neither. She just wanted to be around Olivia as much as she could, no matter how she got it. Olivia caught on to that too, so she would let Lena stay in her bedroom at Sara's house, while she was gone with her car. She would even let Lena spend the night with her. That made everything all right with Lena after Olivia would be gone with the car all evening. Sara knew what was going on between the two of them, but she didn't mind. Lena was very content when she was able to stay the night with Olivia, so it all worked out.

Olivia enjoyed the high she got from main lining that first time, but the second time she did it, was with someone else who was a mutual friend of hers and Hank's. His choice of drug to main line was heroine. Now this was more Olivia's speed. Boy did she like the high she got from shooting heroine. It made her feel warm inside, very relaxed, more confident than she already was, with more heart (which she already had) and it just made her feel all unnecessary. Heroine is equally a dangerous drug as cocaine, in similar, but different ways. "It ain't nothing nice to fuck with", said Olivia, even though she liked it as well as she did. It's no wonder she enjoyed the nod affect she got from doing heroine. She has always moved slowly and took her time doing most things she did. Back in the days, she used to be called, Pokey and Slow Poke. She had been teased that she was as slow as Christmas or molasses and she's been told she was gonna be late for her own funeral, so heroine was all right with Olivia during that time. Besides, being the freak she was, Olivia got off on the warm sensation that would flow through her body when she did heroine. She wasn't having a lot of sex when she was wherever she was, with whomever she was with when she was getting high. She was basically a one-guy kind of girl. Olivia just wanted to get high and hang out with the big guys and girls, mainly guys. Kicking it the way they did, anything could and would jump off and heroine gave Olivia more guts than she already had, that was needed to be down with whatever went down.

Shooting up got to be an everyday thing for Olivia. Sometimes she wouldn't come home until one or two o' clock in the morning. She could hang out like that because Sara kind of let her do what she wanted to do after she moved back home from Brenda's home. To pacify Lena, Olivia would let her spend the night more often, to give Lena incentive for letting her drive her car. Olivia would use Lena's car during the day and go and get high until late at night. While Olivia was going place-to-place getting high, she ran into the brother of one of her neighborhood friends, whom she had been admiring since she first seen him. Warren was a fine, chocolate brother who had this really cute way he walked and seemed to have money. The way Olivia felt about money, she was attracted to anyone and anything that resembled dollar bills and Warren had that look. Come to find out, Warren was a dealer of pharmaceutical drugs, marijuana, heroine and cocaine. He wasn't a big-time dealer, but one could get a small sack from him. Olivia used to check Warren out getting in and out of his gangster green Lincoln Continental car, with the kissing doors and she wondered what he was about. She thought, "Whatever he does, he's got it going on". Warren was a married man though, who had children, but of course Olivia was captured by his charm, looks, popularity, financial status, that walk he had and killer smile, so it didn't matter to the young girl, that he was married. Actually, by this time, Olivia was more focused on Warren being her connection to getting drugs. He was someone

29

she could trust since his mom and siblings were neighbors on the street block Sara's house was on and they were practically like family. After getting drugs from him a few times, Olivia and Warren started dating (more like messing around, having sex). As shameful as it is, Olivia admits she and Warren even had sex in the house he, his wife, and children lived in, while his wife was at work and his kids were at school or the day care. She never gave much thought to the wrong in it, she was just trying to get her fix and her freak on. Warren wanted the sex more than Olivia did. Olivia probably would have wanted the sex just as much if Warren had to work with, what she was use to jumping up and down on, but he didn't. Olivia liked Warren a lot though, so she didn't mind having sex with him. On the real tip, she didn't want to have sex when she was getting high. Warren didn't shoot dope, he just smoked weed and tooted a little caine (cocaine), so his motive for getting Olivia high was strictly to fuck her. Olivia knew that, but she was okay with it because she had her own motive. She liked Warren, but the fact that he was married forced her to keep her heart from getting too in to him. She kept in mind that he was a supplier for free drugs and at that time, that was the most important thing to her. Oh she was clever and became more clever about the drugs and men as time went on. Olivia found out early in her drug using days that cocaine is not only dangerous, but it is cunning. For men, cocaine gives them a false sense of that, "I can fuck all night", thinking and feeling. For real, the feeling may be there, but more often, their dicks won't get hard. With heroine, your body is all hot and bothered and the drug stimulates the sex organs, but the nod, to heroine attics, is more enjoyable. "Hell, you can't or don't want to come out of your nod long enough to start a sex session, so you ain't trying to get with no sex when you're high off heroine", said Olivia. She peeped that (checked that out) by observing the way others were when they were high off the drug, just as she was when she did heroine and she played on that whenever she was propositioned by someone who wanted to get her high or get high with her. If it was a guy who did cocaine, Olivia knew he was gonna go on a blazo from the rush, that he wouldn't want to be still long enough to get his freak on and if he did, the dick wasn't gonna get hard. If it was a guy she used heroine with, she and the guy were gonna go into a nod and forget all about fucking. Olivia smiled and said, "Shit, I had it going on". "Most of the time, I just wanted to enjoy the comfort I had when I was into my nod", she added.. Everyone who did heroine or knew anything about heroine, knew not to bother someone when they were gettin' their nod on, so Olivia escaped the plan any man had, to go up in her (have sexual intercourse with her) after getting high with her. "Even though I usually went into a nod after doing heroine, I was flexible. I could get with this or I could get with that. It didn't make any difference. I felt I could deal with whatever went down", said Olivia. Little did she know, that she was playing Russian roulette with the drugs she used, but they were her choice of entertainment. Around this time in her life, Olivia started going to nightclubs too, while hangin' with the older folk. She would dress up all sexy, with high heels, lipstick and other makeup on, just like she remembered the ladies had done, when they went to the tavern next door to the house she grew up in. Usually, she would be with an older guy or a couple of people older than she, so she didn't have any problems getting into the clubs. Even though Olivia was somewhat of a dope fein, but didn't know it, she was always a lady. She still didn't come on to guys, she didn't show her ass and she was, usually, seen and not heard. She talked trash with the girls, but was disciplined with her conversation when she was around men. Olivia was always cordial. She kept herself clean (hygienically speaking) and tried to look cute every time she stepped out (went to the clubs) or left home. She may have been a bit vain, but had no idea that would, at one point in her life, save her. She had this, "I'm the shit", attitude, aura and way of carrying herself. Most people still liked her in spite of the things she got involved in. While all this getting high and swangin' it with Warren was going on, Olivia was feeding Lena to keep her satisfied, so she would keep doing the things for her that she was doing. All the while, Olivia was spending most of her time where the drugs and partying were going on. Lena didn't like it and was getting tired of Olivia leaving her at Sara's house in her bedroom and not getting any time with Olivia. Meanwhile, Brenda was still calling on the telephone every now and then, wanting Olivia to come and visit her. Olivia would still, sometimes, tell Brenda she would visit her, but would stand Brenda up. She kept in mind what Brenda did to her and learned how Brenda played games, so she wasn't trying to get with her. She didn't even feel Brenda like that anymore. Even though she didn't really want to be with a woman, if she were going to be with one, it would have been Lena. Olivia believed that Lena or any other lesbian could handle her messing with a guy, even though Lena or the lesbian wanted their mate to themselves. What people like them could not accept more, was their mate being with someone else of the same sex (another female). Olivia didn't kick it too much with girls or ladies who didn't indulge in the things she did or kicked it the way she did. She didn't kick it with girls or women too much anyway, but she finally hooked up with her long time girlfriend, who wanted to kick it with her Olivia style (the way Olivia did), so the two of them started hangin' together and became, damn near, inseparable. Shannon (was her name) was cool with everything Olivia was about and so Olivia was content with the select people she flocked with. When she thought she really needed to, she did something special with Lena. She didn't want Lena to interfere with her drug using and kickin' it time, so she let Lena spend the night with her, which she felt was quality time. It worked for a while.

Apparently, Brenda was really missing Olivia and had been asking around, checkin' up on her, because somehow, Brenda found out Olivia was shooting drugs and told Sara. Olivia had been discreet with drugs at home. She never got high that way at home, but she kept her work (syringe) hidden under her mattress. In the streets, Olivia didn't advertise what she got high on. Whatever she did with whomever she got high with didn't go any further than those involved. One day, after being out all night the night before, Olivia came home about eleven AM and was questioned by Sara as soon as she walked through the door. You could tell Sara had been sitting there, just waiting for Olivia and had this really concerned look on her face. Sara asked Olivia, "Are you high"? Of course Olivia didn't admit to anything. Sara asked Olivia, "What are you high on"? Olivia still didn't say anything. She just sat there looking down at the floor. Sara then told Olivia to go upstairs and get herself cleaned up, that her probation officer wanted to see her. After the first time Olivia was sent to the juvenile detention home, a probation officer was assigned to follow-up on her behavior, so Olivia did what Sara told her to do, went upstairs, bathed and got dressed. After doing so, off her and Sara went to the juvenile court. Sitting there in her probation officer's office, Olivia was afraid and very nervous because Sara and the officer had such serious looks on their faces. Per the officer's request Sara began to tell him all of the things Olivia had been doing and about Olivia shooting-up drugs. The officer began to question Olivia, asking her if the things Sara was saying were true and asked Olivia why she was doing those things. Olivia really didn't have a good answer to the questions, except to tell the officer that she was just doing the things she liked doing. The officer then asked Sara what she wanted to do with Olivia at this point. Sara not knowing what options she had and knowing the detention home was for temporary placement, sat there shrugging her shoulders and said, "I don't know". The officer began asking Sara if she wanted Olivia permanently removed from her home and told Sara about G.I.S, Girls Industrial School. Olivia didn't even wait for Sara's response. She immediately panicked and started crying, begging and pleading to not be sent to G.I.S. The officer went on to say, "I think that is the best place for her since she won't obey you (talking to Sara) and you can't do anything with her". The shit was getting too deep for Olivia. Sara was quiet as the officer seemed to be convincing, so Olivia got up from the chair she sat in, got on her knees and pleaded with Sara. Sara was still quiet and didn't respond to Olivia's plea, so Olivia got off her knees and got on top of the officer's desk to plead with him. She was so out of control, that Sara and the officer couldn't even talk, so the officer suggested to Sara that the two of them go to another room or office to talk further. Olivia cried and pleaded with them as they went out the door, trying to hold on to Sara's clothes to keep her from leaving the room. Sara pulled loose from the grasp Olivia had on her and the officer closed the door behind them,

32

leaving Olivia in his office. Olivia sat in the room alone crying and wondering if Sara was going to leave the building without her, for the officer to handle the process of sending her away. Olivia thought, "I don't want to be sent to G.I.S., I've got to do something". She sat there a minute to pull herself together so that she could think and then to listen for voices outside the door, to hear if anyone was out there or coming down the hall towards the office she sat in. She didn't hear anyone, so she got up from the chair she sat in, walked over to the door and put her ear up to it to make sure no one was in the hallway. Then she quietly turned the knob on the door, still listening and opened the door slowly. Before peeping out, she stood there a minute and listened once again. She didn't hear anyone, so she peeped out, looking both ways down the hallway. No one was seen, so Olivia took off running towards the front door of the building, past the receptionist, pulled the door open and ran out of the building as fast as she could. She ran between two houses, through back yards of other houses and jumped fences to get out of sight from anyone seeing which direction she went in. Finally, when it seemed she was blocks away, she stopped running and caught her breath while looking in every direction for anyone or anything that looked suspicious. After she was calm, Olivia went to a house and knocked on the door. An elderly lady answered the knock on her door. Olivia told the lady some story about being stranded and asked the lady if she could use her phone. The lady didn't want to let Olivia into her house, so she gave her coins to use a pay phone. Olivia then carefully went to a nearby coin phone and called Hank. She didn't go into detail about what had happened, but asked him to come and get her. Hank didn't come, but he sent someone to pick her up. As Olivia waited for the ride, she stayed out of sight, but she felt pretty safe because when she ran from the juvenile court, she ran in the opposite direction from home. She figured if anyone was looking for her, they would probably look for her to be going in that direction. Oh, she was clever alright for a young girl and about a lot of things other than drugs. The driver who came and got her, took her straight to Hank's home where she hid out in his basement. Olivia had Hank to call the mutual friend of theirs who made arrangements for her to be hidden. When night fell, she was transported to Daniel's (Danny) home, which is where she spent most of her time when she was getting high.

Olivia and Danny were real tight (close). They were just friends and really cared about one another, platonically speaking. Danny was an older guy about fourteen years older than Olivia, so he was more like a big brother or uncle to her. Olivia would hang out at his house all day and all night sometimes. He was a dealer and was cool with most people. A lot of people were in and out of Danny's house as well. Some of them did their dope there, sat around and kicked it. Therefore, Olivia being as clean and neat as she was, would straighten up

Danny's house, wash the dishes sometimes and would even run to the store for him if she had Lena's car or could use someone else's car. Everyone who hung around was cool like that. Most of them scratched one another's back. In return for Olivia's unconditional kindness and help that she gave and showed Danny, he would give her a fix every six or eight hours. Just like clockwork. Olivia didn't have to pay him a dime. It wasn't a plan of hers to get free dope from Danny. It just turned out that way. Olivia could get free dope from Warren and a couple of others. Danny knew that too, so he knew Olivia wasn't trying to play him. He knew she liked hangin' out at his house, kickin' it with him. Shit, sometimes Olivia and Shannon (Olivia's long time girlfriend) would go to hotels with Danny when he would seem to be there to take care of business. The three of them would shoot dope and kick it around there. They really enjoyed one another's company. Olivia and Shannon never gave a thought about the police raiding the room they were in or of some dope fein robbing and possibly hurting or killing the three of them. They were just hangin' with Danny, trying to get their buzz on (get high). Knowing how serious Olivia was about not being found by her mother or the authorities though, Danny worked everything out for her to go underground. He had planned to drive to a city in the state of Kansas, to do some drug business. Danny had a friend who lived in the city he was going to, told Olivia how cool this guy was and that he would watch out for her if she wanted to go there and stay for a couple or few weeks. Olivia trusted Danny and knew he would not put her in this guy's care if the guy wasn't cool, so she was down with that (going to the city in Kansas). At nightfall, after packing some things and getting their fix, Olivia and her girlfriend Shannon, hit the road with Danny and a male friend of theirs who drove his car. All four of them were, literally, riding high. As they were rolling down the freeway several miles outside of the town they lived in, a police officer pulled them over. "Man", they all thought when the driver first spotted the cop. "Oh shit", is what they all said and the way they all felt when the officer turned his siren and lights on, because they were dirty (had drugs on them and in their systems). To top it all off, Olivia and Shannon were minors. After pulling them over, the cop got out of his car, came to the drivers side of the car Olivia and the others were in while shining his flashlight inside the car and asked Tony (the driver) for his drivers license and registration. Tony's credentials were straight. He didn't have any warrants, everything checked out. An unfortunate thing happened though, while the police officer was checking out Tony's I-D. Because they all had shot-up some heroine before they left Danny's house, Olivia got the dog food (heroine) willies (nausea), had to open the back door (where she and Shannon sat) and vomit. The others knew what the deal was, so when the officer asked Olivia was she alright, she (being a quick thinker when there was trouble) replied, " I'll be okay, I'm just pregnant". The officer bought the story and replied to Tony, "you might want

34

to stop somewhere up the road so that she (talking about Olivia) can eat something". Tony replied to the officer, "we're gonna stop at the next restaurant, diner or truck stop so we all can get something to eat, sir". The officer replied, "Okay, you all be careful and have a safe trip". Olivia and the others in the sound of an echo said, "okay". The officer then, let them go. "Damn that was close", someone said and the others agreed as they proceeded down the highway. After driving a while, Danny and Tony thought they all should chill somewhere overnight, so they reached a motel where they got two rooms and spent the night there. Olivia had been digging (liking) Tony for a while, but had never slept with or had sex with him until this night and Shannon slept with Danny. At the break of dawn, they all arose, showered, got dressed and got back on the road.

Early that evening, Olivia and the others arrived to their destination. Tony knew Jimmy, so Danny introduced Olivia and Shannon to him, whom Olivia was going to be staying with. Being the drug addict she was and being exposed to all the things she had seen or been a part of, Olivia didn't worry about being left in a strange place with this guy who was a stranger to her. Then again, she trusted Danny. After doing the business he came there to do, Danny, along with Tony and Shannon hit the road and headed back home. Olivia was cool there with Jimmy. He never came on to her or tried anything with her. The two of them became good friends. Jimmy was separated from his wife, but still spent time with her and their two children. It was the month of October when Olivia stayed with him. She even went trick-or-treating with him and his kids.

Olivia was away from home almost two weeks without calling or contacting her mom. As mischievous as she was, she loved her mom, Jean and her siblings and missed them terribly. She only wanted to do what she wanted to do and didn't want Sara or anyone else to stop her or interfere, but after being away as long as she had, Olivia got concerned about how worried Sara must have been. She also wanted to peep (find out about) the situation at that point, so she called Sara from a coin phone. That way, no one could trace the exact whereabouts she was calling from. Sara was really happy to hear from her baby (what she would refer to Olivia as) and was relieved to know Olivia was alive and well. Olivia didn't shoot-up any drugs while she was away. Sara, the probation officer and Brenda reacted as though she was a dope-fein junky who was lost and turned out, unable to return. Olivia didn't even know what that was like, so she didn't feel or see herself to be in that category, to that extreme. Therefore, she had no problem withdrawing from the drug she had been using. She wanted to be clean when she returned home or if she were caught. She also wanted to show or prove Sara's, the probation officer's and Brenda's suspicions or assumptions to be wrong, so when she talked to Sara on the phone, she was honestly able to say she had not been shooting drugs. While she was away from home, as she was letting her system clean itself, Olivia even used toothpaste to clear up the tracks (needle marks) on her arms. She continued to smoke weed, but she knew that marijuana was more acceptable and easier to clean from her system, so she took a chance with that. Of course she told Sara she wasn't using any drugs and that she would never shoot-up again. At the time, she meant it. Olivia never told Sara where she was during their conversation on the phone. Sara just kept asking her to come home, but Olivia thought she would be set up. She was afraid Sara would have the police there waiting for her. Sara told Olivia she wouldn't do that and that she just wanted her to come home so the two of them could talk and that the State would take full control and custody of her if she were picked up by the police. Sara told Olivia if she came home willingly, the two of them could talk things over and work something out. That's what Olivia wanted also, but she was afraid of what could be waiting there for her when she returned, so she asked Sara to promise and even swear that she would not let her be or have her arrested. Sara did what Olivia asked her to do, promised and swore that she would not involve the police or juvenile authorities. After being convinced that Sara was sincere and trustworthy, that it was okay to come home, Olivia finished talking to her and called Danny to have him arrange for her to be taken home.

When Olivia arrived to the neighborhood she lived in, she had the driver to circle the block to see if there were any police cars in the area or anyone suspiciously hangin' around. There were no cops, probation officer or authority figures to be seen, so Olivia thought everything was cool and had the driver to let her out of the car in front of Sara's house. When she walked through the door, there was just Sara, Jean and Olivia's siblings waiting and welcoming her with open arms. After everyone there hugged Olivia, Sara asked to be alone with her so the two of them could talk. The others obliged Sara's request. When the two of them were alone, Olivia showed her arms to Sara so that she could see there were no tracks. Tracks are marks made from continuous injections of drugs. There weren't any. You see, one of the tricks you learn in the drug and streetlife is how to cover your ass and also to clean your biological system. For main-liners, a common way of gettin' rid of tracks is to rub toothpaste on them everyday until they are no longer visible. This method is most effective if one is not using the drug on the days they use the toothpaste and until the marks are gone. Olivia used the toothpaste daily while she was in hiding. As strange as the toothpaste method for getting rid of needle marks seems, it really works. Sara then figured that Olivia could not be strung out on drugs because the tracks were gone and because she looked well rested and healthy. Sara told Olivia how much she loved her and cared about her well-being. Sara had done her best to raise Olivia and steer her in the right direction, but it didn't seem she could change or put a stop to the things Olivia was determined to do. Sara told Olivia that she prayed everyday, asking God to watch over her because she was letting go and leaving her in His hands. Sara told Olivia she could now do what she wanted to do, with the exception of Olivia disrespecting her and her house. That decision was great for Olivia, that's all she wanted. Sara told Olivia she didn't think she could take of herself, but since Olivia claimed she could, Sara told her she was on her own. Sara didn't mean she was putting Olivia out of the house or that Olivia couldn't eat at home if she were hungry. She only meant that she wasn't going to tell Olivia what to do. Olivia didn't know what to think or expect from this point on, but she was happy to hear what Sara told her. Somehow, she felt the sincerity of Sara's words and felt safe from being taken away. That made her exhale. After hers and Sara's talk, the two of them cried together, hugged one another and agreed to the resolution of the dilemma.

Though this seemed to be the end of Olivia's wild days, it was the beginning of wilder days. Now that she could do what she wanted to do, she really got busy getting high and hangin' out. She started going to nightclubs more often, that were for those who were twenty-one years of age or older and she always had her mind altered (was always high) from doing one drug or another. Olivia even started shooting-up heroine again. She was only sixteen years old, hot-to-trot and game for almost anything. In the click she kicked it with, the drugs that were often used, were angel dust and TAC, both of the PCP family. Olivia and associates would use one of those forms of PCP, sit wherever they were, usually someone's home or apartment and go on their trip. Olivia still did heroine, but she liked all drugs. Damn near whatever was available to get high on, was cool with her. She rationalized in her mind, that if she didn't do the same drug all the time, she wouldn't be dependent on one drug in particular (addicted). It was years later, when she learned differently about drug addiction.

At sixteen years of age, Olivia had dropped out of senior high school her eleventh grade school year, because she didn't want to make up some tenth grade classes she flunked the previous year. It was the end of her tenth grade school year when she lived with Brenda. With her and Brenda being lovers, Olivia didn't have anyone pressing her about going to school, even though that was the deal she made with Sara in order for her to stay with Brenda. Of course Olivia agreed and probably swore to Sara, that she would go to school and she did just that at first. Brenda didn't say anything when Olivia stayed home from school, so Olivia missed a lot of schooldays. Sometimes Brenda didn't know when Olivia didn't go to school, because Olivia would be somewhere getting high until school was out.

Past her days with Brenda and not having to go to school, Olivia just hung out wherever the drugs were plentiful. When there was a concert she wanted to go to, she would get money from Lena to buy a ticket and would get a ride or catch a ride there, whichever came first. Sometimes she was able to buy a ticket to a concert or whatever else she wanted, with the money she made selling weed. Olivia always wanted to have money or have access to money. What she would do is buy a q-p (quarter pound) of weed (which was a lot back in that era) and walk up and down the neighborhood boulevard where she sold nickel and dime bags and joints for one dollar each. Sometimes she would sell a little weed at the concerts she went to. She was far from being a big-time dealer. She only dealt enough to keep seventy-five or one hundred fifty dollars in her pocket. She knew everyone who hung out or was getting high, so she made her money just selling to those she knew. Selling weed was fun to Olivia. Making money and getting high were the two most important things on her daily agenda. She hadn't dated anyone except Lena and Warren, occasionally, since she moved from Brenda's house, so she was just drifting at this time. She had sex with Hank a couple of times, but it really wasn't about nothin' Mostly, she had sex with Warren when the two of them hooked up. That was all it was with Warren though. Just sex. Olivia knew and kept in mind that Warren was married and had children. He wasn't going to leave his family for anyone and Olivia didn't want or expect him to. She continued to date him, basically because when he got a small three room duplex, he would bring her there to have sex with her and would give her a free fix of heroine. A lot of times, he gave Olivia a capsule of dope, even if they didn't have sex. "Warren was cool", exclaimed Olivia. He was also the middleman she copped the weed from that she was selling. The more she hung out and kicked it with other folk though, the less she saw Warren and depended on him for what she wanted. She used heroine and occasionally, other main-line drugs, less, when she didn't see Warren. Danny had gotten a hold of some bad dope and had gotten very, very ill, which also brought the heat down on him or coincidentally during the same time, the heat was already on him (being watched by the police), so Olivia's resources were all, folding. Because she was down for being high on whatever drug was available to her and not give in to one particular drug, Olivia was not physically affected by her connections drying up. She just went with the flow and indulged in whatever the drug for the day was (sorta' speak).

One night, while kickin' it at one of the nightclubs, Olivia noticed a guy she had seen a few times, as he got out of the big pretty Cadillac he was driving. "This guy is sexy and looks like he's from Hollywood", she thought. Olivia was the kind of girl who checked a guy out from a distance on several occasions, before getting with him or letting him know she was interested in him. Joseph (Joe) was tall, about six feet, medium built, had a light golden skin-tone, wore his hair processed with finger waves in it, he had diamond rings on a couple of his fingers and to top it off, he had a gold tooth. Olivia was very attracted to guys who had a gold tooth or two. Joe seemed to have money. He was dressed nicely this night and the other times Olivia saw him. He was a guy who was more seen than heard, which was also appealing to Olivia. Being attracted to money and expensive things as she was, Olivia was very curious about Joe. After having her eyes on him all along, Olivia noticed Joe was a partner (buddy) of a slickster everyone knew, named Freddie. Freddie was flashy also and drove a Cadillac too. Olivia saw Freddie around town on numerous occasions when, at different times, a lady or two would get out of his Cadillac, all dressed up. The girls, who were with him, wore high-heeled pumps, makeup and longhaired wigs. They seemed to be rich or something. Olivia wondered who they were and what they were about. Somehow, she was introduced to Joe the night she saw him out kickin it with Freddie. Joe talked to her for a while that night as they sat in the nightclub and he later asked her to ride with him and Freddie when they left the club and so she did. Apparently, a lady, who left the club with them, was mingling inside the club earlier, because Olivia didn't meet her inside the club or even see her get out of Joe's car. Casey (was the lady's name) rode in the back seat of the Cadillac with Olivia, as Freddie rode in the front seat with Joe, the driver. The Cadillac ride was smooth. Joints of weed were being passed around as they all sipped on (a new drink to Olivia) Hennessey cognac they bought along with some cups of ice from a nearby liquor store. Olivia felt like she was on Rodeo Drive as they rode the streets in the big car. After turning a few corners, they all went to Freddie's home, sat around, drank more Hennessey and smoked more weed. Joe and Olivia sat closely to one another and talked, as he told her a little bit about himself and Freddie's lady. Olivia didn't trip (think about it) at the time, on why Joe was telling her about Freddie's girl. She just listened and enjoyed the atmosphere and the buzz (high) she had, as slow music played on the stereo. "Freddie's girl is a money-maker", said Joe. He didn't go into much detail, but Olivia had an idea of what he meant. Before daybreak, which was soon after they arrived at Freddie's house, everyone had wined down, so Joe took Olivia home and gave her his phone number. "Call me", is what Joe said as Olivia got out of his car. Olivia went into Sara's house where she still resided, put on a nightgown and laid in bed that morning, trying to figure out the people she had just left and if she wanted to get more involved with them. She liked the way they kicked it and was curious about them all, but she fell asleep before she made a decision. A couple of days later, Olivia talked to Joe on the phone, then Joe came and picked Olivia up. The two of them went for a long ride in Joe's Cadillac, while talking and getting more acquainted with one another along the way. After a while, Joe pulled into a driveway of a small, but cute house. That's where he lived. Olivia spent the night there and had sex with Joe for the first time. Joe was very sexy and charming, but sexually, he was too much man for her. Joe had the fattest, longest dick Olivia had ever felt or seen. "Man", she said, "Joe's penis was the size of a horse's dick", it seemed. She didn't back down from it though, but the next day after she got home, Olivia thought she didn't want another dick up in her for a long, long time. She also thought she was gonna have to go to the hospital to have her pussy checked out, but she really didn't. Her pussy felt like it was hurt. Joe just went further up in her than anyone else had gone and broke her off more than she could handle. While doing Olivia that night (fuckin her), Joe said some things that stayed on her mind and asked her a couple of those "take this good dick, "will you", "are you", "don't you" questions. You know the way a guy asks a girl questions while fuckin' her, thinking he's dickin' her so good, that she'll say yes or agree to anything he ask her or ask of her. Something Olivia didn't know anything about at the time. She kinda' liked Joe, but she was probably more fascinated with him, so she said yes to the questions he asked her while he was fuckin' her and she continued to date him, even though she didn't feel him the way she felt Troy or the other guys she dated and felt she was in love with. Then came the punch line. While visiting Joe at Freddie's home one evening, Joe sat with Olivia to talk to her and told her how Casey, Freddie's lady, went out and made money. Casey was a whoe and Freddie was her pimp. Casey would go to the part of town where truck drivers deliver cargo, lay over, rest or have a meal at a truck stop. Joe told Olivia how Casey brings home three or four hundred dollars a night, sometimes more. He talked about all the things the two of them could do, places they could go and things they could have if they made that much money every night. Mind you, Joe spoke of himself and Olivia making the money. Being young and naive, at the time, Olivia didn't think about how her making money selling her pussy, would be the money she and Joe made. She had not figured out or learned how the pimp game was played. She did have sense enough to know that Joe was not gonna do anything to help her while she was dating a trick nor would he be there when and where the date would take place. She remembered how Troy stayed in his apartment while she went to the janitor's apartment and dated him, so she knew she would do all the physical work and she would be alone with the trick when she did it. She just didn't know yet, what part a pimp plays in the game, what his job as the pimp was and when he works or does his part. Joe sugar-coated it though. He talked fast, said things to Olivia that made her feel she was a star and he always touched her body gently in different places while he talked to her. Oh, he used all the artillery he had and all the techniques he knew and it worked. When dusk fell, he told Olivia he wanted her to go to work with Casey, that Casey would show her how to work the stroll (the street hookers work) and look after her. With Joe being as convincing and influential as he was, Olivia agreed to go to the stroll with Casey. When it was time for Casey to go to work, the two guys, Joe and Freddie, rode in the front seat and Olivia and Casey rode in the back seat of the Cadillac (like pimps roll when they have whoes in their car) as Freddie drove to take the girls to work.

Olivia stayed close to Casey the first couple of times she worked the stroll, then she got the game and ran with it. She even did very well, financially, the first night she worked. Some nights she worked the stroll, she would have a shot of heroine before going to work. Joe didn't shoot-up drugs, but Freddie and Casey did. Unconsciously, heroine gave Olivia the heart that's needed to endure the risk and everything else whoes had to endure. When she put on her short dress or tight fitting pants with her make-up and high-heel pumps, she thought she was the shit. When she walked that stroll, guys would drive by and slow their cars down while turning their heads back to check her out as they drove by. They would eventually come back after turning a couple or few corners. "You want a date honey", is what Olivia would shout out in a sexy tone, whenever a guy would slow his car down or stop it. That was one of the things she learned from Casey when she first got down (as they say in the game). Other things she was taught were safety precautions with tricks (johns) and watching out for the police or decoys. She also learned to get the money from a john first, before having sex with him and to never quote a price or sex act. She would agree to do what was solicited to her by the trick if he quoted the right price. Olivia got paid. She worked the stroll and gave all the money to Joe until the last few days she was with him. Then she held back on him, which was grounds for an ass kickin' in the game, if found out. Pimps want and demand every dollar and every dime made on the stroll or elsewhere for that matter. Joe was a dog too, as Olivia found out after a short period of time she was with him. He had that new Cadillac to pay for and the house he was renting or buying. He enjoyed riding around in that big car, going to different nightclubs, buying cognac, eating out at diners and restaurants and he had an expensive desire for cocaine he liked putting up his nose. Joe also enjoyed smoking weed frequently throughout each day. These types of activities seemed to be the lifestyle of all pimps. They all seemed to enjoy going to breakfast before sun-up, after picking up their whoe or whoes if she or they made any real money (a few hundred or more) or after checking their trap or traps (whoes out as bait to catch a trick) as they call it. Most pimps are super-fly. They dress well and like being flashy. That's the way Joe was. He was really trying to live above his means, which made him a dog about money. Olivia quickly peeped (figured out) what he was about though. He wasn't really a pimp, he just had friends who were pimps and he finally caught a young, naive girl, who was digging (liking) him enough to be influenced by him. Remembering that Olivia was really turned out by Troy. That is why it wasn't that hard for Joe to put her down on the stroll.

During the short time Olivia was with (dating) Joe, one day while Sara, Jean and Yulonda (the only child of Sara's other than Olivia, who still lived in Sara and Jean's home) were gone to work, Joe came to visit Olivia and got into bed with her. The two of them fucked and took a nap before Joe left. Everything Olivia owned was in her bedroom, so Joe saw all the stereo equipment she had, along with her other belongings. There must have been three sets of stereo equipment in Olivia's bedroom. Two sets of equipment were given to her by Lena, one of which was very expensive. Being as though Olivia was surrounded by music and partying while she was growing up, that stereo equipment was her pride and joy. She cherished her equipment. Everyone knew how she felt about it, so no one bothered the stereos without her permission. As a matter of fact, Olivia recalls being very stingy about her music. The time when Joe was in her bedroom was after Olivia had been working the stroll for about two weeks. By that time, Olivia was a lot more comfortable with Joe and trusted him, somewhat. One night, a few days or a week later, after Joe had picked Olivia up from the stroll, he told her he wanted to throw a party for her at his house, but he didn't have a stereo. Joe asked Olivia if she would like to have a party in her honor and of course Olivia said, "Yes". Joe asked Olivia if they could use some of the equipment she had. Excited about him throwing her a party (since she had never had a party before), Olivia told Joe they could use some of her stereo equipment. The next day or two, while everyone at Sara and Jean's house, except Olivia, was away, Joe came and picked up the most expensive set of equipment Olivia had and as usual, Olivia met with Joe later at Freddie's house where he took her from, to the whoe stroll. One or two days past, but there was no party, so Olivia asked Joe, "when are you gonna throw my party"? Joe told her the party was gonna be on the next Friday. The Monday after that Friday rolled around and there was no party. As Joe was taking her to work, Olivia asked him about the party once again. Joe finally told her there wasn't gonna be a party. Olivia didn't trip about the party being cancelled, but she did ask Joe about him bringing the stereo equipment back to Sara and Jean's house. Joe told Olivia he sold the equipment. Olivia was quiet for a minute because she was shocked about what Joe told her. She really couldn't believe what she heard him say and was hoping he was kidding or that he was gonna say something more in regards to getting the equipment back to her, but Joe kept driving and didn't seem to have anything else to say about the matter. After Olivia realized he had nothing more to say, she asked him," why did you sell my stereo equipment"? Joe replied, "Shit, I needed money for my car note". "It's been slow on the stroll, so I did what I had to do". Olivia was so angry she didn't know what to say or do, but she didn't argue with him or start any shit with him about the matter. Joe knew Olivia was angry too, because she didn't say much else during the remainder of the ride to the stroll.

When they got to the stroll where he usually let her out of the car, Olivia got out of the car with nothing to say and just walked away. It was after Joe drove off when she let her tears fall. She didn't break down and cry, she just shedded some tears. Olivia walked the stroll for a few minutes, trying not to get a date until she pulled herself together and figured out what her next move would be. She was not okay with what Joe said he had done, but knew she couldn't make him get her stereo back to her. She grew more angry as she strolled along, thinking about everything that had happened and how nice she had been to Joe, giving him the money she made selling pussy and blowjobs. Rather than her breaking down, Olivia got mentally stronger whenever she was as angry as she was, so she took some tissue from her purse, dried the tears from her eyes and face, put some more lipstick on and went to work. You should have seen her. She worked that stroll like a real pro and made as much money as she could, which was about three hundred dollars, a nice sum of money in that era. When things got really slow, that usually indicated all the real tricks had done what they were gonna do for the night. Instead of waiting around for Joe to pick her up as usual, Olivia took a taxi from the stroll. She had the taxi driver take her to Sara's house where she drew herself a bath, cleaned herself up, put on a nightgown and chilled while she played music on one of her other stereos. Olivia laid in bed, listened to the music and gathered her thoughts about everything until she fell asleep. She knew Joe was going to be looking for her on the stroll, but she didn't care. She actually hoped he'd figure out what time it was, that there wasn't gonna be anymore of him picking her up from the stroll. He couldn't get a dime from her anymore. Even though he didn't know it, he was fired when Olivia got out of his car on the stroll that night. She wasn't worried about him coming to Sara and Jean's house looking for her because he knew he couldn't come or call there that time of night. Olivia was very shook up about Joe selling her stereo equipment. She even filed a police report the next day, but the equipment was never recovered, so she got played and had to charge it to the game. Olivia didn't have anything else to do with Joe neither.

Olivia laid low from the stroll a few weeks. She was avoiding Joe riding up on her and bothering her about being with him again and about her making whoe money without him or another pimp. That's how the game goes. After Olivia figured Joe had gotten the message that she wasn't down for him anymore, she got back down and made money for herself. She continued to keep what she was doing undercover though, because Sara had no idea what she did when she would leave the house in the evening and Olivia wanted to keep it that way. She was fast and in the past she didn't want to mind Sara like she should have, but she always respected Sara and Jean. At least three or four times a week, Olivia would get dressed up (which was really nothing unusual or suspicious to Sara), go to the stroll and make some money. When she wasn't on the stroll on weeknights, she kicked it at someone's crib (house/apartment) getting high and on weekends (which to children of the night began on Thursdays), Olivia kicked it at one of the nightclubs. Occasionally, she would stay home on weekends. After all, there was always a party going on with family members and friends at Sara and Jean's house.

Olivia kicked it up and kicked it around, pretty much, the same way week-after-week. She was always into something, high all the while doing whatever it was she did. She wanted to be high everyday. Not that she had problems she couldn't cope with or anything like that. She just enjoyed the feeling she got from the different drugs she did. She loved drugs. She even thought that she was going to be smoking weed when she was sixty years of age. However, Olivia vowed that she would stop doing drugs if she was to ever be or begin to be controlled by them or one particular drug. Until then, she was gonna get her buzz on every chance she got. She also enjoyed hangin' out with or being at someone's crib where she could do what she liked doing. Things she couldn't do at home at Sara and Jean's house. She had grown up so much, so fast in such a short period, that she started thinking it was time she got her own crib. Like most girls are after graduating from high school or even after they start having sex, Olivia wanted to sleep with the guy she called her man or boyfriend, after having sex with him or every night if possible. She wanted to have whomever she wanted over to her place, where they could do whatever she allowed them to do at whatever time of day or night she wanted. She had been buying things she would need for an apartment, every time she made some money, so she began looking for an apartment to rent. She had not even thought about getting a real job to get an apartment and it worked out that she didn't have to.

After being approved for a one bedroom duplex, Olivia paid the deposit required and agreed to pay the first month's rent on the first day of the following month. Now it was time to celebrate. Olivia really felt as though she was grown at that time. No one could tell her anything. She really got down on the stroll (put forth more effort) to make some money then because she wanted to have the money she needed for the rent and for all the things she had big ideas of having and wanting to buy for her duplex. The nights she didn't work, Olivia usually went to her favorite nightclubs nearby Sara and Jean's house, still getting her celebration on when one of those nights, she saw a fine brother she had never seen before. As she noticed him, the brother noticed her (it seemed like) at the same time. This guy stood across the room in the club and stared at Olivia with this "you know you ought to be with me" look on his face. Very confident-like. The brother was looking so fine and sexy, very neat and nicely dressed in a suit.

A couple of other brothers seemed to be with this guy. The other brothers were dressed accordingly. Olivia checked out the brother she noticed first. He was the one she was interested in. When he sat down, Olivia observed the way he sat with his legs crossed and his hand resting on his thigh when he wasn't holding a drink. She even checked out the way he responded when someone spoke to him, the way he moved when he got up from the chair he sat in, the way he walked and even the way he moved his head when he looked around the room of the club or the way he profiled when he was standing. The brother was smooth and seemed to have much finesse'. He was fascinating. Finally they met. Brother man came over to the table Olivia sat at and asked her for a dance. Bernard was his name. He didn't have too much rapp on the dance floor, except to exchange names with Olivia, which was cool with her. When she danced, she wanted to listen to the music, feel the music and just dance. For her, that was not the time for talking. The only talking Bernard did, was with his eyes and the way he held Olivia's body close to his as they danced to the slow love ballad the DJ played. After the dance, Bernard thanked Olivia and walked her to her seat. After getting to the table where Olivia sat at, Bernard stood next to the table until Olivia sat down and then asked her what she was drinking. From hangin' with older folk she had been kickin' it with, of course Olivia told Bernard she was drinking cognac, Hennessey on the rocks. Bernard said, "okay". That's all he said. Then he walked away, went to the bar, ordered what Olivia said she was drinking, brought it back to her and told her he would talk to her later. He didn't try and hang around, didn't ask Olivia any personal questions or come on strong with some lame rapp like some guys do and he didn't seem to expect anything in return, just because he brought her a drink. Olivia was impressed. As she sat in her seat, sipping on her drink and smoking cigarettes (like she had seen women do in the tavern next door to the house she grew up in), she followed Bernard with her eyes as he mingled around the club. Their eyes met a few times, so Bernard could tell she was checking him out and that she was interested in him. Olivia gathered the same thing. Bernard would stand wherever he was and stare into Olivia's eyes until she turned her head. Olivia, as laid back as she was, would stare back into Bernard's eyes for a minute while sipping her drink or maybe drawing on the cigarette she may have been smoking, then she would smile and look away. She likes to think she was pretty smooth herself. There was definitely chemistry between the two of them and that is the way they both communicated with one another that night. At about one o'clock AM when the club was about to close, because they both were looking into each others eyes and kept up with one another all through the night, Bernard motioned his head for Olivia to come over to where he was standing. You know she went to him. There the two of them stood closely, still looking into each other's eyes. Bernard asked Olivia, "What's up"? "Where are you going when the club closes"? Olivia replied, "I don't know, what's up with you"? Olivia wasn't driving and was there alone, so she really needed a ride home, even though Sara and Jean's house was only a few blocks away from the club. Bernard told Olivia he and his friends were going down the street to one of the guy's apartment and asked her to come with him and so she did. Olivia left the club with Bernard and the others, went to the friend's apartment and hung out there until the next morning. A girl and her two young daughters who apparently lived there, was at the apartment, so Olivia was pretty comfortable with the strangers. She wanted to be with Bernard and him, her, so Olivia wasn't worried about anything happening that she wasn't ready for or couldn't handle. She and the others kicked it at Bernard's friend's apartment, playing LP's, 45's and eight track tapes. Of course they were getting high off some good bud (marijuana) as they socialized. Olivia and Bernard shared a comfortable lounging chair as they got more acquainted, until it got to be daybreak. Some of the people who were there, left, Bernard's friend who lived there and his lady went into their bedroom where they had taken the children earlier and Bernard and Olivia went into the other bedroom that apparently, was the children's room. That's where Olivia and Bernard laid down in a twin bed that forced their bodies to touch. As they lie there in each other's arms, the two of them talked for a while and got better acquainted than they already were, until they fell asleep. It was all good because they both were fully dressed. Bernard didn't even attempt to get undressed nor did he ask Olivia to get undressed. It was as though sex was the furthest thing from his mind. Olivia was very impressed by that, but was also curious about the kind of guy Bernard was and what he was gonna do with her. You know, what kind of relationship he was going to have with her, if at all. Olivia was all the time approached by guys who wanted to have sex with her, but Bernard didn't come to her in that way. As impressive as that was, it made Olivia wonder. When they both awakened, Bernard sat on the side of the bed and commenced to put his shoes on, so Olivia did accordingly. Bernard asked Olivia if she was ready to go and Olivia replied, "Yes, if you are". It was afternoon by that time. The two of them went into the living room where Bernard chatted with his friend for a couple of minutes, who sat in the living room smoking a joint while he read that day's newspaper. As Bernard and Olivia were leaving, Olivia told Bernard's friend it was nice meeting him. The guy was very nice. He told Olivia she was welcome to come back and said something slick like, "don't be a stranger". Olivia guessed that his girl was still in bed because she didn't see her anymore after she went into their bedroom that morning. Bernard then took Olivia home to Sara's house and gave her a phone number to call and reach him at. He leaned on the arm rest in the Cadillac he drove and slowly but gently gave Olivia a nice kiss with a little bit of tongue, before she opened the car's door. "Call me", he said. Olivia replied, "I will".

Olivia waited a couple of days before calling Bernard. She didn't want to seem anxious or desperate to get back with him. She got back to business, making money on the stroll and doing what was necessary to get into her duplex in (by now) a couple of weeks. She told Bernard she was getting her own place and that she would be moving into it the first of the next month, but she didn't tell him about the kind of work she did. She didn't know if Bernard was gonna be around for a while or what kind of relationship they were going to have, so she didn't want him to know too much about her too soon. Bernard lived in the city east of the one Olivia lived in, which was right across the bridge or as some called it, "across the water", so Olivia didn't see him around town. She imagined that he only came to the town she lived in, on occasion or to take care of business. She knew no shame in selling pussy, but she wanted to wait until she saw where Bernard was coming from, before letting him know what she was about. Olivia talked to Bernard on the telephone a few times before she saw him again. After all, Bernard wasn't easy to get in touch with. When she did see him again, it was at the nightclub where the two of them first met. They both seemed really glad to see one another that night and were more cozier with each other this time. Bernard asked Olivia how things were going with the duplex she was trying to get and she was happy to tell him that she paid the rent for the month, got the keys to the doors and paid for the electricity to be turned on. The water was furnished, but she didn't have enough money to get the gas turned on. She told Bernard she also had to replace some fuses to have electricity in all the rooms. Bernard then asked Olivia if those items were all that was needed for her to move into the duplex. Olivia told him, "yes". When the club closed, Olivia left with Bernard and had him drive to where the duplex was located so he could see it and know where she was going to be living. She was able to turn the lights on in the living room, so she invited Bernard in to show him around the place. After seeing the duplex, the two of them left and went by Bernard's friend's apartment. There they sat for a while and visited, but after they smoked a couple of joints with Bernard's friend, Bernard took Olivia home to Sara and Jean's house where she still resided since she had not moved into the duplex yet. When Olivia and Bernard arrived to Sara and Jean's house, Bernard put the car in park, but left the engine running, turned on the park lights, sat there and talked to Olivia for a few minutes. As the two of them were sitting there, Bernard reached into his pocket and pulled out a wad of money. Olivia didn't know where Bernard worked or if he even had a job. She knew he made money somehow, by the car he drove and the way he dressed, but she wanted to kick it with him (date him), so she never asked Bernard about his financial status because it didn't matter at the time. She just sat there in his car while he peeled off a few bills and handed them to her. As she was hesitant to take the money not knowing what it was for, Bernard told her to pay the deposit for the gas to be turned on in the duplex, buy some fuses for the electricity and that he would come the next day and put the fuses in the fuse box. He then gave Olivia a kiss and told her to call him the next day after she was done taking care of the business with the duplex. Olivia got out of the car, went into the house and chilled until the next day. She thought to herself, "this guy is unbelievable". Because of all the games Olivia had seen men play, by this time, she couldn't help but wonder if Bernard was kickin' game too and if so, what his game was. That didn't stop her though. She went after whatever she wanted and she wanted more of Bernard, so she was going with the flow, wherever it took her.

The next day, Olivia went and paid the deposit for the gas to be turned on in the duplex and bought some fuses with the money Bernard gave her. Then she had some boxes of items and some used furniture that was given to her, taken to the duplex. After her furniture and things were put in the duplex, Olivia went back to Sara and Jean's house and called Bernard. She was so happy about everything Bernard had done or said he was going to do thus far, so she chilled and kicked it around Sara and Jean's house until he arrived. Sara was cool about everything. Probably to an extent, she wanted Olivia to get her own apartment because Olivia had gotten a little too big for her young britches (an old figure of speech). Also, one of the times she and Olivia had a disagreement, Olivia told her she could take care of herself. Sara didn't think she could, so Sara probably thought if she let her go, Olivia would see for herself how hard things would be and come back home where she should have been. Since Sara previously told Olivia she was gonna let her go and do whatever she wanted to do, she was living up to her words.

Bernard finally came and got Olivia and the two of them went to the duplex to spend their first night alone together. After arriving at the duplex, Bernard kicked back (got comfortable, relaxed), rolled a couple of joints to smoke and watched TV while Olivia put things away, arranged the furniture and got things in order. During the course of getting things situated is when Olivia told Bernard what she was about. You know, that she goes down by the truck stop and make money. She didn't even think about the wrong in the way she made money and never gave it a thought because Troy, who supposedly cared about or loved her, made her feel it was okay to make money by having sex with men. Selling pussy was also okay with Joe and other men Olivia knew, so she thought it would be okay with Bernard and it was. Bernard didn't trip when she told him. He didn't shy away, look surprised, turn his nose up or go off (get angry). He had been nice to Olivia from day one, he seemed to be genuinely interested in her and he was generous enough or liked her well enough to give her money for the duplex. Olivia felt as though, at best, Bernard would ask her not to sell pussy anymore,

48

but he didn't. Bernard was no square (by the book). Olivia didn't know where or how he made money, but his car, his clothes, the way he was always spending money, having weed all the time and the wad of money he had the night he gave her some money, was evidence that he was getting paid well, whatever his occupation or hustle was. Things between the two of them seemed to be going really well. Olivia was no gold digger by nature. When she liked a guy, money was not her main interest. A man having his own money is attractive and a necessity, but Olivia's motive for wanting to be with a man who had or was about making money, was not because she wanted to be taken care of. She was taught how to get paid when she had sex with someone who only wanted sex from her, but it wasn't like that when she was dealing with someone she wanted to have a relationship with, who made her feel they wanted more with her than just a one night or occasional fuck. "Some men, well, to be truthful, a lot of men will fuck you, use you, leave you, and never offer a girl anything when they fuck her", said Olivia. "Not even a meal, a douche or a night out on the town", she added. She said that some of them will never come back to see a girl after they get that first piece of pussy from her, so she doesn't see any wrong in a girl getting money or whatever is agreed on, from a man who only wants sex and a one time affair. It wasn't like that with Bernard though. He still seemed as though he was gonna be around for the long haul and that's the way Olivia wanted it, so with that, it was a give and take, do for one another thing they had going on.

Olivia was more at ease with Bernard than she was before, now that she had told him what was really going on with her and he seemed to be okay with it. By this time, she was just about finished with her housework, so she sat down, took a couple of tokes off a joint Bernard was smoking and then went and drew herself a bath. Bernard continued to chill in the living room, watching TV while Olivia bathed. After her bath, Olivia put some sweet smelling lotion all over her body, sprayed a little cologne on her neck, between her breast and on her inner thighs and put on a short nightee gown. She knew how to entice a man and that's what she wanted to do to Bernard. This was the first night she and Bernard was spending alone and they had not yet had sex yet, so Olivia figured or hoped this would be the night they would consummate their relationship. After combing her hair, which was the final touch of her getting herself all dolled-up, Olivia walked slowly into the living room where Bernard was. She remembers doing something like emptying the ashtrays and cleaning the coffee table off, while at the same time, telling Bernard she was getting ready to go to bed. Oh she was flaunting her stuff, still on her mission to entice Bernard. The only light in the front of the duplex was from the TV, while Olivia went from the living room to the kitchen to empty the ashtrays. She knew Bernard was going to be watching her walk from room-to-room if at no other time. Being as smooth as he was (you know the type), Bernard didn't show how much he was in lust, but knowing men the way she did (even at her age), Olivia knew he would be looking at her ass as it moved like two puppies playing underneath that little nightee she had on when she left the living room. She also knew he was going to join her in the bedroom, soon after she went to bed. Still keeping his cool, Bernard didn't join Olivia until about fifteen minutes after she turned the light out in the bedroom and climbed into bed. She knows the approximate time it took because she was lying there listening for his footsteps and to not hear the voices from the TV, which would indicate Bernard was coming to bed. From all the activities that went on that day (by this time, the day before), she was very tired and sleepy, so she started to doze off after lying there for about ten minutes. It seemed that just as she was going into a deeper nod, Bernard entered the bedroom, stood by the side of the bed and took his clothes off, which brought Olivia out of the nod. She then did one of those woman-like stretches with her eyes slightly opened as she looked up at Bernard and then slowly moved her legs under the covers, as though she was trying to get situated or more comfortable. Olivia didn't know if Bernard knew it or not, but she was performing. She knew before this point, that Bernard wanted her sexually as well as in general. She also figured by this point, Bernard was feeling a little horney, so she was doing everything she knew to do, to make his dick hard so that he would fuck her. She wanted him to go up in her and she wanted their relationship to go to the next level, wherever that was. Bernard was so cool, that he was puzzling. He was there with Olivia thus far, but Olivia wanted to know how things were going to be after he got the pussy. The bedroom was lit up with moonlight and the street corner light, so Bernard could see Olivia fairly well and she could see him. When he took off his boxer shorts, he already had a slight woody (hard on). Olivia thought to herself, "could this be my dream man"? Bernard's penis was very large in width and had great length, which was a good quality added to all the other things Olivia liked about him. As he climbed into bed, Olivia pulled the covers back so they wouldn't be in the way of her feeling Bernard's body touching hers. Bernard immediately put his arms around her and began caressing her body and french-kissing her. Enough time had already passed between then and the time they met, so the foreplay was short, but sweet. Bernard climbed on top of Olivia and she commenced to rub his body gently with her hands, while stroking his legs with her feet. She opened her legs to receive what Bernard had to give and he gave it to her. The two of them bumped and grind slowly for a while, to savor the smell, taste and touch of one another. As it seemed they both reached the height of ecstasy at the same time, it was on then. Bernard and Olivia started fucking. You would've thought they were wrestling or trying to tear each other apart. "It was wonderful", said Olivia. So wonderful that the two of them climaxed and passed out (it seemed), as they laid there wrapped up in each others arms. About four hours later, Olivia was awakened by Bernard as he stood at the bedside getting dressed after having a shower. It was afternoon by this time. Bernard wasn't the type of man who laid around all day. Olivia asked him, "Are you leaving"? Bernard replied, "Yeah I've got some business to take care of". Olivia asked, "are you coming back"? Bernard replied with certainty, "yeah, I'll be back later on". That was exactly what Olivia wanted to hear. She thought to herself, "he's coming back. Maybe he's gonna move in with me and be around long enough and be my husband". You know, the same thing every girl thinks about when she meets a guy who turns her on the way she likes it. Olivia got out of bed, went and drew herself a bath as Bernard sat in the living room, rolling some joints. He told Olivia he was leaving a couple of joints there for her to smoke and of course he rolled one for him to smoke while he rolled (drove). That seemed to be the usual thing he did when he was driving or riding in his or someone elses car. Olivia walked him to the door as he was leaving and he gave her a kiss on his way out. You know what she thought as she watched him walk to his car. "He's so sweet", is what Olivia thought. A typical thing women think when a man does something that mesmerizes her. Olivia then went and took a bath, put on her robe and took a nap.

Later that day, after getting some more things done around the duplex and getting dressed, Bernard returned. You should have seen the smile on Olivia's face when she saw his Cadillac pull up in front of the duplex. She was cool when he came inside though. She had to play things off as though she wasn't desperate or anxious about him returning. Bernard kicked back the way he did before, with half of a joint he had been smoking on, between his index and middle fingers. Bernard smoked a lot of weed. He had to have some weed daily (it seemed). As the two of them were talking about nothing in particular, Olivia told Bernard she wanted to go down by the truck stop to work because she wanted to be able to get some things for the duplex. Bernard was cool with that. He said to Olivia, "I'll take you down there if you want me to". Olivia thinking about how nice it was of him to offer and give her a ride to work, took him up on the offer. The sun was about to set by this time, so she went into the bedroom and got dressed for work. When she dressed to go to the stroll, she dressed as though she was going to a nightclub or party. She dressed to impress and even to entice. In this case, she was hoping to catch as many men as possible. Olivia and Bernard left the duplex after dusk fell. Bernard dropped Olivia off at the truck stop, gave her a joint to smoke later when she wasn't busy and even gave her a kiss before she got out of the car. Things that Joe didn't do. As Olivia was saying bye to him, Bernard asked her if she wanted him to come back and get her. Feeling as though he was her man now, Olivia told Bernard she would like that. She was feeling earlier, that she wanted Bernard to spend the night at the duplex with her again. Even though she might have sex with several men this night, she desired and wanted some more of Bernard, plus, she liked the idea of him being there with her, at the duplex. With whoes, having sex with tricks is not a fun thing, it's work. It's a job. It's not emotional. Therefore, it's not enjoyable. Olivia said, "I didn't find ninety-eight percent of the tricks I dated attractive, and it ain't nothing fun about that kind of sex". She says that having sex with a trick, is probably close to what it must be like for a woman who was raped. It's just not as mentally disturbing as that of being raped. Olivia didn't know how Bernard would feel about making love or having sex with her after she had been working the stroll, so she would let him initiate their having sex, if they were to. She wanted it to be his decision, but she still wanted Bernard to pick her up from work, in hopes that he would spend the night with her again, even if he didn't sex her that night.

As agreed, Bernard was on the stroll to pick Olivia up around one thirty AM that morning. After getting to the duplex, Bernard sat on the sofa, took his shoes off, laid a bag of weed on the table and got comfortable as though he was getting settled for the night. "Hum", said Olivia to herself. "It looks like he's gonna stay the night after all". She didn't show it, but inside herself, she was elated because she wanted Bernard there with her, to live with her if that were possible. She was really starting to dig this guy deeply. After she got a little more comfortable, she sat down on the sofa with Bernard and began pulling money from the places she hid it when the tricks paid her. Olivia always got her money up front and stashed the money somewhere on her person, when a trick wasn't looking. She had a very good payday this night. After gathering all the money from the table and counting it, Olivia took a few dollars from the pile of bills and handed the rest to Bernard. She didn't ask, but she knew Bernard was impressed with all the money she made in such a short period of time. She got her damn hustle on when she worked the stroll that night. Olivia also knew Bernard (or any man) was pleased about her handing over as much money to him as she did. He was nice to give her money she needed for the duplex, was understanding about the work she did, took her to work and picked her up from work. He had, basically, been supplying her with weed and seemed as though he wasn't going anywhere (had decided he was going to be her man). Because of all this, Olivia didn't mind giving him the money to hold on to. She believed that if she needed anything, Bernard would make sure she got it. Bernard didn't ask any questions or anything. By this time, he had rolled a joint, fired it up and passed it to Olivia. As she sat there toking on the joint, Bernard pulled out a bottle of cough syrup from the pocket of his suit-jacket and began shaking the bottle while Olivia smoked the joint. He took the cap from the bottle and took a swig (drink, sip). Now this was something Olivia had not seen before. She asked Bernard if he had or was catching a cold. He kinda' smiled and said "no". Olivia asked, "What is that for"? Bernard told her it was robo and asked her if she wanted some of it. By then, Olivia had figured out that the syrup was something to get high on. She could see the formula through the bottle and how it seemed to look thicker or different in some way, so she told Bernard she wanted to taste it. Being the drug addict person she was, Olivia was curious of what drinking cough syrup was all about. She took a sip at first and sat there holding the bottle while seemingly listening to her taste buds. Bernard told her to take another swig and so she did. Olivia could taste the bitterness of the formula, which indicated there was a lot more medicine in it than usual. She then passed the bottle to Bernard and fired up the joint that lay in the ashtray. After taking a couple more tokes off the joint, Olivia passed the joint to Bernard, lit a cigarette and told Bernard she was going to take a bath. She always took a bath, cleaned herself up and cleaned herself out (if you know what I mean) after she worked the stroll. After having a bath and getting into a nightgown, she joined Bernard in the living room where he was still chilling, watching TV. By then, Olivia was feeling very sexy from the effect of the syrup she drank, the weed she had smoked and the high she had from just the thought of Bernard being there. She liked the effect of the syrup because of the similarity it had with heroine. It made her very relaxed, so she placed herself on the sofa in a sexy position and began telling Bernard how her night was on the stroll. It was all good sitting there sharing with Bernard. He seemed to be interested in what Olivia had to say. That's how the night went for an hour or so and then Bernard said to Olivia, "let's go to bed". Olivia was surprised Bernard asked her to come to bed with him. The syrup had her ass hot, but she stuck to her decision to let Bernard initiate their making love and he did. There was hardly any foreplay this time. The two of them fucked. Sex with Bernard was wonderful the first time (the night before), but this night it was more intensed. The two of them were a lot closer than before, with all they shared in such a short period, a matter of hours and they both were stimulated from the syrup they drank. The sex was almost breath-taking for Olivia. Bernard went up in her full force, like a mack truck and she enjoyed every minute of it. If anyone is not clear on what sex is like with a pimp, Olivia can verify from experience and girl-talk with other whoes, that pimps are sex freaks and have really large dicks. "I guess that's one of the reasons they are confident and sure of themselves. Men tend to think their dicks are magic wands. Pimps don't have a problem with having sex with their girl or girls, after the girls have been out all night having sex with other men neither. Most pimps are clean, hygiene-wise and expect the same of their whoes. A whoe must handle her hygiene business after working the stroll. It was a must, but that went without saying with me", said Olivia. Sara, Jean and the five sisters she had, taught her at a young age, to keep her body clean.

Bernard got up early as usual that morning and went across the bridge where he was from. He always had business to take care of. He told Olivia he would be back later. Shortly after he returned, Olivia was dressed and ready to go to the stroll, so Bernard took her to work again and later picked her up from work. Olivia was feeling more as though Bernard was going to hang around. She felt he cared for her and was concerned about things that were needed for the duplex, so she gave him all the money she made that night. She had a meal at the truck stop while on a break from work and she bought herself cigarettes. Anything she needed the next day, she would ask Bernard for. Bernard had it going on. Olivia didn't worry about him running off with the money because he had it too good and there was more in stored for him. He would've been a fool to mess up what Olivia was giving him. This night, Olivia didn't even wait until she and Bernard got to the duplex to hand the money she made to him. As they rode away from the stroll, she began pulling money from her hiding places on her person. Bernard didn't ask Olivia for the money or anything. She willingly gave him what she had and wanted to share everything she had with him. Bernard just drove and listened to her as she told him about her night. Olivia noticed that Bernard was going in a different direction from the direction the duplex was in, but she didn't ask any questions about where they were going. She didn't care. She wanted to go wherever her man was going. When Bernard pulled over to park the car, it was in front of the apartment building Bernard took her to, where his friend lived with his girl and two children.

It was cool to go to Bernard's friend's apartment because the party was always on there, it seemed. Upon arriving, music was playing as Bernard's friend sat there smoking a joint. Olivia peeped the bottle of robo cough syrup on the coffee table, so she could tell Bernard's friend kicked it and got his buzz on like Bernard did, on daily basis. Olivia liked that in them because that was the way she liked to flow. She and Bernard sat at his friend's apartment for an hour or two. Long enough to be there when his friend's girl walked through the front door. Olivia wondered where the lady had been, that she was getting home that time of morning. The girl had children and seemed kind of square, that Olivia didn't even imagine where the girl had been. "Maybe she was just getting home from clubbing (being at a nightclub)", thought Olivia. The girl wasn't very talkative and didn't seem very friendly, so Olivia didn't say too much to her. She respected the girl's home, so she spoke to the girl and was very cordial. Olivia just sat there grooving to the music that played and got high off some good weed and robo, while Bernard kicked it around (talked a little shit) with his friend. She and Bernard went back to the duplex from there.

Olivia worked the stroll at least five days a week for a couple of weeks since she moved into the duplex. Bernard took her to work, picked her up from work and stayed the night at the duplex every night from day one. He was cool about everything from the beginning, but had gotten to where he would ask Olivia, "What's up", when she had not or wasn't getting ready for work by a certain time. Olivia would be like, "what", when Bernard would ask that question. Bernard would then ask, "Aren't you going to work"? Olivia would reply, "yes". Bernard wouldn't say anything else, as though that was all he wanted to hear. Olivia didn't really trip on Bernard questioning her about going to work because her working the stroll had become such a routine. She thought Bernard only wondered if she had a different agenda when she wasn't dressed by a certain time. Olivia did go to work that night as planned. Nothing had changed, yet. The next day, (which was in to the third week she lived in the duplex), when the sun was about to set that evening, Bernard told Olivia he wanted her to do something different that night. Olivia (trusted Bernard and knew that what she did was for his best interest as well) said, "okay". She didn't even ask Bernard what he wanted her to do. Around seven thirty or eight o'clock that evening, Olivia was dressed for work, got into the Cadillac with Bernard, sat back and rode with the flow. The ride was a bit longer than it usually took to get her to the stroll by the truck stop. Checking out the sights as they rode, Olivia knew that Bernard was taking her to the nearby city where he was from, which again, was right across the bridge from the twin city she lived in. Olivia was familiar with the city because Sara and Jean used to take her and her siblings with them on some weekends when they would party at one of Sara's sisters home. After crossing the bridge, Olivia and Bernard were downtown in the twin city where Bernard drove around for a while. On the sidewalks and street corners, between the tall skyscrapers and big hotels, were girls standing or strolling. There were even girls riding around in Cadillacs and Lincoln Continentals. Olivia saw girls bent over, as they talked through car windows of men who pulled over to the curb or just stopped their cars in the middle of the street. The girls looked like movie stars or showgirls. Most of them wore pretty, skimpy dresses that were short up to their asses, long dresses with the split up the back or the front almost showing their cunts, while others wore hot pants that were cut so far up, they could've been worn as panties. Whatever the attire was, most of the girls were nice lookin' girls. These girls were serious about catching men. With their three or four inch high heel shoes on and makeup with red or dark lipstick, Olivia could hear the girls shouting out to men as they rode by, "you want a date honey". "Auh man! You could see and feel all the money floating around downtown there", said Olivia. She said businessmen were walking in and out of the hotels; some were driving into or out of the hotels parking lots. It was amazing to her. There were bright lights and action just like she had seen in the movies. Unlike the stroll down by the truck stop where she had been working. Bernard asked Olivia what did she think. Olivia replied, "It looks like a lot of money can be made". Bernard told her some things about working downtown, he told her about the police and he showed her some places to duck into if the heat was on. So fascinated with what she was seeing, Olivia didn't think yet, about the knowledge Bernard seemed to have about the game. Bernard circled the main area of the stroll. He then slowed down the car and motioned to one of the girls that stood on the street, to come to his car. The girl ran over to Bernard's car and hopped in the back seat. Bernard drove off and rode around, circling the whoe stroll as he introduced Olivia to the girl and asked the girl questions. All he had to ask is, "what's happening" and the girl immediately ran down the scoop to him. Basically, what Bernard wanted to know is if any money was being made and if the vice squad (police) was riding tough. You know, keeping the girls from making money or making a lot of busts. Asia (was the lady's name) told Bernard a little money was being made and that it wasn't too hot. Asia was Bernard's older and eldest sister. She was a chocolate girl who was built really cute and was flashy. She was cool and seemed to be a real pro at the game. Bernard told Asia he wanted to put Olivia down, that Olivia worked the stroll down by the truck stop, so she was familiar with the game, but to watch her back for him. Asia said, "cool, okay". Bernard then turned a corner, pulled over and let the two girls out of the car. As Olivia was walking away, Bernard spoke out to her, telling her he would be back to get her.

Olivia strolled along with Asia for a minute and then she trailed Asia from a distance. She was quite proud and didn't want to follow Asia around as though she didn't know what to do, so she utilized the skills and techniques she learned and used on the stroll she had been working. She observed the way things were done on the stroll downtown and figured out how to work it. Things were pretty much the same, only a little faster with more money, more whoes, more people and more traffic. Therefore, the cops were more slicker and dedicated to busting whoes and tricks. They knew their job and was out to get it done. Because of all this, even though Olivia knew what to do, she was being extra cautious. She asked men if they wanted a date, but she didn't work as hard as she knew how to. She wanted to feel her way around and check things out a little bit more. Asia told Olivia about the vice squad (undercover cops) and pointed a couple of them out to her. These cops were dressed in street clothes and usually rode two deep (in pairs). Olivia peeped the way these cops worked and was a bit leery, so she didn't do too well financially, the first night. Bernard picked her up from the stroll that night and understood why she didn't make any money. Besides, he remembered how Asia said it was on the stroll that night when he talked to her. Asia had a couple of dates, but she told Bernard it was slow that night (tricks weren't plentiful or weren't biting). Bernard went back to the duplex with Olivia that night and told her they would try it again, working the stroll downtown the next night. After working the new job site a few nights, Olivia came all the way live. She started getting dates back-to-back. It was the atmosphere. The lights were bright and business was going on, that reeked in the atmosphere. There was so much money downtown there, you could smell the dollar bills, success if you will. Olivia remembered Asia telling her one night, that she was green. That was an insult to her, especially because Asia said that to her in front of some other whoes. Being the street person she was, Olivia verbally defended herself. Asia calling her green was almost like being dared. Olivia had it in her mind that she was going to show Asia how to work the stroll. She knew Asia was impressed with what she had seen so far since she made that remark to her, because when a whoe is not seen on the stroll for fifteen or thirty minutes at a time, sometimes longer depending on how much money a trick is spending, either that whoe is making money or she got busted. Olivia often disappeared, so Asia knew she was making money. Olivia thought to herself, "I'm gonna show her" and she did. As Olivia worked the stroll, she thought about the whole picture of what she was about now: How she started selling pussy; how she started working the streets; how she started giving Bernard the money she made; and how she got from there to this point. She was busy making money or trying to get a date when she was having these thoughts, so she didn't complete them or come to a conclusion about anything. Things were different now. It almost seemed her working the stroll daily, was mandatory. Bernard seemed to have expectations now. Olivia knew for sure at this point, how she felt about him. She was in love with Bernard, so she knew she was down with him for the long haul, however things would be. It seemed when she worked the stroll and knew Bernard was gonna pick her up when she would give him all the money she made, she hustled the stroll as tough as she could. She wanted to impress Bernard with the amount of money she made. Looking back on her life with him, Olivia believes the object of giving Bernard money was for what he gave her (whatever that may have been), to please him and keep him around. She tried to make as much money as she could when she worked the stroll because she thought the more money she gave Bernard, the more he would think of her and see her worth. Growing up without her father and based on her relationships with men, Olivia believes that she, along with other children are affected in one way or another when they grow up without one of their parents. She believes that girls need their father or father figure to teach them about men (amongst other things) as they are growing up and guys need their father or a father figure to teach them how to be a man (amongst other things) as they are growing up. Children are affected when they grow up without their mother or a mother figure as well. Olivia used to wonder if her father thought more of the twin girls he fathered with another woman, than he did her. She wondered if there was something she could have done, to make her father be with her more. When she was a child, Olivia didn't know that the differences her mom and dad had, were the reason her dad wasn't around. Children can't figure out things like that. The parents or an adult should explain these things to children so they won't blame themselves or get the wrong idea. Olivia never asked Sara nor her father, why he wasn't there. She never asked Sara nor her father about the birds and the bees, relationships, boys or men and true love. She had to learn the hard way, from experience. Over the years, Olivia seemed to have felt that she had to go the extra mile to please the men she dated. She thought that was the key to keeping a man around. Therefore, she did what she could to please the men in her life that she or Sara didn't do to please her father and keep him around. It wasn't until she got older, that Olivia learned and realized that a girl or woman does not and should not have to do bad things or whatever a guy wants her to do, for him to love her and be with her. Either a guy loves a girl for who she is or he doesn't. If he does not, that girl will feel it in her heart even though her mind may justify his actions. Today, Olivia has a cliche' she lives by in all her affairs: If you smell a rat, there's one close by. "Thinking this way has saved me from a lot of heartaches, losing money and wasted time, amongst other shit", she said.

Bernard had it made when he caught Olivia. She had already been turned out (trained). Bernard didn't have to bring the game to her, (which would have been more work and effort on his part), she brought the game to him. She wasn't even shy to tell Bernard she was selling pussy when she did. Troy turned Olivia out to selling pussy, Joe turned her out to selling pussy on the stroll without even knowing she had sold pussy before, Freddie's girl sold pussy and there were others, so Olivia began to think there was nothing wrong with it. Besides, she was comfortable with Bernard when she told him about her work. She knew Bernard was one of the children of the night, so he couldn't have been square to the pimping game and other hustles. Little did she know, Bernard was more hip to the game than she was. Bernard didn't present the real image of himself when he hooked up with Olivia. He was trying to be subtle and at the same time, let Olivia lead the way to where he could take her and she did. When she did, she started something that she couldn't later stop, change nor control. She came to realize, Bernard was a pimp. I mean a real pimp and was very serious and true to the game. At the time Olivia met him, Bernard had a whoe who was incarcerated for sixty days, for soliciting for the purpose of prostitution. He and Kelly (was the girl's name) were living together in an apartment in the twin city on the side of the bridge Bernard was from. Off and on, Bernard had other whoes or girls who worked the stroll for him, so he knew his business.

With pimps, whoes don't have a say-so in what they do. Pimps plan the agenda of each day for their whoes. Basically, whoes are to work six days a week, Monday thru Saturday. They are required to turn in every dollar and every dime, to their pimp. Holding back some of the money was grounds for an ass kickin', which Olivia already knew of, but she was soon to see that for herself and more about Bernard that she never before imagined.

When Bernard put Olivia on the stroll downtown in the twin city, the real image of him was presented and there was no turning back for Olivia. Bernard began to expect a lot of things of her. One of them was that she had to start getting ready for work by a certain time and she had to do this everyday of the week except Sundays. This was a program for Olivia because it came to be what she had to do. That was stressful for her. Olivia liked the fast way of making money. Getting paid for what other women did for free was the shit to her, but she wanted to do it if and when she wanted to. If she decided she wanted to go out and party or whatever she decided to do, she wanted to be able to do that, which was unacceptable to Bernard. After working downtown six days a week for a few weeks, Olivia just didn't want to go to work one night. When Bernard asked her why she wasn't getting dressed around the usual time she did, Olivia replied, "I don't feel like working tonight". Bernard said to her, "what do you mean you don't feel like it"? Olivia replied, "I just mean that I'm tired, I don't want to work tonight". Man! Bernard went off verbally, in this quiet tone, moving his head from side-to-side as he spoke. What he was saying was nothing nice. "What the fuck do you mean you're tired, you don't feel like working"? "Your punk ass don't do nothing all day and you're talking about you're tired, you don't feel like working". "You punk bitch, you haven't done nothin' today to be tired about". Olivia could not believe Bernard was saying the things he said. As she sat there listening to him, tears rolled down her face. She wondered when selling pussy by choice, changed to a mandatory thing she had to do damn near everyday of the week, week after week. Olivia really wasn't a punk. For her age and being as new to the stroll as she was, she had a lot of heart. She wasn't what they call a veteran in the game, but she was certainly a cadet. As time went on, she learned that calling a whoe "punk" was one of pimps' favorite names for a whoe who could not handle the trials and tribulations of the game. A whoe who wasn't a soldier. With men as well as with women, there's something about being called a punk, that does something to a person. It can and has made one do what they had to do, to show or prove they weren't a punk (wimp or weak person). Sometimes that is the idea of being called that name. Bernard's motive for calling Olivia a punk, was to make her tough and dedicated to the game and to him. Besides, he wanted to provoke  (if you will) her to work the stroll everyday, like clockwork so that she would get paid if there were any money out

*Jerri L. Smith*

there to be made. Some days were slower than others, but Bernard wanted Olivia
out there to get whatever she could get. In the game, it's not safe for a whoe to be
a punk (whimp). There's no telling what she might run up on or stumble into.
"Shit, whoes have to jump in and out of strangers (tricks/johns) vehicles", said
Olivia. "Whoes ride off with strangers to secluded areas to date these men in
their cars when the johns don't have a hotel room and whoes walk the streets,
slipping into and out of darkness", she added. "It takes a lot of heart to be a
hooker", she says. "And just for the record ladies, hookers don't really want to be
with your man or husband. Just like that man or husband only wants a quick
piece of strange pussy, a good blowjob, something freaky or kinky sex, whoes
only want some quick cash and a hooker is gonna do as least as possible for the
money. Get the money, do what you gotta do and get the date over with as
quickly as possible. That's the way it goes", she explained. "It ain't nothin'
personal and also ladies, don't think that if all hookers were banned or wiped off
the face of the earth, a man, your man, husband or whomever, would not cheat.
Most men who cheat or have affairs, are not trying to have an intimate
relationship, even though having sex is an intimate act. These guys already have
an intimate relationship with their mate they may or may not live with, they may
or may not be married to. Men like something different occasionally. Some need
to feel they still have it, whatever "it" is and others need to feel or think that
someone other than just one woman wants him. If there were no hookers, these
men would do whatever they have to do to get some different pussy. Even if they
have to start out as friends with a woman, wine and dine her, take her shopping,
pay a bill, take her to the movies, etc.. You know, date that woman or make her
feel there's more to the relationship than it is. All so that he can have someone
different to go up in. When a man cheats, he may not have intentions on leaving
his woman or wife, loves her dearly, can't and don't want to live without her in
his life. He just wants someone new or different to play with now and again. If a
man is going to cheat, he's going to have a one-night affair or a long-term
relationship with one woman or another and he may have to and will pay, use his
charm and/or lie to get what he wants. If he cheats with a hooker, he may never
see her again. If the woman he cheats with is not a whoe, the affair may get more
intimate than just a suck or a fuck, which almost makes buying a piece of pussy
seem like, merely, going out and buying a beer", Olivia included. Seeing as how
she believes that at least ninety percent of men have and will cheat, this is
something whoe-haters should think about. While neither cheating with a so-
called respectable woman, is any better than cheating with a whoe, some men are
gonna cheat. It's wrong for them to do so, but it's a fact of life. Yes, men have a
strange way of loving. Some women do too.

60

The first time Bernard, verbally, went off on Olivia, it confused her and hurt her feelings, but at the same time, made her angry. She wasn't used to being fussed at or cursed out by a man, so the things Bernard said to her, made her defensive. The more Bernard fussed and cursed, the more defensive Olivia got. One thing led to another and Bernard stole on Olivia (hit her with his fist) right in her face. Of course Olivia swung at Bernard to defend herself, which pissed him off more. Bernard began fighting, non-stop, as Olivia tried to duck and dodge the licks. Olivia was taught to fight back when someone hits her, but she couldn't win a fight with Bernard or any man for that matter. That didn't stop her from trying though, but Bernard was too much for her to handle. He wasn't backing down or backing off. Olivia being a girl didn't matter. Bernard physically fought her (slapping, fist-hitting and grabbing), until she pleaded with him to stop. "I'm sorry", is what she shouted out until Bernard finally stopped hitting her. Pacing around the room, Bernard continued to talk shit to Olivia until he got tired (Olivia assumed). When it seemed he was mellowing out, Olivia went into the bedroom, laid across the bed and cried until she fell asleep. A while later, she went into the living room where Bernard was, sat down on the sofa with a humbleness about herself and appologized to him as though she did something wrong. Nothing like this had ever happened to Olivia, so she was very pathetic, which is understandable.

She doesn't know if Bernard was sorry, remorseful or just playing a game of being concerned after what he had done. However, She didn't have to go to work that night. Bernard didn't hang around the duplex all evening neither. It was one or two o'clock the next morning, when he returned. Olivia chilled at the duplex while Bernard was gone. As she laid there, sleepless, can you believe she wondered and hoped Bernard was coming back? Being wiser now than she was then, Olivia believes she was feeling at the time, as though she had been a bad girl and had to be disciplined. Kinda' like Bernard was her daddy. The next day, she wanted to show him (daddy) she could be a good girl so he wouldn't go away. Now at the time, Olivia didn't know the sadness and sickness of what was going on. She didn't think of Bernard as a father figure nor did she realize the connection her relationship with Bernard had with her growing up without her father. All Olivia knew was that she loved the feeling of Bernard being there and she was crazy about the idea of a man being there with her. The next day, she got dressed for work around the usual time and Bernard took her to the stroll downtown. Even though she had that feeling of being wrestled and slapped around, she put her all into her work that night. She wanted to make up with Bernard about her not going to work the night before, so she made all the money she could, which was quite a bit. Bernard was pleased with the night Olivia had on the stroll, so to make her feel better, he was very charming that night. Instead of going to the duplex after he picked Olivia up from the stroll, Bernard took her over to his friend's apartment where they, along with others, played music, sang, danced and got high. They kicked it. Kinda' like happy hour after a day's work. Now that Olivia had been around the click (group of people who flocked together) for a little while, she was more comfortable with everybody, even Bernard's friend's girl, whom Olivia had seen on the stroll downtown. Now Olivia knows why the girl, Misty (was her name), came home so late or early in the morning the other times she was at the apartment. Misty had just left the stroll. Olivia finally realized she was cool. She just didn't care for Bernard though nor him, her, but Misty respected Bernard and kept her distance from him. Later that morning when Bernard and Olivia left his friend's apartment, Bernard took Olivia to breakfast. That was sorta' like a treat pimps would give their whoes when their whoe or whoes had a good night at work. Otherwise, a whoe would have to fix herself something to eat at the crib (home). After having breakfast, Bernard took Olivia home where he laid on the sofa, watched TV and smoked some more weed until Olivia showered, cleaned herself up and got ready for bed. Then he joined her in the bedroom and made passionate love to her, more intensed than he did before. He didn't say he was sorry about the day before, but he made Olivia feel he was sorry. Knowing what she knows now, she figures that Bernard was probably protecting his investment. All a part of the game. Anyway, this was the usual routine, at least during the time Bernard didn't have any other whoes other than the one who was incarcerated. Kelly was the girl's name who was a year older than Bernard and had supposedly, turned him on to the game a few years before Olivia's time. Olivia knew that Kelly was gonna be around and didn't know what that was gonna be like, but was happy to have Bernard all to herself for the time being. She didn't know what Kelly looked like or what Bernard felt for her, but her plan was to steal Bernard's heart while Kelly was away and then steal her position.

Knowing a little more about Bernard by now, Olivia had a pretty good idea how things were going to be and she still wanted to be with him. She tried hard to please Bernard and be about the game the way whoes are expected to, but there were days when she just wanted to be Bernard's woman, not his whoe. She did what was expected of her for a couple of weeks after the last altercation she and Bernard had, but again, there came another day when Olivia just didn't want to go to work. Even though she figured Bernard was gonna go off on her the way he did before, Olivia still didn't want to work that day. She was aware that Bernard was a pimp and she was familiar with the laws of the game. To be with a guy like him, there were requirements, but being that as it may, Olivia knew she still had a choice. She never stopped believing that she really didn't and shouldn't have to do something such as selling pussy and other sex, if she didn't want to. Knowing this sometimes made her say, "fuck the laws of the game" and the consequences she would suffer by not abiding by those laws. Having to work when she didn't want to and getting her ass kicked were the things Olivia didn't like most about the game, that continuously caused problems in hers and Bernard's relationship, but day-by-day, it got harder and harder for her to even contemplate leaving Bernard, so she rolled with the punches (sometimes, literally). Sure enough, she got her ass whipped again when she refused to go to work. Bernard was more angry this time, than he was the first time. He felt Olivia either, didn't care about disobeying him or she wanted an ass kickin'. Yeah, that was a really sick ass way of thinking, but pimps actually rationalize on why a whoe should get her ass kicked. They believe a whoe won't do wrong or disobey, if she doesn't want an ass kickin'. Bernard Thinking the way he did made things tougher on Olivia this time, than before. So much so, that he hurt himself more than he hurt her, while trying to teach her a lesson. After hitting Olivia with his fist a few times, Bernard backed off and started walking around the room, still fussing and cursing at her. He tried to play it off, but after a couple of minutes, he sat down on the sofa and held one of his hands with the other. As it was, after he swung at Olivia the last time that day, Olivia ducked as she did each time Bernard swung, to keep him from hitting her in her face. When she ducked the last time Bernard swung at her, her head took the lick, causing a bone to break in one of Bernard's hands. He didn't say so at first, but every minute that passed brought him greater pain. Pretty soon, he couldn't play it off anymore. There was no telephone service in the duplex and Bernard was in too much pain to drive, that he had Olivia to go and call his friend Dwight, Misty's man and ask him to come and take him to the hospital and so Olivia did. Olivia was sorry about Bernard's hand, but more than being sorry about his hand, she was glad the accident stopped Bernard from hitting her. Dwight arrived to take Bernard to the hospital (it seemed) a few minutes after Olivia called him. Bernard was in some pain, but not as much as he was at first. That is, before he drank the rest of the robo syrup he had. On the streets, robotussin cough syrup is what is called "brewed", which has at least ten codeine pills (to a four ounce bottle) added to it. Bernard had a couple of ounces left in the bottle he had the night before, so he drank what was left while he waited for Dwight to arrive. Olivia waited at the duplex for Bernard to return from the hospital. She just knew he would be angrier than before when he returned, because of his hand being broke and because she didn't go to work. Whatever his state of mind would be, Olivia knew she was out of the woods from that ass kickin' Bernard wanted to give her. Bernard's state of mine was quite the contrary though. The robo syrup he drank and the medication he got from the hospital mellowed him out. He was also exhausted from the whole ordeal, so he was cool and didn't say anything to Olivia about her going to work. Again, Olivia apologized to Bernard for causing the ass kickin' he gave her and she spent the night at home pampering him.

After Bernard's hand got broke, Olivia worked everyday for weeks, except Sundays, on the stroll downtown. There had been too much trouble between her and Bernard the past couple of months that she just wanted to get along with him. During the daytime, Bernard would go to the other side of the bridge and would come back to the duplex around the time Olivia would be ready for work. Olivia had become more curious of the places Bernard went and the things he did on the other side of town, but she didn't question him. Once he had taken her to meet his mother, his three younger sisters and his young brother, but other than that, the only time Olivia went across the bridge was to go to work. She was familiar with some of the areas across the bridge because of the times Sara and Jean took her and her siblings over there and because she used to hang out over there with some lesbians during the time she was living with Brenda. Because of those times, Olivia knew the vicinity Bernard's mom lived in, of which she later learned the exact location was an alley-like street right off another whoe stroll. As it is with most people who are in love or falling in love, after weeks gone by, Olivia was more involved and more concerned about what her man did when he was away from her on the other side of town and who he was doing it with. She didn't know exactly when Kelly was getting out of jail or if she had already gotten out and Bernard was going across town to be with her. "Maybe he caught another girl and was spending time with her to turn her out", is what Olivia also thought. Every now and again, she would ask Bernard if she could go with him when he was leaving the duplex, but Bernard would just say, "I'll be back later or pretty soon". Even though Olivia wanted a different response, she accepted the one she got because she knew not to press Bernard about his actions or decisions, until one Saturday morning. That particular morning after Bernard had gotten dressed and went across town, Olivia's curiosity got the best of her. She was tired of not being able to spend the day with her man and going with him to the places he went, so she decided she was going to look for him and would start at his mom's apartment. She really didn't mind if Bernard wasn't there because being at his mom's apartment would be like being where a part of him was. Besides, Bernard's mom was cool and his sisters were too. Everyone except the youngest girl and Bernard's brother, smoked weed and indulged in other drugs. Everyone except the two youngest of Bernard's siblings, were pretty much, children of the night, to one degree or another. If nothing else, Olivia figured she would sit at Bernard's mom's apartment and kick it with his family until he called or came through there (arrived). Olivia didn't have a ride across the bridge where Bernard's mom lived, but she was determined to get there, so she planned to do what she had done many times before, start out walking until she caught a ride with someone she knew or not. Preferably someone she knew. "Whatever", is the attitude she had. The side of town she lived on wasn't very big and it seemed she knew everyone, either from growing up with them, getting high with them or by association with one of her six siblings. Olivia was gonna get a ride across town with someone, so she got dressed after Bernard left that morning and started out walking early that afternoon. Olivia headed in the opposite direction of the turnpike that would take her across the bridge, but she knew if she made it to the boulevard that everyone traveled on sometime or another each day, she was sure to run into someone she knew who might give her a ride. The boulevard was Olivia's main stomping ground, so she knew how to work it (handle herself; maneuver) as well. Being a whoe, she was used to getting into strangers vehicles, so she was prepared to get a ride with a stranger. She always carried a weapon and knew how to use it, but always hoped not to have to. She never wanted to hurt anyone, but would if they tried to hurt her, so even though she took the risk she did, she did it with a dangerous mind. That way she would be ready for any funny shit. If she decided to get a ride with a stranger, it would be with someone who had a license plate on their car that would indicate they lived across the bridge. Olivia felt if someone didn't know her and wasn't going her way to the other side of town, they would probably have a hidden agenda for offering to take her as far as she was going. She was no fool and didn't trust that, so she did use her head and better judgement in the things she did. As it turned out, she made it to the boulevard and stopped by an older guy's house, who tried numerous times to get in her panties. Olivia wasn't interested in the guy, but she knew he wanted her, so she was always cordial to him and used his interest in her to her advantage. She associated with the guy whenever she saw him and got high with him on several occasions, but just didn't like him the way he liked her. The guy wanted Olivia badly though. Enough so, that he would do what he could for her. Including take her across the bridge and he did. Olivia was desperate to get to Bernard. She wasn't going to and didn't stop at nothing to get to her destination. After getting to the other side of town, but still far from where she was trying to get to, her friend's car was stalled. Olivia appologized to her friend, but she didn't let that detain her from her mission. As cold-hearted as it may have seemed, she didn't hang around to help her friend get his car started nor did she invite him to come with her. She just told him she would get back with him later (whenever that was). While walking from where the car was stalled, as Olivia got a little ways down the road, she caught a ride with a stranger who took her to where she was going, to Bernard's mom's apartment. It was cool. Knowing herself and the way she did things back when, Olivia figures she probably offered the stranger a phone number after he tried to rapp to her or push-up on her. She didn't give him her phone number. She didn't even have a phone, but she gave the stranger a phone number she made up. In situations like that, Olivia made like she wanted to see the guy again or that she liked him. That way, if the guy had any thoughts of foul play, her seeming to be interested in him would make him feel he had action at her (a chance with her), but just not at that moment. It worked that time and other times as well. After getting close to her destination, Olivia got out of the stranger's car around the corner from Bernard's mom's apartment and walked the rest of the way. She was always careful not to let strangers and others she knew, know her exact whereabouts in certain situations. Bernard wasn't at his mom's apartment at first, but Olivia stayed and visited his family anyway. It was all good until Bernard finally arrived. Since Olivia was in the neighborhood, Bernard figured she could be out making some money and wanted her to get down on the whoe stroll around the corner from his mom's apartment. Olivia didn't come as far as she did on a sunny, summer afternoon, to work the stroll. She knew she had to work the stroll downtown that night. That afternoon, all she wanted to do is spend some quality time with her man, but Bernard wasn't trying to get with that. While discussing the matter as the two of them stood in the hallway of the apartment building, one thing led to another, which was nothin' nice. Olivia knew Bernard would hit her without any warning if she pressed him or made him angry, but she was a person who, a lot of times, wouldn't accept "no" for an answer and questioned being made to do something she didn't want to do. She was that way and even got into trouble with Sara and Jean when she would always ask the question, "why". That's what she asked when she didn't get the reply she wanted or didn't understand someone's actions. Sure enough, her questioning what Bernard wanted her to do made Bernard angry. No matter what answer he gave her, if it wasn't what she wanted to hear, she would still ask, "but why". At that point, Olivia knew that at any minute, Bernard was going to swing at her (hit her) or grab her, so finally, she said something smart (sarcastic) to him and took off running down the stairs and out the door of the apartment building. Of course Bernard ran after her, chasing her to catch her. As she got to the end of the road Bernard's mom lived on, Bernard caught her by grabbing the hair in the back of her head. From the sudden impact, Olivia's head was pushed forward, causing her forehead to hit and break the window on the side of the building that sat on the corner. You would think that Bernard would have been sorry and sympathetic, but he wasn't. The breaking of the window made him angrier. He thought the police would be at the scene at any minute, so he told Olivia to get back to his mom's apartment. Olivia had grown angrier than before. Especially since Bernard showed no remorse, so she didn't want to go back to the apartment. By then, blood was running down her face from the cut on her forehead, as a result of her head breaking the building's window. Bernard didn't want to cause a scene or be around if or when the police arrived, so he began to push Olivia along, back to the apartment building. Bernard's mom got upset when she saw the blood running down Olivia's face. She tried to assist in stopping the bleeding, but it was clear that Olivia needed medical attention. Bernard didn't want to take Olivia to the hospital because he may have been questioned by physicians or possibly the police, so he asked his mom to use his car and take her. The cut on Olivia's forehead turned out to be pretty bad, so after getting x-rays, her head was stitched up and she was released from the hospital's care. Bernard's mom took her back to the apartment where Bernard was waiting. By then, he had calmed down and was even caring of Olivia's feelings. There the two of them sat, drank some robotussin syrup Bernard bought for Olivia, smoked some weed and ended up spending the night on Bernard's mom's sofa.

Each time it seemed Olivia would leave Bernard after a fight they had, she only got closer to him. There was no recovery time after the night she got stitches. The next night, she was back to work, walking the stroll downtown, in and out of tricks cars and the hotels, doing damn near whatever a trick wanted and could pay for. "Some of the men square women date and some of the men some women marry, are kinky and even perverted", says Olivia. Which is probably one of the reasons these men seek money-hungry women such as hookers, to date. Even though whoes date these men and do the things these men want to do, they get disgusted with some of them. That's when a whoe ask for bigger money. As they smile and put on an act of enjoyment with these guys, their stomachs turn inside. These men couldn't possibly expect a respectable woman to do some of the things they want to do for sexual pleasure. Olivia dated guys who wanted a straight lay (sexual intercourse) or blowjob, to guys who wanted a golden shower or have their mouth browned. "If you don't know what a golden shower is or how the mouth is browned, ask somebody", said Olivia. Some of the things some of these men want to do or have done to them, ain't nothin' nice and whoes oblige them if the price is right, but also, it's better to piss on them, than to piss a pimp off by turning down some money. Therefore, Olivia did what she had to do. She clocked dollars (made money by the minutes or hour).

Seeing as how Olivia was cool with his family and very familiar with the whoe stroll downtown, that she didn't need her hand held, Bernard rented an apartment downstairs from his mom and moved her across the bridge. He even took his furniture from the apartment he and Kelly lived in and moved it into his and Olivia's new apartment. That made Olivia feel he had love or deep feelings for her and that she had bumped Kelly from her position. She felt she was part of Bernard's family now, that Bernard really wanted to be with her and that their relationship was more official than ever, so she was willing to put more effort into making money than she had been. She worked the stroll around the corner from the apartment building by day and worked the stroll downtown by night. Sometimes she didn't have to work her day job, depending on if she had a good night the night before. She worked when Bernard wanted her to and where he wanted her to work. After work, she and Bernard would usually gather somewhere with colleagues, even at their apartment sometimes where they all got high and kicked it. Olivia got busted from time-to-time, but not too often. The first time she went to jail, she was a bit worried, but Bernard got her out in a matter of a couple or few hours. After she saw how quickly Bernard posted bond for her, she was relieved. Besides, the only charges against her were misdemeanors, so Olivia quickly realized she couldn't be kept in jail for too long of a period, on that type of charge. Being in jail for a long period of time is one thing about her job that concerned her more than some other things. Olivia knew Bernard was concerned about her being locked down. If for no other reason, he wanted her out on the streets to make money, so she believed that he would come and get her as soon as possible. There was always someone to call who would get the word to Bernard or Dwight and let them know their whoe or whoes were in jail, so that made the risk-taking less frightening. What Olivia still worried about was explaining to Bernard how she got busted. Bernard didn't like having to give the police or courts the money he had to pay when he had to make her bail. He did it because that is one of the jobs of a pimp, but after Olivia got out of jail, after a successful night's work or even if her night wasn't prosperous, Bernard wanted a report (damn near) of the night she had. Olivia didn't have a problem with reporting to Bernard though. It made her feel he cared.

By now, Kelly had gotten out of jail. Olivia met her, but she wasn't around very long. "In fact, it seemed as though she wasn't going to be with Bernard anymore and Bernard didn't seem to care. Bernard had a money-maker in having me", Olivia says. He knew it too, even though pimps don't stop trying to catch whoes or bitches and put them down, just because they have one good whoe. Their motto is, "the more whoes they have, the merrier they are and the more money they will have". The way things were with her and Bernard, Olivia believes that he was making good money with her and was digging her quite a bit, so for that time being, he was content. Olivia wasn't bad-lookin', she had a bad (nice) body and made good sex, so she was pretty easy to like. She also made a good housewife, so Bernard probably did like her a little more than most pimps like whoes. That is, in a personal way. Olivia's main work location was downtown and after she figured out how the vice squad worked, she rarely went to jail. That was unusual for some whoes, but Olivia studied hard and used strategies when she worked. She strolled alone, didn't hang around groups of whoes when money was slow coming, she didn't drink alcoholic beverages at all when she worked nor did she smoke more than one joint before or during work hours. Especially until she broke luck (had her first date) or had a few dates. "You see, there is more to being a pro, being good at what you do, than just being able to work your ass or give good head (blow jobs)", said Olivia. "You have to know the game in every aspect", she said. "Different strolls are worked in different ways at different times of the day. There is an art to being a good, money-makin' whoe", she added. There was too much white-collar work going on downtown during the daytime, for whoes to stroll. Lawyers went from their offices to the courthouse, employees went to and from lunch and consumers shopped and took care of their personal business, so whoes worked the downtown stroll after eight PM. During the daytime from about nine AM until around six PM, the more fancier whoes like Olivia worked the stroll near hers and Bernard's apartment and at night, the gay queens and the less fancy, cheap whoes worked that stroll. There was a lot of money to be made on both whoe strolls if they were worked properly and at the right time. Everything was all good for several months. Olivia had even dated a trick who wanted to get with her on regular basis which is a good thing. If all else failed on a slow day, she could probably get one hundred dollars from just that one trick, so she was pleased with that. She had to think dollars and cents at all times because she wanted to please Bernard and make some kind of money everyday she got down. Another thing about the game Olivia learned, didn't like and had a hard time with, was being of whatever assistance she could be, in Bernard catching, training and keeping another bitch or whoe. That was very difficult for her. Especially since she had Bernard to herself for months, almost a year. She tried to be what they called, "a big bitch", by dealing with and handling another woman being with Bernard, but she wasn't too good at it. It was all good when someone else was giving Bernard whoe money and Olivia was okay with another woman or other women kickin' it with her and Bernard after work, going to breakfast, dinner or something like that, but when it came to the part where Bernard had to give up the dick and spend the night with a girl, Olivia was a punk. She wasn't good at that at all, at least not at first. She was doing all she could to get the money though. When a trick didn't have a hotel room, she directed him to a secluded spot and dated him in his or her car. To stay on top of things and to keep the upper hand, Olivia would have a trick pull his pants down to his knees or his ankles. She would sit next to him with her hand wrapped around his dick, moving her hand up and down until the dick got hard, all the while looking out the car windows around the area they were in, to make sure the cops didn't sneak up on them or that no one was coming or watching. When the dick was hard, Olivia would straddle over the trick, sit on his dick and ride it until he got a nutt. In this position, she could get the job done and be on the lookout at the same time. Lots of times, it took a few minutes if the trick paid for a straight lay and a blowjob. Olivia had to suck the dick and get it hard before she sat on it. When a trick pays for a half and half, usually he gets his dick sucked until it's erect and then he gets his nutt when he gets the pussy. Getting a blowjob and some pussy, two nutts, takes more time, which takes more money for the job, but also requires a hotel room. Whatever a trick had money to pay for, was cool with Olivia, but after a while, the thought of Bernard having another whoe who would increase the cash flow, became more appealing, so Olivia thought she would try and handle another girl being with him. If he caught another whoe, Olivia didn't really have any choice but to handle it because that's the way it is in the game. Maybe, just maybe if Bernard had one or more whoes other than her, she wouldn't have to work as hard or as often as she did.

While out and about one day, Olivia was off duty just kickin' it and ran into the long-time girlfriend of hers who used to hang out with her at Danny's house when she used to shoot dope. After talking to one another for a while, Olivia and Shannon exchanged addresses and phone numbers and Olivia told Shannon she would call her. A couple of days later, Olivia did call Shannon. The two of them talked on the phone about what Olivia was about and how much money she made. Olivia also spoke highly of Bernard, telling Shannon how suave Bernard was and how big and long Bernard's dick was, to arouse Shannon's curiosity. Shannon was very interested in what Olivia was saying and responded by saying, "really girl and damn, his description and qualities sounds like he's someone I should know". Olivia replied by saying, "yeah girl, you would like him". Olivia called Shannon again a couple of days later, when she talked Shannon into coming across the bridge to visit, meet Bernard and possibly choosing him to become her stable sister. That's what whoes are, who have the same pimp. Shannon was undecided about everything at the time, but agreed to come and visit the following day and she did. The day before Shannon came to Olivia's and Bernard's apartment, Olivia told Bernard she was trying to pull Shannon and told him quite a bit about her. She told him some of the things she and Shannon had done together and told Bernard that Shannon was coming the next day to meet him and to visit. Bernard was proud of Olivia and was game for the hook-up (in agreeance with). He felt more that Olivia was down for him and was game like he wanted her to be, like she should be. The next day, Shannon made it to their apartment, sat a while, smoked some weed and talked with them. Bernard then took Shannon for a ride around town so they could be alone and get better aquainted. Olivia was still cool with everything because she knew Bernard was about the Benjamins (money) and wasn't quick to give up the dick unless he was gonna get paid. "All it took was that one interview (sorta' speak)", said Olivia. The following day, Bernard told Olivia he wanted Shannon to go to work with her. Olivia was okay with that, even though she didn't have a choice. She always enjoyed hangin' with Shannon (going places and doing thangs) and vice versa. The two of them got along great and always had. At one time, they were inseparable. When you saw one, you saw the other. If not at that moment soon after. Of course they had never shared a man before, so the results of that was yet to be seen. Early that evening, Bernard came home and had Shannon with him. Olivia was just about dressed for work, but had to add some finishing touches. She then joined Bernard and Shannon in the living room. That's where Bernard sat down with the two girls and gave them some last minute advice and instructions. Then he took the two girls and dropped them off downtown. The night went okay. Olivia really couldn't work like she knew how, because she had to kinda' hold Shannon's hand. She had two dates the whole night. One of the guys she dated wanted a double date, meaning, he paid to have both her and Shannon. That was cool since Shannon was just getting broke in (having her first date). Olivia wanted to be with Shannon on her first few dates, not only because Bernard would want and expect her to be, but because she loved and cared a lot about Shannon. She wanted to make sure Shannon was alright and as comfortable as she could be with dating tricks, before being alone on a date with one. It was pretty slow that night on the money side, so nothin' too much was going on anyway. The first night was basically to break Shannon in. Strolling, watching the other girls work, watching the vice squad in action, getting familiar with the faces of the vice officers and the unmarked cars they drove, as well as dating her first trick. Those were the main objects of Shannon's first night down. Bernard didn't expect too much of her. He knew how it was for beginners. Bernard picked the two girls up from the whoe stroll at about two AM the next morning and rolled off into the dusk with them. Shannon smoked weed and indulged in other drugs too, so Bernard passed her a joint of weed to fire up as they rode through the city to his and Olivia's apartment. Bernard had to be bouta-bout-it to make his game strong and make it work, so it was time for him to go to work now, meaning, he had to put in some work with Shannon, schooling her, brainwashing her, promising her, mesmerizing her or even sexing her. Whatever he thought he needed to do, to tighten up his game so that Shannon would stay around and pay him. He wanted her to be gamed and ready to go back to work the next night. That's the way the game goes, so Bernard didn't stay home that night. He dropped Olivia off at the apartment and told her he would be back. He then took Shannon to one of the most popular hotels in town, where street people stayed the night, a week, a month or several months. Nobody legit who was in town for business or a vacation, stayed at this hotel. It was strictly where the street people got a more reasonable rate for a place to spend the night or establish residency. It was cool for those people. They could do their business (whatever that may be) from this hotel, but they had to be about the money because the people who owned or ran the hotel were trying to get theirs too. They probably were or used to be about street hustling also, to an extent. They pretty much had to be, to allow the activities that went on there to get off. Bernard got Shannon a room at that hotel for that night and stayed with her so that she wouldn't be there alone and so that she wouldn't run off. With new recruits, you never know if they are going to stay or get weak and punk out. Bernard expected Olivia to understand what he was doing if he didn't come back home that night and he expected her to be strong about it, but she couldn't and she didn't. Olivia really understood how things were done in the game and she tried to be strong, but she punked out (got weak). She didn't sleep well at all that night. She even cried herself to sleep, even though she didn't sleep very long. Early that morning, at about six AM, she woke up and noticed Bernard still had not made it home, which made her very sad and hurt. She knew he stayed the night or morning in the hotel room with Shannon, which put a lump in her throat. Olivia thought it was possible and probable that Bernard went up in (had sex with) Shannon like he did her and the thought of that was tearing her up inside. She dreaded the day that she had to go there (think about and have to deal with that) because she knew or suspected she was gonna feel just the way she was feeling. She wasn't sure about what went on in that hotel room that morning, but she wanted her man and she wanted to prevent, interrupt or break the monotony of whatever may have or may be going on. Bernard and Olivia only had one car, which Bernard drove to the hotel and there was no one to call for a ride, so Olivia showered, got dressed and walked to the hotel. It was a very long walk too, but she didn't care. Walking the streets was a big part of her job, so she could handle it. Besides, that didn't matter at a time like this. What mattered was some other woman jumping up and down on Bernard's dick and laying in bed next to him. Olivia was not cool with that at all.

It took Olivia about forty-five minutes to reach the hotel. When she got, there, she couldn't just go up to the room. Management looked out for their guest and didn't allow un-announced visitors to go up to the rooms, so Olivia asked if there were guest there under Bernard or Shannon's name and had the desk clerk to ring the room. There was no answer at the room the clerk rang, which really disturbed Olivia. All she could think about was Bernard and Shannon being up in the hotel room, fuckin' and suckin'. She didn't want to nor was she going to leave that hotel without her man, so she sat down in the lobby and waited for Bernard to come downstairs. There was only one way in and one way out, so Bernard could not leave the hotel without Olivia seeing him. Olivia just sat there and waited patiently, with a puppy-dog look on her face, as though she had just lost her best friend. She couldn't be angry because she knew the game and besides, she caught Shannon and hooked her up with Bernard. After sitting on the sofa in the lobby of the hotel, watching TV for about an hour and a half, finally the elevator doors opened and out stepped Bernard. Olivia was probably the first thing he saw when the doors opened and he wasn't surprised to see her, but was his usual cool calm self. Olivia sat there looking into his eyes as he walked over

72

to her and sat down in the chair across from the sofa she sat on. "What, are you doing here", he asked. Olivia replied, "I wanted to see you". Bernard just looked at her because he could tell by the look on her face that she was sad and figured she was hurting because he slept with Shannon. Olivia wouldn't have felt any better if Shannon wasn't her friend. She wasn't ready for anyone sleeping with and having sex with Bernard. When Bernard asked her how she got to the hotel and she told him she walked, Bernard knew then, how badly Olivia felt. He had to have cared about her feelings and empathized with her. Otherwise, he would have been angry about her coming to look for him and he would have fussed at her. Bernard went to the front desk, handled some business with the desk clerk, turned to Olivia and said, "let's go". Olivia stood and followed him out the door of the hotel building and got into their car that was parked across the street in the hotel's parking lot. Bernard took her home and chilled out there with her until later that day. Olivia didn't ask Bernard any questions because she knew not to. She was just glad he was home with her. Bernard was really sweet about the whole ordeal. As he drove to the apartment, he and Olivia talked about things and he had a caring smile on his face the entire time they rode. With Olivia having him all to herself for as long as she did, Bernard understood her being affected by him being with someone else. Jealous is probably more like what she was, so Bernard didn't trip when she did what she did. "I know, I know all the squares are saying, "Shit, how else is someone supposed to feel when their mate sleeps with or is fuckin' someone else. What kind of shit is that", Olivia explained. "I know what you mean", she said. "Shit, I ain't trying to flow like that anymore my damn self and haven't for a long time. After Bernard and I got closer, when I knew I was in love with him, I didn't want to turn tricks or screw anyone except him, didn't want him to be with anyone other than me and didn't understand how he could ask or allow me to do it", Olivia added. "Again, that's how the game goes", she said. "I had a choice to either be with Bernard and be about the game, accepting the game as it was and always had been long before I got down or to leave the game and Bernard. By this time, I was so in love with him and naive too, that it seemed I was breathless at times. When I let Bernard know I wasn't a square and involved him in my work not knowing that pimping was his profession, Bernard would then not have things any other way. I was stuck between a rock and a hard place and fought long and hard about what to do with myself. I figured I would stay with Bernard, in the game, until the day came when I would go to work, look around at the whole scene and walk away, never to return or I would leave the apartment Bernard and I lived in and not come back to him or the game", Olivia remembers. From this point, that didn't happen anytime soon. "I was just, too weak for Bernard and caught up in some of the advantages and fun things about the game, to let it all go. Not at this point anyway", she admitted.

Later on that Saturday when dusk was about to fall, Olivia started to get dressed for work. Bernard told her that Shannon was going to be working that night also. Olivia was still a little bit sad about Bernard spending the night with Shannon and Bernard could see that, so he asked Olivia if she was alright. Even though she really wasn't, Olivia told him she was. After getting dressed, she rode with Bernard to the hotel where Shannon was. Olivia sat in the car and smoked a joint while Bernard went up to the room to get Shannon. When he returned with her, he took the two girls downtown and dropped them off on the whoe-stroll. Olivia was still cool. She wasn't angry at Shannon, but still feeling the way she did, she just wasn't as talkative as she usually was. She worked that stroll though and still looked out for Shannon like Bernard expected her to. Shannon was a little bit more familiar with everything this time, so Olivia didn't have to hold her hand as much as she did the night before (Shannon's first night). It was a warm Saturday night and there was a lot of men walking and riding around, so it turned out to be very prosperous. Olivia had several dates and Shannon had a few. Olivia was able to really get down this night since she didn't have to go on dates with Shannon. She just made sure she saw the type and make of the cars Shannon left in when she went on dates. It was all good. After things had slowed down which was around the usual time, two or two-thirty AM, Bernard picked the girls up from the stroll. This time he took Shannon to the hotel first before going to his and Olivia's apartment. Bernard parked in front of the hotel when he got there and told Olivia to wait in the car, he would be right back. He then escorted Shannon to her room in the hotel, which took about fifteen or twenty minutes for him to return. Olivia figured Bernard was up in the hotel room chatting with Shannon, while getting his money (according to the laws of the game). Olivia guessed that he was probably also up there in Shannon's face as he talked to her, giving her instructions and then a slow and sexy peck on her lips, patted her on her ass and told her he would be back. She knew his style and techniques very well. She knew how he played the game, but not as much as she was gonna know. For now, she knew quite a bit. To buy himself some time and not have a girl tripping at times like these, one of the slick things Bernard would do was to say, "I'll be back". Just, "I'll be back". He never said, "I'll be back later", "I'll be right back", "I'll be back shortly" or "I'll be back tomorrow". He left that statement wide open. Especially when he probably wasn't or didn't think he would make it back to a girl that same day or anytime soon. Not knowing his moves, of course Shannon and even Olivia at times, would think he was coming right back or coming back shortly, meaning the same day. A girl would probably (at that time of night or morning) fall asleep while lying there waiting (maybe watching TV) for a guy to return. By the time a girl will have noticed and gotten really angry because that guy hasn't returned yet and it's hours later, it will be close to the time that guy or Bernard was planning on getting back to her. Then she would (that girl/whomever) be alright again, now that he's back. "See, that's game", said Olivia. That's one of the ways Bernard use to operate. Bernard returned to the car where Olivia awaited and went home with her. He waited for her to bathe and get cleaned up and then he fucked her really good for the longest time. He didn't eat pussy too often. Other pimps were probably the same way. Not all of them though. The ones that didn't do it that often probably didn't want to eat the pussy because of all the dicks that were going up in their girl. For Bernard, it was something he did on special occasions, which was seldom. Olivia was cool with that. More than getting her pussy ate, she wanted the dick. Preferably one like Bernard's that could go way up in her where no man had gone before. At least, at that time. The good fuckin' Bernard gave Olivia that night was game too, she said. "Shit, he stayed the night in a hotel room with another girl the night before and I still wasn't all smiley like I usually was. Plus, I still managed to do what he wanted me to do. He had to reward me (so he thought he was doing) and make it up to me. That was one of the ways he did it", Olivia admits. For the time being, she was okay with that because her pussy was purring like a little kitty afterwards and her man was at home with her in their bed for Olivia to fall asleep up under. That's all she wanted, for now.

The next day was Sunday and Olivia didn't usually work Sundays, but Bernard (probably feeling that Shannon was a little shaky) didn't want Shannon to have too much idle time this early in the game, to change her mind and quit on him, so he wanted Olivia to get down and work her. Olivia didn't want to go to work that day and of course she didn't tell Bernard that, but she did what she had to do. She figured Bernard was trying to get paid by Shannon, as much as he could, while the gettin' was good. After dark that evening, Bernard took the girls downtown to the stroll and dropped them off once again. "It was like a ghost town down there", said Olivia, which she said wasn't unusual. That was one of the reasons whoes didn't work on Sundays, but Olivia wanted to do what she could for her man, which was also for herself, so she got her hustle on. It was like trying to draw blood from a turnip, but finally, she got a guy who had two passengers, to pull his car over. Olivia was counting dollars before her tricks hatched (sorta' speak), figuring how good it would be for her and Shannon to get three dates in one. That would set the night off right for the girls. A hooker's first date was called, "breaking luck". "Call it a whoe's intuition or superstition, but when a whoe breaks luck, the rest of the night seems to go well. If the first guy a whoe catches, is bullshitting or gives a girl a hard time, the rest of the night seemed to be filled with problems or trouble', Olivia explained. She figured if she and Shannon could take care of all three guys that were in the car, they would take home some kind of money if nothin' else jumped off. The chances of having

75

a good payday this night, was slim, so Olivia did most of the talking to try and get the guys to date and spend as much money as possible. "Hey baby, (talking to the driver), do you guys wanna party", said Olivia. That's what a whoe asked when she was talking to more than one guy. The guys replied, "yeah, we want to party". After talking to them through the window of the driver's side of the car, Olivia looked around to see if the coast was clear. The guys were saying, "come on, we want to party", so Olivia told Shannon to come on as she jumped in the back seat. Shannon jumped in the back seat of the car from the passenger side. "Keep straight", said Olivia to the driver, who proceeded to drive after both girls were in the car. Olivia and probably all whoes, would tell tricks where to drive to when riding with them. Olivia asked the questions about what the tricks like to do sexually as she ran her fingers through the hair on the head of the guy in the back seat, with her right hand. While sitting on the edge of the seat talking shit to the guys, watching and directing the driver where to drive to, she was able to reach over the front seat with her left hand and rub on the driver's chest. Before long, they had come to a secluded area where the driver stopped the car. Still sitting there talking shit and questioning the guys, Olivia came to the conclusion that the guys didn't have any money, didn't want to spend any money or was just bullshitting, so she told the driver to take her and Shannon back to the stroll. Not remembering exactly what was said, whatever it was made her decide that she and Shannon would walk back to the stroll. As they motioned to get out of the car, the front passenger tried to detain Shannon, while the guy in the back tried to restrain and detain Olivia. The front passenger couldn't get a good grip on Shannon as he reached over the seat, so Shannon was able to open the door on her side. Having a hard time getting loose from the guy in the back seat, Olivia shouted out to Shannon, "go, go". All at the same time, the driver was putting the car's gears in the drive position, so Olivia shouted to Shannon once again, "go, run Shannon, run". Shannon was able to pull away from the loose grasp the front passenger had on her and jump out of the car right before the driver commenced to drive off. Olivia motioned with her right hand for Shannon to see through the rear window of the car, "go, go", waiving to Shannon to leave. You see, Olivia figured in a situation like this, it was better for Shannon to get away, than for both her and Shannon to get caught up. This way, the one who gets away can be a witness and go and tell someone, if and when necessary. "Those guys would have been fools to do something tragic to me, when Shannon could identify them and the car they were in", said Olivia, so she didn't trip out, even though she was in a bad situation. Shannon was new to the game, but could have and should have helped Olivia get out of the clutches of the guy in the back seat after she got the car door open on the side of the car she was on, but she panicked, which was understandable. She would have been more terrified than Olivia, if it was she who was left with those guys, so Olivia rather it be her. The guys knew they couldn't catch Shannon and hold on to Olivia at the same time once Shannon ran away from the car, so they drove off with Olivia and took her for a long ride. After riding a little while, Olivia didn't know where she was. She had lost her since of direction while she was keeping an eye on the guys, watching their hands and listening to what they were planning to do with her. She ended up with them, riding down the freeway somewhere, still in the back seat of the car that had been going too fast for her to jump out. Olivia had no choice but to go along with the ride to play out the situation she was in. As the driver drove down the freeway, he began to go a little bit slower than he had been and should have been. As she listened to the guys talk to one another, Olivia knew they were going to fuck her and probably try and make her suck their dicks too. She seems to remember one of them saying something about getting some rubbers (condoms). Olivia just rode and listened. The guy in the back seat then asked her to take off her pantyhose and panties. Trying to cooperate for fear of what the guys might do, Olivia was no fool, so she took one shoe off, took one leg out of her pantyhose and panties and left them hanging on the other leg, just like she always did when she dated a trick in a car. She wasn't sure what the guys were going to do, but she was waiting and wanted to be prepared for the opportunity to do whatever she could to get away from them. As the driver drove down the freeway, one or more of the guys spotted a service station on the other side of the freeway. While they were discussing what they were going to do, Olivia peeped (checked out) a police officer sitting in his car in the service station's lot. While the guys were engrossed in deciding what they were going to do, Olivia was thinking on how this was a good time for her to make a move. She didn't think the driver would make any sudden or drastic moves that would attract the officer's attention, but she couldn't let that stop her from taking a chance at this opportune time. Playing it off as though she was going along with their program, as Olivia noticed there were no cars traveling behind them and noticed that the guy in the back seat stopped focusing on her a minute too long, she grabbed the handle on the car door and pushed the door open to jump out. As she pushed the door open, the guy in the back seat grabbed her at the same time. At that time, Olivia's left foot was hangin' out the door of the car and the driver was still going about thirty or thirty-five miles an hour, maybe forty. Still slower than the speed limit, so Olivia jerked away from the hold on her clothes the guy in the back seat had on her and jumped out of the moving car. Of course she fell on to the pavement of the freeway when she jumped, but she quickly got up and ran to the wide island that separated the freeway's traffic. As she ran to make it to the island, the driver of the car she jumped from, drove off with a little more speed so they could get away before Olivia made it to and alerted the police officer. Olivia stopped and looked to make sure no traffic was coming on the other side of the freeway before she ran from the island to get across to the service station.

Then she ran with a limp, yelling and waiving to get the officer's attention and she did. She had not shedded any tears the entire time she was with those guys, because she had to keep her head so that she would be more astute and she also didn't want to show any fear or aggravate the guys. After she reached the police officer, she broke down and cried. Olivia was afraid the whole time she was with the guys, but she couldn't give in to her fear and get weak. When the police officer saw Olivia approaching his car yelling and waving at him, he hurried and got out of his car to see what was wrong. When Olivia told the officer what happened, (well, everything except her trying to hustle the guys for a date), the officer helped Olivia into the back seat of his squad car, got on his radio to report what had happened and requested another squad car be on the look-out for the type and make of the car the guys were in. The police officer then took Olivia to the police station, let her go to the lady's room to clean herself up and then let her use the phone to call for a ride. Bernard wasn't at home and no one was at his mom's apartment, had a car, so Olivia just told Bernard's mom what happened, that she was alright and that she would try and get a ride home. Meanwhile, a couple of people at the police station overheard her tell the person she was talking to on the phone, that she would try and get a ride home. After she hung up the phone and told the officers her ride wasn't where she called to, one of the persons at the police station, whose car was parked outside, offered to give Olivia a ride since they were going to the same part of town Olivia lived in. After going through what she had gone through, ordinarily Olivia wouldn't be up to dealing with anymore strangers, but since the police knew who she was getting a ride with, Olivia took the nice people up on there offer. After getting home, she went upstairs to Bernard's mom's apartment, to let her know she made it home and was physically alright. She then went downstairs to hers and Bernard's apartment, took a bath and waited for Bernard to come home. She called the hotel to find out if Shannon made it back to the room, but there was no answer when the desk clerk rang Shannon's room. Olivia was worried, but she chilled until Bernard came home. After telling Bernard what happened the minute after he walked through the door, Bernard left in his car and went to the hotel to see if Shannon had returned, which she had not. She left a message with the desk clerk for Bernard though. Shannon didn't say where she was in the message she left, just that she was alright. Bernard stayed down at the hotel for about an hour or so, to see if Shannon would come or call again, but she didn't, so he went back home. There he stayed until the next day. He even let Olivia take off work that Monday night. Olivia spent the day regrouping and being a housewife. She knew Bernard was expecting her to get back to business on Tuesday, so she built her courage up and prepared herself mentally, to be ready for any bullshit she might run into again, while working the stroll. For this day though, she just wanted to enjoy being off work. Olivia called the hotel once again and had the desk clerk to

ring the room Shannon was in, but the desk clerk said that room was vacant. She
then called Shannon's grandmother's home where Shannon had been residing.
Shannon wasn't there neither, but her grandmother told Olivia that Shannon had
just left not long before she called. Olivia was glad to hear that and knew
Shannon was alright. Three days had passed since Olivia got back to work. She
had not tried to reach Shannon nor Shannon her. Knowing Shannon as well as
she did, Olivia knew Shannon got spooked the night they had the trouble with
those guys and she wasn't coming back to be in the game nor with Bernard.
Olivia figured as much when Bernard told her that Shannon left the message at
the hotel that morning after the ordeal with the guys they had the trouble with.
Olivia was cool with that though. She realized she wasn't ready to share Bernard
with another girl. Especially her long-time girlfriend. Days turned into weeks and
weeks turned into months, but still, neither of the girls tried to contact one
another. Olivia was still cool with that. Even though she loved and cared about
Shannon, she decided she didn't want Shannon around as a stable sister and left
well enough alone.

Olivia continued to work the stroll downtown at night and sometimes worked
the stroll around the corner from home during the daytime. Sometimes things
went really fast when the money being made was flowing and plentiful. Other
times, things were really slow and the hustle was greater. It wasn't all work and
no play though. Bernard took Olivia to concerts and the annual players balls.
Pimps were in clicks, sorta' speak. They all, basically, respected one another, but
mostly kicked it with those who were (they felt) of the same caliber, according to
their standards. Sometimes the ones who kicked it together, would go to concerts
in groups and they all attended the players ball. Pimps went all out when they
went to the ball. Everyone looked like movie stars, flashing and spending big
money, buying the best cognac and the best champagne the bartender had. Some
of the pimps arrived to the ball in stretch limousines, while others were in their
Cadillac, Lincoln Continental or Mercedes Benz, detailed (professionally hand
cleaned or designed) just for the occasion. "It was quite an event", said Olivia,
but the next day and days after, these guys pimp their whoe or whoes with full
force, to make back the money they splurged at the gala affair. The whoes didn't
mind though, because they knew everyone who was really down in the game
making big money, was going to be at the ball and they wanted to be amongst
them. This was a night for everyone to shine. "The life was fun sometimes, but
most of the time, it was hard work", said Olivia. All the weight was on her, being
Bernard's only whoe before and after Shannon, but she loved her man and
continued to do what she had to do to be with and get along with him. Olivia still
worked alone, but from time-to-time, she went on double dates with other whoes.
She was cool with all of those who worked the same strolls she worked because

they all respected her and Bernard and because she was very professional about her work. When she got down on whichever stroll she worked, she got right to work and didn't bullshit around, she knew how to handle the tricks and she knew how to get the money. She also knew how to dodge the po-po (police). A lot of whoes would have alcoholic drinks or get fucked up off one drug or another, including robo syrup, before and/or during work hours, but not Olivia. Even though Bernard didn't play that, Olivia didn't want to be down like that. Crazy shit can happen on the streets or while dealing with a trick, so she wanted to have a straight head so that she could be alert as possible. Other than a joint of weed here and there, Olivia stayed sober until she finished working for the day or night. Besides, she couldn't get her buzz on and enjoy the high like she wanted to, when she had shit to do. She took the game as serious as it was. "Shit, the life ain't no joke", she said. "Not only will a whoe be going to jail everytime she turns around, but her ass can get played and or come up missing if she don't keep a straight head about herself, to use when shit gets faulty", Olivia stressed. Prime examples of the kind of shit that could happen is the shit that went down when she and Shannon got caught up with those three guys. Another example is what happened a few or several months after the incident they were involved in. One night, Olivia hooked up with a girl who was from the same side of town she was from. Valerie (Val) was really a square. She just met and fell in love with a hustler-slash-player (an old friend of Olivia's) who knew a little bit about the pimp game, but wasn't a real pimp. Valerie's man was bringing her downtown some nights, dipping and dabbing in the game, but didn't work Val every night like real pimps work their girls. "If I remember correctly, I believe Val had a part-time square job, so she was fairly green (inexperienced) to the game", said Olivia. Val only knew the basics about selling pussy, but what Olivia recognized and admired about her, was that she liked money and she had heart. Because of that, Olivia didn't mind working with her, just on double dates. Otherwise, Olivia still walked and worked alone as usual. This particular night she hooked up with Val, was late one weeknight around two AM, when most of the other whoes were raised (picked up) or got up from the stroll (stopped working). Only a few whoes were still down, trying to get any leftovers or kibbles and bits they could put with what they already had, as a result of a really slow night. Because it was so slow, Olivia conversated with Val a little more than usual, just to entertain herself until a vehicle rode by that she wanted to shout out to. Finally, a van rode by. "You want a date honey", is what Olivia shouted. You know, the usual shout-out. There was also a guy in the passenger seat who leaned forward to see who was calling out to the driver as they rolled past Olivia and Val. As far as Olivia could see, there were only the two guys (the driver and the passenger) in the van. The van only had the two front windows and two small windows on the doors that opened at the very back (tail end) of it. There were no windows on the sides of the van, so at the time, Olivia only saw the two guys in the front seats. The driver didn't stop right then, but drove around the block, came back around and pulled over down the street from where the girls stood, so Olivia and Val walked down to where the van sat. There the two girls stood at the curb on the driver's side of the van and talked to the guys to negotiate a deal. The driver seemed pretty friendly and got out of the van to talk to Olivia, as did the passenger. Not wanting to be seen talking to the guys, both Olivia and Val walked to the back of the van to continue the discussion with the guys and come to an agreement or conclusion. After standing at the back of the van for a few minutes, somehow, the driver of the van stuck what felt to Olivia, to be a big long blade (knife) in her back, just enough for her to feel it, while the passenger grabbed a hold to Val. The two guys then demanded Olivia and Val to get into the back of the van. With no one else around to see what was going on and not knowing the mentality of the guys, Olivia and Val did what the they told them to do. After climbing into the back of the van, the driver (who seemed to be calling all the shots) told Olivia and Val to lie face down on the floor of the van. The passenger got into the back of the van with the two girls, to keep them from jumping out or trying anything and the other guy drove the van. It was very dark in the back of the van since the only windows it had, were tinted. After riding twenty minutes or so, when it seemed to Olivia that they were on a freeway, (no stops were being made), the guys demanded she and Val take off their clothes. In their line of work, the girls didn't have a problem with taking off their clothes. What Olivia had a problem with, is someone taking the pussy or some head (her giving them a blow-job), without paying her. She was just not a girl who gave the pussy or any kind of sex away to any or every guy who wanted her. She gave the pussy or sex up for love or for money. That freaky deaky shit, just for the fun of it or for the hell of it, was meaningless to her. She also had a problem with violent or any other kind of force. She was very angry with these guys, but they had a weapon, so she played it cool and went along with the situation. After getting undressed, the guys demanded Olivia and Val lay back down. As they rode for a while, it seemed to Olivia that they were on a dirt road with no streetlights. She could tell because there was no occasional light flaring into the van, as it does when a vehicle is passing streetlights. Plus, the road they were now on, was bumpy. All of a sudden, the engine in the van died out. The driver tried a few times to restart the engine but was not successful. In an angry tone, he then told the girls to get out of the van, so the guy in the back opened the doors for the girls, while the driver climbed over the front seat to the back of the van. Olivia started to grab her clothes, but the driver told her to leave them, so she did. When they all were out of the van, the driver closed the back doors of the van, leaving Olivia's and Val's clothes on the floor of it. Then the driver grabbed Olivia by her arm, as did the other guy to Val and told the girls to come on. Olivia was right in what she sensed. They were on a narrow dirt road that was only wide enough for one vehicle. Along one side of it were trees and bushes and along the other side of the road was a wide-open field that could barely be seen since there were no streetlights. The driver led the way up the dirt road a little ways and then across the mass of land. It was very dark out, but Olivia could see there were no houses or buildings anywhere near, as the stars and moon provided a little light. After walking quite a distance from the road, the driver stopped walking and told Olivia to get down on the ground. The other guy had Val to do the same. As the driver stood over Olivia, he began to take his clothes off. The other guy and Val were a few feet away, but Olivia couldn't see them too well. She only guessed that the other guy got undressed too. The driver then kneeled down, got on top of Olivia and commenced to fuck her. He really didn't have too much to say at that point. Not even "open your legs" because after he kneeled down, he used his legs to spread Olivia's apart. The driver didn't have much stamina neither. Olivia could smell alcohol on his breath as he huffed and puffed a couple of minutes after he stuck his dick in her pussy. The fuck was very brief which was good for Olivia and was over in a jiffy. Olivia was glad because she didn't want to give the non-paying man a drop of the pussy, not to mention a long drawn out fuck. After getting a nutt, the driver just laid there on top of her. Olivia didn't say anything to the man; she just laid there going along with the program for the time being. The next thing she knew, was the sound of the driver snoring. She couldn't believe this guy fell asleep while lying on top of her. She wanted to say something to Val, but she came up with a plan, so she just chilled and waited for the driver to get into a deeper sleep. As she laid there, she was able to look to the right of her at the driver's left hand. She could see the glare of the weapon he had and was more out-done with the whole situation than she was before. The weapon the man had was a blade alright. That's why she could see the glare from it, even in the darkness, but the so-called knife, weapon this guy had was just a pin knife, probably the blade of a nail clipper. Olivia could hardly believe it. "Shit, if I had known that was all these guys had to work with, they would have had a problem with me, especially bringing me all that way", said Olivia. The size of that puny little knife pissed her off, but she laid there and waited for the right time to execute her plan. The plan was for her to wait until the guy was sound asleep and then she would make her move. Olivia figured, the heavier the man got while laying on top of her and the louder he snored, the more sound asleep he would be. At that moment, which was about ten minutes later, she slid her body to the right a little bit and waited to see if the man was gonna wake up, move or stop snoring, but he didn't. Olivia waited a minute, slid to the right a little bit more and waited another minute. The man didn't wake up, move or stop snoring. What Olivia was doing was trying to slide from under the man. By this time, the man was still on top of her, but only on the left side of her body, so

Olivia slid once again which moved the man on to his right side with his face down over her left shoulder. The right side of the man's body was on the ground and as he slept, his left hand relaxed, so he no longer had a grip on the piece of knife he used to threaten the girls. Now that Olivia could reach the knife, she slid it out of the man's hand and threw it away from where they lie. She then waited another minute as though she was counting to three to make her move. Hearing the man snort as he snored, Olivia quickly rolled to the right and pulled her left arm from under the man's head. All in the same movement it seemed, she went from being on her right knee on the ground, to being on her feet, then she took off running. Shortly after she took off running, she ran into and fell over a bob-wired fence, but that didn't stop her. She immediately got on to her feet and continued to run as fast as she could, across what seemed to be a field. She couldn't see where she was going, but she hauled ass (an African American expression), ran like the wind and didn't look back. Finally, she made it to the dirt road and guessed or hoped it was the same road the van was traveling on before it stalled. Naked and bare-footed, Olivia just kept running on a straight path. She didn't know where the path would take her, but the road had to end somewhere or lead to another road. She didn't trip on running into someone who would see her naked. Olivia didn't care about that, she just wanted to be found and to get away from the guys she was with. She was concerned about Valerie as she ran, but figured if she got away, she could alert the police so they would go back, find Val and arrest the guys who abducted them. "Oh yeah, those guys were gonna get busted", said Olivia. The van they were in was stalled, so when the police found it, they would find her and Val's clothes still in it and they would also find out whom the van belonged to. Olivia wanted Valerie to get away too, but she didn't want to risk at least one of them getting away from those guys, so she did what she could do for herself, as well as for Val. It seemed she ran for miles, but she finally made it to the end of the dirt rode, which led to a freeway. Cars were zooming by, so she ran down the shoulder of the rode, waiving at the cars that passed, to try and stop someone who would help her. Several cars passed her by, but finally, a car was pulled over and the driver let down the powered window on the passenger side of the car. Huffing and puffing from nearly being out of breath, Olivia was crying as she told the driver of the car that pulled over, what had happened and asked the male driver to take her to get help for her friend. The man didn't say anything. He just reached over and opened the door for her. The man drove about a half mile down the freeway looking over at Olivia's naked body. The only thing Olivia could think about was how nice it was of the man to give her a ride, but what a dog he was for lusting on her titties and ass at a time of distress. She also hoped the man didn't start no shit with her, but she was mentally and physically prepared to jump out of the man's car if she had to. Soon after, she could see a small building off the shoulder of the freeway that was lit up on the outside as well as the inside. The driver saw the building also and pulled over off the road into its parking area without Olivia asking him to. Olivia was so glad to find that the building off the side of the freeway was a highway patrol station, so she jumped out of the car as soon as the driver stopped and ran inside. Still crying, she told the officer inside the building what happened (except for the part about her and Valerie trying to pick the guys up for a date) and told the officer the two guys who abducted her, still had Valerie. Olivia told the officer it should be easy to find Valerie and the two abductors because the van they were in was stalled on the road of which she ran from. She also told the officer that hers and Valerie's clothes were still in the van. The officer immediately called a police dispatcher and requested cars to come to the patrol station. It didn't take long for police officers to respond to the call neither. The patrolman gave Olivia a jacket to cover herself with when she first came inside the station, so when police officers arrived, she ran outside, told them what happened and pointed down the road, showing the officers, approximately, where the dirt road was that she ran from. As the officers quickly got into their cars, they sped off, burning rubber to get down the road and find Valerie and the abductors. Right as they drove off, another squad car arrived, went into the patrol station to talk to the patrolman and then took Olivia to a nearby police station. After giving her statement and calling for a ride but not reaching anyone, one of the police officers who was getting off duty, offered and took Olivia home. Bernard wasn't at home when Olivia got there and her keys were left in the abductors van, so Olivia went upstairs to Bernard's mom's apartment and stayed there until Bernard arrived. Bernard finally got there and took Olivia downstairs to their apartment. He was very sympathetic and charming when Olivia did what he wanted her to do, so he comforted her to make her feel better and told her they were in the game together. Bernard told Olivia to stay strong and that everything was gonna be alright. After having a bath, Bernard gave Olivia some robo syrup to calm and relax her. Olivia got her nod on, but she didn't sleep very well because she was worried about Valerie. She wanted to call Valerie's man to fill him in on what happened, but she couldn't because she didn't have his phone number. There had been no contact from the police before daybreak, which wasn't very long after she got home. It must have been between three and four o' clock AM when she escaped. It was probably five-thirty AM when Bernard made it home. "Shit the incident got to be a big ordeal", said Olivia. The shit made the news that morning. "Damn", she said, "after daylight, the news reporters filmed the police running through the woods with dogs, trying to catch the driver of the van who was dragging Val along with him as he tried to get away". The police captured the other guy and found the stalled van. Olivia and Valerie's clothes were still in it, which shedded more light and truth on what Olivia told them. The police were on their jobs though. They even had a helicopter soaring over the wooded area, assisting in finding and capturing the fugitive and Valerie. "It was crazy", said Olivia, "seeing shit like that on TV, knowing I was involved in it". "Damn, that's the kind of shit I thought I would only see in the movies or on the news involving a criminal I knew nothing about", she added. She said it was a trip. The police finally captured the man late that afternoon. They found Valerie first though. Apparently Val was slowing the man down from his attempt to get away, so he left her behind and kept running. The man didn't physically hurt Valerie, even though she was exhausted and pretty shook up. She was alright though. Her man brought someone with him to pick her up from the police station, so she made it home safely. "Now you know more than you knew before, the pimp and whoe game ain't no joke and a whoe's biggest problems ain't always with her pimp", said Olivia. "By the grace of God, I lived to tell this story", she admitted with a smile but sad look on her face. She and Valerie got past the ordeal they went through and they appeared in court to testify against the two guys so they would be prosecuted. The girls were to appear back in court at a later date, for the sentencing of the guys, but neither of them showed up. Olivia was back to work and her usual schedule by that time, but Valerie quit the job after that incident happened, which was smart of her. Once again, you would think Olivia would quit the game as well, but that meant she had to quit Bernard. She was just too mentally and emotionally weak for him to do that at the time, so she shook it all off and kept on going.

Olivia worked months, taking care of Bernard in every way she could. They didn't have an elaborate apartment, but Olivia kept it clean and fed Bernard well. After living downstairs from Bernard's mom for about six months, Bernard's mom was able to get a house south of the area the apartment was in, so Olivia and Bernard were able to have the apartment his mom moved from. The landlord had to renovate the apartment before it could be occupied, so Olivia negotiated a no deposit deal in exchange for her doing the painting and cleaning of the apartment. The landlord paid for the paint and supplies and bought new carpet. She even let Olivia choose the color paint and carpet she wanted. "It was way cool", said Olivia. She had ideas of how she wanted the apartment to look, so she was happy to have it like that. Seems like right around the time she started her project in the upstairs apartment, Kelly came back to Bernard. Shortly after she came back, Bernard caught another whoe. That was great for Olivia in a way. Bernard got busy putting Kelly and the new girl down, so he cut Olivia some slack. On the other hand, Olivia was sad because she knew Bernard was gonna have to spend time with and sex the other girls some time or another. She didn't press Bernard about that though. She wanted a nicer place to live, which was very important to her, so she focused mainly on that. Olivia took advantage of the time it seemed Bernard was giving her, to rest and get the upstairs apartment ready for them to move into. It took about a month and a half, to get the rooms in the upstairs apartment painted and for the men who delivered the carpet to lay it. Bernard came home everyday to hang around a little while and help Olivia out a little bit. Then he was off again to take care of business with his other whoes. After the walls in the new apartment were painted and the carpet was laid, Bernard came home and helped Olivia move their furniture and things into the upstairs apartment. He allowed Olivia a few more days to get everything in order and then it was back to work for her. She worked the stroll downtown a few weeks until it got really hot (harassment from the vice squad). That's when Bernard, along with some of the other pimps, raised their whoes from the downtown stroll and put them down on another main strip (street, boulevard) in the city. Even though Olivia didn't want to, she had to ride to work and work with her stable sisters (Bernard's other two whoes). With Bernard, it was a must that his girls got along with one another and act like they liked it. Olivia thought Kelly was cool, but the other bitch (which is what the other girl acted like) was jealous of Olivia's position and was a troublemaker. "The shit the new girl used to do to play for Bernard's attention and more of his time, used to piss me off", said Olivia. CeCe (the new girl's name) couldn't be trusted, so Bernard had to watch her. She was a moneymaker and had heart but she was like a rabbit on one hand and a snake on the other. After Olivia peeped (saw, checked out) CeCe's game, she figured out how to play (deal with) her. Bernard knew both Kelly and CeCe liked fuckin' off from time-to-time (too often). He knew CeCe was easily detoured by drugs, alcoholic beverages and smooth-talkin', good-lookin' brothers (African American men) and Kelly could be detoured by drugs and alcoholic beverages. Therefore, he depended on Olivia to be the queen bee (sorta' speak) and his eyes, to see that Kelly and CeCe did what they were supposed to do. Both Kelly and CeCe sensed that, but CeCe didn't like it more so than Kelly. CeCe knew what time it was with Olivia also because Olivia had an apartment, which was where Bernard called home, while she and Kelly lived day-by-day in the same hotel Shannon stayed in the couple of days she was with Bernard. Bernard knew that Olivia was crazy in love with him and was pretty confident that she wasn't going anywhere (to run off and leave him), but he wasn't too sure about Kelly and CeCe. Olivia, Kelly and CeCe got along pretty good when Bernard wasn't around, only for the sake of not getting their asses kicked. When Bernard wasn't around, the animosity between Olivia and CeCe was clear to see, even though they behaved themselves. When Bernard was around, all three girls were like little troopers. The attitudes of Olivia and CeCe to one another were still there, but they didn't start no shit. Actually, Olivia was digging (liked) Kelly and even enjoyed working and kickin' it with her. Kelly was what they called a veteran in the game. She knew very well how the game went and she was crazier for Bernard than Olivia was. Kelly was sick with it though. The way she used to play for attention got her beat down (got her ass kicked) badly. Those things she did for attention were different from those CeCe used to do though. Kelly didn't run off and choose other pimps or do devious and backstabbing shit that caused problems with or for Olivia. Her shit was targeted at Bernard. Shit that she knew Bernard would get angry about. Bernard didn't have any remorse neither, when he kicked Kelly's ass. Olivia said she wondered sometimes if that was what Kelly wanted, because she did the same kind of shit time and time again. Sometimes Olivia felt sorry for her because Bernard would be fuckin' Kelly up when he got with her (went off on her) and Olivia really liked Kelly, but that CeCe, Olivia couldn't stand on the for real. Olivia played CeCe though. She sweated about things to Bernard when no one else was around, but she didn't let a bitch see her sweat. And just to clear things up with the squares, Olivia said she refers to a woman as "bitch", but don't always mean on four legs as a dog. As it is defined in dictionaries, Olivia said she usually means, "evil woman/female", when she says the "b" word. "Sometimes I do mean "dog" when I say "bitch", says Olivia. "There are women, females out there who do moral-less things or (to better classify them) doggish things to other women or men for that matter. Just so that everyone is on the same page I'm on, I'm speaking about the women or girls who fuck their mother's boyfriend or their stepfather, their aunt or sister's man or their girlfriend's man or ex. Women who are devious and backstabbing. You know the kind of shit I'm talkin' about", she said. . "There's a lot more shit those kind of women do that are doggish", she adds. Anyway, CeCe was a bitch in more ways than one, but Olivia handled her. All three of Bernard's girls clocked dollars though (made money). By this time, they worked the main strip mostly, but also worked downtown some nights. Things were different downtown though. Because of a new ordinance of loitering for the purpose of prostitution, whoes could no longer stroll downtown, they had to drive around or sit in their cars to catch a date. "It was cool though", said Olivia. Because it was different than the usual way of working the stroll, the money came slowly at first. When things first changed downtown, there really wasn't enough money being spent for all the whoes that worked that stroll, to have good paydays. Therefore, Bernard said "fuck it" and had his girls put more time and effort into working the strip. That was cool with Olivia too. She could work any stroll. Her stable sisters didn't do too bad themselves. They were also versatile about where they worked. All three of the girls were better known as international whoes. They had to be, to be with Bernard. He wanted his whoes to be wherever the money was being spent most. After his bankroll got a little fat and things got a little slow on the strip the girls worked, Bernard made plans for his girls to roll out of town and go up north to work for a minute (a few weeks or so). Their destination would be Oregon, but had to stop in Wyoming and work there for as long as money was being spent, before they went on to Oregon, selling pussy to anyone anywhere along the way. When Kelly came back to Bernard this time, she had a small new car she was able to get because she worked a square job the time she was away. She thought she was slick, but Bernard was on to her. Even Olivia could figure out Kelly's shit. That was another of her biggest problems that clashed with Bernard. Kelly tried to be slick about a lot of things she did and even tried to run things sometimes. Probably because she was a year or two older than he and supposedly turned him on to the game, so she thought she knew some things that he didn't know and thought that she could pull some shit that he wasn't hip to. Kelly had a car note, which wasn't a problem just yet. She, along with Olivia and Ce Ce made big money before the drought, so Bernard was in pocket (financially able) to give his girls two hundred dollars each, without it even putting a dent in his bank-roll and sent them on their way to Oregon in Kelly's car.

The girls hit the freeway, took turns driving and took turns paying to fill the gas tank up in Kelly's car. They drove continuously for about nine or ten hours, so when they reached Denver, they decided to stay the night there in a hotel room, to get some rest. When they woke up the next morning, the girls showered, got dressed and got back on the road. It was near the end of summer, 1978, so the weather was still very nice. Olivia and CeCe were just following the directions, but Kelly, better knew how to get where they were going because she had driven to Oregon to work before Olivia's and CeCe's time and she worked Wyoming that time as well. The three girls stopped a few times to gas the car up, get something to eat, drink or use a restroom. Then they hit the road again. After riding through and past Utah, the girls finally made it to Rock Springs, Wyoming and got a hotel room. Kelly and Whoes that belonged to other pimps, had worked Rock Springs before, so Kelly was still a little familiar with the town. The biggest event or excitement in Wyoming was the rodeo or some shit like that, so when some whoes came to town, every man there, knew about it. Probably every woman too. Olivia, Kelly and CeCe stayed there two nights and three days and made big bucks and no whammies. "We would have stayed longer, but it got to where no one wanted to rent us a room and we had to check out of the room we were in on the third day", said Olivia. The desk clerk there, told Olivia and her sisters that the room they were in had been previously reserved for that third day, but Olivia and her sisters knew that was bullshit. The girls had gotten paid though, so they didn't press their luck any further. While they were in that town though, the girls only went to one bar that was like a saloon. They didn't have to go any further because there were plenty of men in and out of that saloon, who wanted to buy some chocolate pussy. Olivia and her two sisters took turns and sometimes went together to the hotel room with one man or another, so many times, you would have thought there was a revolving door connecting the hotel room to the saloon. "It was the shit", said Olivia. During the daytime, the girls went to a laundry mat to wash or went shopping for toiletries and then they would take some fast food back to the room to eat. There they would stay until dusk fell. In two nights, the three girls made big money. Olivia made the most because she was bouta-bout-it like she was supposed to be. Even though Kelly and CeCe didn't think Olivia knew it, Olivia knew when she went back to the hotel room to date a trick, that Kelly and CeCe got their drinking on (had alcoholic drinks). Olivia didn't say anything to the girls though. She just waited and reported them to Bernard when she talked to him on the phone. Olivia checked in and touched bases with Bernard everyday. Bernard wanted to know how things were going, how much money each of them made and anything else Olivia thought he should know. One of the times Olivia called Bernard from Wyoming, Bernard told her he bought her a Cadillac, so Olivia was really trying to be a soldier (sorta speak). Lieutenant if you will. She wanted to make her man proud of her. Bernard always rewarded Olivia when she stood tall (as he called it) and strong. Even though she gave him all the money she made when she sold sex, Bernard spent money on her, for the things she needed and some of the things she wanted, so Olivia didn't trip about giving it to him. On the last day in Wyoming, she gathered all the money she and her sisters made (with the exception of the money Bernard told them to keep for expenses), went to a western union and wired Bernard his money. Then the girls got on the road and headed to Oregon. They only stopped when it was necessary, but other than that, they drove straight to their destination where Bernard was going to meet up with them a few days later.

It was daytime when the girls got to Oregon. After getting a hotel room and getting their luggage into the room, the girls chilled out until it was time for them to go to work. They really didn't know where the whoe stroll was in Portland, so the girls went to the city's downtown area where whoe strolls usually are and got their hustle on or at least tried to. After approaching the second guy she came in contact with, Olivia approached an undercover officer and was taken to jail. The judicial system was a little bit different in Portland, Oregon than what Olivia was accustomed to where she was from. She had to stay in jail for twelve hours in the Portland jail, before she could make bond. She had been to jail several times before and had even done thirty days in the correctional institute of the city she was from, so she was cool with this as long as she knew someone was on the outside, doing what had to be done to get her out. Kelly and CeCe made Olivia's bond late that next morning. When Olivia got out of jail and she and Kelly were able to be alone for a few minutes, Kelly told her that she and Ce Ce called Bernard after she was arrested. Kelly wanted Olivia to know that CeCe had the ordacity to ask Bernard if he wanted them to get her out of jail. Kelly told Olivia that Bernard went off on CeCe, asking her, "what the fuck do you mean, do I want you and Kelly to get her (Olivia) out of jail". Kelly wanted Olivia to know that was the reason CeCe had an attitude. Olivia didn't say anything to CeCe about what she asked Bernard, but she peeped CeCe's attitude. Olivia loved it. She was glad Bernard set the bitch straight about being in her corner when he wasn't around. Olivia continued to play CeCe off and the girls took a nap after they ate the food they bought back to the room with them. Olivia slept hard because she didn't get any sleep all night while she was in jail. She would have slept longer in the hotel room had Kelly not woke her up. When Kelly did wake Olivia, it was to tell her that CeCe was gone. Kelly apparently woke up and noticed that CeCe wasn't in the room. Kelly then noticed some of their things had been moved around and the bags CeCe's clothes and things were in, were gone. Olivia got up and looked around the room with Kelly, to see if anything of theirs was missing. Olivia didn't want to call Bernard with a false alarm, so she thought they should wait an hour or two, to see if CeCe would return. Right before it was two hours later, Olivia knowing the snake and rabbit CeCe was, knew CeCe wasn't coming back, so she went ahead, called Bernard and told him what was going on. Bernard didn't seem to be surprised or worried about CeCe being gone. He just instructed Olivia and Kelly to go on with business and that he would be there in a few days. Bernard talked to Kelly on the phone for a few minutes and apparently asked Kelly how she was holding up. Kelly told Bernard she was cool. Bernard was minus one whoe. He probably wanted to check Kelly out to find out where her head was so that he could make sure his game with her was strong. Olivia and Kelly went on with business as though nothing had happened. They did everything together, day after day. They both got ready for and went to work around the same time everyday, when one wanted to get something to eat, the other ate too and when one rested, the other chilled out also. The two of them worked and got along well together. A couple of days later, was Olivia's nineteenth birthday. There wasn't any celebration or anything. Just another workday, but Kelly managed to sneak away sometime or another and buy Olivia a birthday card, so that was nice for Olivia. Especially since there was no one else around who would recognize what day it was. Olivia called her mom on the phone to let her mom know she was alright and to hear her mom tell her happy birthday. Her mom didn't like what she was doing, but Olivia was still her daughter. She loved Olivia and always let her know that. Even though Olivia felt the need to do whatever she wanted to do, she needed to know her mom and family loved her and was always there for her. With all that she had been through, Olivia's nineteenth birthday seemed like her twenty-ninth birthday, but that's the way it is in the life, living in the fast lane and growing up too fast. It was the day after Olivia's birthday when Bernard arrived. Bernard didn't forget Olivia's birthday neither. After he got to the hotel room, he got settled in, put his

OLIVIA
For the Love of Money

hand in his pants pocket, pulled out a diamond ring and handed it to Olivia. He probably would have put it on her finger had Kelly not been there. Olivia was so happy. The nice things Bernard did sometimes, made all the bullshit she went through and had to endure, seem worthwhile. "Well, at least it did during the happy times", said Olivia. "When things were bad, they were really fucked up", she said. Olivia kind of felt badly about getting the ring from Bernard. Only because she could imagine what Kelly must have felt. She cared about Kelly, but she also felt good about Bernard making her feel he loved her, that it was more personal with her than it was with Kelly or any other woman and that she was his number one girl. You know, the way every girl or woman wants the guy she's involved with to make her feel. The only thing Olivia was missing now, was Bernard making love to her. It was kind of hard getting that working, being that they were in a hotel room that had twin beds and Kelly was there in the same room. Both Olivia and Kelly were excited about Bernard being there and they both spent the early part of the evening talking with him. At the usual time, the two girls got ready for and went to work. It was probably five or six AM when they got in from work. Bernard was asleep when the girls arrived and only woke up long enough to get his money from them. Then he went back to sleep. The two girls took turns showering and cleaning themselves up. Bernard always tried to respect his girls feelings by not being intimate with neither of them when the other was around, so Olivia and Kelly slept in one of the beds and Bernard slept alone in the other. With some pimps and their stable, they do the freaky-deaky with one another where everyone joins in, suckin', fuckin', lickin' and what have you. Olivia only wanted to be with her man, to spend time and freak with him. She couldn't get with that freak shit, with someone she was in love with as she was with Bernard. She didn't know about Kelly, but she was exhausted, so she went fast asleep after her head hit the pillow. When she awakened, Kelly was lying next to her, dressed in some shorts and a t-shirt or something, seeming to be asleep. Kelly wasn't very feminine, so she had a habit of sleeping in pajamas or some type of summer wear. She wasn't prissy-like. You know, not tomboyish, but not girly or sexy neither. Kind of hard to describe. Maybe she was self-concious of showing her body or wearing sexy shit. Anyway, Bernard was awake, lying in the other bed watching TV. Olivia was on the side of the bed she and Kelly slept in, nearest to the bed Bernard slept in and Kelly was next to her with her back to Olivia and Bernard. After awakening, Olivia looked over at Bernard as he laid there looking at her. She had a good morning smile on her face, happy to wake up and see her man and wanted to be lying there next to him, touching him. Olivia wanted Bernard to make love to her, but a good fuckin' would also work. Either way would've been fine with Olivia at this point. "Shit, I had not had sex with my man for days. I wanted him badly", said Olivia. Bernard had the same look on his face as well. He wanted to go up in Olivia as badly as

91

she wanted him to. Finally, Bernard motioned his head (on his shoulders "smile") to Olivia. You know, one of those come here motions. When he did that, Olivia smiled, looked back to see if Kelly was watching or if she had awakened. Kelly seemed to still be asleep, so Olivia quietly and gently got out of the bed she and Kelly were in, trying not to make any noise or move the bed too much so she wouldn't wake Kelly. Bernard was lying on his right side and scooted back from the edge of the bed to make room for Olivia to lie in front of him with her ass backed up against his dick. His dick was already hard when Olivia's ass pressed against it. Olivia enjoyed sleeping in something sexy, so all she had on was a long gown with no panties underneath it. Bernard knew it too. He knew how Olivia slept draw-less (panty-less) so her pussy could get some air while she slept and also to make it easy for him to get to the pussy. The two of them laid there for a few minutes, waiting to see if Kelly would awaken. As Kelly seemed so still as though she was sound asleep, Bernard made his move by taking his dick out of his unzipped pants and sticking it in Olivia's pussy from the back entrance. Olivia assisted by grinding on the dick until it was all the way up in her. There the two of them lie with Bernard's front to Olivia's back as Bernard pushed his dick in and pulled all of it out repetitiously, except the head of it. Olivia rocked to and fro on the dick as Bernard pushed it in and pulled it out of her pussy. They had it going on until all of a sudden, Kelly just jumped up from the bed. With an attitude, she grabbed her purse and car keys, slid sandals or some kind of shoes on her feet and stormed out the door of the hotel room. Bernard and Olivia stopped grinding when Kelly jumped up from the bed, but Bernard didn't take his dick out of Olivia's pussy nor did he say anything to Kelly as she was leaving. He and Olivia laid there and listened for Kelly's car engine to start and her drive the car off. That's when Bernard really went up in the pussy. Olivia gave it up too. From the front to the back, there was some serious fuckin' going on in that room. Olivia and Bernard fucked like minks. They both took showers afterwards and got dressed before Kelly came back. Again, Olivia felt sorry for Kelly, but she felt Bernard was her man and she was going to be with him whenever and however she could if Bernard allowed it. Bernard wanted Olivia's pussy, plus, he probably felt it was time he gave her something for her to keep up the good work. "You know how men think their dicks are like magic wands", said Olivia. "They think a good dick is all a girl needs to motivate her to do the things she does for a guy". Kelly came back to the room about an hour later. No one said anything to the other about what happened, but Bernard did get Kelly her own room later that day. He and the girls stayed in Oregon for about thirty-two days. Bernard stayed in Olivia's room most of the time. When he did go to Kelly's room, he was only there for about four or five hours, then he would come back to Olivia's room where his luggages were. Olivia was cool with everything. Since Bernard told her he bought her a Cadillac, he put a diamond ring on her finger, he acted as though he really only wanted to be with her and he acted as though being with Kelly was a job, it was easier for Olivia to bare. Kelly seemed to be okay, as long as she didn't have to see what was really going on with Olivia and as long as Bernard spent some time alone with her. She and Olivia still got along pretty good and worked well together. "It was all good", said Olivia.

Olivia went to jail one other time while in Oregon, but Bernard got her out as quickly as she went in. The money wasn't too plentiful in Oregon, but Olivia was trying really hard to make something happen. That's the reason she was busted the second time. The first time she was just eager to make her man some money and got careless. It seemed like there was a drought in Portland on the whoeing side. The tricks weren't biting or was scarce. After being there about three weeks, Olivia started to see it was time to move on, but that was Bernard's call and he had already peeped that. "The money was so damn slow in Portland, me and Kelly even drove to Seattle and Tacoma Washington to work one night, but it was slow in both of those cities as well or either we didn't hit the right areas", said Olivia. She did get one date in Tacoma, so that was cool even though she said it wasn't about what she wanted to take home. Bernard could see the girls were trying really hard to get him some paper (money), but it just wasn't happening, so a week later, he flew home and had Olivia and Kelly drive and work their way back home. The girls left Portland, Oregon the day after Bernard left. Olivia was glad to be going home. She, Kelly and CeCe left home about thirty-five days ago and the going had being rough since they left Wyoming, so she was more than ready to get back to the norm. Things weren't exactly smooth after getting back home though. Everything was okay between Olivia and Bernard, but things weren't too kosher between Bernard and Kelly. When Kelly was away from Bernard and bought the car she had, only her name was on the title. She used the credentials of the square job she had, to get the car, but wanted to sell pussy to pay the car notes. Everyone who knows the game, knows that a girl can't sell pussy on the whoe stroll without having a pimp. In the game, any pimp can (what they call) arrest a whoe and charge her if she is an outlaw or renegade (without a pimp). That goes back to the saying "it's a man's world". Therefore, Kelly came back to Bernard, even though that wasn't the only reason she came back to him. Kelly loved Bernard's dirty draws (underwear). However, she wanted something to call her own and she wanted to pay for it with the money she made on the whoe stroll, Bernard's money. Trying to be slick or do things the way she wanted them done. The car Kelly was buying was a small economy car that really wasn't Bernard's style. Bernard preferred Cadillacs, but a Lincoln Continental or some other type of luxury car would even do, so he didn't give a shit about the car Kelly had. Anyway, Kelly had been making money, so she wanted Bernard to pay her car note that was due after they got back to their home town. "As I said before, Bernard didn't give a shit about Kelly's car", said Olivia. Especially with his name not being on the title. He wouldn't give Kelly the money she needed, but still expected her to keep doing what she was supposed to do if she was gonna be with him. "As I mentioned earlier, Kelly's problems she usually caused with Bernard was that she thought she was slick. She had it all planned when she got the car and then came back to Bernard, but her plan backfired", Olivia said. Kelly tripped about Bernard not paying her car note and started doing stupid shit she knew Bernard would kick her ass for and sure enough, he did. "I wasn't around when it happened and Kelly must have done something really bad because in kickin' her ass, Bernard broke her nose", said Olivia. She didn't find out about it until Bernard called her and told her Kelly would be arriving at their apartment soon and would be staying there with her for a week or so. Olivia didn't like it, but of course she told Bernard "okay" and didn't ask him any questions. When Kelly arrived to the apartment, the questions Olivia wanted to ask, were answered. Bernard wasn't about to pay for Kelly to stay in a hotel room and not go to work every night. That's the reason he had Kelly to stay at his and Olivia's apartment. Olivia understood. She didn't like the feeling that she was providing for Kelly or that she had to go to work every night while Kelly laid at the apartment, but knowing Bernard as she did, Olivia knew that he was gonna pimp the shit out of Kelly once her nose healed and she was back to work on the stroll. Olivia also knew that her understanding and cooperation was making the position she held, stronger and stronger, so she went along with the program, gracefully.

It was near the end of October now, autumn was approaching and everything seemed to be going fine. "In the life, so many things happen in such a short period, that when you look back on them, it seems like those things happened over a stretched out period of time", Olivia remembers. "Actually, many things could and did happen in two months, two weeks or even two days", she adds. Kelly was back to work a couple of weeks after her nose was broken, but ran off and came back since then. That time she left, she was gone for almost two months. "I don't know what she did that time neither, but one day that really seemed of autumn, Bernard had me and Kelly with him and had reached one of his friends home where he bought robo syrup. I can't remember what was said on the way there, but after getting to the syrup house, Bernard pulled Kelly out of the car and commenced to kickin' her ass and beat her with a small tree limb on his friend's lawn. The ass kickin' was so intense, that I started to cry, pleading with Bernard to stop hitting Kelly", Olivia confessed. Bernard was nobody nice when he was angry. He never beat Olivia down as badly as he did Kelly. Olivia got her ass kicked, but it seemed as though Bernard was always careful not to make her feel he was dogging her or that he didn't care about her, so he was more lenient on her ass when he got with her (kicked her ass). The way he kicked Kelly's ass, was so uncaring. Olivia believes even Kelly started to feel Bernard didn't give a fuck about her anymore, so she ran off again a few days later. Once again, Olivia had Bernard all to herself. On the personal side, that was wonderful for her, but on the money side, she wasn't happy. She felt Bernard loved her, but he was a pimp first, so how he felt about her didn't stop him from pimpin'. Bernard was used to and wanted money in his pockets. When his money was low or his pockets were empty, he wasn't very nice at all. Olivia loved that man though and her love for money was mutual. She just had a cut cord, but pimps don't. Not about the pimping game.

For reasons unknown, in November, the landlord of Olivia's and Bernard's apartment informed Olivia along with other tenants, they had to move because she was closing and boarding up the apartment buildings. Olivia never learned what the deal was, but Bernard moved his furniture to his mom's house and got him and Olivia a room at the same hotel the other girls used to stay in. That really wasn't Olivia's style, but that was the best move Bernard could make at the time, so Olivia stayed there with her man for about three or four weeks. She could tell Bernard wasn't too happy about something or another, but she couldn't pinpoint what the matter was. All she knew was that little bitty shit would piss him off. One night, he whipped Olivia's ass pretty good, so she ran off when he thought she was on her way to work. While sittin' around kickin' it in his brother-in-law's room, Bernard fell asleep, so Olivia let him sleep and went back to hers and his room without waking Bernard. That's why Bernard kicked Olivia's ass that night. As he was hitting her, he said he could have been robbed on the count of her letting him sleep amongst his brother in-law and the other pimps and hustlers who were in his brother in-law's room. "Shit, he just walked in our room and started hittin' me upside my head without saying anything or asking me any questions", said Olivia. "Whatever", she said. "It still wasn't worth gettin' my ass kicked. Hell, they didn't rob him and personally, I don't think they would have gone there in that place at that time", Olivia stressed. Anyway, she spent the night on the other side of the bridge that night, called Bernard and told him she wasn't going to work nor was she coming back to the room that night. She was pissed at him. She did go back to the room the next day and went to work that night. She and Bernard were okay with one another again and she went to work every night there after, like she normally did. She had checked on an apartment a few blocks from the one she and Bernard moved from and told Bernard she wanted to move into the apartment the first day of December, the following month. That meant she had to really be down so they could pay for the room they were staying in, the deposit down on the apartment and the first month's rent for the apartment. It wasn't easy handling everything there was to take care of, but

Olivia got some help from the trick she met downtown months ago, who became a regular date of hers (a trick who only wanted to date Olivia when he wanted sex). After that first date she had with this john (trick), Olivia didn't see him for months. As she was working the strip one night after she got back from Portland, Olivia ran into and dated the trick again. That night, the second time she dated this guy, the trick told her he wanted to date her on regular basis, which was cool with Olivia, so when all else fell, she called Tom (the trick's name).

Tom gave Olivia the money she needed to pay the deposit on the new apartment. Since she ran into and dated him the second time, she had dated him many other times and he had even given her money or bought her things when she didn't give him sex. He had given her his work phone number and even gave her his home phone number, so Olivia could and did call on him whenever she felt the financial need to. Having him was all good. On the first day of December, Olivia paid December's rent and moved into the apartment. It didn't take much for her to move into the apartment since the only furniture she and Bernard had was two lounging chairs. Bernard's mom didn't have any furniture for the living room of her new house, so when Bernard and Olivia moved to the hotel and Bernard moved his furniture into his mom's house, his mom put the furniture to good use and didn't want Bernard to take it back. Olivia didn't think that was fair, but she didn't dare say anything. She just made due with what she had. Hers and Bernard's stay at this particular apartment was as brief as could be. The winter weather had gotten really bad, lots of snow had fallen since mid November and money came slowly and close to none on the whoe stroll. Olivia managed to make some kind of money each night she worked, but it seemed as though the small amount of money she was getting was far from what she was use to making and not enough to amount to something that would really add up. Therefore, there wasn't really enough to manage, so Bernard didn't manage it at all. Just like whoes have their moments when they just don't feel the game and fuck off from time-to-time, pimps have their fuck off periods too. As things were rough enough during this time, they got worse for Olivia when one dreary day in January, she was informed that her father (her birth father) had been killed. Even though he never lived in the household with her as she grew up and Olivia didn't see him that often, she loved her father very much. She always hoped that as an adult, she might get the chance to establish a closer relationship with him and get to know him. She was even looking forward to him teaching her some things about love and men, along with other things in general. Now that he was gone, Olivia was sad and very hurt to know she would never get the chance she wanted, to get to know him and spend time with him. Bernard didn't expect too much of Olivia or press her to be about the game during this time. It seemed as though he felt if Olivia went to work as she usually did, that would be good, but if she didn't, he understood. Some days he had an attitude if Olivia didn't go to work, but he didn't say anything to her about it. Olivia didn't care about the game at this point, but she knew that to be with Bernard, she was gonna have to get back to work soon after her father's funeral. For the time being, she didn't give a shit about what he wanted or expected neither. She was all shook up about her father's death and was in morning. She respected her father while he was alive and was gonna respect him until he was in his grave, as well as she would the rest of her life. While being off work the days she were, things got to be unmanageable. She and Bernard got behind on the rent. A few weeks after the funeral, the both of them ended up moving out of the apartment, went and stayed with Bernard's oldest sister, her husband (who was her pimp) and two sons on the other side of the bridge where Olivia was from. Weeks later, just when it seemed things were at there worse, Olivia discovered Bernard was shooting dope in his arm. "That was crazy and unbelievable to me", said Olivia, "since Bernard was the one who stopped me from shooting-up drugs". Olivia never would've thought Bernard would shoot dope. He was so against her doing it and even went off on her verbally, the last time she did it. Bernard was so good-lookin' and so smooth (suave), that Olivia couldn't imagine and didn't want to see him go down that road. "It goes to show you that anyone, no matter how good-lookin' or suave they are, how intelligent they are, how popular or successful they are or how much money they have, can get involved with and even addicted to drugs and/or alcohol", said Olivia. She didn't get carried away (literally or figuratively speaking) with mainlining drugs like she could have when she was into that or like she had seen so many others do, but she knew how possible it was that Bernard could get caught up in that mix. She tried talking to him about what he was doing, but it didn't do any good, so she did the one thing she hated for Brenda (the woman she used to live with) to do, she told Bernard's mom what he was doing, which was a bad idea because no one could stop Bernard from shootin' dope. Not even his mom. Bernard got really angry with Olivia, just as she did when Brenda told Sara about her shootin'up. Olivia was Bernard's moneymaker though, so he couldn't or wouldn't dis (dismiss) her as easily as she dissed Brenda, but he was nobody nice for a minute (a short period/a few days). His dope shootin' days didn't last very long though. It was on for a couple of months and he and Olivia didn't get along with one another neither, but Olivia didn't leave him. Bernard started hangin' out with a dope-shootin' player, a friend of his, who happened to get his girl to sell pussy every now and again. Therefore, Bernard got involved with what his friend was about. He was so engrossed in hangin' out with his friend that he didn't keep up with Olivia and what she was doing. He wasn't pimpin' her like he had been, which was cool with Olivia, so she did what she could for herself and Bernard and let him do his thang. Olivia didn't like living with Bernard's sister or anyone else for that matter, so while Bernard was doing his thang, she started planning for the future and getting another apartment of hers and Bernard's own. Because she had already told Tom she was sleeping on the floor at a girlfriend's apartment, she was able to get him to take her to look at furniture and buying her a pretty, white and gold bedroom set. Olivia was happy about getting the new furniture. She had Tom pay all but fifty dollars on the bedroom set so it could stay in the store (kinda' like storage) until she got an apartment to move it into. Getting the furniture gave her encouragement and the desire to get back to work like she was supposed to be anyway. She was grateful to be able to live at Bernard's sister's apartment, but was happier when she had her own place. It was a must that she did.

In March of 1979, Olivia leased another apartment that was a couple of street blocks from the stroll she sometimes worked during the daytime. This apartment was only a few blocks down the same street from the last apartment she and Bernard lived in before they went to live at his sister's apartment. The new apartment was the bomb (pretty fancy). It had a sunken kitchen that was two steps down off the living room, bars on the windows and brand new wall-to-wall carpet. The building the apartment was in even had a TV monitor and automatic buzzer to open the secured door of the building to let visitors in. "It was the shit", said Olivia. It was the kind of place she had been wanting and could put her all into decorating. There must have been a couple of back-to-back conventions in town during this time, because Olivia started making big money again, which she was happy about since she had big plans for the new apartment. It took all kinds of tricks/johns for her to make the kind of money she made. One night as she was going to her car on the stroll downtown, a trick rode up beside her and propositioned her to buy her pantyhose from her. Easy money. Olivia was game for the offer and charged the man fifteen dollars for the pantyhose she was wearing. After she got the money from the man, she went into the ladies room of one of the hotels downtown, took her pantyhose off, balled them up in her hand and went back out on the stroll. When the man drove back around, Olivia handed the pantyhose to him and the man drove off. As Olivia proceeded on her way, the trick pulled up beside her once again about twenty minutes later and propositioned her for the panties she was wearing. Olivia was thinking, "Shit, for the money, I don't need any panties on", so she sold them to the man for twenty dollars. "Shit, the pantyhose didn't cost me but one dollar plus tax and the panties probably cost two dollars and cents and they weren't even new", said Olivia. That was a thirty-five dollar trick she turned, just for her underwear. "Which is a prime example that turning a trick does not always require a whoe to do some suckin' and fuckin", Olivia explained. A whoe does whatever she has to do, but no more than she has to do for the money. It seemed everyone who was really down in the game, was gettin' paid. You could see it in the way whoes were flossin' (dressing, carrying themselves and what have you). Bernard's sister was obviously getting her share and then some of the money that was floating around on the whoe stroll, because she, her husband and two sons flew and moved to Anchorage, Alaska about a month or two after Olivia and Bernard moved into their new apartment. Bernard, his sister's husband and several other pimps and hustlers knew a big time pimp from their home town, who had taken his young wife-slash-whoe and relocated to Anchorage a few years ago from this point. Olivia met the pimp once when he was in town and came to visit Bernard at the first apartment he and Olivia had on the side of the bridge Bernard and the pimp were from. Olivia had not met the pimp's wife yet. The word was that the pimp was in Alaska getting fat with one hundred and fifty dollar bills, so Bernard's sister and her pimp husband went up north there, to get a piece of the action (sorta' speak). Around the time when all the prosperity was going on downtown and on the strip, Kelly came back to Bernard and even CeCe was back and forth from Bernard to whomever. Bernard didn't seem to care about CeCe running off at first, as long as she paid him the little time she was with him. Olivia was trying to get all she could too. Being that Bernard was busy pimpin' and wasn't trying to buy things for his and Olivia's new apartment, Olivia got what she wanted and needed from Tom. Her pride and joy was still music and dancing, but she didn't have a stereo, so the second major purchase she had Tom make, was a seven hundred dollars set of stereo equipment from Macy's department store. Tom charged the purchase on one of his credit cards. "You think he didn't when he did", said Olivia, with a tone of boasting. At this point, Tom was crazy for her, but no matter what he bought Olivia or how much he paid for what he bought her, he only got the pussy or some head (blowjob) when he gave her cash money. When he just wanted to have a meal or spend time with her, she went shopping even if she only got a pair of shoes, a purse, an outfit or something. A trick has to pay for whatever time he spends with a whoe and Olivia was down to get what she could for her time, at all times. Tom was a white male who had three teenage children and a really heavyset wife whom he said he had not had sex with for two years when Olivia first met him. "Hum! Who knows", said Olivia. Tom had a big thing for chocolate girls, so Olivia put the whip appeal on his ass. "Shit, Tom had it bad for me, that he was gonna try and give me whatever I wanted if he could", Olivia stated. It was nice having someone want you that badly, she admitted. Even though he was a trick, Olivia was grateful for everything he bought her or did for her because he was very generous and cared a lot for her. She gave Tom the pussy though, whenever he wanted it and had cash to pay for it. He didn't have much dick to work with and hardly any stamina, but that was great for Olivia because it made her job easier, plus, it wasn't about Tom or any trick having a big dick and being able to last a while, unlike what some people may think. A real whoe has many skills. One of those skills is to focus on the money at all times and not on finding pleasure in the sex she has with tricks/johns. To some, that may seem impossible, but it is very possible and that's the way it was with Olivia.

It seemed like the spring season brought the stars out (as in movie stars). Whoes were dressing (wearing nice clothing) better than ever, looking like they were making big money. Kelly was no fancy dresser, but CeCe was. Whomever CeCe had been with, pimp or trick, she had a few nice things to wear when she came back to Bernard. Bernard always made Olivia's bond when he had to, he paid the rent and utilities when they were due to be paid, he kept the fridge full with food and he made sure Olivia had cigarettes and the toiletries she used for her person, as well as the items she needed for the apartment, but he didn't spend too much money on clothing for her. Even though Olivia made good money, the more she needed or asked for, the harder Bernard was gonna pimp her, so she went another route and got what she wanted. A few weeks after Tom bought her the stereo equipment, Olivia told Tom she didn't have very many clothes to wear and talked him into taking her shopping. Olivia was attracted to fine things. They seemed to call out to her, so she suggested Tom take her to the plaza where one had to have a bankroll or credit cards to shop. Olivia saw many pretty things she wanted and ended up leaving the plaza with eight new dresses, a skimpy short outfit, some nice black leather high-heeled sandals and a black leather purse. "Auh, I went for the gusto when I got mine", she said "and when I let Tom take me to dinner, I ate lobster, Alaskan crab legs and steaks". She had it going on with Tom and if he couldn't set out the Benjamin's, the Grants or any of the other dead presidents, plastic (credit cards) was acceptable.

With Tom's money and credit cards, Olivia was able to be more fashionable than ever when she dressed for work. She was really slangin' the pussy (selling a lot of it all over the place). Bernard had been in touch with his sister in Alaska, keeping up with the status of the money being made up there. According to his sister and brother in-law, there was enough money up there in Anchorage, for everyone and then some, so Bernard decided he wanted to get a little bit of the Eskimos money too. For a task such as that, being so far away without him there to watch over a whoe, making sure she did what she went there to do, someone dedicated, faithful and trustworthy was required. The chosen one was Olivia, Bernard's queen. Olivia was the best girl for the job, so Bernard purchased an airline ticket for his queen and off to Alaska she flew. Olivia was glad to make the trip for the tour she would get and for the experience, but also because Bernard told her he would probably join her there. That meant Kelly and CeCe were gonna stay home and work. Olivia would then get the chance to be alone with her man, on vacation sorta' speak, away from his other whoes for a couple of weeks. When Bernard took her to the airport, Olivia got on the airplane with bells on (figuratively speaking). The trip was a business trip, but Olivia was cool with that. She felt like a big bitch (someone of clout, important, v.i.p.), so she was ready to get there and get down. She stayed at Bernard's sister's apartment for about ten days. "Shit, when I did get down, all I saw was fifties and hundred dollar bills just as I had heard about", said Olivia. Basically, all she did was rest, dressed and clocked dollars (made money). Four days after she arrived in Anchorage, Olivia wired Bernard two thousand dollars and kept one hundred fifty dollars for food and other necessities. A couple of days later when she talked to Bernard on the phone and asked him when he was coming to Anchorage, Bernard told her he had business at home and wasn't going to be able to make the trip at that time. That pissed Olivia off, but she didn't trip (nag or complain). She felt it was too good to be true when Bernard mentioned to her that he might join her. She knew Bernard's other girls weren't making nearly as much money as she was, but they were able to see and be with him everyday, so she said, "fuck it", in thought. Before she hung up the phone from talking to Bernard, she told him as soon as she moneyed-up (made some more money), she was coming home and that's what she did. She still didn't come home broke (money less), even though her flight cost her almost six hundred dollars. Not only did she make her airfare, she brought close to five hundred dollars back with her. Olivia was straight bouta-bout-it from the moment she arrived in Anchorage, til the moment she got to the airport in Anchorage to return home. "The set up in Anchorage was so sweet, a bitch can't and shouldn't do anything but get paid while there", said Olivia. She said there was a, somewhat, sleazy cathouse (hotel) right on the stroll, that had rooms that were rented for fifteen or twenty dollars per four hours occupied. "Shit, the owner of the hotel was gettin' over like a fat rat", Olivia said. Most tricks didn't spend the money it took to have a girl for four hours since it cost them one hundred dollars for a half-and-half (half suck, half fuck), which only took or lasted about twenty minutes tops. Therefore, the rooms were only occupied for twenty or thirty minutes at a time, at best. Sometimes a trick would hang around in the room for an hour or two after a whoe did her job, but usually not. There must have been at least thirty or forty rooms in that cathouse. "Myself, along with several other whoes were in and out of the hotel rooms like that cat house was a convenient store", Olivia said with a smile. "Well, in a sense, it was a convenient store", she added. There were like five strip bars around the corner from, but a couple of them joined to, the square the cathouse was a part of and/or connected to. After guys went into the strip bars, watched some semi-naked women and queens (gays and/ transvestites) shake their pussy, asses and titties in the their face or maybe pay one of them for a table dance where the girls would grind or jump up and down on their dick, filled with alcoholic beverages by then, the guys would come out of the bars where whoes would swarm them and put the mack on them (solicit them). All intoxicated, hot and bothered, the guys were more than ready by then, for some head, pussy, ass, a whipping/beating, a golden shower or whatever their desire or fantasy was. Olivia was one of those who was more than willing to oblige any and every guy who had enough money, to pay for their preference.

Olivia left Alaska and arrived at the airport in her hometown where Bernard was waiting outside in his new car, to take her home. With the two thousand dollars she wired him, Bernard bought a nineteen seventy-three Fleetwood Cadillac that was canary yellow with a gold vinyl top and gold velour interior. "It was clean", said Olivia. That's the kind of shit pimps spend whoe money on, more so than anything else. Olivia was cool with that though, since Bernard bought her the nineteen sixty-nine cocoa brown Cadillac sedan with chocolate leather interior, when she was in Wyoming. "My car was older, but it was cute, clean and it ran good", said Olivia. She said it was all good in the late nineteen seventies. Bernard had a friend ride to the airport with him. When Olivia walked out the doors at the airport, she was lookin' like Bernard always wanted her to look to catch a date. She was wearing her longhaired wig and lipstick, with a long skimpy turquoise wrap-around dress. Olivia also wore four-inch heels that had straps that wrapped around her ankles and thong panties, but no bra. She was dressed (as usual) to impress any man who wanted to spend some money on her. "Shit, the way the game goes, I would have walked out the doors of the airport with a trick who wanted to take me to his hotel room and spend some money on me", Olivia said with certainty. "I would have held on to the trick's arm, winked at Bernard or did something to let him know what time it was (what was going on) without letting the trick see a man (Bernard) who could only be my pimp (or so the trick would think), there to pick me up. Tricks get nervous to date or talk to a girl when there's another man looking on, who seems to be the girl's pimp", Olivia explained. Bernard would have been happy if she walked out the doors at the airport, with a trick. He wouldn't have minded driving the long distance to the airport from the part of town they lived in and not picking Olivia up. He didn't care where a whoe was, whether he was around or not, he expected his whoe (s) to get the money. Just like m.o.b, money over bitches, is what some men say. That's definitely the way it is with pimps. Anyway, Olivia was happy and impressed to see her man and his new car she bought. She strolled to the bright flashy Cadillac with her sunglasses on and sort of slithered into the back seat of the car in a sexy motion and off her man drove. The new Cadillac was riding so smooth as she sat in the back seat like a movie star or entertainer, smoking a joint of weed her man passed to her. When they got in town, Bernard dropped his friend off, took Olivia to their apartment and made strong, mad and passionate love to her for about an hour. Then the two of them sorta' passed out and napped until early that evening. Even though they had bullshit times when they fought, Bernard cared a lot for Olivia and was proud of her and Olivia was very much in love with Bernard. Usually, the two of them were cute together. Bernard used to call Olivia "mama" in a sexy way. The two of them were kind of like a married couple who were also business partners. When Bernard awakened from his nap that evening, it was back to business for him with Kelly and CeCe. A couple of weeks later, CeCe ran off again. This time when she left, CeCe left behind her clothes and other belongings in the hotel room she stayed in and chose an older guy who was one of the state's most prominent pimps. Mace, was the pimp's name who CeCe chose, was flashy, had big jewelry, a new Cadillac along with a couple other cars and he had three other whoes. Mace dressed nicely, dressed his whoes accordingly and kept their hair laid (professionally done). His whoes didn't usually wear wigs. He had his stable (of whoes) in order and they were as a big happy family, but Mace wouldn't have had it any other way. He was competition enough, but he had bigger action at CeCe with his other girls. One of them in particular. Mace's newest girl he caught before CeCe chose him, had been with Mace for about six or seven months when CeCe joined his stable. Oh girl was bisexual, so Mace sicked (as in commanding a bitch, a dog) her on CeCe. Mace had big game to catch a whoe. "Shit, taking or letting a whoe go shopping and keeping her hair done by a beautician, was a plus", said Olivia, who didn't have it like that with Bernard. He just as well bought a whoe a wig and be done with spending money on hair. A lot of pimps buy their girl or girls wigs and tell their girl or girls to piece together some clothes to make an outfit. "I ain't stupid", said Olivia. "That's why I hooked a trick like Tom and had him buy me some clothes", she said. Bernard did good paying for the immediate necessities, which was most important to Olivia. The rest of the money was spent on Cadillacs, weed, robo syrup and showboating. Bernard always kept money in his pockets though. He was just not into spending money on a whoe, for things he couldn't claim as his property if a bitch left him or ran off. "You see, that shit pimps talk about we, us, and ours, the money, the cars and other assets are only things of ours (the pimp's and the whoe's) for as long as a whoe is with that pimp. When a bitch leaves, she ain't taking shit with her except her clothes. She may only be taking the ones on her back when she leaves and if she's got anything worth money, such as furs, jewelry or leather and suede ensembles, she certainly may not be taking shit like that with her and that's the way it is with a lot of pimps", Olivia explained. "I am not saying these things to blow anyone's game or cause any problems with anyone's game, but if a pimp is really bout-about it, it don't matter what a whoe knows about him and the way pimps are or about what I say anyway", she added. A woman loves her pimp because of who he is and how he does whatever he does that she likes, regardless to how a brother is or plays the pimpin' game. Therefore, that woman will stay with the pimp, be down for him and pay him anyway if she wants to be with him and that's what he's about. "I was true to the game and loyal to Bernard. There was no other pimp for me", Olivia admits. She paid Bernard because he was good to her from the beginning and with the money she made and gave to him, Bernard provided her with what she needed. She continued to pay him because that's what he was about, because she loved him and because she still wanted to be with him after she learned that he was about the pimpin'. As long as he continued to pay for her to rent an apartment with the money she made and gave to him, along with the utilities and kept the refrigerator filled with food, Olivia didn't have a problem with none of it because she was working for herself as well.

When CeCe left Bernard and chose Mace, Bernard took it more personal than he ever had, for some reason. He didn't trip with Mace or anything like that, but he did sick (command) Olivia and Kelly on CeCe. That was right up Olivia's alley too (figuratively speaking). Olivia had been waiting for the day she could get in CeCe's ass without getting in trouble with Bernard. Ordinarily, Bernard didn't tolerate shit like that, but now, since Olivia had permission, she schemed and took advantage of the opportunity. For weeks, she and Kelly rode the stroll downtown, with CeCe's clothes and other shit in the trunk of Olivia's car. Olivia's plan was to lure CeCe into the car so she and Kelly could drive to a secluded area and beat her down. This mission went on for about three weeks. Once, Olivia and Kelly managed to talk CeCe into getting into the car so she could get her clothes. Olivia had instructed Kelly, who was driving, on what to do if CeCe took the bait. Because Kelly was driving like a senior citizen, CeCe was able to jump out of the car and escape before they could get her to a secluded area. There were other times when Olivia caught CeCe and Mace's girl who was bi-sexual, in their car at stop signs or stop lights, when Olivia jumped out of her car, ran over to the car CeCe was in and tried to cut CeCe's face with a knife or hit CeCe in her face. Olivia wasn't able to strike CeCe those times because CeCe's stable sister, who was always the driver of the two, would speed off before Olivia could strike CeCe, when she saw Olivia running towards the car they were in. One night though, Olivia finally got the chance she had been waiting for. She and Asia were riding together this time, had been down that night for a couple of hours and decided to stop at a Quik Trip convenient store for cigarettes or something. When they turned the corner on to the one-way street Quik Trip was on, right away, Olivia noticed the car parked out front of the store was Mace's car that CeCe and her stable sister rode in. CeCe and her stable sister were inside the store. "Looka'-here, looka'-here", is what Olivia said when she saw Mace's car his girls were riding in. Opportunity had arrived. This was Olivia's chance to get her hands on CeCe without CeCe getting away. She had

Asia to park in front of the building next door to Quik Trip. That way, CeCe nor her sister would see her car. Olivia then got out of her car, stood with her back against the wall of the building next to Quik Trip and waited for the girls to come out of the store. When they did, Olivia rushed CeCe and commenced to kickin' her ass. Finally, CeCe's sister was over the element of surprise and responded by picking CeCe up from the ground. That also gave Olivia the opportunity to use her fist and drill CeCe in her face. CeCe's sister then swung CeCe around, placing herself between CeCe and Olivia and said, "That's enough". A few words were exchanged between Olivia and the sister, the fight ended and both stables of girls got in their cars and left the scene. Olivia doesn't know what CeCe and her sister did from that point on, but she and Asia got back to work. One other time previous to this one, Olivia was trying to get with CeCe on the stroll, but CeCe's stable sister (the same whoe) decided she was gonna run interference. As she and Olivia were face-to-face exchanging words, Olivia told the whoe to step (get out of her face), but the whoe didn't, so Olivia ended up stabbing her in her head with a screwdriver. You see, whoes can be dangerous and Olivia was no punk about handling herself. After the altercation she had with Mace's other whoe and after she got in CeCe's ass, the conflict ended. The night Olivia beat down CeCe, Mace rode through the whoe stroll and mugged (looked at) Olivia as he rode past her car. He didn't seem to have any animosity, but then again, he always wanted Olivia to choose him, so he was cool. Bernard and Mace never had any words about the matter neither. Mace probably knew how flighty CeCe was anyway and didn't want to jeopardize anything by tripping with anyone over her. Everyone just chilled and this too passed. Now that everyone was back to their corners (sorta' speak), Olivia and Kelly put forth their best efforts on a daily basis, to make as much money as they could. Things were lookin' up (well and prosperous) and Bernard was looking like he was having money with his new Cadillac and all. He and Olivia had a nice apartment and Bernard was still two whoes deep (an old saying in the game, whoe count), so he wasn't doing too badly. Olivia, being in hers and Bernard's modern apartment, was ecstatic and carried herself in a different manner as though she was livin' large and Kelly seemed to be content living in a hotel room, so all was well.

Of Bernard's siblings, Olivia was more tight (closer) with the one who was the same age as she and a few years younger than Bernard. Bernard's mom looked at Olivia and treated her as a daughter in-law, but even though Olivia was cool with or got along with them all, she wasn't one of Bernard's younger sister's favorite people. Olivia and Shawn (the younger sister's name) were alright with one another up until Olivia returned home from Oregon wearing the ring Bernard gave her. As it was, the ring originally belonged to Shawn, who was a year or two younger than Olivia. Shawn had pawned the ring a couple of months before

Olivia and her stable sisters went to Oregon. By the time Bernard was leaving to come to Oregon, Shawn was about to lose the ring since it had been in hock for nearly ninety days, so Bernard got it out of pawn and gave it to Olivia. Shawn didn't like that and despised Olivia for that reason. Bernard ended up pawning the ring himself when things got a little rough so neither Olivia nor Shawn was able to have the ring. Still, from then on, the two of them got along with, but really didn't care for one another. "I believe Shawn took it personal that Bernard gave me something that belonged to her", said Olivia. Shawn felt her brother cared for Olivia more and that Olivia was taking or had taken her brother away from her. Bernard was Shawn's idol and protector. He was Shawn's only brother for about twelve years, until their youngest sibling was born. The two of them were very tight (close). On the other hand, Olivia wasn't too fond of Shawn because she felt Shawn played games with different guys (players, hustlers, other pimps) who Bernard previously had altercations with about her. Olivia felt Shawn was putting Bernard in positions that could get him hurt or killed and she didn't like it. Olivia and Shawn didn't trip with one another though, because Bernard wasn't gonna stand for it. For the reason Olivia had a problem with Shawn, sure enough, Bernard finally got into a bigger altercation with another real pimp, than the altercations he got into those previous times. The pimp Bernard got into it with, was as down in the game as Bernard was (true to the ethics of the pimpin' game), so the situation was bound to get worse before it got resolved. One summer day around the end of July in nineteen seventy-nine, Bernard was hangin' with his buddy and co-worker (pimp), whom Bernard also rented a room from in his buddy's duplex, for CeCe to stay in. While hangin' with Alvin (Bernard's friend's name) as he had his whoe in the back seat of his Cadillac, taking her to the stroll around the corner from Olivia's and Bernard's apartment, Bernard had Alvin to stop and get Olivia so he could put her down too. After picking Olivia up and getting to the back street off the stroll, with the whoes still in the back seat, Alvin parked his car, but left the engine running while he and Bernard sat there and scoped out the activities of the other whoes who were already down. As they sat in the car parked a few feet from the street corner of the street that led to the stroll, another pimp's whoe who had seen Bernard sitting in Alvin's car, ran down the street to tell him the well-known pimp-slash-dope dealer was around the corner beating on his sister Shawn. With a quickness, Bernard jumped out of Alvin's car, ran around the corner and up the street to where the altercation was taking place and Olivia immediately responded by following her man. When Bernard reached the scene, he just commenced to putting the beat-down on the pimp (Vance was the pimp's name) who was beating on Shawn. Vance's white girl who was his whoe, grabbed Bernard from behind, but Olivia grabbed the white girl, pulled her off Bernard, pushed the bitch and held her ass back while Bernard dealt with Vance. Bernard didn't show any mercy on him. Vance's brother sat in Vance's white Fleetwood Cadillac for a minute (a short period), probably thinking Vance was gonna handle the situation. Seeing Bernard getting the best of Vance, the brother finally jumped out of the Cadillac with a gat (pistol) and immediately tried to aim it at Bernard. Bernard having had his eye on the brother as well and being the quick thinker he was with quick reflexes, reacted before the brother could get his aim on, by picking Vance up from the ground and shielding himself with Vance. That way, if Vance's brother fired the gat, the bullet would have hit Vance. "Pretty clever, Hun"? Said Olivia. Meanwhile, there were other pimps and whoes standing a few feet from Bernard and Vance. Some of them were further away than others, but they all were standing near and had a good view. When Vance's brother first got out of the car, Alvin, Bernard's buddy, was walking up on the scene with one of his hands behind his back holding a gat in it and another pimp who was really cool with Bernard (his whoe was the one who informed Bernard what Vance was doing to Shawn), was behind a tree diagonally across the street from where Bernard and Vance were, aiming his gat at Vance's brother. The shit was on, but after Vance's brother saw that he couldn't hit his mark (which was Bernard), after he saw Alvin walking towards him and after he peeped the other pimp standing behind the tree aiming a gat at him, the brother got his ass back in Vance's car. Right after the brother got back in the car and closed the car door, Bernard pushed Vance away from him and took off running. Olivia and Shawn took off running right as Bernard did and all the other whoes and pimps scattered, running in different directions. Vance then ran to his car, jumped in it and burned rubber getting away from the scene. "It was a trip", said Olivia, but that was the end of the incident that day and everything was under control, at least for a minute. If Vance was putting Shawn under a pimp's arrest, Bernard should not have interfered. "Because I know how Shawn wanted to play with the big dawgs (men, pimps, hustlers), but was really mettlin' in the game and other areas that could have been hazardous to her health, I'm sure Vance had a legit reason for gettin' in her ass", said Olivia. "Oh yeah, I know the game very well", she added. She said it is exactly like a wise man named Mr. Whitefolks, a well-known pimp stated during a televised interview, "a bitch is not supposed to be in a pimp's face unless she's gonna choose and/or pay that pimp". "Shit, Mr Whitefolks say a bitch shouldn't even be caught lookin' at a pimp unless she's choosing because as he said and I am a witness to the rules and regulations of the pimpin' game, that bitch can also be arrested and/or charged with reckless eyeballin' (making eye contact with a pimp)", said Olivia. According to the pimpin' game, if a bitch is placed under a pimp's arrest, whatever she has that is of value, is confiscated by that pimp. That means her fur coat (if it is of value), any money a bitch has, her jewelry, etc. That's the way it was in the seventies and some macks/pimps are still pimpin' like that", Olivia expresses. "I'm sure that was the reason Vance was handling Shawn the way any real pimp would. Bernard knows the game as well or better than the next pimp, but Shawn is his sister, which don't and shouldn't make any difference to a real pimp", Olivia adds. Now that she's not with Bernard and have retired from the game, Olivia is callin' it as she saw it then and how she sees it now, Bernard was out of line. As you know or may suspect about street folk, most of the times when shit happens, such as what happened between Bernard and Vance, it don't just end at that, especially when colleagues or an audience of folk witness the beat-down. Things were pretty calm and ordinary for the next day or two after the altercation, but the ordeal changed Olivia for the rest of her life, as well as others who were involved.

On the streets, when something happens, such as what happened between Bernard and Vance, even though days may pass, any child of the night knows that the matter is not necessarily squashed (over), so it is safe for one to keep his or her guards up (be alert) at all times. As a result of the altercation Bernard had with Vance, early one evening about three days later, Bernard was riding with Alvin, Olivia and Alvin's whoe was in the back seat of the car after a day's work on the stroll they worked during the daytime and Alvin was about to stop at Olivia's and Bernard's apartment to take Olivia home when a Cadillac drove by and someone fired a couple of shots at Alvin's car. It was Vance and another dude, probably Vance's brother as the passenger, retaliating from the ass whoopin' Bernard put on Vance. After the shots were fired, Vance sped off, so in return, Alvin chased him and he and Bernard fired shots at Vance's car. A couple of days later, the drive-by shooting happened again, so Bernard decided he wasn't gonna have Olivia in his nor Alvin's car with him. Olivia began driving her own Cadillac that Kelly sometimes drove when she and CeCe worked together. Apparently Vance realized the drive-by shooting wasn't the way to get to Bernard, so there was no activity of this matter for about three or four weeks passed. On Friday night, September 3, 1979, Bernard and Alvin threw a party in the upstairs unit of the duplex building Alvin owned. CeCe was already there since she lived there, so Bernard picked up Olivia and Kelly and brought them to the party since Olivia's car had stopped running or was no longer around. There were several other pimps, whoes and hustlers at the party. It was all good. CeCe's birthday was at the end of August and Olivia's was a few days after the day of the party, so the party was kind of a celebration for both girls. Everyone who came to the party brought their own bottle and sack (alcoholic beverage and bag of marijuana or drug of their choice), the seventies music played loudly while everyone got fucked-up (got high) and they all kicked it. Because CeCe was such a rabbit (hops from man-to-man or pimp-to-pimp), Bernard damn near had to baby-sit the bitch. "I was no fool. I knew the bitch's game", said Olivia. "I was lookin' good that night and knowing that I was a dedicated money making whoe, I was respected, I was cool with everyone, other pimps/macks tried to catch me or obviously, noticed me and Bernard always acknowledged me and what I meant to him. Therefore, even though he felt he had to pay CeCe a lot of attention, he didn't let me go too long unattended at the party", Olivia explained. The minute he started dancing with me and giving me some time, CeCe purposely started getting more fucked-up and doing silly shit. You see, Olivia didn't do silly shit like CeCe did when Bernard spent time with his other whoes, except the time when she tripped about him staying the night with her friend Shannon. Olivia had learned since then, to control her feelings a lot better because Bernard spending time with his other girls or whomever was paying him, was just business. Olivia saw what the bitch, CeCe, was doing the night of the party and because Bernard seemed to be playing right into the bitch's game, Olivia got pissed off, but she didn't trip and she didn't clown (act a fool). She just waited for the right moment, eased out of the party, out of the building and took a taxi away from the joint (party place). Not really ready to go home, she took the taxi to her aunt's home. After there, Olivia knocked on the door to discover everyone there was asleep, which was unusual for them on a Friday night, so Olivia decided to walk home and blow off some of the steam that built up inside of her. She was very angry at Bernard for letting CeCe manipulate him and she was kind of hurt because she wondered about all the reasons it seemed important to him, that he have a snake bitch like CeCe. Finally, Olivia made it home. The building hers and Bernard's apartment was in, was a secured building. After getting up the stairs and on to the porch of the building, one had to go through some glass doors that were always unlocked and would lead one into the hallway of the building. In the glassed-in hallway, there was a telephone system built into the wall, so that visitors could call the tenant they were visiting. Also in the hallway mounted on the wall near the ceiling, was a video security camera that was also a monitor which allowed the tenants to see the hallway if their TV was on channel two and there was a steal door that only the tenants had a key to, to get inside the building where the apartments were. After making it home and entering the hallway through the glass doors of the apartment building, as Olivia stuck her key in the lock of the steal door to get inside the building, a man entered through the glass doors of the hallway, grabbed her from behind before she could get the steal door open and pulled her out of the hallway on to the porch of the building. That's where Vance, the pimp Bernard had the fight with, was waiting. Struggling to get out of the grasp the other man had on her, Olivia wiggled and tried to pull herself away. Seeing Vance told her what was going down. It seems that the plan was to get her away from the building. Olivia's logic about being in a situation like that, had always been for the villain to take her out right then, especially if it seemed he was gonna kill her. That person may even torture her before killing her once he got her to a secluded area or place. Olivia didn't think it made any since to go with someone willingly, if that person or persons were gonna kill her anyway. Of course she would fight to stay alive and get away. The guy who grabbed her was trying to man handle her  and Vance assisted in trying to restrain Olivia, getting her off the porch, but Olivia fought hard with all her might and broke away from the hands that were holding on to her. The next thing she knew, was a relative's face, three days after the night Vance and the other man tried to abduct her. It was then, the day after her twentieth birthday. There she laid in a hospital bed with all kinds of machines surrounding her. Tubes ran from the machines, to Olivia's mouth, nostrils and throat. She was fucked up, but she kinda' recognized the faces she saw as she came to for short periods at a time from the coma she had been in. As it happened, when she pulled away from the would be abductors' hands, Vance shot her in the back of her neck, where the twenty-two caliber's bullet hit a nerve by Olivia's third cervical.  As high as his aim was, apparently Vance was trying to shoot Olivia in her head. "For all of those who think a twenty-two caliber pistol ain't shit, I'm a witness to the damage that caliber weapon can do. It aint no punk", Olivia admitted. Only by the grace of God, did she open her eyes again, because the doctors didn't think she was gonna live. After getting shot, it was thirty minutes later when the ambulance reached her and thirty minutes after the last breath Olivia had taken. Therefore, the paramedics had to, immediately, make an incision on Olivia's neck right at her throat, to put oxygen tubes down to her lungs. Before she came out of the coma, the doctors told Sara if she did live, she would be brain dead. Some people are when they go too long without oxygen. Well, after Olivia had come to from the coma and went back into that zone between life and death a couple or few times, she finally came closer to the side of life and recognized whomever was in her room visiting her at that time. That meant her brain wasn't dead. From what she was told, several relatives of hers took turns going into her room, standing at her bedside, calling out her name and talking to her until she responded. The idea was to keep her from slipping into the dark side. With that, but first of all, of God's will, it worked. After hearing about and seeing for himself that Olivia recognized her family members and relatives, Olivia's doctor told Sara if Olivia didn't have brain damage, she would never walk again, but Sara didn't tell Olivia that. The day after Olivia came to and was more alert, but wasn't able to move from her neck down, she was able to stay awake a few minutes at a time longer than she could the day before. Unable to talk because she still had a tube in her throat giving her oxygen, Olivia just laid there and nodded when she was asked questions. "I didn't feel like talking anyway. I was physically and mentally exhausted, I was confused and I didn't know or couldn't remember what had happened, so I just existed and rested", she explained. She said she didn't even develop a thought as she laid there. People were saying happy birthday to her, Sara read birthday and get well cards to her and Olivia saw birthday balloons, so she knew it was her birthday, but it really wasn't. Her birthday was two days before this day. The third day after Olivia's awakening, there Bernard sat on the floor looking up at her. He looked very sad and didn't say too much to Olivia the entire time he was there visiting. He had Kelly and CeCe buy and bring to Olivia's room, some roses and a card, the day after she was shot. Olivia was told that her brother and one of her sisters went looking for him the night after she was shot, with pistols on their persons. Olivia's mom, Jean, Olivia's siblings and other relatives knew Bernard was Olivia's pimp. They weren't too fond of him or what Olivia was about and they all assumed right off the bat, that Bernard shot Olivia. Thank goodness her brother and sister didn't find him that night they went looking for him. For on the third day after the shooting, Olivia shook her head "no", when she was asked the question "did Bernard shoot you". She couldn't remember exactly what had happened, but she knew that Bernard didn't and wouldn't hurt her with a gun or weapon. Apparently Olivia's mom and family were then told about the feud between Bernard and Vance, so Olivia was then asked if Vance shot her. Olivia's response was a positive nod. Vance had been arrested the day after Olivia was shot, but the police let him go for lack of evidence, a witness or Olivia being able to tell them he was her assailant. Now that Olivia was awake and fingered him, Vance was indicted, but made bond, so there was an officer or security guard placed outside Olivia's room. Knowing how Olivia's family must have felt and knowing he was probably the number one suspect at first, Bernard waited until what happened to Olivia was established, before he came to see her.

Olivia was more coherent now that she had been out of the coma for four days. She could now move her right leg and foot, although, they were very weak. Because she could move one of her legs, Olivia didn't think she wouldn't be able to walk again. She always believed in God and had faith in Him, that He would allow her to walk. That faith allowed her to strongly believe that she would be alright after she got some rest and probably some therapy. For now, she was content with lying in the hospital bed, getting her rest on (resting). Olivia believes that God was with her the entire time and kept her at peace with the situation. "It was Amazing", she said. Since she was out of the woods, her doctors talked to her and explained things to her when they came to examine her. While they were having a talk with Sara and Jean at Olivia's bedside, Olivia listened and learned from her doctors that everyone's spinal cord is in what they call a bag. From the injury Olivia suffered, the bag her spinal cord was in, was swollen or inflated (sorta' speak), which was part of the reason she couldn't move her other limbs. When the doctors first ran the tubes and I-v's through Olivia's body, they intravenously ran a medicine that takes the swelling from the bag outside her spinal cord. That's why she was able to move her right leg. From where the bullet hit Olivia's cervical, it damaged the nerves on the left side of her body more so than the right side. Moving her left leg and other limbs took God's will and a little more time and effort on Olivia's, the doctors and therapists' part. Still, Olivia didn't get discouraged. She just looked forward to waking up each day and seeing what movement and improvement the new day would bring. As days went by, fewer of her relatives camped out at the hospital or came to visit her. Now that they all knew she was gonna live, everyone was able to exhale. Sara and Jean didn't miss a beat though. They came to the hospital Olivia was in and stayed until nine or nine-thirty pm, everyday. "They were the best", said Olivia, with tears in her eyes. In spite of everything she did or didn't do, her mom, Jean, Olivia's siblings and relatives never gave up on her, stopped loving nor respecting her. They were always there for her and welcomed her with open arms. "It don't get no better than that", Olivia proudly and gratefully said. Under the same circumstances, some other kids, teenagers or even adults who run away from home, get caught up in the streetlife, drugs and/or alcohol, don't have it like Olivia did, which is very sad. Family is family and Olivia was raised and taught to never turn her back on a family member. Although he or she may live a lifestyle that is different, that is no reason to not care about that person or disown him or her, even if you don't like or approve of what they do. "Their wrong doing is between themselves, God and maybe the law. It is something that person has to work out and overcome, but he or she still needs the love of his or her family", said Olivia. She says she couldn't have a more loving family than the one she has. A lot of people look down on others because they are different or because they do and enjoy things that others may not indulge in. That is often the case because some people, a lot of people think and may even believe that others are suppose to or should be like them, but that's not so and it is not right. People are different in many, many ways than others. Olivia was certainly different from most of her family members, but they gave her the love she needed to know was always there and they always did what they could for her. At this point, there wasn't anything Sara and Jean could do to speed up her recovery, but their presence was like therapy for her. Everyday, she sensed the time Sara and Jean would be arriving to see her. She even developed a sharp ear and recognized the sound of Jean's footsteps as she and Sara walked down the halls of the hospital towards her room. When they entered her room, Olivia would be smiling, even if she laid in the hospital bed with her back to the door. She knew Sara and Jean were gonna walk through the doorway of her room at any minute. Knowing they were coming to see her, gave her something more to look forward to everyday, which was good for her because it took her mind off other things. She missed Bernard, but she didn't trip off the fact that she had not seen him for about a week since he came to see her that one time. She knew her man and knew he was still about the pimpin', even though one of his whoes was off her feet. Olivia understood, but when it got to be two weeks since she last saw him, she started to get sad and ask questions. Finally, Bernard's mom came to see her. Olivia was pleased to see her, but when she asked where Bernard was, she broke down and cried like a baby when she learned that he left town. Bernard's mom knew how much Olivia loved her son and because of Olivia's health status, didn't want to tell her Bernard was gone, but Olivia kept asking. She got all hyped when Bernard's mom would try and evade the questions she asked, by telling her "don't worry about Bernard, you just concentrate on getting well". Olivia knew somethin' was up. It took Sara and Jean about forty-five minutes to calm her down after she was told Bernard was gone. His mom told Olivia he would be back, so Olivia stopped crying and kept that in mind as she drifted off to sleep that night. It was that night after Sara and Jean left the hospital, that she started thinking really hard about getting well and getting back on her feet. She was surrounded by love though. Even her regular trick, Tom, came to visit her and brought her food or whatever she wanted or needed, so she was very well cared for. Still, Olivia wanted to be where her man was. For her, it was almost just as Bishop Don "the magic" Juan, a retired pimp said on a televised interview, "one of his whoes got shot five times and when he went to the hospital to see her, right in front of her mother, the whoe told Bishop she wanted to get up from the hospital bed she was in and go and get his money". "Bishop called that dedication, which is quite true, but take it from me", said Olivia, "that whoe loved Bishop and wanted to please him by doing what he wanted or expected her to do". More than being dedicated to the game and what Bernard wanted her to do, Olivia wanted to get up from her hospital bed so she could be with Bernard, period. She believes that was the way it was with Bishop's whoe and most other whoes as well. Pimpin' Ken, another well known pimp also said on the same televised documentary of the pimpin' game, that all women or just any woman is not gonna choose and pay a pimp. Ken stated that the kind of woman that pays a pimp, needs to prove her worth to a man, she's been sexually abused by her father, brother or other male adult and/or she has a very low self esteem. Ken said she probably or may be looking for that father-figure image in a man that she lacked while growing up. "I can attest to a woman choosing and paying a man because she likes his style and because she loves him", said Olivia. In some instances such as hers, a girl meets a guy and falls in love with him for whatever she sees in him. Just to please him and show him that she loves him, she will do anything or damn near anything. That's the way it was for Olivia. She fell in love with Bernard before she knew the real deal about him. Then it didn't make any difference. There was truth to what pimpin' Ken said though. It was after Olivia fell in love with Bernard, that she felt she had to prove her self worth so he would recognize what he had in having her. She needed to have a man around, who thought a lot of her and would not leave her, but different whoes had different hang-ups or character defects, that stem from one or another of the things Ken mentioned. After Olivia pulled herself together from the heartbreaking news she got about Bernard leaving town, serenity seemed to hover over her. It seemed as though angels and other good spirits (literally) were in her room watching over her and telling her everything was gonna be alright. "It was wonderfully unbelievable", said Olivia. She would sleep so much during the daytime, that she sometimes would only sleep a couple of hours at a time through the night. During those times, she would lay awake in the dark with just the light on the nurses call button, the stars and the moonlight shining. With the blinds on the window raised by her request, Olivia would lie in bed and look out the window up at the stars until daybreak. Even after daybreak, there seemed to be a morning star outside her window every morning, that wouldn't disappear until the sun rose and outshined it. Olivia believes that star was shining down on her through the night, to keep her from darkness. "It was the brightest of the other stars in the sky and was so pretty, I couldn't take my eyes off it. When I couldn't see it anymore, I was able to go to sleep in physical and mental comfort", she described. Knowing Sara and Jean would be there to see her in the early evenings and knowing the brightest star of them all might be outside her window at night, gave Olivia something to look forward to everyday and not think about how quickly or how slowly she was recovering. It seemed to all work together as a plan, to keep her at peace.

A month later from when Olivia was shot, she was now off the respirator machines and I-v's and there was nothing more the doctors could do for her. A bandage had been put on the incision on her neck where the tracheotomy (to get oxygen to her lungs) was done, since she could breath on her own and didn't need to have her lungs or throat suctioned (ridded of phlegm). It was time to let the incision close. Therapy was the next phase at this point, so Olivia was taken down to the therapy room of the hospital one afternoon to have her first session of therapy. The session didn't go too well. The therapist who was working with her, tried to put Olivia on her stomach, moved her left arm the wrong way in doing so and dislocated her shoulder. The therapist knew right away that she had fucked up too, because the dislocating of Olivia's shoulder made a loud noise when it popped out of the socket. Olivia didn't know how serious the injury was and didn't feel any pain, so she didn't trip. The therapist knew the extent of the injury though and she knew the seriousness of an employee injuring a patient, so she was very nervous. That day was the beginning and the end of Olivia's therapy at the hospital after the therapist took her back to her room. That's what Olivia needed though, to wake up the muscles and get them back in use, so she was transferred to a rehabilitation institution for in-patient therapy, a few days later. She was taken from the hospital, to the rehab institute via ambulance. After she arrived and was all settled into her room, nurse aides came, told her the doctor wanted x-rays of her, used the draw sheet on her bed to transfer her on to a stretcher and took her to have pictures taken of her cervical and spinal cord. It was a normal request for a doctor to want x-rays of a new patient, so Olivia didn't think nothin' of it. She pretty much just went along with whatever was being done to her because she had faith that she was in good hands. Everyone was doing whatever they could to help her. After all, it was their job. It took about thirty minutes for the x-rays to be taken. Apparently, the doctor viewed the x-rays one-by-one as they were taken because she informed the nurse aides of her diagnosis of the pictures before Olivia left the x-ray lab. From what the doctor saw on the x-rays, the nurses aides were instructed to take Olivia back to her room, put a hard collar (brace) around her neck and to not move her under any circumstances that weren't absolutely necessary. The x-rays that were taken, showed that Olivia's fifth and sixth cervical were closing in towards one another, causing her neck to break. That explains why her head would always fall to the right as she laid in bed. She noticed her head leaning towards her right shoulder all the time before she left the hospital and went to rehab, but she thought it was because she was too weak to hold it up. As she laid in bed, turning her head back and forth from the TV to the doorway as the nurses, doctors or visitors came into her room, eventually she had to ask someone to straighten her head, aligning it with her body. When she attempted to raise her head on her own, she was actually sliding her shoulders to the left. Of all the times she asked someone to straighten her head while she was in the hospital, no one had any idea her neck was about to break. A person has no idea how many times God saves their life, but this is one story, testimony that sets an example. If Olivia's neck had broken, she wouldn't have lived to tell this story. God spared her life after the gunshot injury and He whispered in the doctor's ear, to get x-rays of Olivia's cervical and spinal cord just in the nick of time, not to mention all the other times He saved her life that she's not aware of. "He is awesome", said Olivia. The next morning after the x-rays were taken, she was taken back to the same hospital she came from, via ambulance and went to surgery immediately. It must have been five or six o' clock AM when she arrived to the emergency room of the hospital and was hours later, when she came from under the anesthesia. Olivia's throat was very sore when she awakened and she seemed to be weighed down as she laid there really still. The surgery the doctors performed was a cervical transfusion, which was to take a piece of bone from Olivia's right hip and fuse it between her fifth and sixth cervical to stabilize it. To also stabilize the surgery that was done, the doctors screwed a halo-like brace into each side of Olivia's skull, which had five or ten pounds of steal weight hanging from the brace. That was to keep her from moving her head too freely. The surgery she had was definitely in the major surgery category. As a result of it, Olivia's head didn't hurt or anything like that, but her throat was swollen inside. To perform the surgery, the surgeon made an incision in the front of her neck right below her right jawbone, to the right of her throat. That's where he went in and fused the cervical. Scary for Olivia to even think about. The surgery was a work of art though and it saved her life. It would have been just as scary for Olivia to see the brace hooked up to her head, but thank God she didn't see nor have a clue what really went on. She didn't even know the brace was screwed into her skull until it was taken off. "Man", said Olivia, "what I went through after having the surgery, was painful, more miserable and harder to bare, than what I went through after I came out of the coma". In fact, she didn't feel any pain or discomfort from the gunshot wound. Recovering from the surgery she had, was the mother (mf). For days, she couldn't eat solid foods and could barely swallow liquids because of the swelling inside her neck. It was agony for her, but most of the time, she was still able to smile and maintain her pleasant personality. Three weeks after the surgery, it was time for the halo-like brace to be taken off. The brace was put on after the doctor fused Olivia's cervical while she was under anesthesia, but she had to be awake when it was taken off. Olivia was ready for the brace to come off because that meant her cervical was healing and she could go on to the next phase, back to rehab for therapy. Not knowing the brace she wore was screwed into her skull, Olivia lay there, ready and waiting for her doctor to do his thang. When the doctor placed himself over her to remove the brace, Olivia closed her eyes and then it happened. "I yelled to the top of my lungs the entire time it took the doctor to finish what he was doing. It seemed like the longest time, but actually it only took about two or three minutes at best", said Olivia. By the time it was done and she stopped yelling, she cried like a baby. She was even a little angry at her doctor for doing to her what seemed like torture. As she tried to stop crying, she was waiting for the pain to come and wondered how intense it would be, but there wasn't any. What Olivia felt when the bolts were unscrewed, was the pressure being released. She finally stopped crying, but still sniffled as she realized there wasn't going to be any pain. She then calmed down with Sara's and Jean's help. The two of them comforted her (as though she were a baby or a child) and told her, "see there, that wasn't so bad was it". Olivia replied by nodding her head, "yes". Of course Sara said, "Well it's all over now". After Olivia was calm, a therapist arrived with another brace that had been ordered for her. Olivia's doctor couldn't have taken the halo brace off unless the somie brace (the new brace) was available. After showing it to Olivia and assuring her the somie brace wouldn't hurt or be uncomfortable to place on her nor to be removed, the doctor placed it around her neck and fastened it across her chest and back. A slim steal rod went from the chest of the brace, up to the pad that Olivia's chin was to rest upon. Still predominately paralyzed from the neck down, Olivia laid in bed wearing the somie brace for two weeks. That brace got to be more uncomfortable than the other after a week or so, but it was a part of healing and recovery too, so Olivia stayed strong by the grace of God and accepted what she could not change. During this episode of her recovery, things weren't too bad. Not only did Sara, Jean and Tom visit her, spent time with her and pampered her, for some reason, Olivia attracted one of the hospital's employees to her. This lady was the supervisor of one of the hospital's departments. She was an older lady who was gorgeous and also bi-sexual. Olivia said it was cool though. She needed to feel loved, wanted and needed and she needed all the help she could get, so it was all good. Nothing she wasn't familiar with. She had been there more times than one, so she went with the flow. Olivia has never understood it, but the lady at the hospital who was attracted to her, got attached to her in an intimate way. The lady was no pervert or anything like that. She didn't try and do Olivia right there in the hospital bed or anything like that, but she watched over Olivia and took care of her each day, until Sara and Jean arrived. "The lady even started kissin' me after saying hello or goodbye and started callin' my mom, "mom", said Olivia. I don't like pussy", she admitted. "I have no idea how I attract women to me in that way", she added. "Because of the freak in me, I do like to get my pussy ate, sucked or what have you and I like to get freaked, so I wasn't mad at the lady for wanting to get with me. As long as a woman don't expect me to eat pussy, we may be able to work out a little somethin' somethin'", she said with a smile.

Olivia ate like a pig (hardy) for the next two weeks, since the swelling inside her throat had gone down. Everyone called her a bottomless pit. It seemed there was no end to how much food she could consume, but all the food and dairy products she ate and drank, were helping to make her strong and give her energy. Olivia not only ate the food prepared in the hospital's dietary department, she also ate the food Sara, Jean and Tom brought to her. Tom was great and stuck by Olivia through her entire recovery. Either he had fallen in love with her or he liked her pussy so well, that he wanted to do good deeds so that he could get it again, if and when she was back on her feet. After two weeks of the somie brace and the feasts', Olivia was transferred back to the rehabilitation institute for in-patient therapy, once again. It was autumn now, but there were occasional warm, sunny days. Under the circumstances, it was still a very pleasant time for Olivia. A change to the next phase and the change of seasons. The rehab institute was a clean and pleasant establishment too, so Olivia settled into her new room quite nicely and did what she had to do. After getting her settled in, the same doctor Olivia had the first time she was admitted into the institute, wanted x-rays of Olivia's cervical again, so the nurses aides took Olivia to have the pictures taken. The x-rays that were taken showed positive results, so Olivia's doctor ordered for the somie brace to be taken off Olivia's neck and to replace it with a hard collar brace. A couple of days later, Olivia's occupational and physical therapy began. "It was cool", said Olivia. She was anxious to have therapy and see how well she would recover back to her normal physical being, so she cooperated and tried her hardest in whatever exercise the therapists' had her do. After two weeks of therapy, Olivia was then able to move and raise her right arm. She was very excited about that and was more motivated to keep up the hard work in therapy. As part of her occupational therapy, she even cleaned and painted ceramics. Her left arm wasn't showing any signs of muscle movement, so when she was sitting and/or having therapy, her left arm was in a sling. It was all good though.

Olivia's right leg had gotten stronger and by now, she could also move her left leg from side-to-side. She just couldn't lift it, but being able to move it as much as she could, was good enough for her, for now. Olivia had greater hope that she would be able to walk again. She was in a bad and difficult way, but not as badly as she could've been or as she saw others at the institute. Her physical condition didn't change her desire for money and/or fine things though. Her disability income that Sara got working for her, had kicked in, so Sara brought her what she needed and some of the things she wanted. Olivia hustled Tom for most of the things she wanted. She had Tom buy her a diamond watch, diamond earrings and even decorative pots to have her plants repotted in. "Shit, I really reached for something to have him buy me and had him purchase an oak wood cabinet with a glass door. That was to put my stereo equipment in, that he bought for me before I got shot", said Olivia. A few days after she had come out of the coma, Olivia had Sara, Jean and other family members get her furniture and things out of her apartment she and Bernard rented, so even though she was on her back, she still asked Tom for things she wanted to have when she got back on her feet. Now that she could sit up in a wheelchair and had return of some of her muscles and limbs, Olivia was able to go home with Sara and Jean and spend the weekends there. Her sister next to her in age, still lived at home with Sara and Jean and offered as much help as she could give when Olivia was there. Olivia's sister was pregnant and couldn't tolerate being in Olivia's room when Olivia was in the hospital, but she and Olivia were and always had been close. Olivia's sister even relieved Sara sometimes and fed Olivia her meals. Everyone was wonderful during this trying time for Olivia. Sara had it the hardest though, because she was the one who put Olivia on the bed pan when necessary, she wiped Olivia's ass, washed Olivia's ass and got Olivia dressed and undressed. Usually, Olivia's sister did her hair, French-braided it or what have you and Jean did her share of helping too. Jean handled Olivia when she needed to be lifted or transported. Jean was gentle but strong and physically fit, so she was good at stuff like that. Both Sara and Jean worked in another hospital on the other side of town. Jean had worked in dietary of that hospital since Olivia was one year old and Sara started working in that same hospital as an LPN when Olivia was thirteen years old, so they both had lots of experience working with the physically ill. By this time, Jean was a supervisor in dietary, but at home, Sara was the cook, so Olivia had it made. "Man, I was and still am very blessed to have the family I have", said Olivia, all teary eyed. For weeks, she had physical therapy lying down. Basically, her therapist ranged her legs and feet and then had her practice sitting without anyone or anything supporting her back. Olivia could now sit up on the edge of the bench she did her therapy on, with her feet on the floor. She had fun doing that because she felt more normal than she did sitting in her wheelchair. Now that her balance was pretty good and she could tolerate gravity, it was time for her to try standing, so that was the next phase she went to. Olivia had what therapist call drop foot, so she wore a hard plastic brace on her left foot, (the foot that dropped), that went from the bottom of her foot, up the back of her left leg, with velcro straps that fastened around her leg and held the brace in place. The brace was to hold her foot in a flexed position so that she wouldn't drag it. The brace was made of thin plastic so Olivia was able to wear her shoe with it, but the shoes she had to wear were kind of a desert boot. They were the best shoes for her to wear at the time because they gave her support and they seemed to be the idea shoe to be worn with the brace. Not Olivia's style of shoe nor the kind of shoe she wanted to be confined to wear the rest of her life, but it served the purpose at the time. Olivia had not shown any sign of being able to flex her left foot on her own because the muscles in it were too weak, so the therapist was pretty sure she would have to wear the brace the rest of her life. Olivia wore a brace around her left knee also because the doctor and therapist said she didn't have a back knee. The muscle in her leg behind her knee, had deteriorated, turned to mush or something, so that brace was to keep her leg from snapping back when she tried to stand on her feet. Oh she was fucked up, but against all odds, she had recovered more than some people thought she would. When the therapists', nurses and Jean transferred or moved Olivia around, they fastened a belt made for this, around her waist. That's what they held on to, to keep her from falling. That belt is what the therapist used when she began Olivia's therapy on standing.

Not only was Olivia going home with Sara and Jean on the weekends, but she also spent Thanksgiving and holiday weekend at home. She had not seen her relatives and family friends since she came out of the coma she was in, so she was kind of excited to see everyone, but also kind of shy for everyone who would be at the house this holiday, to see her in the physical condition she was in. All through the day, people were arriving and the house got a little crowded, so Jean thought it would be better for Olivia to sit in a regular chair instead of the wheelchair. Olivia had just started her standing therapy. She had not began taking steps yet, but when Jean put the belt around her waist and stood her up, Olivia was able to assist Jean by pivoting around on her right foot until her back was to the seat she was gonna take and then Jean held on to her as she sat down. While doing so, Olivia began to cry from embarrassment because she knew everyone there was watching. Jean consoled Olivia after telling her to straighten up (pull herself together), that everyone understood and were all just glad she was alive and had come as far as she had in her recovery. You see, of Jean and Sara, Jean was the tougher, more firm one and Sara was the softer, more sensitive one. In some instances, Olivia needed someone firm and strong who cared, but didn't feel sorry for her. That person was Jean, who was able to help Olivia tremendously by being firm, so after she verbally straightened Olivia out that day and got her situated in the chair she sat in, Olivia felt better and had a wonderful day. After the Thanksgiving weekend, she returned to rehab to continue her in-patient therapy. It wasn't until then, when she noticed the sensation she felt in the toes on her left foot. When she first noticed the sensation, she kept telling her physical therapist what she felt, but the therapist didn't see any motion when she massaged and ranged her foot and had her try and wiggle the toes, so she figured Olivia was feeling an illusional sensation that those with nerve damage often feel. Actually, what Olivia felt was the nerves in her foot and toes waking up, so slowly but surely, the therapist was able to see a slight movement each time she had Olivia try again to wiggle them. The therapist then began additional therapy with Olivia's left foot. The next level of treatment was for her to sit on a table that had stirrup-like mechanisms of weight attached to it, that Olivia lifted with her feet. As she used all the muscles in her body to help lift the weight, she began flexing her left foot unconsciously, at first, which was good because her left foot got stronger and didn't drop as much as it did before. During the same time, Olivia's therapist started having her take steps, so Olivia was ready to begin her therapy on walking. One step at a time, a short distance at a time is the way the walking therapy went. At the end of November through December, Olivia continued her therapy and was able to walk a further distance around the therapy room, than the distance she could walk before. Her balance when she was standing wasn't all that great or so the therapist and Olivia thought, so the therapist didn't let Olivia stand or walk without holding on to the belt she had around Olivia's waist. Still, Olivia wore the braces on her left leg and foot for support and she was alright with that because the progress she made thus far, was grand.

All while Olivia was hospitalized, she thought about what her physical status would be by Christmas that year, because she knew there would be some partying going on at Sara and Jean's house. Even if she couldn't get her boogie on, she would be happy to be able to stand on her own and take steps. That would be her Christmas present from God and from herself. Now that Christmas was near, Olivia put forth more effort to get stronger and learn to walk. She was a joy to all the therapist and nurses aides the entire time they cared for her. Even her doctor who was a female, called Olivia "Sweet Pea". Olivia's physical therapist spent a lot of time with her. Probably because Olivia didn't complain and wasn't a bitch about not being able to do things she used to do. Olivia tried as hard as she could and left the rest to God. Of course she promised Him she wouldn't do this, that and the other anymore, if He would let her walk again. You know how some people do when they get into trouble. That's what Olivia did, but weeks after making that promise, she was downstairs of the rehab institute from the floor the patients rooms were on, in the restroom with one of her girlfriends who came to visit her, smoking weed. She was sincere about the promise she made to God at the time she made it, but she didn't know how to be different yet. Being different was something that had to be learned or by the grace of God, gradually happen. Olivia's will had always been and still was to get high. It took a greater lesson for her to not do her will, but until that time came, she did whatever came to mind and what was natural to her. She believes that God is very forgiving and understanding. He had a plan for her and was going to straighten her out in due time. Olivia still had lessons to learn, so God laid low and allowed her to experience whatever she needed to experience, before she was to spiritually and morally excel. Because she was physically stronger now and was getting therapy on standing and taking steps, when she went home on the weekends, Jean would put her braces on her, put Olivia's shoes on her feet, fasten the transfer belt around her waist, stand Olivia on her feet and have her walk from one end of the dining room of their home, to the other end. When Olivia told Jean she couldn't do it, Jean told her she could, that she wouldn't let her fall. Olivia trusted Jean with her life, so she did what Jean told her to do and she kept trying. It must have been like de ja vu for Jean, for she was the one who held Olivia's hand when Olivia was a baby just learning to walk. Sara and Olivia's sister sat in the living room and watched Olivia and Jean. As Jean and Olivia did Olivia's walking therapy, they began laughing and having fun, making up games to play as Olivia walked. "Those were very special times", said Olivia. Having fun with her family while doing her therapy was one of the things she did while at home on the weekends in the month of December before Christmas. Before she knew it, the week of Christmas seemed to rapidly creep upon her. Two days before Christmas, Sara and Jean came and got her from the institute and took her home with them to stay through the holidays. Olivia didn't have to go back to rehab until the second day of January, 1980, so she was excited about going home, even though she wasn't on her feet like she had hoped to be. Sara and Jean packed her clothes since she would be home for a week. They even arranged the furniture in the dining room of their home, so that the rollaway bed Olivia slept

*Jerri L. Smith*

on, was not in the way of all the visitors they would have during this time. Olivia still wasn't able to walk on her own yet, but it was all good because the steps she was able to take, had improved quite a bit. Therefore, she had greater faith than before that she would be able to walk again. It was just gonna take a little more time and therapy, along with the grace of God. Christmas Eve was the bomb (great, neat, super, etc.) though. That was the day that everyone came to Sara and Jean's house to eat, drink, be merry and exchange gifts. Olivia had selected items from a catalog that she purchased for family members. Sara and Jean placed the order for her. When dusk was about to fall on that day, people arrived all through the evening. It was a B.Y.O.B. affair, so everyone arrived with a sack or bottle in their hands when they came through the door. The party was on early in the evening before visitors arrived though. As usual, the radio was on as it always was on weekends and holidays at Sara's and Jean's house, Sara had a cocktail of her favorite scotch she drank and Jean had already popped the top on a can or two of the beer she drank. It was a normal way of life at those times, for them to kick it like that. All the relatives and friends knew where to go for a good time, where there was no nonsense, so Olivia, along with everyone else always looked forward to the get-togethers Sara and Jean had. Sara had gotten Olivia bathed and dressed late that afternoon. Jean got Olivia up from her bed and put her in her wheelchair early that evening, so Olivia was ready for the evening of fun to begin. After all of her sisters and brother were there, along with several other relatives and family friends, everyone was getting their buzz on, mingling, socializing, dancing, laughing and joking with one another. Everyone who was drinking, had cups in their hands because Olivia's grandmother was there, who was a born Christian and didn't tolerate the drinking of alcoholic beverages. Even the beer drinkers drank their beer out of cups. Everyone respected Granny. She was the big cahoona of the clan (sorta' speak). Someone always picked Granny up from her apartment to bring her to any holiday function or occasion she wanted to attend (some were traditional) and took her home at a decent hour. Usually around ten o' clock PM. When that time was near on Christmas Eve, everyone who had a gift for Granny, gave it to her. Including Olivia. Olivia bought her granny a gift from one of the department store's catalog too, but the ultimate gift for Granny, was from God and Olivia. After Granny opened her store bought gifts, Sara announced to Granny and everyone there, that Olivia had another gift for her. The introduction of Olivia's gift to Granny was prompted with everything except a drum roll. The music was turned off, everyone was instructed to be quiet and all eyes were on Olivia. At that time, Jean walked over to Olivia as she sat in her wheelchair that was parked on the far side of the living room away from the front door. She then fastened the transfer belt around Olivia's waist, bent down with her face to Olivia's and asked her if she was ready. Olivia nodded "yes". Jean then held on to Olivia's right arm (the good

122

arm) with one of her hands, she grabbed the transfer belt around Olivia's waist with the other hand and assisted Olivia as she scooted to the edge of the wheelchair seat. When Olivia was in a position to stand, Jean held on tightly to the transfer belt and Olivia's arm, as Olivia placed her right hand on the arm of the wheelchair to push herself up. Now that she was in a standing position, she and Jean looked at one another as though they were establishing a start point or mark. Jean waited for Olivia to get her balance and then asked her again, if she was ready. Olivia nodded once again, "yes", so Jean slowly let go of Olivia's arm and the belt around her waist as Olivia stood there. Jean was really quick with her hands and reflexes, so she was prepared to grab a hold to Olivia if she lost her balance. She told Olivia to take her time and start whenever she was ready, so Olivia took a step with one foot, a step with the other foot and just kept going. Step after step she walked from where the wheelchair sat, across the living room to the front door. Jean walked beside Olivia, facing her the entire time. When Olivia got to the front door, she stopped. Slowly, she took baby steps to turn around and then she headed back to her wheelchair. As she walked towards her chair, she could hear sniffles of joy, from tears of amazement and happiness. "That time was so special, that I get tears in my eyes when I think about it", said Olivia. Her family, relatives and family friends were so happy she could walk. The sight of it warmed their hearts. Olivia could tell some of them were crying, but she didn't look up to see anyone's face. She just kept walking, looking down at the floor and her feet to concentrate step by step, until she reached her wheelchair where she took baby steps once again, to turn around and sit down. After doing so, everyone started applauding her performance (it seemed) and giving her hugs. Olivia's granny being the Christian she was, was very happy to see Olivia walking, but wasn't too surprised because she always had that sureness about her belief in God and what He could do. Still, her face was filled with the look of joy and relief. "Thank You Jesus", was the look she had on her face as though her prayers were answered. She was taken home shortly afterwards and the party was really on then. Folk started pouring whiskey, beer drinkers slammed down the beer they had in their cups so they could get another and drink it the real way (to them), out of the can and the pot (marijuana) smokers fired up joints in the kitchen (respectfully away from those who didn't smoke weed and didn't like smelling it). "Now that's what I was talking about", said Olivia. Kickin' it like that with family and friends at Christmas time and other holidays, is what she didn't want to miss out on and wanted to be on her feet for. With the use of her right arm and hand, she reached for a joint that was passed to her, took a few tokes and then passed it on. Someone gave her a can of beer with a straw in it, so Olivia sat in her chair and got her buzz on (got high). After Granny left, the volume on the stereo was pumped up (turned up) and everyone got his or her damn boogie on, even the kids. Christmas Eve at Sara's and Jean's house, still is and probably always will be the bomb (the shit, great, fantastic, etc.). At midnight that eve, the tradition continued with everyone exchanging gifts while the music still played and they all still sipped on their drinks and/or smoked their weed. The party would soon be over around one thirty or two AM because those who had children, had to go home and get their kids to bed so they could play Santa Claus. Olivia couldn't hang quite that long because that one beer along with the tokes off the couple of joints she had, got her fucked up. Plus, she had been sitting up for a long while and her tolerance for hangin' like that wasn't very high. While keeping an eye on her all through the night, Sara frequently asked Olivia if she was alright and if she was ready to lie down. Finally, Olivia was ready to retire or at least recline for the evening, so Sara and Jean pushed her wheelchair to the roll away bed she slept in since the bedrooms in the house were upstairs on the second floor. Jean assisted Olivia from the chair on to the bed and Sara took her shoes off. She didn't undress Olivia because the party was still on. She just made sure Olivia was comfortable and able to rest. When everyone finally left, Sara got Olivia undressed, put her nightgown on her, covered Olivia, told her she loved her, kissed Olivia's forehead and told her goodnight. "Is she a wonderful mom or what", asked Olivia. After Sara raised her children, she damn near had to raise Olivia once again, which Olivia don't think Sara minded too much because Sara used to sometimes say, "she wished Olivia was a baby again". Sara got her wish to a certain extent. On Christmas day, several relatives came to Sara's and Jean's home, but not as many of those who were there the night before. Being with her family at Christmas time and being able to walk, were two of the greatest gifts God had given Olivia. Even though she had not given it a thought, she was also given news two days after Christmas, that Vance (the guy who shot her) was killed in his home-slash-dope house on that day, nineteen seventy-nine. One more example of the power of fait and the old cliché' "what goes around comes around". God's will was done. Olivia wasn't happy nor sad about Vance's death, but she was relieved that she didn't have to deal with him in court or have to keep looking over her shoulders for him. New Years Eve at Sara and Jean's home was as busy as Christmas Eve. Most of those who were there on the eve before Christmas, also brought in the New Year there. As it was on Christmas Eve, everyone got their partying on and they all kicked it until two or three AM New Years morning.

On New Years Day of nineteen eighty, everyone at Sara's and Jean's home just lounged, ate and recuperated. On the second day of January that year, Olivia was taken back to rehab once again, to continue her therapy. The following day, before her therapist assisted her to a standing position, Olivia told the therapist she wanted to show her something. After standing, Olivia told the therapist that she didn't have to hold on to her. The Therapist asked Olivia if she was sure and

Olivia replied, "yes I'm sure". Olivia then took off walking with baby steps, while the therapist just walked along beside her. The therapist was very happy to see Olivia walking without anyone's assistance and jokingly told her she was supposed to learn to walk at the rehab institute, not at home. The therapist was excited and very proud of Olivia's recovery. Now that Olivia's balance had improved tremendously and the therapist didn't have to hold on to her, the therapist took Olivia a little further by having her walk around the entire first floor of the rehab building (which wasn't too much area) to build up her endurance. It was tiring for Olivia, but she kept going when she wanted to stop because she knew the results would be all good. Olivia's occupational therapy for the upper part of her body, had pretty much ended. Her right arm and hand were just about back to normal and would gradually recover fully with time and the use of it, but there was still no sign of movement with her left arm. At this point, she was told there probably wouldn't be any return of the use of that arm. With all the progress she had made, Olivia was okay with the diagnosis the occupational therapist gave her, but she still had hope that she would use or just be able to move her left arm again. She knew that all things were possible through the grace of God. For now, being able to walk again and use her right arm and hand, was enough and was the greatest thing she could ever ask for, next to being alive. The following weekend after she returned back to rehab when she would be going home with Sara and Jean for a visit, Olivia was released from in-patient therapy at the institute and was only to return for outpatient therapy. She was excited about being released, even though she walked a little different than she did before the gunshot injury. She didn't have a problem with the way she walked though. Naturally she would walk a little wobbly, just as she did when she was a baby learning to walk. She figured the more she walked, the stronger her muscles would get and the better her balance would be, so she didn't trip. Besides, she was too grateful for what she had and what she could do, to worry about what she didn't have or what she couldn't do. There was one thing that concerned Olivia though. She often wondered about having to wear the brace on her left knee that kept her leg from snapping back when she walked. Olivia wondered if the back knee (as they called it) would get stronger so that she wouldn't have to wear the brace. One of the things that was and had always been important to her was being able to wear high-heeled pumps. From day one after being out of the woods (sorta' speak), Olivia wanted to know and asked Sara if she would be able to walk again and if so, would she be able to wear high-heeled shoes. When she asked, Sara just told her she didn't know and to not worry about that at that time. Sara knew how important wearing high-heeled shoes were to Olivia. After all, Olivia used to get into trouble as a kid, for playing in Sara's and Jean's high-heeled shoes. Olivia didn't dwell on her curiosity of her physical outcome though. She didn't have to wear the brace on her foot anymore, so she knew how possible it was that her back knee would form and get stronger or that she would eventually get stronger and learn to control her leg so that it wouldn't snap back when she walked. For now, she just took things one day at a time and asked the Lord for His will.

Now that it was a new year, Olivia was no longer an in-patient at rehab and was back on her feet. Possibilities were endless. The stronger she got, the more she took notice in herself again and started buying the fancy and sexy clothes to dress in, that she was accustomed to wearing. Olivia always had great determination to succeed in whatever she wanted to accomplish. Regaining as much of her bodily functions had top priority in her accomplishments at this time, but although determination was a natural part of her character, she had a hidden agenda that gave her even greater determination to get back to the norm as much as possible. Still a bit naive in thinking that she had to prove her self-worth to a man, Olivia wanted to show Bernard how strong, capable, true to him and the game she was. She was on a mission to get back with her man, but she only deceived herself in thinking that because of all she had done, all she had been through and because of her physical condition, things would be different if she went back to Bernard. All those times she thought he loved her, she had yet to learn that himself and pimpin', were the two most important things to Bernard. He may have had a little bit of love for her, but himself and pimpin' came first. Before she would see Bernard again though, Olivia wanted to get back to feeling about herself, the way she had and always wanted to feel, which was sexy. She even cut off her shoulder length hair, began wearing the curly hair-do called the Geri Curl and had Tom buy her the seventy dollar sunglasses she wore, that gave her a classy, sophisticated look. She had the idea that she was gonna leave town and go where Bernard was if he didn't come back home to stay. That's why she wore the curl. She wanted her hair to look good at all times and be manageable since she only had the use of one of her arms and hands. "I felt myself wanting to be different, but still was unsure on how different I would become or how to become different", she said. She just reacted to whatever came naturally and let nature take its course. As she made herself up, she continued to go to rehab for outpatient therapy three times a week. Her social security benefits paid for her transportation to and from therapy, so she had even declared her independence again, by taking a taxi to rehab and making her own decisions. Olivia was glad for this new era she was entering where she didn't have to walk or ride the streets, selling pussy, blowjobs and other sexual acts. It was nice for her, getting a social security check every month that enabled her to take care of herself and some of her wants and not have to hustle for a date. The social security check was small change compared to the money Olivia made on the whoe stroll, but it was honest and respectable and she didn't have to suck or jump up and down on a dick to get it. "Don't get me wrong, by this time, even though I had gone through all I had, I had not yet vowed to not sell sex again, but it was great being able to put my hands on some kind of money and not have to do the things for it, that I had previously done", said Olivia. Finally, Bernard had come to town for a visit. He had not planned to stay and only stayed in town for two nights and three days. When he left their hometown after visiting Olivia in the hospital that one time, Bernard went to California and took CeCe with him. Since then, he had gone from Los Angeles, to Anchorage, Alaska. Anchorage is where Bernard had come from and where he was going back to after his visit. Olivia was ecstatic to see him. As he used to do, Bernard took Olivia to his buddy and play brother Dwight's apartment, sat around there, got high and kicked it. After leaving Dwight's apartment, Olivia went with Bernard back to his mom's house where she spent the night with her man and made love with him. As she gave up the pussy, Olivia had tears of Passion and of sadness because she loved and missed Bernard very much. She also cried because she knew that he was leaving town without her the next day, going back to Alaska and she wanted to go with him. When she asked him when he was coming back, Bernard told her he didn't know. Of course she asked if she could go with him, but Bernard didn't think that was a good idea and told Olivia she wasn't ready. Olivia was still recovering, so Bernard knew she wasn't ready. At least not for what he would do with her if she went with him, but Olivia wasn't thinking about that (the game). She was thinking that Bernard cared enough about her, that he wouldn't try or even want to take her there (back to the way it was), so when he told her she wasn't ready, she thought he meant she wasn't ready to leave town and be out on her own again. The thought had not crossed her mind that Bernard didn't think she was ready to get back to what he was about. Other than Olivia selling pussy, Bernard didn't have a need for her, but again, she had yet to find that out. After Bernard left town, Olivia made it up in her mind that she was going to Alaska to be with her man or at least, be where he was. She didn't tell Bernard of her thoughts. She wasn't even sure she would make the trip, but that was the plan. In March of nineteen eighty, she was released from treatment all together. All that could be done for her had been done, so any other return of muscle use would only come from her using the muscles she had use of, to make them and the weaker ones stronger, but first and most of all, by the grace of God. After being released from out-patient therapy, Olivia started counting her dollars she had saved and checking the airlines to get rates for a flight to Anchorage. She could not get in touch with Bernard's sister about staying at her apartment and Bernard had an apartment with CeCe, so she contacted a trick she met when she was in Anchorage. The trick was an older, African American man who was pretty cool, which was unusual for Olivia. As a rule of hers, which was also advice from Freddie's whoe who trained her and instructions from Bernard, Olivia didn't date or shall we say, trick with African American men. "They be long strokin', wanting to keep a bitch hemmed up all day or night and may even take their money back after they have a whoe suck their dick and after they fuck the shit out of a her all night", said Olivia. "Oh no, it wasn't that kind of party when I dated a trick or john", she added. She dated the brother in Alaska though, who was married, so she hooked up with his brother by phone. The trick's brother was a widower and a much older guy, old enough to be Olivia's daddy, who was real cool with her. She didn't want to date neither one of the brothers. She was just trying to hook up a place to chill if and when she went back to Alaska, until she made other arrangements. Olivia staying at the widower's apartment was confirmed, so all systems were go. Mid March, it was air Alaska for her. Sara and Jean didn't want her to go, but they knew how she was when she had her mind set on doing something, so they just stepped aside, let her go and left it to God to watch over her. When Olivia arrived in Anchorage, she took a taxi to the widower's apartment where she was going to stay. After getting settled in, she called Bernard's sister. Asia (Bernard's sister) was glad to hear Olivia was in town, came right over to the apartment where she was and picked her up. Of course she took Olivia to see Bernard. Olivia was very happy to see him, even though she felt differently than she felt when he was in their hometown for a visit. What she now felt for Bernard, was not as intense as it was before, being that she had not been with him for over six months, except for the one night she spent with him when he came home. It felt good to her knowing she was no longer under what seemed like a spell (hypnosis, a trance) and knowing that she wasn't obligated to go to work on the stroll. She didn't have to do what Bernard wanted or expected her to do anymore. Olivia wanted to be with Bernard, but not under any circumstances and she didn't want to sell pussy everyday. In fact, she didn't want to sell pussy at all. Not really. She did visit with Bernard, his sister and her family though. CeCe was locked down (in jail) for thirty or sixty days, so she wasn't around at the time, which was cool because Bernard could be just the way he felt like being, however that was and not have to front for CeCe's benefit. The visit was all good. The next day or so later, Olivia spent the night with Bernard, the two of them fucked and they slept together on the sofa. Olivia could tell Bernard wanted to charge her because that is probably what he felt he was supposed to do, but Olivia almost died for something he did, which really wasn't his fault. "To be honest, I didn't think Bernard ought to ask me for another dime, ever again in life, but I respected what he was about and understood", Olivia said. The next day, she went back to the apartment where she was temporarily residing and she chilled for about two or three weeks. "Man, I was bored to tears at that apartment", said Olivia. By that time, something she felt told her it was time to make a move, so Olivia thought about things one night while she was trying to go to sleep. After weighing her options, she decided to go back to her home town, so she called Asia the next day, told her she was ready to make a move and had Asia come and get her. When Asia arrived, she damn near had to break Olivia out of the brother's apartment. "I don't know what his trip was, but this guy pulled a gun out of nowhere (it seemed) and wasn't going to let me leave. After Asia and I both talked with him and got him to chill, we got out of the apartment (left there) with a quickness (quickly)", said Olivia. That trip with the brother was very eerie and uncomfortable for her, being that she was, physically, in the shape she was in as a result of a gun (weapon). She could hardly believe she was in a situation like that again so soon after the gunshot injury she had just suffered, but she thanked God for allowing her to walk away that time, unharmed. After leaving the brother's apartment, Olivia had Asia take her to a small motel where she got a room. That's where she stayed for a few weeks, until she found an apartment. While staying at the motel, Olivia decided to stay in Anchorage, so she worked the stroll at night and went to government agencies during the daytime to apply for assistance. Being that she received income for disability, she was already getting Medicaid as well, but was also granted food stamps and what the state of Alaska called, "rent assistance". That assistance was an additional monthly income that Olivia and others who were eligible, were granted because of the cost of living in the state of Alaska. That was all good for Olivia because as long as she had legit income to cover the rent and bills, she would hustle for anything else she needed or wanted. On the first day of May that year, she moved into her own duplex. The duplex had two bedrooms, one of which was furnished since the duplex was a furnished unit. The living room and dining room were furnished with furniture that was very nice, considering Olivia didn't pick it out and buy it herself. She had pretty good taste in material things and was impressed with the furniture as well as the apartment. All she needed now was a TV, iron, bath and wash towels, linen, a few dishes, pots, pans, silver or flatware and a few other items to start with. Just the necessities until she got settled in and got her cash flow and other things working. Things were coming together nicely though. After getting moved into the apartment and working the stroll that first week, Asia took Olivia with her and hooked up with Monae. Monae was the estranged wife of the big-time pimp who was from the same hometown Olivia and the others were from. Monae's husband was the pimp Olivia met at hers and Bernard's apartment in their hometown a few years earlier, but she was just now meeting Monae for the first time. Monae was taken to Alaska by her husband when she was in her late teens. By now, Monae had a whoe of her own and owned a massage parlor of which her whoe and other hookers worked in. The parlor was also Monae's home too. The parlor had a business side with four bedrooms, a kitchen and a full bathroom and a private side where Monae slept, which was like a studio apartment. The floor plan of the parlor was off the hook (clever, very well planned). There were separate entrances and exits in the front and back on both sides of the building. The parlor also had a big walk-in closet between the two sides of it that had a secret door that led from one side of the parlor to the other. With all the clothes Monae had, the secret door was hidden and Monae had an intercom system that ran from one side of the parlor to the other. Olivia said she was impressed with what Monae had going on. With the intercom system, Monae could listen from the private side of the parlor, to the happenings on the business side of the parlor, but one could not hear the happenings on the private side, from the business side of the parlor. "Oh she had it hooked up and business was, apparently, great", said Olivia. When Asia took her to meet Monae, she and Monae hit it off right off the bat (immediately) and the three girls hung out with one another that entire day. Before the girls departed, Monae and Olivia mutually let each other know they wanted to keep in touch with one another, so even when Asia wasn't around, the two of them kicked it together. Seeing as how Olivia was getting around pretty well and trying to have a little somthin' going on, making whoe money and all, Bernard started coming around as though he was reclaiming something that belonged to him. He didn't make any demands or put the rush on Olivia because he was sure of himself and knew Olivia very well. Bernard knew that Olivia still had love for him, so he knew that if she was in the game, she would be in the game with him. He also knew that Olivia wanted some more of him, so he felt all he had to do was come around and was confident that she knew and would do what it took to please him or expect any of his time. Bernard was right too. Just like before, Olivia initiated choosing him or reenlisting herself into his stable. After checking out her new apartment and seeing that she didn't have a TV, Bernard brought a small TV from his and CeCe's apartment, to Olivia's apartment for her to use. He certainly wasn't going to buy her a new one, but Olivia was cool with the used TV because she wasn't sure about being with Bernard again like she was before her injury and plus, she really had not given him too much whoe money yet. Before long, CeCe got out of jail and was back on the scene, so Olivia knew what she had to get ready for. It didn't take very long for her to have a problem with CeCe neither. A couple of months after CeCe got out of jail, Olivia and Monae were really cool with one another by then and were on the stroll one night, walking and chatting with one another between dates. It was pretty cold outside that night, so after strolling a while, the two ladies of the night jumped into a taxi that was sitting on the stroll as the driver was waiting for a call from the taxi dispatcher. The girls didn't take the taxi anywhere though. They only wanted to get in it and get warm since it was slow at the time, getting dates. All of a sudden, CeCe got down (showed up on the stroll) while Olivia and Monae were still sitting in the taxi. Olivia could hardly believe her eyes and was surprised to see that CeCe had the audacity to be wearing her first leather jacket that her trick Tom bought her. Obviously   while she was laid up in the hospital not knowing if she would live or ever walk again, CeCe was hanging out with Bernard at his and Olivia's apartment and took Olivia's jacket when she left town with Bernard, going to California. Olivia mentally tripped (was flabbergasted) when she saw CeCe in the jacket. She found it hard to believe the bitch had the nerve to wear the jacket, knowing that she would see her in it and think that she would be okay with it. Being that it was as cold as it was outside, Olivia and Monae continued to sit in the taxi that was parked right on the stroll. The taxi driver had some idled time and was one of the cool drivers who would let hookers sit in his taxi for a few minutes, to get warm during the cold months. Olivia didn't want to react too hasty, but after seeing CeCe in the jacket, she told Monae what the deal was and told her the bitch CeCe, was gonna have to come out of the jacket (take it off). Monae understood and had Olivia's back (was on Olivia's side). Monae really liked Olivia a lot and was down with her on whatever she had to challenge, so she handed Olivia a derringer pistol undercover, just in case she had a problem getting her jacket from CeCe. After getting the pistol from Monae and sliding it under the seat in front of her, Olivia, with Monae's help, came up with a lure to get CeCe into the taxi cab. Monae sat on the passenger side in the front seat of the taxi, while Olivia sat on the passenger side of the taxi in the back seat. Knowing CeCe was cold standing outside, Monae rolled the front passenger's window down and hollered out the window at CeCe, telling her to come there to the taxi. CeCe was hesitant, but walked over to the taxi to find out what Monae wanted. Monae told CeCe to get in, so CeCe walked around the taxi to the drivers side to get into the back seat on that side. After she got in the car, Monae started making small talk with her to play off the set up and she asked CeCe bullshit questions to throw her off of the lure plan. When Monae finished her role in the play, Olivia took over and started out by asking CeCe what was up. CeCe thinking the question Olivia asked her was just a general question, responded by saying, "shit nothin' right now". Olivia then told CeCe, "that's my jacket you're wearing and I want it". CeCe kinda' smiled and said, "you have to ask Bernard about that". Olivia got a little bit louder in her tone of voice and said, "that's my jacket and Bernard didn't buy it, so I don't have to ask him shit (nothing)". Even if Bernard giving CeCe the jacket, was part of the way things were done in the pimpin' game, Olivia wasn't trying to get with that with all she had been through. Especially with this punk ass bitch she didn't like and didn't give a fuck about. CeCe knew Olivia was in town, so Olivia felt as though the bitch was throwing in her face, the fact that Bernard let her have or take something that belonged to her. After all, Olivia didn't burn out (leave) on Bernard or the game. She was temporarily removed from the game, but that bitch CeCe didn't give a fuck about that or Olivia. She was a dog and shit like this is the kind of games the bitch played. However, Olivia didn't like her response, so she told CeCe, "I want my jacket now". CeCe

131

responded again by saying, "you can have your jacket, but you have to ask Bernard for it and take it up with him". Just as she said that, she reached for the door handle to open the car door. Seeing that the bitch was getting ready to evade anymore talk about the jacket or any drama she felt was coming on, Olivia grabbed a hold to the jacket trying to keep CeCe from getting out of the taxi, but CeCe jerked away from the grasp Olivia had on her while opening the door at the same time and jumped out of the taxi. When she did that, Olivia opened the door on the side of the taxi she sat on, grabbed the derringer pistol from under the seat in front of her, got out of the taxi and started walking in the direction CeCe was going. CeCe never did get on the sidewalk when she got out of the taxi. She walked (damn near) down the middle of the street, looking back at Olivia as she walked along. One of the times CeCe looked back, Olivia was aiming the derringer at her. When CeCe saw what Olivia was doing, she took off running, so Olivia walked faster towards her and fired two shots. Of course the bullets didn't hit CeCe, but it wasn't because Olivia wasn't trying to hit her. After firing the shots, Olivia didn't trip, panic or anything. She was cool, but Monae thought she should leave and stay off the stroll the rest of the night, so Olivia got back into the taxi and the two of them took the taxi to Monae's parlor. After riding away from the stroll, Olivia thought about things and thought it was a good idea that she stay away from her apartment as well, because when Bernard found out what went down, he would go there looking for her after he looked for her on the stroll. Sure enough, Bernard was out and about looking for her and came to the parlor where he figured she was. When he rung the doorbell, Olivia and Monae knew it was him, so Monae had Olivia stay on the private side of the parlor and lock the secret door, while she answered and opened the door for Bernard on the business side of the parlor. The intercom was on, so Olivia could hear the discussion Monae had with Bernard. Basically, Monae told him she had not seen Olivia since Olivia left the stroll. Bernard told Monae he hoped they didn't fall out (have an altercation) behind Olivia (because of) and Monae, being the strong afro-American woman she was, told Bernard that she hoped they didn't fall out as well. The two of them sat there and smoked a joint while they shot the breeze (chatted) for about twenty minutes and then Bernard left. That night and the next two days, Olivia stayed at the parlor where she and Monae tried to come up with a plan for her situation. Even if it was the next week or maybe even the next month when she ran into (saw) Bernard, he was gonna go off on her (verbally or physically punish or discipline her) for what she did to his whoe. Olivia interfered with Bernard's whoe getting his money and knew that he wasn't too happy about that alone, so she knew she had to avoid him for a while to allow him to get over the anger he probably felt. After having to take Olivia to her apartment a few times to get changes of clothing, Monae suggested to her that she move out of her apartment and come live with her at the parlor and so Olivia did. While still trying to figure out how to put some distance between what happened on the stroll with CeCe and the day when she would run into Bernard and have to face him about what she did, Olivia kept a very low profile. She knew that Bernard wouldn't just be hanging around the stroll, so she did go to a nightclub that was downstairs from one of the strip joints, just to get out of the parlor and get some air. As soon as she walked into the club that night, she went to the ladies room. Just as she walked back to the stalls in the restroom, CeCe opened the door, walked out of the stall she was in and ran right into her. The look on her face was the look as though she saw a ghost. With the aisle leading to the area the stalls were in being so narrow, CeCe couldn't get through unless Olivia turned sideways, so Olivia could see on CeCe's face, the fear she felt. If Olivia wanted to, she could have stole on CeCe (spontaneously hit CeCe in her face) and commenced to kickin' her ass, but she was trying to let things die down to bypass the ass kickin' that Bernard probably wanted to give her, the ass kickin' that was really due her according to the pimpin' game. Noticing right away that CeCe was afraid, Olivia quickly responded to her being startled, by saying, "tell Bernard everything is cool". Meaning, she didn't want any trouble with him and wanted to squash the matter she started about her jacket. She then stepped aside and let CeCe pass. Olivia can't remember CeCe washing her hands. She got out of the ladies room with a quickness. Olivia went ahead and did her business in the ladies room, then joined Monae at a table she was seated at in the nightclub. Monae saw CeCe come from the ladies room and quickly leave the club, so she asked Olivia what went on in there. After filling her in on what she said to CeCe, Olivia told Monae she thought she ought to leave the stroll because CeCe might call Bernard and tell him she was there. Monae agreed that Olivia getting away from the stroll was a good idea, so the two of them got up (left). CeCe wasn't wearing Olivia's jacket that night. Olivia never saw the jacket again, which was cool with her. She didn't have the jacket, but CeCe didn't wear it neither, so she was cool with that. The day after Olivia ran into CeCe at the club, Monae talked with her cousin who lived in Honolulu and hooked Olivia up with him. Olivia chose Cash (Monae's cousin) over the phone and flew to Honolulu two days later, to be with her new pimp. You see, according to the way the game goes, Olivia knew that as long as she was an outlaw, she was as good as being Bernard's whoe. Bernard could charge her if she made any whoe money and could whip her ass about fuckin' with his whoe whenever he caught up with her, but if she chose another pimp, Bernard had to take it up with him, whatever problem he had with her. He certainly would no longer have any claims on the whoe money she made. Bernard getting with her about shootin' at CeCe, was the only reason Olivia chose Cash though. She wasn't the kind of girl whose only goal in life, was to be a whoe nor to be obligated to give a man her money, no matter where she got it from, but at that time, choosing another pimp was the best thing for her to do, other than go back to her home town. Going back home is not what Olivia wanted to do at the time, so she did what she had to do to dodge Bernard. When Olivia arrived in Honolulu, Cash was standing at the gate lookin' so good. "Damn he's fine", is what Olivia said to herself when she saw him. She said Cash was not all flashy like most pimps are, but he was well groomed and was dressed in casual clothes that were sporty. The only thing that made him look like a gigolo, player or pimp, was that he was a pretty boy kind of guy. Cash wore conservative suits and was funny (humorous) as hell. The brother, like most pimps, had extravagant taste. Cash was a gentleman, which was unusual for a pimp, but he was nobody nice when he got angry. While in Hawaii, he practiced karate and didn't mind using it. He was usually cool though. When Olivia walked through the gate from the airplane and approached him, Cash gave her a peck (kiss) on her lips, told Olivia, "aloha (hello, welcome)" and got her bags/luggage for her. Olivia then chose him like a pimp is supposed to be chose, purse first, ass last and gave him the money she brought with her as choosing fees. She knew the game and the way it goes is the way she came to Cash. So far, she was impressed with him and was more impressed with Cash when she followed him to the small, two-seater, convertible sports car he was driving. She had never rode in or known anyone who owned a car like the one Cash was driving. Olivia thought to herself, "being with this guy may not be so bad after all". After leaving the airport, Cash took her to his apartment and introduced her to his whoe. There the three of them sat and drank Mums Champaign that was forty dollars a bottle at that time. Cash then made a call and took Olivia with him to pick up someone. The person he picked up was a short, physically fit and cute white girl who had red, thick, Mary Hartman kind of hair that she could sit on. Malissa's hair was so long, the length of it hung beneath her ass. She was very cute and nice, intelligent and successful as well. It turned out that the sports car Cash drove, belonged to Malissa, but Olivia was still impressed with him. After picking Malissa up, she, Cash and Olivia went to dinner. The restaurant they dined at was very extravagant with the dimmed lights and waiters who wore the neatly folded towel over one of their arms and cummerbunds around their waist. Olivia enjoyed the service that was offered at the restaurant. She had dined at fine restaurants, but they weren't quite as formal as the one she dined at with Cash and Malissa. One of the waiters assisted her and Malissa in taking their seats, served them and Cash water and left menus at the table for them all to take their time and view. Cash joked around with the two ladies while the three of them waited to order. The restaurant's menu had really fancy, expensive entrees on it, but Cash seemed to have dined at the restaurant before and didn't take long in deciding what he was going to have. Olivia can't remember what she had, but Cash ordered escargot with his meal. Olivia had rich taste in most things, but escargot was never one of the things she had a desire or taste for. In fact, she thought it was a gross thing for anyone to eat. Anyway, the waiter arrived with the trio's meals and flame sautéed the escargot in a chafing dish at the tableside the trio was seated at. Olivia felt like a big bitch (someone important, a v.i.p. if you will). The fancy restaurants she previously dined at had great service, but none of them cooked food at the tables their customers were seated at. However, Olivia carried herself very well. "I thought I was the shit (of an elite caliber or group of people)", she said. As soon as Cash's escargot was served to him and the waiter left the tableside, just as Olivia began dressing her food with salt, butter and what have you, Cash wanted her to taste the escargot he was having. With her nose turned up (frowning), Olivia didn't have anything good to say about escargot, but Cash insisted she taste it. When Olivia refused to taste the snail, Cash threatened to not pay for her meal and to walk out of the restaurant leaving her at the table without money to pay the tab. Because Cash was so convincing about sticking her with the tab, Olivia tasted the escargot. To her surprise, the snail was very tasty, but she didn't want anymore than the small bite she had. Even though sautéed escargot is tasty, Olivia couldn't stomach the thought of what it actually is. It was after she tasted the snail, that she realized Cash was bluffing about not paying for her meal. She later learned that he often joked in that way. He was the kind of guy who could tell an absurd tale that was believable because of the way he told it, all serious and shit. Because Olivia enjoyed comedy and humorous people, she thought Cash was quite a guy. In such a short time, she liked him a lot and liked his style. The two of them hit it off and quickly got comfortable with one another as though they had known each other a longer period of time than they had. Malissa was cool also. She and Olivia hit it off right away as well. After dining that evening, Olivia, Cash and Malissa left the restaurant and went to Malissa's home. More impressed than she was with Cash, Olivia was more impressed with Malissa. She had it going on. The lady lived in a condominium on the eleventh floor of the building, which had a balcony that overlooked the island. That's where she, Cash and Olivia hung out the rest of the night and did the freak. It wasn't even Olivia's style to participate in threesomes unless she was getting paid, but being that she was across the waters, miles away from home or Anchorage, because she knew when she decided to go, that she would have to be down (ready and willing) for whatever her new pimp's program was and what he wanted her to do, Olivia did what she had to do. She didn't understand what the three of them freaking was all about, but she assumed that Cash had his reasons for doing it. It was a hell of a way for her and Malissa to bond, but Olivia figured their closeness played a big part in Cash's game and that had everything to do with the get-together. After her second night in Honolulu, Olivia had it going on. She worked the stroll on Kalikawa Boulevard the second night there, but Cash left Honolulu that third day she flew to Anchorage to take care of some business he had there. While away, he had Malissa to look after Olivia, so Olivia stayed in the condo with her. Now the pieces of the puzzle were fitting together, of why Cash wanted Olivia and Malissa to bond. He had some serious business in Anchorage because Olivia didn't see him in Hawaii, the remainder of the time she was there. For thirty-four days, Olivia stayed in Honolulu with Malissa and Cash stayed in Anchorage. That was cool with Olivia though. Cash, didn't give her any instructions on working (selling pussy) in Honolulu, so he couldn't expect her to be down while he was away with her not knowing the ropes. Olivia just chilled and kicked it with Malissa whenever there was something going on. Malissa owned a massage parlor that was a lot more legit than Monae's. Olivia believes that Malissa sold pussy and other sexual acts on the side, but her parlor was just for what it was, massages. Some of the parlor's cliental probably wanted to buy sex as well, but Malissa didn't date guys at the parlor like what went on in Monae's parlor. Malissa was no square. She was quite a lady, but it was obvious that she loved money and she also enjoyed getting her buzz on (getting high) when she wasn't doing business. Malissa had money, made money and seemed to keep handy, the things she needed. She even had a brick of Tai stick (marijuana) that was the first Olivia had ever seen. It had to have cost Malissa several hundred dollars and wasn't for sell. It was for her personal use. Staying with Malissa at her condo, was the bomb (the best) for Olivia. While Malissa was away taking care of business, Olivia chilled there smoking weed and viewing the island through the binoculars she looked through from the balcony. She was livin' large, even though it was at someone else's expense. She didn't have any plans at the time, except to wait for Cash to return so that he could give her the knowledge and the backup she needed to properly get down (work the stroll). Meanwhile, she enjoyed a life of leisure and the island.

While Olivia stayed with Malissa, from time-to-time, Malissa had dates whom she visited with at the condo. At those times, she gave Olivia twenty-five or thirty dollars to go see a movie or something. Olivia was okay with that. Shit, she didn't mind hanging out for a couple or few hours and get paid for it. One night, there was a social event for masseuses of various massage parlors, that Malissa took Olivia to. The event was at a small cottage on the island and turned out to be a get high party, basically, which was right up Olivia's alley (her kind of party). The get-together was all good (to Olivia). As Olivia sat amongst several people in the dimmed lighted living room of the cottage, plates of cocaine were passed around. After using the rolled up dollar bill to snort a couple of lines of the powdered drug, Olivia passed the plate to the person sitting next to her. A few minutes later, another plate was coming her way. As she did before, Olivia snorted a couple of lines of the drug from that plate and passed it on. That's how the night went at the social gathering. All night long, plates were going around the room like clockwork. Wine was also served as everyone mingled and socialized. Everytime a bottle of wine was opened, it was a different wine as though the gathering was a wine tasting event. Oh it was happening in Honolulu. Olivia left the affair around two AM. Malissa had a friend take Olivia to the condo because she had an extended, but private engagement to attend. Olivia wasn't mad at Malissa (didn't mind; understood Malissa wanting to get her freak on). She was ready to retire for the evening anyway, even though she was wide awake and knew she wouldn't be able to go to sleep for a while. There really wasn't anything left for her to do except chill, other than make some money and it wasn't that kind of party with the people who attended the get-together.

On most days, Olivia sat at the condo, watched TV, got her buzz on and viewed the island from the balcony of the condo. A couple of weeks after she arrived in Honolulu was her twenty-second birthday. Without her asking for anything in particular or any recognition of her birthday, Malissa made the day a day for Olivia to remember. First off, she took Olivia with her to the marina to meet up with one of her friends who was in the navy. Malissa's friend had just gotten off a ship that was so huge, Olivia couldn't even see the top of it as she stood near it. It was a sight for her to see since the only time she saw a ship was on TV. She was amazed. After meeting up with Malissa's friend, the three of them went to a small residential community where a lady and another guy awaited. The community had a private inlet for the sail and speedboats owned by some of the residences of the community. That's where Olivia, Malissa and the others boarded a sailboat owned by one of them and sailed from the inlet out to the Pacific Ocean. After getting well out into the ocean, Olivia was afraid when she learned how sailboats shift from one side to the other. In doing so, one has to hold on to something or brace themselves to keep from falling, which was hard for Olivia to do with only the use of one of her hands. After the sailboat shifted to both sides a couple of times, Olivia couldn't hang any longer, so she went below the deck of the boat and fell asleep. When she awakened, she and the others were back at the inlet. Olivia was very pleased about that. The ocean was beautiful, but she didn't stay up on the deck long enough to see much. The short time she was on deck, she did see a small mountain or piece of rock in the ocean, called the Chinaman's Hat, so she did see that tourists' attraction. After getting on their way, Malissa took Olivia to a couple of shops and bought her a pair of shoes and a purse. Then she told Olivia she was taking her to a concert at the coliseum after they had dinner, so the two of them went back to the condo, had their shower and redressed. After dining elegantly at a very nice restaurant, the two of them enjoyed the Isley Brothers and The Brothers Johnson (two very popular singing groups back then) in concert. The concert was the bomb (a blast). When it was over, Malissa took Olivia to a nightclub where they had drinks and heard live jazz while a female crooned and scatted. After enjoying the jazz show for about

137

an hour and a half, Malissa began to nod from the exhausting day she had, so Olivia suggested they go to the condo. By far, this birthday of Olivia's was one of the best birthdays she had ever had. She couldn't thank Malissa enough, for the wonderful day she had, but not enough to freak with her again.

Olivia spent two more weeks in Honolulu after her birthday. While there, she wrote Bernard a letter of apology for what she did to CeCe and told him that she wanted to squash the matter. She knew she would be going back to Anchorage sooner or later and knew from the jump that her choosing Cash was not a permanent arrangement nor would it last for months. Therefore, she wanted to make amends to Bernard while she was protected, before she became an outlaw again or just without a man. After realizing Cash wasn't coming back to Honolulu anytime soon, Olivia packed her bags, thanked Malissa for her hospitality and all she had done for her, took a flight from the island and flew back to Alaska. When she arrived in Anchorage and got to Monae's parlor, Cash wasn't there, but he was still in town. When he did arrive to the parlor, he wasn't angry, surprised or affected in any way about Olivia leaving Honolulu without his knowledge or instructions. Somewhere along the way, Cash caught two young girls too young to be away from home, whom were with him at their own will and was placed in the parlor to work there since they were too young to work the stroll. Both girls seemed to be happy in doing what they were doing. One of them was an oriental girl, the other, dominican. In a short period of time, both girls were in love with Cash and was down for whatever he wanted and asked of them. They were the reason Cash was detained in Anchorage. He didn't even try and pimp Olivia. As a matter of fact, he seemed to care a lot for her in a different way. For some reason, he had a soft spot for Olivia. Maybe it was because of her handicap, not being able to use one of her arms, which would be the unusual. Usually, pimps don't give a shit if someone is blind, cripple or crazy. If that person can make money it don't matter, nothing else matters. If a pimp can make money off an individual, they will get paid with no remorse. Cash didn't press Olivia about money or anything. Olivia didn't know what the deal was, but she wasn't mad about it. A few days after she returned from the island, Cash went back to Honolulu and had Monae watch after his new girls and send him the money the new girls made. Olivia just chilled and hung out with Monae. While she and Monae went to nightclubs and party houses to kick it, the parlor was jumping (busy) and Monae collected big money twenty-four seven (twenty-four hours a day, seven days a week). Her girl worked the parlor, along with Cash's two girls. The set up for collection of the whoe money was very clever too. Monae bought a large box of envelopes just for the business side of the parlor. The girls who worked the parlor were instructed and required to put the money they were paid for a date by each john, into an envelope after they placed the john in the room the date was going to take place in. The girls were instructed and required to then, slide each envelope under the locked, secret door that led to the private side of the parlor. "I know, I know. The set up Monae had, was off the hook (brilliant, clever)", said Olivia. Everything flowed smoothly and consecutively for the next three months. Before Cash went back to Honolulu, he didn't bring the pimpin' to Olivia, but he got the pussy a couple more times. "Cash was one pimp I couldn't figure out at the time, but I didn't question him though", Olivia said. While in Anchorage, Olivia sold sex sometimes, but she didn't have to because she didn't have a pimp and that's the way she liked it. She finally ran into Bernard and wasn't sure about what that would bring, but Bernard was cool by then. He really knew how Olivia felt about him and knew how she felt about CeCe, so he understood and knew he should have figured she wouldn't be nice after seeing CeCe in her jacket. All of that was behind her now though and she was glad about that because she didn't want any trouble with Bernard. She didn't mind not getting her leather jacket back neither, just as long as CeCe didn't wear it. Bernard didn't pursue Olivia to be down for him because he never had to and thought his presence was enough to catch her, but apparently he was a little slow on his game or was too damn sure of himself. He had not figured out yet, that Olivia wasn't as weak for him as she once was. Therefore, it would take a little more effort on his part, for her to get back down for him like she used to be. Bernard, along with a lot of others thought Olivia and Monae were fuckin' or suckin' because every time they saw Monae, Olivia was with her. Everyone knew Monae was pimpin' and wondered if Olivia had chosen her, but it wasn't like that. Monae never came to Olivia in that way. The two of them were just buddies, but Olivia didn't give a fuck about what anyone thought. She wasn't gettin' pimped and was doing what she wanted to do, so everything was all good.

After Cash had been in Honolulu for about a month or so, he returned back to Anchorage. After midnight of the day he got back to Alaska, he arrived at the parlor all happy like a kid on Christmas day and wanted to turn Monae and Olivia on to a new high he had been introduced to. The drug used was nothing new to neither of the ladies since the two of them had their own separate experiences with cocaine. Monae had never main-lined (shot up) cocaine as Olivia once did, but she was experienced with the drug as well. Just when Olivia, more so than Monae, thought she had used cocaine in all the ways it could be used, including putting the powdered drug on the purr-tongue (clitoris) of her pussy, to putting the powder on the head of a lover's dick, Cash came along with, yet, a different way of using the very powerful, habit-forming and dangerous drug. Freebasing is what he called it, which neither Olivia nor Monae had ever heard of. The year was nineteen eighty-two. At that time, there wasn't really a name for the form of cocaine that derived from cooking the powdered drug, which is what freebased cocaine is. Cooked cocaine. Freeing the base. I take that to mean that the cut, which is the substance used to step on the drug (decreased the potency, while increasing the amount/weight of the drug) is freed from the base (the drug)", Olivia explained. That's what happens when the cocaine is cooked, freebased. Freebasing cocaine cooks all the cut from the drug, transforming it back to it's purest form. Cash had quite a bit of the drug too and had all the tools (paraphernalia) needed to smoke it, which is how (the only way) the drug is used once it is cooked. "Cash showed us everything involved in smoking the cocaine, except cook it. The drug was already cooked when he set it out on the glass-top table, so the only thing to it at that point, was to do it. Business at the parlor had slowed down early that night, so even Monae's whoe and the other two girls Cash had working at the parlor, were allowed to join in on the smokathon (sorta' speak). Everyone had their share of smoking the drug," said Olivia. With all the drugs she had previously done, Olivia considered herself a connoisseur of drugs, so it didn't take long for her to figure the drug out, form her opinion of it and decide if it was what she thought was a good high that she wanted to frequently indulge in. She believed that every drug offered it's user some type of fulfillment or enjoyment so she carefully analyzed the affect of the freebased drug to determine what it offered. In not time, Olivia came to conclusion that smoking freebased cocaine was a waste of money and time. Speeding was not her idea of a good high anyway. That's the affect cocaine gives it's users, no matter how it is done. When the drug is smoked, it gives it's user a rush to the brain that first hit (draw, toke) that's taken, that it's user will never feel again, except maybe after a long abstinence from smoking the drug. It didn't take Olivia but a few hits of the freebased cocaine, to realize she couldn't get the affect again, that she got from the first hit, even if she sat up all night smoking. "So what I got a rush when I took that first puff. That's not shit to me, not my kind of high", said Olivia, "so I wasn't impressed with freebasing", she added. Olivia said she had never enjoyed speeding. If she needed energy, she would spend less money on some iron pills and some vitamins. She said she liked things nice and slow and the only thing she wanted fast, was a speedy way of having lots of money. Just because it was available, she continued to indulge (or so she thought) in the smoke-out, but she didn't feel she would smoke cocaine again. Especially if she had to pay for it. When day was about to break, the smokathon had finally ended and Olivia said she was glad. Cash left the parlor while Olivia and Monae sat there wide awake, trying to figure out what to do with themselves. "It was horrible", said Olivia. After feeling as dumb as she did, sitting there not really having anything to say like a cat had her tongue, with not a damn thing to do, she really thought smoking freebased cocaine was stupid and was more convinced than she seemed to be a couple of hours before now, that she didn't like the affect this way of doing cocaine gave her. All she wanted to do at this point, was to go to sleep so that the drug would wear off, but that didn't happen no time soon. Later that day when she and Monae awakened, everything was back to the usual, but never again the same. Neither Olivia nor Monae knew that though. It wasn't until a few days later when Cash returned and brought back with him some more of the freebased cocaine, that it became apparent. Olivia got to hit the pipe (paraphernalia tool used to smoke cocaine) a couple of times. Then Cash took his dope and tools to the other side of the parlor and called out Monae's name for her to come and join him. Olivia wasn't mad about being excluded from smoking anymore of the dope Cash had. In fact, she wasn't in the mood for being all hyped anyway. Besides, giving her a couple of hits of the cocaine and then excluding her from the rest of it, was a trick and she knew it, but she was okay with that. As soon as Monae and Cash went to the other side of the parlor, Olivia got her chill on (kicked back to relax). A couple of hours later, she had come down from the high enough to start drifting off to sleep. Just as she was going into a nod, Monae came over to the side of the parlor she was on and asked her to loan her some money. Olivia knew what the deal was. Monae and Cash had smoked all the cocaine Cash had and they both wanted some more. Feeling the way she did about freebasing, not even wanting to spend her money on the drug for her own pleasure or misery, Olivia told Monae she didn't have any money to loan out for some dope. Even though Olivia had indulged in drugs for years, she never did and didn't have to spend a lot of money on them as she quickly realized one was forced to do when they smoked cocaine. "It was nonsense", said Olivia, "to indulge in something that never satisfies". She could see how one could get into financial debt, fuckin' with cocaine in whatever form it was in and she knew she couldn't force Monae nor Cash to pay her back any money they borrowed, so she knew that loaning Monae money was a bad idea under the circumstances. Monae didn't trip at the time she was denied of the loan. She just went back to the side of the parlor Cash was on and didn't press the issue any further. At least not at that time. By late morning that next day, she and Cash seemed to have been up all night tripping. Olivia kind of remembers hearing the back door of the business side of the parlor open a couple of times through the night, but she continued to get her snooze on (continued to sleep). After getting dressed and just chilling on the private side of the parlor that morning, Monae came and asked Olivia once again, for a loan and once again, Olivia denied her of the loan. The two ladies didn't have a disagreement about it or anything when Olivia denied Monae of the loan. However, Monae did go with an attitude to the business side of the parlor where Cash was probably awaiting, hoping she came back with the money she asked for. A few minutes later, Monae returned to the private side of the parlor once again, but this time, she told Olivia she had to leave (move from the parlor). Olivia wasn't really prepared for that, at least not mentally, but she obliged Monae of her request. Olivia knew Monae really didn't want her to go and felt it was Cash's idea for Monae to play her that way to see if she wanted to stay at the parlor bad enough to give Monae the money she asked her for. Olivia couldn't give in and let Monae nor Cash punk her like that, think that she was weak or think that she wasn't down enough to get busy and do what she had to do to take care of herself. In situations like this, Olivia knew that once a person gives in, he or she will get played like that by the same person again. She wasn't going out like that (having Monae think that she could manipulate her), so she called for a taxi after collecting and packing most of her things. More than she hated a lot of things, Olivia hated for someone to play games with her, try and run a game on her, try and treat her like a trick and last but not least, try and play on her intelligence. Cash put Monae up to the bluff they tried to play on Olivia, but Cash didn't know how bout-about-it Olivia was and that she was a real money-getter, and apparently, neither did Monae. Therefore, the two of them probably thought that rather than Olivia be alone in a far away place such as Alaska with no place to go  (or so they thought), she would punk out and give in to them, but their plan didn't work out like they thought it would. Little did the two of them know of the rude awakening they were in for.  Olivia's taxi arrived and she got on up (left the parlor) with her bags in hand and had the taxi driver take her to the motel she stayed in before. That is where she went for what she knew and ended up staying there for about five weeks, paying forty dollars a night for her room. "Shit, I got my damn hustle on", said Olivia. For about four weeks, she didn't see nor talk to Monae nor Cash. Then she ran into Monae on the stroll. The two ladies spoke to each other and was cordial to one another.  Olivia didn't bring up the mishap to Monae nor did Monae mention the ordeal. The encounter was very brief, Olivia went her way and Monae went hers. The fifth week Olivia was at the motel, she got an unsuspected phone call from Monae who had the desk clerk ring her room. Monae didn't beat around the bush.  She was very frank, came straight out and told Olivia she wanted her to come back and stay at the parlor. Monae even offered to come get Olivia. Hearing in her voice how serious she was, Olivia accepted Monae's proposal, Monae came and got Olivia, the two of them went back to the parlor and carried on as though nothing had ever happened. From then on, Olivia had Monae's genuine respect and the two of them remain friends even as I speak.  Even though neither of them knew it, their not so innocent introduction to freebasing, changed their lives forever. It wasn't until years later though, that they individually realized how so. Olivia stayed with Monae at the parlor through the renovation of a couple of rooms on the business side of it and through Monae's eviction from the parlor. After Monae left the parlor, she was sentenced to sixty days in a correctional institution.  Olivia stayed in a two-bedroom motel room with Monae's husband for a week and helped him find an apartment for Monae to occupy after she was released. After finding an apartment, Monae's husband paid the deposit along with the first month's rent. Then Olivia flew back to her hometown to chill. When she went back, she had a new attitude and a new walk. Olivia had her trick Tom, pick her up at the airport and take her to her mom's and Jean's home. Her family was very impressed when they saw her. She didn't walk with the limp she walked with before she left home and she had a few more items when she returned, looking like she had money. Olivia was feeling really good about herself at that time and was glad to be back home.

Not sure what to do with herself, Olivia just kicked it around or chilled during the daytime and went to the nightclub (where she first met Bernard) on some Thursdays, every Friday and Saturday and some Sunday nights. On some days in the early evenings, she frequented a strip bar where Bernard's sister (her age) danced. That's where she kept running into Randy, her former colleague Misty's brother. Nothing jumped off between them when they ran into one another at the strip joint, but there was a lot of chemistry between them. Neither one of them made it a secret that they were attracted to one another. For now though, they were just checking each other out. Finally, Olivia caught Randy who wasn't in the pimpin' game, but grew up around it being that Misty was a whoe and her man who was like a brother in-law to Randy, was a pimp. Misty's brother was a year younger than Olivia, but advanced for his age. The brother was good-lookin' too. He had a sexy style for his age, that said he was flexible and was not a square to the game and hustling. One night while kickin' it at her favorite nightclub, Olivia ran into Randy who was there with another of his sisters who was younger than Misty. The sister Randy was with, was a year older than Olivia, but was in Olivia's class in senior high school, so Olivia knew her as well and was able to sit at their table and get into their mix to get more acquainted with Randy. Randy was just what Olivia was lookin' for in a guy during this time, because he wasn't a pimp, but neither was he a square. Olivia being with a square guy at that time, would have been too slow for her because of the lifestyle she had been livin' and her being with a pimp was too fast for her, but Randy being in the category between the two style of men, was the right speed for her, both physically and mentally. Randy was in deed a hustler, so he was versatile about most things. He didn't put the demands on Olivia though, like those Bernard put on her. As the night moved along, Olivia kicked it with Randy at the club and there was bigger chemistry between the two of them than the chemistry they previously noticed and felt was there before. So much so, that Olivia invited him and Randy accepted the invitation to come home with her that night, to Sara's and Jean's home and spend the night there with her. "Yes, I gave up the pussy to him that night", said Olivia. She said it was obvious they were gonna fuck, so there was no since in prolonging the ecstasy. Randy hooked

Olivia up and she him. The two of them then fell asleep holding on to each other as though they had been waiting for one another all their lives. "It seemed so right", said Olivia. There was an instant connection between her and Randy, so they became, damn near, inseparable. For two months, Olivia and Randy spent everyday together. Sara, probably happy to see someone want Olivia in spite of her physical status and not try and pimp her, allowed Randy to stay the night in Olivia's bedroom as often as he and Olivia wanted to sleep together. The third month, on March twenty-fifth, the two of them were married at the courthouse. They didn't tell anyone they were gonna get married, so it was a surprise to everyone. After they took their vows, the both of them went back to Sara's and Jean's home and broke the news to them. Sara and Jean were surprised in deed, but happy Randy did right by Olivia. Olivia's aunt broke out a bottle of Harvey's Bristol Cream and they all toasted the newlyweds. After the intimate celebration, Randy took Olivia to his mom's home on the other side of the bridge and broke the news to her, who wasn't pleased at all. It wasn't that she didn't like Olivia, she didn't even know her, but she felt her son was too young for one and two, she knew Randy and Olivia had only dated for three months. It was too late for anybody to doubt or disagree at this point though. What was done, was done. However, Randy's sister Misty, didn't even like the idea of Olivia and Randy dating, not to mention the two of them being married to one another. Being that Olivia was a semi retired whoe and street smart, Misty thought she was going to use Randy and dog (mistreat) him, so she was totally against the marriage and her attitude showed it. Misty wasn't too fond of Olivia anyway. She and Olivia never had any bad words with one another or anything like that, so her not being fond of Olivia was one of those girl things. You know how women player-hate for stupid reasons like: "I don't like the way the bitch walks"; "oh, her butt is too big, she thinks it looks good but it don't"; "that bitch thinks she's all that"; "that bitch thinks she's cute just because her hair is long". You know, shit like that. Misty didn't like Olivia because of some shit she was tripping on, but she had been and still was cordial to her even though Olivia had often felt the bad vibes. There were things about Misty that Olivia had her own opinion about as well, but it was no thang (big deal) to her because she never really gave a shit about the way someone else is or chooses to be nor of what someone thinks of her. Especially a bitch (female). Misty wasn't a problem for her so Olivia didn't dislike her. She didn't know Misty well enough to like or dislike her and she didn't have to live with her. Olivia didn't even see Misty that often, so she never gave her too much thought. She got along well with the rest of Randy's family and relatives though. Even Misty quickly grew to like Olivia a lot. After Randy got the okay from his mom, he did the honorable thing and brought Olivia to his mom's home to live there with him until the two of them could get their own place. That worked out very well. Although Randy was a hustler, he also kept a job. As a matter of fact, he had a full-time job and a part-time job when Olivia came to live with him at his mom's house. Randy enjoyed getting high too. That was all good with Olivia because she enjoyed being high everyday, even if it was just from smoking weed. Randy didn't smoke weed though. He smoked PCP (sherm, water, wet daddies or what have you) and he drank beer, gin or brandy. Olivia wasn't big on drinking alcoholic beverages, but she did smoke PCP-slash-wet with the best of them, so she and Randy had that in common, along with some other things they both enjoyed and indulged in. After getting wet (high on pcp), Olivia could and would chill out though, but Randy wanted to be all over the city, visiting or trying to talk his way up on some money. He came home every night and he always touched bases with Olivia, so she wasn't mad at him about the way he liked kickin' it nor did she have a problem with him gettin' his hustle on. Olivia stayed with Randy at his mom's house for two or three months. After being there a couple of months, she started having thoughts about what was going on in Anchorage. Sometimes she thought about Bernard, but most times not. The new lifestyle she was living was nice and she loved her husband, but it seemed she was caught between the new lifestyle she was livin' and the old one she lived. Still today, Olivia can't say that she wanted Bernard during that time, but it seemed something in Alaska was calling her, drawing her back there or that there was something there she had to finish. Therefore, she told Randy she had to go back to Anchorage to take care of some business. Randy wasn't in agreeance with Olivia going to Anchorage at first, but because of his love for money, Olivia was able to convince him to allow her or go along with her going back to Alaska. "The only thing that convinced Randy to let me go back to Anchorage, was my telling him I was gonna send any money I made, back to him", said Olivia. She said she believed Randy loved her, but he loved money too and because of the things he was exposed to while growing up, he was also under the influence that one could be in love with their mate and have their mate sell their body too. Just as Olivia was under the same influence. Randy didn't really want Olivia to have sex with anyone else, but could except it for the money. Anyway, he nor Olivia said anything to anyone about Olivia going to Anchorage, until the last minute (couple or few days before she was to depart). No one said anything to Olivia about what they felt about her leaving her husband to go back to Alaska once they learned of it, but again, Olivia felt the bad vibes. Everyone knew Bernard was in Anchorage and believed he was the reason Olivia wanted to go back there, but that didn't stop her from going though. With innocent intentions, she went back to Anchorage, but her stay there turned out to be everything opposite of innocent. She even stayed four months longer than she was supposed to or should have, but that episode of her life in Alaska, summed up the unfinished search she was on to find herself and where she wanted to be or put an end to the streetlife she had been caught up in. That visit to Alaska turned Olivia's life around and although the things she had to do to find herself were sinful, they were a means to an end and for that, it was all good.

Olivia arrived in Anchorage and stayed with Monae in the apartment she helped Monae's husband find for her. The two of them would go and work the stroll together until dawn. Then they would go to someone's home or apartment and sit for hours, smoking freebased cocaine. Since Olivia was introduced to freebasing, she had indulged in the drug several times more, even though she said she didn't like it and was sincere to herself when she vowed to not do the drug again. Calling one back to indulge again and again, is one of the affects the drug has on its user. Therefore, Olivia did the drug anyway and when she and Monae finished working the stroll, it was a mutual agreement that the two of them put their money together (went in on the cost to purchase one rock of freebased cocaine, after another) and smoke cocaine until the early evening. Up all night selling pussy and other sexual acts and then smoking damn near til sunset when they both were broke (penniless), the two friends had no idea how much deeper they were falling under the influence, under the spell of this bad white bitch better known as cocaine. In the mix of their smoke-outs, Olivia was sometimes in the company of Bernard because he too indulged in the drug. "It seemed that was the time (era) when most of the pimps in Anchorage stopped being real pimps and whoes who use to be down for the money to have nice things, became dope feins, doing what they had to do to chase a bitch that couldn't be caught", Olivia remembers. Eventually, she chose Bernard again. CeCe ended up having to do a longer bit (time she had to serve) in a correctional facility and was out of the picture at the time, so Olivia had Bernard to herself and stayed with him in a hotel room. Every night, she worked the stroll faithfully. That's the way it had to be with Bernard. The thing that was worse about being with him then as oppose to the way things were before, was that all Bernard wanted to do was smoke up the whoe money Olivia made. He even wanted to claim the social security money she received, but she refused to let him have what her father risked his life in the service for, so that she or any of her siblings could have the benefit of the income if they were ever in the situation she was in (physically speaking). Olivia continued to let her disability checks go directly to her bank account in her hometown, so that she wouldn't have any problem with getting them. By now, it was hard for her to resist or refrain from smoking cocaine, even though she really didn't like the high it gave her. If she had not been around so many people who indulged in the drug, it would have been easier to resist the temptation (or so she thought), but knowing others were doing it, made the desire to do it more tempting for her. She hated the fact that even though she (or anyone else for that matter) knew to say no, she didn't or couldn't when she should have. "For those who have never experienced this drug, you couldn't possibly know or even have an idea how powerful and evil this substance (cocaine, freebased or otherwise) is. The biggest mistake is that first hit, because that is the beginning of something thousands, probably millions of people can't turn back the hands of time from", said Olivia. She said "that shit (freebased cocaine) aint nothin' nice". Smoking cocaine with Bernard quickly got way out of hand. It didn't take long for Olivia to realize he was deeper on that end (addicted to smoking cocaine) than she cared to be a part of. After working the stroll and smoking cocaine with Bernard for about four weeks, Olivia knew how important smoking the drug was to him and how far gone he was in his addiction when he, along with her, sat in a dope house one morning she met him there after she finished working the stroll and smoked all the money up that she made the night before. When they finally gave up hope that they were gonna get some more cocaine to smoke and went to the hotel room they were occupying, there was a lock on the door that they didn't have a key to. It turned out that Bernard had not paid for that day's rent, which was due at or before check out time, so his and all Olivia's clothes and things were locked in the room until they paid what they owed. This was the second or third time a lock was placed on the door of the room they occupied, so when Olivia hustled and got the money needed to pay what was owed, she took her belongings from the room and left Bernard's things (which were few) there. She didn't know what she was gonna do with her own things at first, but after talking with an older hustler friend of hers, Olivia was able to take her things to her friend's apartment. She still went to work the stroll that night and again, she spent the morning in the dope house smoking cocaine with Bernard. When Olivia got her clothes from the hotel room she and Bernard occupied, she only paid what was owed, which was for that day, but check out time rolled around and the desk clerk had not received the fee for that next twenty-four hours. Just like before, after working til dawn and smoking cocaine in the dope house until early that next evening, Olivia and Bernard had exceeded the time they paid for their room. Olivia didn't care this time because her shit (clothes and things) wasn't in the room, so it didn't make her any difference how Bernard handled the situation. Knowing that Olivia gave him all the money she made, Bernard stopped smoking cocaine when he was down to the last forty or fifty dollars of the five or six hundred Olivia made the night before. He held on to just enough to pay for a hotel room. Since there was a lock put on the door of the room they had been staying in on too many occasions, instead of going back to that hotel and paying what it took to stay there (at the Mush Inn), Bernard got a room at a different hotel that was on a main avenue. Olivia was just about fed up with it all, smoking cocaine, selling pussy and Bernard, but she was still trying to hold on. Once she and Bernard got in the new hotel room they rented and before Olivia could lie down and get some rest or have a shower, Bernard insisted she go back to work. Here it was, two or three pm. Olivia left the other hotel room they stayed in around eight-thirty pm the day before, worked the stroll until five or six this morning, smoked cocaine all morning and afternoon and now Bernard was making her go back to work. "What a lousy ass man he was", she said. That was it for her, she had had it. That was when she realized Bernard didn't love her, didn't care about her and didn't give a shit about her physical condition or what she had gone through. She didn't argue or trip with him though, when he insisted she go back to work. Olivia just politely powdered her nose (sorta' speak) as best she could (considering the fact that she didn't have a clean change of clothes nor any of her toiletries) and left the hotel walking. This was the last straw for her. She didn't know where she was going, but wherever her destination was, she had to walk to get there. She even had tears of sadness and anger rolling down her face, from her discovery. "How could someone treat a person so badly, after that person had done as much as I did and had gone through for Bernard", Olivia mentally asked herself. The answer she learned from this experience, was how heartless and ruthless pimps are. With them, it's strictly business or about the Benjamins (money), nothin' personal. As she walked along, she thought about everything that happened from that moment, back to the year nineteen seventy-six when she was first put down on a stroll. While walking, she came to the conclusion that she didn't want to work the strolls anymore and she also decided the best thing for her was to leave Anchorage and not come back. "The things that were going on in that city were sinful", she said. There were too many people she knew, who were in the pimp and whoe game and/or smoking cocaine. Olivia thought this was a good time to get away from it all. As she continued to walk in the direction the stroll was in, she knew she wasn't going back to the hotel where Bernard awaited. The first thing she needed to do was make enough money to get a hotel room somewhere for a few days and not let Bernard know where she was staying. "While hiding out, I would then sneak and turn some tricks until I got enough money for air fare home, along with money to pay for my meals and lodging", planned Olivia. Just as her survival instincts kicked in and she mapped out a plan, an older brother (African American male) who was really good friends with Monae, rode by, recognized her and pulled his car over to the curb to holler at (talk with) her. Olivia was really glad to see the brother. After all, she was quite a ways from the stroll, so getting a ride there was all a girl with a long walk needed. The brother offered to give Olivia a ride and she accepted, so that worked out well for her. Because she was a little shook up, didn't seem to know where she was going and really didn't want to go and work the stroll, Olivia began telling the brother about her dilemma and how badly she didn't want to go back to Bernard or even see him again. She told the brother whatever she did, would have to be underground because she would have a problem if she ran into Bernard. One word led to another, Olivia asked the brother if she could stay at the apartment for a week or two, with him and his woman (girlfriend) and the brother told her she could. Olivia was relieved. Staying at the brother's and his girl's apartment, was a better arrangement for her because Bernard was going to be looking for her. It would've been hard for her to make some money on the stroll without running into him and she knew he was not gonna be nice when he caught up with her, so this was the safest way for her in buying some time until she could get out of town. For two weeks, Olivia just chilled at her friends apartment and watched TV all day and night. The brother and his lady friend both worked during the daytime, so Olivia had the apartment to herself, which was good for her because she needed time to collect her thoughts, look back on the past and figure out where she was going from here. Since she had shelter, she didn't get out and make money. Instead, she just waited for her next month's social security check to be deposited directly into her checking account at the bank in her hometown. Then Sara and Jean would purchase an airline ticket on their end, for her to fly home. When that time came, Olivia couldn't get to the airport fast enough. She knew that once she got there, she was in the clear from running into Bernard or seeing him again for a long time to come. While flying home in thought along the way, she finally realized she was drawn back to Anchorage to something it seemed she had to finish. Now that the business or what have you was finished, she was able to close the book on her life with Bernard and was completely ready for the new lifestyle she attempted to have when she first married Randy. If he would still have her.

When Olivia returned home, she was a lot thinner in weight than she was before she left. She didn't tell anyone about all the bullshit she had gone through, but it was obvious she had a rough time while in Anchorage. The same day she arrived in her hometown, she called her husband on the telephone and talked with him for about twenty or thirty minutes. It wasn't what Randy said during the conversation, it was the way he said it that told Olivia he wasn't pleased with her. Her going to Alaska, staying as long as she did and not sending money home to him like she said she would, was disturbing to him. His attitude told Olivia he suspected she had some relations with Bernard while she was in Anchorage, but he never mentioned Bernard's name. After the two of them talked to one another on the phone, Randy came and picked Olivia up. Olivia didn't ask to spend the night with him that night and he didn't seem to want to be with her in that way. Olivia was wrong as two left shoes for what she did, so she didn't press Randy for anything or expect anything of him. She knew she had to make it up to him, for all the wrong she had done. She wanted her husband and was sure of that now. Because she was at fault, Olivia was willing to wait as long as it took for Randy to accept her back and she was willing to accept the rejection she was getting at the time, until he was ready to forgive her. For several weeks, things weren't like they should have been, but they got better with time. Randy eventually saw that Olivia really wanted to be with him and settle down, so he gave in and started bringing her to his mom's house some nights, to spend the night there with him. That's when Olivia used all she knew to show her husband she loved him and was ready to be the wife she vowed to be. Not only did she get up in the mornings and cook him breakfast, she was by his side, in her place as his woman, his wife and at night time, she freaked him from head to toe like he wanted to be freaked. "Sometimes you feel like taking your time and making love to your partner, sometimes you just want to have some good butt naked fun, you know, fucking and other times, you just wanna get off (get a quick nutt). With Olivia being in the situation she was in, to make up with Randy, she knew it was gonna take some love-making for him to feel how sincere she was and to help lead the way back to how it was before she went to Alaska. First she started with Randy's lips, giving him tender kisses, wild French (tongue) kisses and then more gentle kisses. As she saw how aroused Randy was getting and felt his dick grow, Olivia gently sucked on his neck just enough to arouse him more, but not bruise him. As Randy began touching Olivia's body, squeezing her breast and rubbing his hands gently across her hard nipples, Olivia could tell he was getting fired up (hot and bothered) and was anxious for more. With gentleness, Randy started pushing Olivia's body downwards while scooting his body upwards. Olivia knew what he wanted. He wanted to feel her warm, wet lips and tongue on his hard dick. Olivia was getting to that, but she wanted to get there slowly covering all the hidden places that makes a man's dick grow, throb and get rock hard. That's the way she wanted the dick to be when Randy went up in her. While working her way to that point with her lips and tongue, Olivia gradually moved her way down to Randy's chest and his stomach, gently sucking and licking his smooth, tan body and nibbling on his nipples. After moving her way down thus far, still kissing Randy's body, Olivia grabbed his dick with her right hand and squeezed it, but not too tight. As she continued to suck, lick and nibble on his body, she rubbed Randy's dick, wrapped her hand around it and began moving her hand up and down while holding on to it. Randy began to grind slowly and then with force. By now, Olivia could feel his dick throb. She said the dick was so hard, she could feel the pulse and each vein that popped out from the flow of the blood rushing to Randy's testicles. Just as Randy squirmed, indicating that he couldn't wait much longer, Olivia slid down on his dick with her wet mouth. Careful not to let her teeth rub against it, she bobbed her head up and down a few times on the entire dick and then she worked the head of it. Gently, she then sucked the head of Randy's dick, but not with too much suction. After keeping up that flow for about fifteen minutes or so, Olivia kissed the head of it, climbed on top of Randy to straddle him with her hot moist pussy touching the head of his dick and gently pushed down on it while Randy pushed so the dick would slide up in her. With a slow grind, Olivia moved her petite, but plump ass up and down on Randy's penis as he held on to and sucked her perky breast. Minutes later, Randy flipped Olivia over, held her legs up in the air and went up in her gently at first, but then with full force before long. "Auh! It was on then" is what she said. There Randy stayed, climbing up in Olivia's wet pussy and grinding for what seemed to be the longest time, just like she liked it, until both of their sex organs exploded in ecstasy. Savoring the feeling, Randy laid there with his dick still inside Olivia, letting his penis drain while soaking in the hot fluid that oozed from his and her organs. While lying there talking to one another with whispers, the both of them verbally shared the love and passion they felt for each another. Finally, Randy slowly came out of Olivia kissing her gently along the way, reached over and grabbed one of the two snifters of brandy that sat on the nightstand next to the bed. Handing that glass to Olivia, Randy reached over and grabbed the other snifter of brandy for himself. While lying there sipping the brandy, the two of them continued to quietly converse with each other. In the early hours just before dawn, the two of them fell asleep all snuggled up with one another. From that morning on, everything else just fell back into place with their marriage. Because they didn't really want to be apart from one another, it wasn't planned, but Olivia just found herself staying with Randy at his mom's house again. She was cool with that for now because she wanted to sleep with her husband every night, but she wanted a place they could call their own, so she began looking for an apartment she and Randy could rent. After residing at Randy's mom's house for two or three months, with Tom's help, Olivia bought a playpen of living room furniture. The first day of the following month, she and Randy moved into their first apartment. Everything went really well the first few months. Most of the times when Randy got off work and got wet (smoked pcp), Olivia was with him. Randy's sister Angel, even hung out with them often times. During that time, Olivia felt Randy loved her even though he didn't seem to sometimes. She knew he wanted her and wanted to be with her, but things seemed different from the way things should have been or probably would have been if she had not gone to Alaska or even if she had done what she said she was going to do when she did go. Not really able to pin-point what the matter was, Olivia felt that Randy lost something he had or felt for her in the beginning or was more cautious with his feelings for her and was being careful of how close to her he would allow himself to get. Emotionally that is. The player in him and Olivia's extended stay in Alaska drove him to reach out and touch girls he had previous relationships with and girls he met while Olivia was away. When Olivia got sick and was hospitalized, things came to the surface. It was after she got out of the hospital, when she discovered Randy was involved with someone else. Randy's game was to get whatever he could from whomever he could get it from. He was good at doing that and would go to great lengths to get what he wanted, depending on how important or how badly he wanted it. It wasn't about him getting some different pussy. That was just one of the perks he got, but rather than him getting the pussy, Randy wanted things he didn't have. He had pussy at home. Good pussy. Money was the number one thing Randy was after, but he would accept some pcp/wet, which was mainly what he wanted money for, he accepted Jewelry, clothes and other accessories. Even if his car needed repairing or parts and he nor Olivia had the money that was needed, Randy would try and play a girl to get his car fixed. When Olivia went into the hospital, of course she couldn't keep her jewelry and wedding ring, so she had Randy take the jewelry home. After getting home from the hospital and getting back to her jewelry, Olivia was missing one ring in particular, her engagement ring. Come to find out, Randy was trying to play a new girl for something he wanted and apparently it was something big because he pretended he was gonna marry the girl to get what he was after. Therefore, he put Olivia's engagement ring on the girl's finger to make his scheme more authentic. From that point on, his and Olivia's marriage was in trouble. As a result of Olivia's anger and Randy's determination to play out his scheme, the couple got behind on their rent and had to vacate the apartment they were renting. From that apartment, they went and stayed with Randy's brother and sister in-law in their townhome apartment. The couple didn't get along very well while they were at Randy's brother's apartment because Randy was still playing with the girl he gave Olivia's ring to, even though he got the ring from the girl and gave it back to Olivia. Randy also had some intimate involvement with his two-year-old son's mother. However, he faithfully slept with Olivia every night because he still had a certain amount of respect for her. Olivia never saw anything Randy did with other girls, but she knew they existed. The allegations she made in regards to the things he did, could not be proven because she never busted (caught) him. That's one of the reasons she didn't leave him. The main reason Olivia didn't leave Randy was because she was willing to take some of his shit for a minute (a little while). She felt that was the least she could do to pay or make up for the wrong she did when she was in Alaska. Even though Randy suspected things she may have done in Anchorage, he accepted Olivia back for the sake of their marriage (she guesses), so Olivia wanted to give her share of acceptance, patience, understanding and forgiveness. All the while she and Randy stayed with Randy's brother, Olivia still did what she had to do while she was dealing with the problems she and Randy were having, applied for and was approved for government housing section eight. Because she took care of business regardless to what was going on and of what the situation may have been, Randy chilled with his games and cheating and let Olivia know it was her he loved and wanted to be with. Probably because he felt secure with her as he once told her. He knew Olivia was about trying to have money. When he told her he felt secure in being with her, Olivia really didn't know how to take him saying so, but for now, she was okay with it.

Getting into the new apartment was great for Olivia and Randy. The apartment was in a good location near Randy's job and it meant a new beginning for him and Olivia in a place of their own where they could work on their marriage. Everything was okay again since Randy gave up on the scheme he had for having the relationship with the girl he temporarily gave Olivia's ring to. The only problem Olivia still had with Randy, was his addiction to smoking pcp (sherm, wet). Everyday, he had to have a stick of sherm (his fix it seemed), maybe two sticks. Olivia wasn't cool with the everyday need it seemed Randy had to smoke the drug, but she went along with it because she enjoyed smoking sherm herself. Along with Randy smoking the drug everyday, was that he had to have an alcoholic beverage to drink while or after he got wet (sherm high). Then he wanted to drive his car here and there, visiting and shit. That was what caused the problem because Randy did not drive as well as he thought he did when he was fucked up (high) as he usually was. He didn't have any wrecks or hit any pedestrians or anything like that, but he did run red lights, stop signs and shit like that. It was only by the grace of God, that he has never had a wreck or run over anyone while driving under the influence of the drug called wet or sherm. The times he did fuck up while driving when he was high, Randy was high enough that he didn't see the police, so he went to jail often, which means the car was towed, Olivia had to bail him out of jail and she had to spend her money to get the car out of tow. She even had to go and visit Randy and put money on the books for him at the correctional institute he had to do time at, as a result of the trouble he got himself into while driving under the influence. Eventually, he and Olivia started having arguments and falling out about the trouble his drug using caused because Olivia found herself constantly having to take care of the rent and household expenses all by herself, as well as the legal fines and fees Randy was charged. Finally, the two of them had a bigger fight than the ones they had before, which caused management of the apartment they lived in, to find out Randy lived in the unit that was only supposed to be for Olivia. Olivia couldn't put Randy's name on the lease because the government assistance for housing she qualified for, was only for her as an applicant eligible for the assistance due to her disability. Management finding out about Randy residing in the apartment Olivia rented, caused her to be evicted. All she wanted from the time she left Sara's and Jean's home and got her first duplex, was to have her own home. A place where she could do what she wanted, come and go as she pleased and preferably, have a man there for companionship and to sleep with every night. From the way things were as she grew up, Olivia wasn't accustomed to moving to a different place to live in every two or few months, not even once a year.

Now she was starting to look back and see that since she got out on her own, all she had done was go from place to place. She didn't sit down and figure too much on it, but she was starting to be more aware of her repeated mistakes. With a couple of weeks left in the month, she started looking for another apartment to move to so that she wouldn't have to go and live in someone else's home. Because she knew how important smoking wet was to her husband, along with the problems it causes and Randy not being responsible as he should have been, Olivia got smart and rented an apartment she could afford by herself, just in case she ended up by herself or if Randy went to jail. The way she had to work things out was cramping her style because she found herself renting apartments in neighborhoods that weren't as nice as the ones she preferred to live in or the neighborhoods weren't bad but the apartments weren't of the quality she desired. That's the way it had to be for now, just so that she could handle the household expenses when Randy fucked up. Olivia still was not ready to give up on her marriage yet, so she found and rented a basement apartment. She didn't like being in the basement of the building she was in or any building for that matter, but the place was clean, she decorated it as best she could and it was affordable. She still had the white and gold bedroom set and the playpen set of living room furniture Tom bought for her, so she had cute things to decorate any apartment, but not for long. Still smoking wet and going to jail causing the car to get towed, Randy made things worse for himself and Olivia by getting arrested, but getting out of the correctional institute everyday on work release and not returning after work like he was supposed to. One time he even escaped from the institute and another time, he pretended to be ill causing the authorities to take him to a hospital. After getting there, Randy dodged the officers and left the hospital. Therefore, a warrant was put out on him for his arrest. He and Olivia did have some fun times in the basement apartment though. One of the good things that happened there, was that Olivia went and studied three months for her G.E.D. and passed the test the first time she took it. Randy graduated from senior high school with his class, so he convinced Olivia to go back and get her diploma. Olivia loved Randy more for encouraging her to do that. Still, there was always dumb shit of some kind with him. A few months after Olivia got her G.E.D., Randy started playing with a girl from the side of the bridge Olivia was from, whom Randy had relations with when he was in senior high school. Randy's mom resided on both sides of the bridge at different times, so during Randy's senior years of school, he lived on that side of the bridge. The girl from Randy's past had been and still was a sucker for him and Randy played the girl whenever he could for whatever he could get. After concocting a scheme to have this girl buy or help him buy a new car, Randy started staying out all night sometimes coming home driving someone else's car. Feeling all disrespected and shit, Olivia said, "fuck this shit" and made a plan of her own. After Randy stayed out all night a few times, that last time, Olivia had someone help her take all of the little shit she had out of hers and Randy's apartment. She took the dishes, whatnots, the TV's, her clothes, everything that she could put into a car. She had made it up in her mind to leave Randy. Because she wanted to get all she could out of the apartment and get away before Randy returned, Olivia couldn't get a truck (just yet) to take her furniture, so she took all that she could take. The only thing left in the apartment was the living room and bedroom furniture, but she planned to go back and get the furniture a couple of days later. When she did go back for the furniture, it was gone. After questioning some of Randy's family members and friends, Olivia found out Randy sold the playpen group of living room furniture. No one knew what he did with the bedroom set, but it wasn't at Randy's mom's house, which was the most likely place he would store it. Olivia was very hurt and very angry, so she was determined to find out what Randy did with the bedroom set Tom bought for her and get it back even if she had to play him to get it. When she left the apartment, she went and stayed at one of her sisters' townhome apartment on the side of the bridge she was from. She was in touch with Randy and it only took about a week or two for her to find out he took the bedroom set and moved into a newly leased apartment with the girl from his past whom he stayed with those nights he didn't come home. Knowing he took her furniture so that he and another girl could use it, hurt Olivia more than it hurt her for Randy to be with the girl. She could not believe her husband could take something that belonged to her and give it to someone else. That was not acceptable to her so she played a game herself and made her husband think she was getting another apartment for him and her to live in so they could get back together. Randy was easily convinced, which didn't take much. He had a new car, which is what he did all he had done for, so he was ready to come back to Olivia anyway. Before he and Olivia got back together, Randy brought the bedroom furniture back to Olivia and gave her a diamond ring. Olivia didn't tell him, but she couldn't then and didn't ever want to sleep in the bed of that furniture again, knowing Randy slept in it with his mistress. She didn't want to have to look at the furniture everyday once she got another apartment and be reminded of Randy lying in it with someone else, so she sold it to her sister and brother in-law she was staying with. Olivia accepted the ring Randy gave her though, even though she knew he took it from that girl. The ring wasn't in a box when he gave it to her. He just pulled it out of his pants pocket and gave it to her. Olivia kind of felt the ring was owed to her since the girl had what belonged to her, her husband and her furniture. For real, Olivia knew having the ring wasn't right because she knew Randy had to have taken the ring from the girl, but she also knew her husband's intentions were good. Randy figured he had taken from his wife to give to the girl (even though he did it to get what he wanted), so he gave Olivia something that belonged to the girl, to make it up to Olivia what he had done. He wanted Olivia to know he didn't cheat for the fun of it, but for the money (sorta' speak), just like she did in her line of work. Olivia knew that was what her getting the ring was about, so she was glad to get it. Her streetlife way of thinking made her understand what was going on and be down (all for, in agreeance with) with the way her husband operated. From all the things she had seen and gone through previously, she had learned by this time how a person reaps what he or she sews, so she had a bad feeling about the games her husband played. She had no control over what Randy did though, so she just went with the flow. Apparently Randy's mistress was in love with him because she traded her car and had her mother co-sign for Randy to get the new car he had. Although, it was all on the strength that he had convinced the girl and her mom that he was going to marry the girl. Taking Olivia's furniture and moving into the apartment with his mistress was just a part of Randy's scheme to give merit to his proposal to her. The plot worked too, well enough for Randy to get the new car he wanted, but it soon backfired on his ass. No sooner than Randy brought Olivia's furniture back to her, took his clothes from the apartment he had with his mistress and started spending some nights with Olivia, he was arrested for having a sawed-off shotgun in his possession, so he had Olivia go and get his car from the scene where he was arrested and keep it for him until he got out of jail. That's what Olivia attempted to do, but two days later, she awakened early that morning, looked out the window of the bedroom she slept in and discovered the car was gone. Later that day, she found out that Randy's mistress and her sister had come in the middle of the night and taken Randy's car. "It was all a mess", said Olivia. For a minute, she plotted on getting the car back, but Randy told her not to worry, he would get it back when he got out of jail. The charge he was convicted of got him ninety days in the county jail, so Olivia chilled out and did her own thing for a while. Now tired from all the shit she had been going through with him, Olivia contacted her aunt who had moved from Los Angeles to Las Vegas and arranged to go to Vegas to stay with her aunt for a few weeks. She was more than ready to get away, but at the same time, she still wanted and was determined to have her own apartment with her own things. Since Randy sold the playpen living room furniture they had and she sold the bedroom set they had, Olivia didn't have anything to furnish an apartment with, so she had to get some more furniture before she got an apartment. Two days before she went to Vegas, Olivia had Tom charge to his credit card, thirteen hundred dollars of living room furniture for her. On the day she was to leave for Vegas, she made arrangements for the new furniture to be delivered to Sara's and Jean's house where the furniture would be stored until she returned from her trip and got another apartment. Then she took her trip to Vegas on a greyhound bus. The long ride to Las Vegas gave Olivia time to be by herself and think about things. She finally arrived in Vegas and stayed there with her aunt and uncle for three weeks.

Because she wanted to be a good wife and make her marriage work, Olivia wanted to stop seeing Tom, but during the course of hers and Randy's marriage since she returned from Alaska, dealing with all the shit Randy was doing helped her decide to continue dating Tom. She felt she had to so that she could make ends meet those times she had to take care of everything by herself plus spend money to help straighten out the messes Randy got himself into. After all that had happened, Olivia had no guilt about dating Tom neither. She knew that at any time, Randy might go up in (have sex with) one girl or another if they had something to offer him. What she did with Tom was for her and Randy. Since Randy was all about himself in his adultery and wasn't responsible in taking care of the household finances he and Olivia had, Olivia needed Tom or hers and Randy's asses would both had been on the streets or always living in someone else's home. Olivia didn't want that for herself, so she was gonna date Tom for as long as she needed to. When she was ready to return home from Vegas, it was Tom who purchased her airline ticket and picked her up from the airport. Even though she didn't desire Tom as a lover, she thought he was one of the best things that ever happened to her. Olivia respected Tom too, so he never actually knew she was married or that Randy (or Bernard for that matter) lived with her in the apartments she had. She thought it was better for her that Tom believed she lived alone, so that's the way she played him. When Olivia returned from Vegas, Randy was still in jail, but got out about forty-five days later. Because he had his business with the car to straighten out, Olivia didn't rush to get back with him right away. She and Randy did spend some nights together at her sister's apartment where she resided and other nights they spent at Randy's mom's house. That's the way things were for a couple or few months after Randy was back on the street (got out of jail). Finally, Olivia found another apartment back on the side of the bridge that Randy's mom lived on. The apartment was clean, but it was small and still wasn't the kind of home she really want to have nor was it in the neighborhood she wanted to be in. It was affordable for her though. The new furniture she had was beautiful, so it decorated the new apartment nicely. By this time, she had gotten a new bed and glass-top dinette set with velvet cushioned chairs that she made layaway payments on to buy. By now, Randy was trying to do right by her by staying away from the mistress bitch. As long as he had that car though, the girl tried to keep up with him and cause problems for him. That's when Randy decided to get rid of the car and get him another one that didn't have the girl's nor her mother's name on it. Thanks to the girl, Randy's plan was blown right out of the water (sorta' speak). When the car was reported stolen, the bitch of a girl told the insurance company where the car was, so the car was confiscated which caused Randy to lose it. That was all good to Olivia though, because she knew that would put an end to the girl's harassing him and being in hers and Randy's life. It was fucked up though, that of the adultery, of all the deceit and of all the trouble, Randy was worse off than he was before he started playing games with the girl. He had traded the Lincoln Continental he and Olivia had when he got the car his mistress helped him get. Randy still had his job though and about a month later, he had another car. He always had one car or another since Olivia first met him when she was with Bernard. A car was one of the most important things to him. Now that he had another one of his own and he and Olivia were back together in their new apartment, Randy chilled and everything was good between him and Olivia with the exception of Randy smoking wet. Olivia still smoked wet too, but she didn't put drugs before business. That's one of the reasons she didn't like smoking freebased cocaine. She loved getting high though. She just didn't believe in allowing drugs to have complete control over her and what she did, causing her life to become unmanageable and causing things to fall beneath the lifestyle she always tried to maintain. As one of the rules she made for herself, Olivia vowed to quit drugs if she were ever faced with a drug addiction that controlled her. Randy, on the other hand, played for help in supporting his drug addiction for wet (wet daddies). That wasn't Olivia's style. She liked having her own money and making her own money to buy what she needed or wanted. However, she and Randy probably stayed in the apartment they had during this time, longer than any other apartment they had. Olivia even enrolled in a business college to pursue her education and get knowledge for a career in accounting. Randy's sister Angel whom Olivia hung out and smoked sherm (wet) with, had graduated with their class from high school and worked a job everyday, so when Olivia returned from Alaska the last time and decided she wanted the "normal" life, Angel was her idol (sorta' speak). Olivia admired the way Angel went to work a job everyday, the way she dressed, the lady-like even preppy way she carried herself, the way she was respected and the fact she wasn't a square about getting high or the streettlife. She just never chose the life. Olivia didn't know what it was like to sit in a restaurant and have lunch with a friend or family member. The only time she went into a restaurant was in the evenings or at nighttime. Those were the times her days started. Suddenly, she began to notice the way she wanted to be different from the way she had been, but didn't know before how to be different or how different she would be once the change occurred. It was happening without her initiating it. "I'm sure now, that because of all that had happened to me, I finally wanted to get away from all the bullshit and nonsense and go to a safer more quiet and calm place or lifestyle. That's how and when the transformation began. Before, the streetlife was appealing to me, but my feelings about it were different now", said Olivia. Now (at that time) she was more comfortable than she had ever been since she first left home and she could let her new and different self transform at it's own pace. Always being attracted to the corporate world, the look or style of businessmen and women, Olivia bought and carried a brief-bag everyday, that was filled with her schoolbooks and she started dressing more conservative. She loved going to school too. She was going at her own will, no one forced her to go, so she was proud of herself and was determined to finish what she started. Looking back on the fact that she had always been down for money in many ways, it should have been obvious to her that the new her was to be a businesswoman. Who knows, maybe that was who and what she would have been in her earlier years, had she not been detoured to the wrong path she took.

Things were going well for Olivia at school. She was learning a lot and made good grades even though she smoked wet most evenings after school. Either Randy, Angel or both of them wanted to get a stick of wet on daily basis, so even when Olivia didn't intend to get high on a school day, all it took was for her husband or sister in-law to suggest it and it was on. "I don't see how I went to school everyday after smoking that shit in the evenings", Olivia admitted. By the grace of God, her mind was stronger than she ever knew it was.

Usually, Olivia didn't consider whether she was mentally strong enough to handle things she indulged in. She just recklessly did whatever came to mind and some things that others had in mind. "Man, it is almost unbelievable what all I put myself through", she said. "I just took a lickin' and kept on tickin", she added. She said it was almost like she was on autopilot. Olivia couldn't keep up with Randy and hang out late with him on school nights though. Even though she got high in the evenings, she had to retire early so that she could try and study or get herself ready for the next school day. Randy still wanted to kick it though, which soon caused problems between him and Olivia. He still went to jail too often and Olivia was sick of that, but when she came home one night being as picky as she is and detected something had gone on there while Randy had her sitting at his mom's house waiting for him to come and get her, that filled Olivia up with all of Randy's shit she could stand, so she clowned (went off on, fussed at) him that night. She then started to feel that he was gonna make her want to physically hurt him, so she decided again, that she was going to leave him. After she secretly found and paid the deposit down on an apartment on the side of town she was from, Olivia waited until the first day of the following month, to leave. She even ordered phone service to begin on the day she was to move into the apartment. That's when her check for disability would go directly to the bank, she would pay the first month's rent and move into the apartment. All the while she waited for that time to come, she arranged for her help to be ready to move her things when all systems were go (figuratively speaking). She did everything hush-hush though because if Randy knew she was going to leave, he would try and stop her or take her furniture again while she was away from home. On the first day of the following month, Olivia took Randy to work and kept the car so that she could go to the bank, go and pay the rent at the apartment she was moving into and get the keys to that apartment. On the second day of the following month, she laid in bed pretending to be asleep while Randy was in the shower getting ready for work. After he got dressed and was ready to leave, he woke Olivia up (or so he thought) to kiss her goodbye just as he did every morning before he left. Then he went out the door. Before he could leave the apartment building, Olivia jumped up from the bed and placed herself to the side of the window in the bedroom so that she could watch Randy drive off without him seeing her. When he drove off, Olivia got on the phone and called her helpers. Once they arrived, everything went like clockwork considering nothing Olivia had was packed. By one-thirty or two o'clock that afternoon, all the furniture and things were moved out of the apartment. The only thing left there was a cooler that belonged to Randy, his clothes and his shoes. Randy didn't pay for anything he and Olivia had in their apartment, so that's what Olivia left him with, nothing. By five o' clock or five-thirty that evening, the movers had all Olivia's furniture and things in the new apartment and had gone on their way. Olivia arranged the furniture and unpacked a few of the boxes she had, but she was exhausted so she fixed herself a couple of sandwiches, ate and then chilled. She was sad about leaving Randy the way she did, but she remembered him taking the other furniture she had and didn't want to give him the opportunity to dog her like that again. She was alright though. She soon fell asleep and had a good night's rest. The next day, she didn't call Randy, but she knew he would be worried about her even though he was angry, so she called Angel and told Angel she was okay. She also asked Angel to tell Randy she was sorry things had to happen the way they did, but she didn't tell Angel where she was. For now (at that time), she just wanted time to herself. After a week or two had passed, she informed Randy and Angel of where she had moved to. Three or four weeks from then, she foolishly let Randy move in. Of course things were all good at first, but a couple of months later, the usual bullshit started up again. Nothing had changed. Olivia was still a student at the business college and got some money back from her grant, so she was able to buy her first car she could actually call her own. Since she had her own wheels, regardless to what Randy did, she did what she had to do. A couple of months later when it had only been four months since she moved into the apartment she now rented, Olivia was more sure than she had ever been, that she didn't want to be with Randy anymore. When Randy came home high one day and Olivia told him that, Randy snapped like a postal worker. The man wanted to take the dinette set Olivia had just bought. Olivia couldn't stop him from taking it, but while the idiot was trying to put the glass top table in the back seat of his car which was not gonna fit, he broke it. While he was busy with the tabletop, Olivia called the police. The dispatcher took so long assisting her (as usual), that Randy had come back into the apartment and busted her on the phone with the police. He wanted to fight Olivia, but he didn't know how long he had before the police would come, so he left. The police arrived a minute or two after Randy drove off and they stayed a few minutes before they left. Ten minutes later, Randy busted open the door of the apartment in rage, grabbed some scissors and began slashing every pillow and cushion on the sofa and both chairs that went with it. Then he slashed the cushions on the chairs of the dinette set. Olivia wanted to stop him, but she didn't want him to cut her. When she motioned to grab the phone, Randy snatched the phone cord from the wall jack, then stormed into the bedroom and snatched the footboard of the new bed from the railing, stripping the wood on it so that the railing could not be attached to it anymore to hold a queen-size mattress. He fucked up every piece of furniture in the apartment that Olivia only had less than one year and all Olivia could do is stand there and cry, pleading with Randy to stop what he was doing. She was taught not to hate anyone, but on that day, she felt hatred towards her husband. Now that everything was fucked up, Randy left and didn't come back to the apartment that day. He did come back the next evening and apologized, but Olivia never accepted nor did she refuse the apology. She didn't have very much to say to Randy, which made him very uncomfortable. Olivia didn't feel there was anything to say at that point. The damage was already done. Because she didn't have any rapp (conversation) for him, Randy just got himself a change of clothes and left. Olivia was very humble and even a little bit angry at herself for giving Randy a key to the new apartment in the first place. After escaping from the last apartment with all of her things in tact, she was foolish or weak and gave Randy another chance to fuck her around again. For that, she was angry and blamed herself. About three weeks later, Randy was arrested for something or another and had to serve sixty days in the county jail. Olivia didn't wish that upon him, but she took advantage of him being gone and moved out of the apartment. This time, she was absolutely sure she was giving up on her marriage and didn't want to try and make it work anymore. Because Randy had marital rights and Olivia couldn't afford to dissolve the marriage at the time, she went and stayed with the same sister of hers, whom she stayed with before. Olivia's sister had moved into a house that was a block and a half from the apartment Olivia was moving from. Olivia put her furniture in the basement of another of her sisters' home who lived next door to the one she would be staying with. She wasn't too choosey at the time about anything. She felt she had paid for the wrong she did in Alaska and had been more patient than enough with Randy, but there had been too many sins committed in their marriage. At this point, she just wanted a place to lay her head, time to recollect herself and a safe place she could stay at until Randy got out of jail and had time to realize, come to terms with and accept the fact that his marriage was over. Olivia needed to give him that time after he was released. That way, she wouldn't have to worry about him busting down the door of the next apartment she got.

The year was now nineteen eighty-four and it was a couple of months past Olivia's twenty-fifth birthday. Already mentally feeling as though she was four or five years older than she actually was, Olivia was ready to settle down more so now, than she was before. She not only was sick of moving from apartment-to apartment, she was tired of it and tired of bullshit ass men. For now, she just wanted to be by herself to figure out what she wanted to do and where she wanted to go from here. She decided that when she did choose another man, he would be what she used to consider a square. This guy would be a man who has a good job, but not so that he could take care of her though. Olivia wanted a guy who had a good job so he could take care of himself and not financially depend on her. This guy would be a one woman's man (if there was such a guy) who was not from the streets, but had street sense. The idea this guy would have for fun would be to watch the ball games on TV at home or sometimes at a friend or family member's home, play dominoes or bid whiz, go to the movies, occasionally go out dancing or some shit like that and this guy would be one who didn't indulge in heavy drugs. It would be okay if he smoked marijuana because Olivia still wanted to smoke some good weed whenever she could. At this point, she felt she could and would quit all the other drugs she indulged in if she had a lifestyle that was fulfilling enough to take the place of the fun she had getting high. The idea guy she would choose when she was ready for another relationship, would be a guy who didn't hang out in nightclubs, but enjoyed going out every now and again. Last, but certainly not least, the idea guy would not have a criminal record or get into trouble with the law. This guy would be very family oriented who would consider her as a part of his family. Family picnics and bar-b-ques would be one of the things this guy would do for fun with Olivia by his side, representing him. Having get-togethers some days at their home or at someone else's home would also be a fun thing Olivia's idea guy would enjoy. This man is the idea man she would choose to be with the next time she got into a relationship. Since she had never expected anything of a man other than him being good-lookin', suave, sexy, clean, a fancy dresser, good in bed and ambitious for nice things, her idea man would definitely be a change for her that might take her to a more positive and productive level. Olivia had no idea how tall an order finding this man she dreamed of would be. She didn't go scouting for him though. She just put her mind and time into her education and existed until her old wounds healed and time passed that would put the distance she wanted to have, between her and Randy. That way, Randy could go on with his life and she could do the same. Olivia didn't make any plans yet because she just wanted to chill for a while and exhale. She expected Randy to come looking for

162

her when he got out of jail, so she had that yet to deal with, to make it clear to him their marriage was over and get past that before going to another phase. Sure enough, Randy came to Olivia's sister's home and pleaded his feelings and desires, but it didn't work. He even tried several more times on different days, but finally, he got the message that Olivia didn't want to be with him anymore. Eventually he stopped coming around. Olivia did some smart thinking when she went to stay with her sister at the time she did. She knew that Randy couldn't exercise his marital rights too well at someone else's home, he couldn't start no shit with her there and that's the way she wanted it. The only thing Randy could do about anything was to say what he had to say and move on. Those were the grounds Olivia wanted to be on when it was time for her to deal with him. It was for her best interest and it worked.

Olivia's sister and brother in-law entertained guest on regular basis. Actually, they had guest everyday. Olivia's brother in-law always had his friends over to the house to drink beer and shoot the shit. "Their house was pretty much a party house", said Olivia, but she said no strangers were allowed. Not only did brother in-law's friends drop by all times of the day or evening, Olivia's other siblings often dropped by. It was cool though. Olivia occupied a bedroom upstairs in the house. That's where she spent most of her time. She never tripped on the guys that came by to visit brother in-law. All of them were quite a bit older than she except one of them, since brother in-law was at least fourteen years older than she. That didn't really matter though. Olivia had always been attracted to men who were older than she, but she just didn't give any of brother in-law's friends a second look or any thought because she wasn't trying to get with anyone at the time. However, one night Olivia's sister and brother in-law were gonna take a ride with one of brother in-law's friends who was a year older than Olivia and another of their male friends was going along for the ride also. Olivia was upstairs chilling and watching TV that Friday night because she had no plans. She was doing what she wanted to be doing when her sister came up the stairs to her room and told her that Anthony (Tony) wanted her to ride with them. The ride they were taking was in Tony's car, so he was the driver at first. Tony wasn't the pretty-boy type of guy, all cool and shit like the kind of guy Olivia had been attracted to, so she felt no instant attraction to him the times she saw him. Tony had his shit together though, but Olivia didn't trip on seeing him or not seeing him. Since she was invited by him to go for the ride, she got up, powdered her nose and rode with the others to wherever they were going. The ride they took was fun. Everyone in the car were drinkers except Olivia, so she was the sober one. She can't say whether Tony was as intoxicated as he seemed or claimed to be, but he had brother in-law take over the wheel a little ways down the road and he got in the back seat where Olivia and their other friend was. Olivia's sister rode in the front seat with brother in-law so Olivia sat between the two guys in the back seat. By the time they all got back to Olivia's sister and brother in-law's home, Tony had flirted with and even gave Olivia a kiss. That was the beginning of their relationship of which Olivia didn't have a clue what she was getting herself in to since Tony seemed to be different from the guys she vowed to stay away from. Even though Olivia had not paid Tony any attention prior to this night, she thought he was a good catch, but she knew he had been and may have still been dating a girl she grew up with and went to school with. That was one of the reasons Olivia didn't give Tony a second look before. She got the four-one-one (information) that Tony was crazy in love with the girl and of all the good things he had done for her. Tony was from the opposite side of the bridge from the side Olivia and the girl were from, but he always hung out on the side of the bridge Olivia grew up on. By the time Olivia met him, he had been working for an airline for about seven years. Everyone who knew Tony called him "Big Bank" (as in Big Bank Hank) because he had or seemed to have money. The car he drove, the clothes and accessories he wore and the things he did made it obvious that he was having money. He was his own man, he was very popular, he was very charming, he wasn't a street-guy and he didn't have a criminal record of any kind. Tony drank beer quite a bit and on weekends or special occasions, he drank Hennessey or Remi Martin cognac, but he didn't do drugs. He didn't even smoke weed nor cigarettes. Tony danced when he was full (intoxicated), but he wasn't big on dancing. Therefore, he didn't go to nightclubs, but he did enjoy kickin' it at a friend or family member's home. He always had a seat somewhere watching a ballgame when one aired on TV. He even went fishing from time-to-time. Olivia didn't know a lot about him, but what she did know consisted of a lot of the qualities her idea man would have. He seemed to be the kind of man who didn't play games with women, he was honest for the most part and was caring or so Olivia thought. She thought Tony was the man she was destined to be with, so she dropped her guards and gave in to the desire she had been ignoring. Nothing physical happened between her and Tony the night they started digging (liking) one another. Tony had to go out of town the next day, but he told Olivia he would be back on a certain day at a certain time and he wanted a date to spend the night with her. Seeming to be a man of his word and being prompt as he was, Tony returned from the trip he took and arrived at Olivia's sister and brother in-law's house to see her on the dot of the time he said he would arrive. Olivia was so impressed. That was the night she and Tony consummated their relationship. Three weeks later, she was to move into an apartment back on the other side of the bridge that she wanted to share with Tony, so Tony had brother in-law and a couple of other friends of his to help move Olivia's furniture. Tony stayed the night with Olivia that night. The next morning, he left and said he would be back later, but he didn't come back that day. In fact, it was three or four days later when he returned. That was the beginning of the fucked up relationship Olivia ended up having with him, but again, was too weak to let go and too determined to make it work. Tony had all kinds of excuses and lies to explain the things that he did or didn't do. One night he stayed at the apartment with Olivia, when the morning after, Olivia's license plates on her car were gone. Another morning after a night Tony stayed with her, one of her tires was flat, so Tony began to use those incidences as his reason for staying away as long as he did. "He didn't come and see me for days at a time before my car was vandalized or tampered with, so that being his reason for staying away was bullshit", said Olivia. When she tried to persuade him to be at the apartment with her more often, Tony also used his job as an excuse for not being there. His job did give him an assignment in New York. He had a choice to go there or to Saint Louis, but preferred working in New York. On his days off, which usually were weekends, he came home, but never let Olivia know when he was coming and claimed he didn't come to town every weekend he had off. From that point to three years later, Olivia still had problems with Tony and that honest guy she thought he was, turned out to be a habitual liar. Tony was very private about what he did and whom he did it with, which was cool, but he was so secretive that he lied even when it wasn't necessary. Not only was he a liar, but the one-woman man Olivia thought he was, also turned out to be as big of a player as any street-guy she knew or knew of. For three years she hung on to the idea of the man she wanted Tony to be and once thought he was. All of the potentials for the kind of guy Olivia wanted to be with, was in Tony. It was as though he was trying to be different or that something happened in his past, maybe a relationship that went bad and hurt him or something, that scared him into being harder than he really wanted to be. However, he was nobody nice. Even though he was raised and went to school on the side of the bridge Olivia had moved to, Tony loved being on the side of the bridge Olivia was from. Therefore, Olivia found an apartment back on that side of town and moved from the apartment Tony helped her move into. This time, Tony didn't help her move her furniture because he had some lame excuse that Olivia accepted. She didn't give up on him though. She really didn't want to live in the city she was from, but since Tony spent ninety-seven percent of his time on that side of town, Olivia thought if she lived on that side, he would be with her or that she would see him more often. She was just so damn weak for a man once her feelings got involved. Olivia wanted to be stronger because she hated the fact that she couldn't walk away from or turn a guy down when she should if he wasn't treating her right. Instead, she would make herself available or do what she thought it took to be with him. That's what she had done with the men she dated before Tony and that's what she did with him as well. The three years she was involved with Tony, Olivia was there for him to be with when he wanted her to be, she hung around his family or anywhere she thought he would be, just to be near him and she continued to hold on even though she knew he was involved with or doing (having sex with) other women. Tony was a true player. He never rode around in his car, any of the women he dated unless it was late at night or if he had a male friend riding with him and he had the top floor of his mom's house set up like an apartment. That's where he supposedly lived, which was believable though. Tony had a double cylinder dead-bolt lock on the door that led to the third floor of his mom's house. On the third floor, was a sink and refrigerator, there was just no stove or bathroom. That didn't matter though because the bathroom is conveniently right next door to the stairway that leads to the third floor. Tony had his own phone service. He also had a sofa and chair on one side of the loft-like room, with his bed, two nightstands and a floor model TV on the other side of the room. He had a nice little set-up at his mom's house. That's why it was so believable that he lived there, but it was all just a game. Tony's room at his mom's house was his headquarters. His mom and family on that side of the bridge, drank whiskey and beer too and they often had guest and parties, so Tony's apartment or room was a place for him to crash (sleep, take a nap) if he wanted to, his office when he was on that side of town and did his business from there and it was a place for him to take a freak that he wanted to get busy with. You know, have sex with. In nineteen eighty-six, it was suspected that Tony was dating a woman a few years older than he, whom one of Olivia's sisters went to school with, but Olivia couldn't prove it and she found it hard to believe since the woman didn't seem to be Tony's type. Tony hardly spent time with Olivia during that time. When he did, it was for one night at a time and the times he did were several days apart. That's when Olivia started smoking freebased cocaine again, by then, called crack. She didn't smoke crack often though. She only did it when she was in the company of certain people. That year on her birthday was the first time since she and Tony started dating, that Tony spent time with her other than to spend a night and have sex with her. Even though Olivia had to buy everything, Tony cooked a shrimp dinner. He even told Olivia what to buy for the dinner, which consisted of the shrimp and ingredients along with a bottle of Hennessey cognac and a rock of cocaine. Olivia had never seen or known Tony to do drugs and was puzzled by him asking her to buy cocaine, but she didn't ask any questions. In fact, Tony didn't even do anything with the drug (the rock) while he was at Olivia's apartment, so she had no idea what was up with that. Since she started smoking crack again, she had gotten high with the wife of one of Tony's friends who worked with him. After giving it some thought, she figured someone had to have told Tony that she smoked crack. The only reason he would ask her to buy some would be if he knew she used the drug and knew where to buy it. Still, Olivia didn't trip. Being in the city where Tony hung out didn't make any difference in the amount of time he spent with Olivia though.

She even filed for a divorce thinking that would make a difference since Tony once used that as an excuse for his actions, but it didn't. After Olivia's apartment was broken into, she needed and was ready for a change, so the following month, she moved from the apartment she was in, to an apartment that was in her hometown, but was on the south side of the town. She stayed in the apartment she moved from, for one year and graduated from the business school she enrolled in to at least get a certificate in the field she majored in when she took classes at the business college she didn't complete. She was at a standstill as far as getting into and having a career in the field of her major, plus her relationship with Tony wasn't moving into a positive direction neither, so Olivia wanted to get away and recollect herself again. Feeling as though there was nothing she could do that would make a difference in hers and Tony's relationship, she developed a "fuck it" attitude and convinced herself that she didn't care anymore whether or not Tony was around. After she got settled into the new apartment and was trying to get used to the fact that she and Tony weren't going to be together, the tiny bit of attention he paid her while partying at her sister and brother in-law's house, broke down her defenses and she let him come back to her apartment with her when the party was over. After that night, Olivia had hope that she and Tony would be together once again, so she fell back into the cycle of calling him and trying to be where she thought she would see him. It was sickening to her how weak she was. She liked her new apartment and tried to focus on decorating it to keep from tripping on Tony, but often times she was lonely because Tony still didn't spend anymore time with her than he ever had. Olivia wanted badly to break it off with Tony and never again desire him, but it just wasn't happening. She heard it said by someone, that the best way to get over one man (or in a man's case, one woman) is to get another. Olivia really didn't want to be with anyone else, but she couldn't be with Tony neither, so she took heed to the wise cliché or solution to her problem and tried to have a relationship with another man. That relationship only lasted for about a minute (a really short period), so she still allowed Tony to come and visit her whenever he got the urge. Everytime Tony spent a night with Olivia, pulled her back under his spell. It was as though he did just enough to keep her feelings involved with him. It worked too. Olivia was still lonely at her new apartment, but she was gonna try and keep it and pray for things to get better one way or another. She ended up moving though, about six months after she moved in. The central air system flooded the apartment a couple of times, which gave her a reason to leave the cute but lonely apartment. Once again, she moved back to the area of town where she grew up. When she moved into the duplex she found, Olivia was very, very weak for Tony by then. The drugs she used didn't help matters neither, but Olivia didn't know that yet. Whenever she didn't have anything to do or when all else fell, she could still have a nice day, but she had a better day if she was feeling good on a high. She didn't jones for drugs as far as she knew at the time, she just enjoyed the way different drugs made her feel. Better than the way she felt when she was high, was the way she felt when she was with the man she loved. That and money were the two main things Olivia ever wanted other than good health. As much as she loved money, she loved and would choose a man over money any day, if he was worth it. The problem was just that everyone she chose, was full of game and full of shit. She wasn't giving up though. A few days before she moved into the new duplex, Olivia did jones (crave) for Tony plus she wanted to let him know where she was moving to, so she drove across the bridge where his mom lived. She wasn't sure if Tony would be there, but if he were, it would be worth the trip and if he wasn't, that would be okay because she took the chance to go and see. When Olivia arrived at Tony's mom's house, one of Tony's friends had just gone inside the house, so Olivia knew Tony was there, but when she got up to the screened-in porch and tried to open the door, it was locked. Olivia didn't even ring the doorbell. She didn't figure she needed to since Tony knew she was there and didn't leave the door unlocked so that she could get in. If he was busy, he could have hollered at Olivia from a window or something, but he didn't. Not wanting to look like a bigger fool than she felt she was, Olivia didn't wait around because it was obvious to her that Tony didn't want her there, so she turned around, went back to her car and left. Feeling all hurt and rejected, this was one time she consciously knew she didn't want to cope with what she was feeling, so she drove to a dope-house right around the corner from Tony's mom's house and bought herself a stick of wet (sherm) so that she could get high. After making her purchase, Olivia headed in the direction that would take her back across the bridge where she was from. Anxious to alter her mind so that she wouldn't think so much about Tony dissing (dismissing) her, Olivia pulled her car over off the road that was a couple of miles from Tony's mom's house and fired (lit) up the stick of wet. There she sat on the side of the road with tears rolling down her face and smoked half of the stick. Then she proceeded to drive so that she could get back across the bridge. Several blocks away when she had just about made it to the freeway, Olivia noticed through the rear view mirror, that a cop was driving behind her. She tried to be cool, but she had the other half of the stick of sherm between her fingers and had to put it away in case the officer pulled her over. Because she could only use one of her arms and hands and because her car didn't have a good wheel alignment, as she let go of the steering wheel just long enough to reach the ashtray, her car weaved to one side. After grabbing the wheel trying to play it off by acting normal and then trying again to reach the ashtray, the car weaved once again causing the officer to turn on his lights and siren and pull Olivia over. Olivia went to jail that day, was charged with driving under the influence and got her drivers license taken from her. After getting out of jail and then going to court thirty days later, she was only convicted of careless driving because the DUI charge was dropped since she was convincing when she claimed that she was on medication the day she went to jail. As a result of her conviction, Olivia's drivers license was suspended for one year, which confined her to only driving on the side of the bridge she was moving to. Actually, she wasn't suppose to drive at all, but like most human beings, Olivia often did things she shouldn't have or wasn't supposed to do. She knew though, that if she got pulled over on that side of the bridge without drivers license, she would only get a ticket. At least that's the way she looked at it. There went her sherm (wet) smoking days though. Distribution of sherm or wet was not common or plentiful on the side of the bridge Olivia was from, where she was moving back to. More common on that side of the bridge, than wet, was angel dust and crack, but Olivia was out of touch with those she knew who use to smoke angel dust (a different form of wet, all of the pcp family) and the dealers of that drug on that side of town. Therefore, she found herself hangin' out with crack smokers. Actually, Olivia only smoked crack with a select group of people and when she did, it wasn't very often at first. Two days after she went to court, she got the keys to her new place. On the same day, a city truck backed into her car, which caused her to be taken to the hospital. Since her cervical was fused after the gunshot injury she had suffered, x-rays were taken of her neck and back, but her only injuries were soreness and muscle spasms, so she was released with a prescription of pain medication, from the hospital's care. The following day when she had to be at the new place so one of the phone company's technicians could get in, she had not moved any of her furniture in, so she just hung around until the technician came. While she waited, Tony arrived unexpectedly since Olivia soon forgave him for dissing her the day she went to his mom's house and was locked out and she had given him the address prior to the day. While there, the two of them started conversating when Tony told Olivia the two of them could do a lot of things together if she didn't talk so much. Olivia took that to mean that Tony would spend more time with her if she didn't run her mouth, telling people what the two of them did together. Being that spending more time with him was all she had been longing for, Olivia assured Tony she could and would refrain from discussing their relationship with other folk. Olivia didn't understand yet, why their relationship had to be a big secret, but if that's what it took for her to have more time with Tony, she would keep quiet. Right after the code of secrecy was established, Tony didn't waste any time and asked Olivia to make a call and arrange to buy some crack and so Olivia did. He even gave her one hundred and fifty dollars for the purchase of a gram and a half of the dope (drug), so Olivia was cool with that. While she continued to wait for the phone technician and the delivery of the order she placed with the dope-man, Tony went and got the works they needed (a pipe, chore girl and grain alcohol to burn on cotton as a torch to smoke the crack with). The phone technician arrived soon

169

after Tony left and then the distributor arrived before Tony returned. About three minutes after the dope-man left, Tony returned and it was on (their intimate get-high party began). As secretive as Tony was, he probably waited around the corner and watched the dope-man leave before returning from the store so the dope-man wouldn't see him. He was funny like that, but smoking crack is not a thing smokers want publicly known, at least not in the early stage of their addiction. After using it a while though and it starts calling it's victim, it's not something a smoker can hide. For six months, Tony spent two to four days a week with Olivia, smoking cocaine, suckin' and fuckin'. Usually when he and Olivia smoked crack together, Tony bought it and he spent one hundred fifty to three hundred fifty dollars each time. "Shit, after about four months of that, I didn't even want to smoke as much as Tony wanted to buy sometimes, but I wanted to be with him", said Olivia, so she kept on smoking. The part she really hated, was the days Tony didn't come to see her or call. Now (by that time) she was on that end for him and crack. Even though she still didn't like crack, she wanted and craved it. That's what cocaine does to it's users. Especially crack. It affects the mind giving its users a mental craving for it, rather than a physical craving. It was exactly like someone once said, "when you've gotten on that end from smoking crack, it be callin' you to smoke more and more". Smoking crack is crazy and it's frightening. "It's like magic", is what Olivia used to say. The days Tony didn't call or come to see her made Olivia feel lonelier than she felt before. She then and had always wanted to be with him everyday. Now that she had two very intense cravings stirring inside of her when she couldn't be with Tony, she would go to her friend's house who was the wife of Tony's co-worker and hang out there getting high until the next day. "I mean late into the next day, not just until daybreak", said Olivia. "It was sinful", she said, when she found herself pawning her jewelry to the dope-man and writing checks for twenty or forty dollars that she didn't even have in the bank. By the fifth month of this madness, Olivia had even considered pawning her TV and other household items, but she didn't. That's when she knew she needed to stop doing this drug or at least slow down, which is very hard for a person to do at his or her own will. After getting home at about four o' clock one morning, Olivia was broke (penniless) and the entire amount of crack she spent her money on, was gone. There she was lying in bed wide awake, depressed because she didn't have anymore money and no more crack to smoke, she couldn't be with Tony and she couldn't go to sleep. That's when she saw a commercial on TV, of what was called the Care Unit. The Care Unit was an in-patient drug treatment facility, that was one floor from the top of one of the hospitals on the opposite side of the bridge. Just about desperate enough to drive to that hospital that morning, Olivia called the number that was advertised on the commercial and pretended she was calling for someone else. She got all the information she would need if she decided to admit herself, but didn't use the information, not at that time. By the sixth month of the crack smoking madness, Olivia couldn't stand herself. After being up all night and through the early morning into the next day once again, she got home already in a state of depression and couldn't chill, that she went into such a state of isolation, she didn't even want to open the blinds on the windows of her duplex that after noon. She was just about ready to try the Care Unit for help, but she calmed down as the time went by and eventually crashed (fell asleep). Two nights or mornings later, Olivia couldn't take anymore of the depression she felt and the craving of the devilish drug. That's when she drove herself to the Care Unit around four o' clock that morning and admitted herself into a thirty day in-patient treatment and twelve step program. After going through two days of detox, Olivia felt better. For thirty days, she was drug-free and for thirty days when she sat with a group in the program, introduced herself and was to state whether she was a recovering addict or alcoholic, she just said her name and looked to the next person for that person to introduce him or herself. She didn't think she was what her idea of a drug addict was, so she couldn't, didn't and refused to classify herself as an addict, but she was. It just took her a little while longer to realize it. Olivia didn't go into the treatment program with the mentality that she didn't want to do drugs anymore. She just wanted to get away from drugs for a few weeks, pull herself together and get a grip on the things that were becoming unmanageable. Admitting herself into the treatment program was a spur of the moment decision. She didn't even mention the program to Tony or tell him she was going. It was a few days after she was admitted, that Tony found out. He was cool with it though. The only question he had about it was when Olivia would be home. That made Olivia feel as though he missed her, so she was anxious to go home. She thought that maybe now, since she and Tony were spending a lot of time with each other and shared a lot with one another, their relationship could be different and better. That's what Olivia thought until the day she was released from the care unit. After going through the twelve step program and the ceremony in her honor on her last day of the program, no sooner than she got home, Tony arrived, gave her a couple of hundred dollar bills and told her to have the dope-man deliver a package to her. Still weak and sick in the head because she was in denial about being a drug addict, because she didn't intend to stop getting high and because she missed Tony, Olivia was game for the plan even though she felt a little bit guilty. She really didn't have intentions on gettin' back to getting high so soon, but since Tony brought it on, she couldn't resist. That first day Olivia got out of treatment and smoked as much crack as she did (even if she only had one hit of it or any drug), set off a repeat of the way things were before she went to treatment, but this time, things got worse like the therapist at the care unit said they would. Olivia and Tony smoked more than they did before. Still, there were days and nights that Tony wasn't around. It became very obvious to Olivia that he only came to see her and was only gonna come and see her if he wanted to get high. She constantly called his phone line at his mom's house, but ninety-eight percent of the time, he wasn't there or didn't answer the phone. What Olivia didn't understand was where Tony stayed when he wasn't at his mom's house. She suspected he was staying with another woman those times though, but he wasn't with neither of the ladies whom were obvious to her he would be with. She knew where those women lived and of course she drove by their apartments to look for Tony's car on many occasions. The older woman Tony met at Olivia's sister's house, came to mind, but she was the least obvious one because Olivia just couldn't believe Tony would choose that lady over her or one of the other women he was fuckin'. The older lady wasn't very feminine, which seemed to have always been a quality in women Tony admired just like most men, but she was the only one Olivia couldn't investigate because she didn't know what was up with her or where she lived. Maybe she was the secret woman Tony spent real, quality time with. By now, Olivia started to feel that if smoking crack and freaking with Tony was the only time she could have with him, she wasn't sure she wanted it. On that end though (mentally trapped), she was powerless and couldn't break away. All along, she told Tony she wanted to live with him where the two of them could share one household. Tony promised her time and time again, they would be together like that and that he was going to move in with her at a certain time. When that time came, he had a bullshit story to tell and claimed he was gonna do it at another time. Whenever it was time for him to put up, he made up some other shit that was going on or that he was waiting for to happen, just to put it off longer. Olivia kept waiting, not really believing the shit Tony told her, but gave him the benefit of a doubt. Even though she was going along with the program, she wanted more, so she figured if she continued to invest the time, she would get what she wanted one day. She had learned quite a bit about relationships and men over the years, so by now, she wasn't as naive as she once was, but she was still weak though and was still a sucker for love. The days she didn't see Tony, gave her time to analyze their relationship from the time they started smoking crack together. Olivia knew she was only able to be with Tony more because he had a private place to smoke and someone to freak with to boot (as a bonus). He was getting what he wanted and didn't want anything more. At least not with Olivia.

Because Olivia had smoked so much crack and couldn't say no to the drug, she started thinking, "perhaps I am a drug addict", but still couldn't turn down the opportunity to smoke. Apparently Tony was tripping on how much she wanted to smoke and how she could freak all night because he became suspicious about what she did when he wasn't around and wanted to get high. Tony wondered what Olivia would do, you know, how far she would go for a chance to smoke crack when she didn't have any money. While tripping, he decided to set a trap for Olivia, to find out just how badly she wanted to smoke and what she would do for it. One night while Olivia was at hers and Tony's mutual friends' home getting her smoke on (smoking crack), all that she had money to buy was gone, so she was basically just hangin' around. Just as a lot of other friends did, a guy whom Olivia met a while back, walked into her friend's house looking for the man of the house (Tony's co-worker). The guy who came to visit also worked with Tony, so Olivia figured he was cool. After one thing led to another, the guy asked Olivia to get high with him and wanted to do it at her duplex. Knowing how men are sometimes when they're alone with a girl or when a girl invites him into her home, Olivia didn't think taking the guy to her duplex, was a good idea. The setting there was too intimate plus guys tend to think they have sexual action (offer, opportunity) with a girl, when she invites them to her home. Therefore as a rule, Olivia didn't do that unless it was someone she was interested in, so she told the guy he could only come to her home if her girlfriend came along. After kickin' the thought around and not wanting to seem he had another motive for wanting to go to Olivia's duplex, the guy agreed to her girlfriend tagging along. Olivia had her car, so naturally, her girlfriend would ride with her and they would meet the guy at her place or he would follow them. She waited for her girlfriend to go to another room and do whatever she had to do before leaving. The guy who wanted to get high with Olivia, was going from room-to-room conversating with Girlfriend and her husband. When both girlfriend and the guy came back into the room where Olivia sat, the guy informed Olivia that girlfriend was gonna ride with him so that she could make the drug purchase, which was believable. None the wiser of what was really going on, Olivia was down with the new plan (in agreeance with), went home and waited. Fifteen minutes later, the guy and Girlfriend arrived. Just in case someone (a non smoker) dropped by, when Olivia smoked at her home, she did it in the bedroom, so that's where she took her guest. The smoke-out was on and poppin', but twenty minutes after it started, girlfriend said she had to make a run back to her house and check on her kids or something. The guy she and Olivia were getting high with, was gonna let her use his car to make the run, but Olivia offered her car, so Girlfriend left and said she would be right back. Olivia really didn't want to be left alone with the guy, not because she thought he would try and take advantage of her because that would've been stupid of him since girlfriend and her husband knew him and knew he was there. Olivia didn't even want him to try and hit on her (push up on, come on to), but she was cool and didn't trip. Sure enough though, the guy tried to get his flirt on, but it was all verbal. After Olivia casually set him straight in the nicest possible way, she and the guy continued to get high and had a nice conversation about general shit, nothing in particular. It must have taken

173

girlfriend forty minutes or an hour to return. Olivia wasn't angry with her when she returned because she handled the situation being left alone with the guy. She just thought it was faulty (a negative move) that her girlfriend agreed to be at the duplex to run interference, but left her alone with the guy. Still today, Olivia wonders if the guy paid or gave Girlfriend a rock (a piece of crack) in exchange for being left alone with her, giving him time to put his mack down (words of persuasion). With the way a lot of people are when they are on crack, that kind of set up is not far fetched. Worse things have, can and will happen while one is under that drug's influence. After Girlfriend returned, the guy left a few minutes later and Olivia took Girlfriend home. No problem. After getting to Girlfriend's home, Olivia stayed and visited a while. Actually, she was waiting around until it was well past the time Tony got off work, which was midnight. The time got to be one thirty or two a.m. Sometimes Olivia hung around Girlfriend's house just so she could, maybe, run into Tony. By that time though, she knew Tony wasn't gonna be through there (stop by), so she went on home and messed around until she came down from the high she was on. A couple of hours later, she nodded out (went to sleep). The next day, Olivia carried on as she usually did, hoping this was a day she would get to spend with her boo (honey, man, lover, Tony). Early that afternoon, the phone rang and she answered it not giving a thought to whom it might be. She certainly didn't think it was a call regarding the night before. Nothing happened that wasn't kosher, so Olivia wasn't tripping. When she answered the phone expecting a pleasant "hello" from the person on the other end though, what she heard was the other party saying, "you took the bait fool" and then a click. The male caller said what he had to say so fast and quickly hung up, that Olivia wasn't sure, but the voice sounded like Tony's. After thinking about how the night before went and mentally analyzing the voice she heard, Olivia came to realize that the caller was Tony. What he had to be thinking was very disturbing to her and she couldn't help but to wonder if others thought about her, the same things Tony apparently thought. All Tony had to do was ride by the duplex when he got off work and see his co-worker's car parked outside, for him to assume the same thing that went on when he was there, was the same thing going on with his co-worker. When Olivia thought long and hard about the way everything went down, what she figured out blew her mind (sorta' speak). It seemed to her, that Tony paid or made a deal with his co-worker (his friend) to approach her about getting high with him, just to find out if she would suck and/or fuck him for a high. Olivia can't say for sure just what the deal was, but from the phone call she got, getting high with that guy was obviously a trap and when it all became clear to her, she could even see that girlfriend had her role to play in the plot, not with Tony, but with his co-worker. She could hardly believe the whole damn incident went down. All that day, she tried to reach Tony by phone to explain to him what actually happened, but she never did get a hold of him. That was the day she said, "fuck this shit" and decided she was going back to treatment for another thirty day in-patient program. Since she was released from the care unit the first time, she thought a few times about going back, but knowing what Tony thought of her, along with other shit she had gone through, Olivia was more interested than before, in the treatment program. This time though, she was going to admit she was a drug addict, that she was powerless over alcohol and drugs, that her life had become unmanageable and that she didn't want to get high anymore. She had gotten sick and tired the last time, but now she was sick and tired of being sick and tired. It had been a long time comin', but now it was time for a change, so Olivia called the same hospital to find out if she could be re-admitted. To her disappointment, she was informed that it had not been thirty days since she was released from their care, so she couldn't be admitted again for the treatment program until then. Olivia really wanted to be re-admitted right away because she knew she wouldn't be able to refrain from smoking crack until she could go back to the care unit. She wanted to get away right then and get the help she needed. Since the city truck backed into her car before she moved into the duplex, Olivia had physical treatment in rehab at another hospital, then she saw a chiropractor three times a week. Even though she got high quite a bit, she still took care of any business she had; kept her hair done; kept her duplex clean and decorated; paid her rent; she made sure she at least paid enough on her bills to keep her phone and utilities on; she paid her tabs and got her jewelry back from the dope-man whenever he held it for her; she kept her appearance up and still dressed well, so she was no slouch. It was very, very hard to do the right thing though, when she had a craving to do the wrong thing. The struggle was too great and that was one of the reasons she didn't wanna do it anymore. Olivia was and had for a long time been a drug addict. It just took that bad ass crack for her to realize it. As tired as she was of what seemed to have been like a rat race, she was actually glad the time had come for her to change a little bit more than she already had. Because she knew Tony wasn't really her man, Olivia still dated Tom, so she always had the things she needed and some of the things she wanted. Tom was the man and Olivia didn't care how much she liked or wanted Tony or anyone else. She vowed that she would keep on seeing Tom until another man would do for her, what Tom was doing or at least be with her the way she wanted to be with a man. In a nutshell (sorta' speak), she knew all along which side her bread was buttered on. Because of the back injuries she suffered from the city truck backing into her car that day, Olivia knew she would be getting a settlement on the claim she made, really soon. All the while she had been smoking crack, getting a new car had top priority on the list she made of the things she was gonna do with the money she would get. Smoking crack was not on the list, but there was no way she would be able to resist spending the remainder of that money on crack after she got a new car. She never intended to spend a lot of money on the drug, so she tried really hard not to make plans to smoke when she got the settlement money. She always hoped the desire would go away when she was broke and not come back when she got money from whatever source it came from, but it never worked out that way. Since she had decided to go back to drug treatment as soon as time allowed her to, Olivia also decided and was determined to quit drugs for good. The things she had gone through while smoking crack, really opened her eyes to the whole drug scene and now (at that time), she wanted to get away from it all. Once again, she found herself wanting to be a little more different than she had been. First it was money, then it was men, then it was drugs, then it was prostitution and now (at that time), more drugs and another man she couldn't have. Those were the desires that caused the majority of the problems and bullshit she had gone through. Olivia really wanted to do good and productive things with the money she got from the settlement she was waiting for. She didn't want to crave the evil drug called crack anymore and wanted to be able to get a good night's sleep when she laid her head down, so going back to drug treatment and quitting drugs was where she needed to start. Now that she no longer worked the stroll, maybe she could see more clearly and make better decisions about money, men and general life stuff, if she were drug-free and clean. Getting to the road of being a better person and having a better life, depended on Olivia getting and staying sober. This was a really good time for her to start on her road to recovery. That way she would be sober when the city settled with her and she would be able to spend the money wisely. Since she had to wait to be re-admitted into the drug program though, Olivia got real with the situation and smoked crack whenever she could. It was two weeks later when she would be able to go back to rehab, so she figured she might as well get her smoke on (smoke crack) because once she went back through the doors of the care unit, that would be the end of her drug using days. She was serious this time. Meanwhile, other bad things happened that positively convinced her that she didn't want to get high anymore after doing another thirty day in-patient treatment program. She didn't tell Tony she was going to treatment this time neither. This time she had it in her mind that she was gonna show him something because apparently, he thought she was some kind of freak who only required to be fucked and was only good enough for him to use. Tony didn't mean Olivia any good and if all the wrong he had done to her wasn't enough for her to realize it, she soon found out the real deal after she got out of treatment. Way before then, it was two days before she was to admit herself into rehab and she felt she couldn't even take one more day of what she was going through. That's why she took the risk of driving to the other side of the bridge and stayed at her aunt and uncle's home, until her admission day.

The time came when Olivia would surrender herself to a higher power greater than herself, whom she chose to be God. Talk about exhaling, she felt a great deal of weight be lifted off her, just knowing a change had come. For thirty days, she worked the twelve steps to sobriety. She even admitted she was a grateful recovering drug addict and potential alcoholic when she introduced herself in the group meetings. Through the fire (sorta' speak, of all the things she had gone through), one of the things about her that had not changed, was her love for money. She was grateful for the social security checks she still got every month, but she wanted nice things and money to buy what she needed and wanted. Olivia always had a desire for extravagant things and a high dollar lifestyle that her social security income couldn't buy her. With the use of only one of her arms and hands, there weren't a lot of things an employer would hire her to do and although she majored in and got a diploma in accounting, company's required an applicant for employment, to have a degree, work experience and even knowledge of computer accounting, which Olivia did not have since that wasn't included in the courses her major consisted of at the time. Not that she wasn't good at accounting or couldn't do certain other jobs, like bookkeeping. Olivia learned that a lot of employers either didn't think she could do a job, they thought that perhaps she could do the job, but wanted someone with the use of both hands who could do the job faster or better or they didn't even want to give her a chance. As soon as her head was a little clearer, she thought of some good financial ideas that were legit. Concentrating more on her sobriety though, organizing a plan was a little bit premature for her at the time. That's where Tom came into play, along with the amateur drug dealing she did. Even though she felt it was wrong and double standard, Olivia still got prescription drugs for illnesses she had and sold them to her select client who had been clients of hers the entire four or five years she got the drugs. Her prescription drug deals were her main source for money to smoke crack, other than Tony sporting her. Tony spent big money on crack, so Olivia didn't have to spend a dime when she smoked with him. The couple of times she did write checks when she had insufficient funds in the bank, she had direct deposit for her disability checks, so the bank cleared the checks that came in because they could get the bank's money back off the top of her monthly deposit. Sometimes Olivia sold the food stamps she got every month too, so as crazy as it all was, it all worked out. She still had her duplex when she went back to treatment though, so she had to do what she had to do to keep her rent and bills paid so she would have a home to go to when she left the hospital. That's the reason when she got her medication slash product in, she had her best client come and visit her, who, fortunately for her, purchased the whole package she had. How sick can a person be? Of course unless he or she was a money dog (loved money) like Olivia was. Olivia had it bad though because she had a lot of character defects that she acquired from her streetlife, she was a drug addict and she loved money. Now that she was getting help, she could look at her defects of character by taking inventory of herself to identify with those defects and then ask God to remove them. It takes a lifetime for all the defects a person has, to be removed, but Olivia had taken the first step and the rest would come one day at a time.

Since she wasn't supposed to be driving, knowing she would be getting a new car soon and wanting a clean slate with her driving record when she got her settlement, Olivia thought it was best to sell her car. Her driver's license would soon be reinstateable, so she got rid of the old car she had while she was ahead. She was trying to get her shit together all the way around so that once she was out on her own, she wouldn't have any reason to sneak around. She was still about the Benjamins though, but she put her all into the treatment program. It wasn't until her last week there, that she contacted Tony and then it was by mail. There was no return address on the envelope neither. Tony's name and address was the only information on it and Olivia also neglected to mention in the letter, where she was. She only wrote Tony because she had some choice words for him about the little set-up he orchestrated and how she felt about it. Just like she now was about drugs, she was just about at her roads end with Tony as well, so she put him on hold. She could never do that before, but she was getting stronger and she wanted Tony to know that. She wanted to feel she could stay away from him because she wasn't as weak anymore as she had been. She felt better about herself than she had ever felt and was now better able to control herself. On her last day of treatment, Olivia attended another ceremony in hers and a couple of other's honor. That was standard procedure for everyone who completed the thirty-day program. Olivia had really learned a lot about drug addiction this time she went to treatment. One of the things she learned and took a good look at, was how she dealt with loneliness and idle time. Many, if not most, drug addicts and other folk have a problem with those things. Some are conscious of it, some are not. For fear of being lonely or that having too much idle time may cause her to want to get high, Olivia made arrangements to go from the hospital's care unit, to a halfway house for drug addicts. She didn't have a desire or thought about getting high and she wanted to keep it that way. The halfway house is where she stayed for five or six weeks. Still doing business with her medication like clockwork, Olivia had always refilled her prescriptions every sixty days. That was the set-up she had with two physicians at two different clinics, so she was still clocking dollars (making money). Seeing her doctors when it was time for her to see them and getting her prescriptions filled, were basically the only times she left the halfway house. She was able to get a weekend pass after being there for two weeks, but since the program told her and she thought it was a good idea that she change her playmates and playgrounds, there wasn't really anywhere she wanted to go to and she was cool with that. It wasn't until she had to leave the halfway house one day, to go to the side of the bridge she was from and get her refills from one of her doctors, that she saw Tony for the first time in almost two months. As she got off the bus that took her across the bridge and walked to meet her sister who was taking her the rest of the way to see her doctor, Tony drove by, recognized her and immediately made a u-turn. Olivia could tell he was happy to see her. He wanted to know where she had been. Olivia told him where she had been and where she was staying, so Tony asked her to spend a Friday or Saturday night with him that following week. Thinking that things might be different between them now, Olivia agreed to spend the next Friday night with Tony. She was making an effort to be a better woman so she hoped Tony would see that and desire her enough to want to do more with her than get high and fuck, but that was just wishful thinking on her part. That next Friday evening, he picked her up from the halfway house and quickly took her to her duplex. He didn't even pass go or collect two hundred dollars (sorta' speak, as in monopoly). No sooner than they got there, Tony commenced to taking his clothes off (with not one fuckin' romantic gesture nor verbal expression), laid a sack of crack cocaine on the table and began preparing it to take a hit (a puff). Olivia was very disappointed in him going there, knowing she was trying to stay sober, but Tony didn't give a fuck. He got her on that end initially, got her on that end after the first time she was released from the treatment program and he wanted to get her back on that end this time. All he cared about or wanted, was a freak to go up in and to get his dick sucked while he sucked on the crack pipe that is also known as a dick (a glass one because of the long stem one puts his or her mouth on, to smoke the drug). Stronger by now and determined to be drug free, Olivia didn't shy away or get bent out of shape (sorta' speak) nor did she participate. She didn't even have a bit of desire to get high, but she was in a trying position. What she should have done, was tell Tony she wasn't about smoking crack or doing any kind of drugs anymore and to put the drug away, but she wanted to be him, so she didn't say anything. After Tony hit (took a couple of tokes) the crack pipe a few times and freaked (had sex) with Olivia for a few minutes, he took a short break and told her he wanted her to get high with him. Immediately, Olivia broke out into tears. She didn't have to say anything. Tony knew right away that she was crying because she really didn't want to get high. After he comforted her, told her not to cry and that she didn't have to smoke if she didn't want to, Olivia stopped crying and Tony continued smoking. Olivia pulled herself together and was there for Tony to freak with, even though she didn't want to be around the drug and shouldn't have been around it at that stage of her recovery. A week later, she discharged herself from the halfway house. She withstood the test and turned down the opportunity to get high with Tony, so she knew just how much stronger she had gotten and figured she was ready to go home. Even though she didn't get high anymore, Olivia still let Tony come to the duplex when he wanted to and do his thang, which for her was like playing Russian roulette. Tony didn't care though. Just as it is with any other man, he also did to a girl what a girl let him do, so as long as Olivia let him treat her the way he did, Tony didn't give it a second thought. This went on throughout the remainder of Olivia's stay in the duplex. Four months after she returned home, she got the settlement from the City and bought the car of her dreams (at that time). In March of the following year (nineteen eighty-eight), she moved out of the duplex and moved into a nicer apartment not too far from the duplex. With no respect for her sobriety and continuing recovery, Tony carried on with his smokathons at her new apartment. Still weak for him, Olivia allowed it. She still tripped on Tony's whereabouts the days and nights he didn't come to her apartment and she prayed for the wisdom of what was best for her. That gave her faith that the truth would be revealed to her and that she would be given the strength to leave Tony alone. Sure enough, in August that year, Olivia found out Tony was and had been living with the older woman she least expected he would be with. It was even revealed to her that Tony had plans to marry the lady, which broke Olivia's heart to hear of. Knowing how some people get shit started by assuming and knowing how Tony lied about everything, Olivia didn't rely solely on the four-one-one she got. She investigated the info herself. That way, Tony wouldn't accuse her of going by he-say, she-say on what she believed. It only took two weeks though, for Olivia to see for herself that Tony was involved with the older woman. She scouted the area where Tony frequented and was usually seen. On different days, she rode the streets from one neighborhood to another, looking for his truck to be parked where he, apparently, resided. Finally she spotted it. Not sure if the truck was parked where it was because Tony was visiting, Olivia didn't jump to conclusions. To be sure of what the deal was before reacting, she drove by the house the truck was parked at, a few more times. That last time, she went by the house during the daytime because Tony worked from three pm til midnight and she figured the lady worked during the day. Kind of surprised but not really, Tony's truck was parked in front of the same house once again, so this time Olivia went to the door and knocked. Autumn had not come yet, so the main door was open behind the glassed storm door on the house. That's why Olivia stood a little bit to the side of the door so Tony wouldn't see her and not answer the knock on the door. Tony did come to the door, was very surprised and of course, had an attitude with Olivia about her coming there. He didn't go off (get violent) on her though. He knew he was gonna want to come to her apartment again, to get some head (blowjob) and some pussy while he smoked his shit (crack). After having words with him, Olivia left, went home and just about cried her heart out. She didn't want to run out, buy some drugs and get fucked up, but she did want to go to sleep temporarily, so that she wouldn't think about all she had been through with Tony. Since she was serious about quitting drugs when she went back to treatment though and being determined to do just that, by this time, her sobriety meant the world to her. She didn't want any drugs. That includes alcohol. Olivia was proud of herself for being clean and sober for almost a year and she didn't want to mess that up, so she just endured the pain in her heart until it slowly eased up and she made it up in her mind that she was no longer gonna be a glutton for punishment she got being involved with Tony.

Finding out Tony was living with and engaged to marry the older lady, was it for Olivia. After she told him she was through with him, Tony took her as a joke and tried to play his way back to her apartment. It didn't work though. He then realized how firm Olivia was with her decision to not be with him anymore, stayed away and didn't contact her for almost three weeks. That gave Olivia time for the heartache she had, to subdue. "I don't know why I was so surprised Tony chose someone else to be with the way I wanted to be with him. For one thing, I was weak. Then too, why would a guy buy the damn cow when he can get the milk free (sorta' speak). Hum! I guess I had to grow a little bit more and experience some things, to learn and see it that way", said Olivia. Now determined to not go back to Tony though, she started going to nightclubs again. It had been at least five years since she did the club scene, but she felt that being noticed by other men might boost her esteem that she always had high levels of and might encourage her even more, to stay away from Tony, so she tried it and it worked. When Tony came around after he probably felt he had given Olivia time to miss him and he tried to resume a relationship with her, Olivia turned him down and sent him on his way. She knew that Tony only stayed away as long as he did because he was hoping she would get weak for him the way she had always done and would let him back in. Finding out he was involved with the older lady was one thing, but Olivia was deeply humiliated, knowing that so many of Tony's friends and his family members knew who he was with and who he really cared about. Realizing how big of a fool she was and how everyone except her knew it, fucked Olivia up. She didn't want anymore of Tony's shit and she didn't want anymore of him, so at this point, there was nothing he could do to get her back. Of course he tried a few more times though, but it still didn't work. Soon after Olivia started kickin' it at the clubs, she saw a gorgeous guy at the club she most frequented. Olivia was very attracted to this guy, was introduced to him by her girlfriend whom she was out with and she ended up dating the brother for the next two years. This guy had a job, his own apartment and his own car when Olivia met him, so she was impressed and pleased to see that the brother was holding his own. A couple of months later, the brother started sleeping at Olivia's apartment most nights, but he didn't move his clothes and things in. Olivia was well over Tony by now, but Tony didn't think so. He had not been around for a little while, but there were times he called. When Olivia talked to him on the phone, he never asked if he could come to see her, but he would pause at different times during the conversation, hoping Olivia would ask to see him, but she didn't. One night he dropped by the apartment building Olivia lived in and rang the doorbell to her apartment so that she would let him in the secured building's door. Olivia answered the door, but she didn't let Tony in because she was expecting the new guy she was now kickin' it with and she told Tony that. She had never kicked Tony to the curb for someone else, so he wasn't too happy to hear she was expecting a visitor. The new guy Olivia was dating, came to see her regularly and spent the night everytime he did, so Olivia liked him quite a bit and didn't want to mess that up. That's why she didn't have a problem telling Tony he couldn't drop by to see her anymore. That was the last time he came to her apartment. Olivia was well into her sobriety also. She was sure by now that she wanted to live the rest of her life drug free and she had changed her playgrounds and most of her playmates, but maybe once a week or usually once every two weeks, she went by her girlfriend's home, whom she smoked crack with when she wasn't getting high with Tony. More often than she should have, Olivia took her girlfriend to pick up a sack (the packaged drug), usually from the dope-lady whose house she and her girlfriend got high at when they weren't getting high at Girlfriend's home. They hardly ever got high at Olivia's duplex. Anyway, Olivia was taught in the drug program, that she should change her playmates. Not some of them, but all of them. That is, all of those who were drug addicts or users. There are many good reasons why a person recovering from drug addiction should do that, but Olivia had yet to learn other reasons why she needed to stay away from   playgrounds and playmates that were associated with any drug, in any way. One evening she made a casual visit to see her girlfriend, just to sit with her for about twenty or thirty minutes and shoot the shit (conversate). Although Olivia was recovering from drugs, Girlfriend was still smoking, but was sitting there at her home all alone without any crack and no ride, so of course she took advantage of the opportunity to have Olivia give her a ride and of course she wanted Olivia to take her to the dope-lady's house. Girlfriend and the dope-lady were real cool with one another and the dope-lady would give Girlfriend a little somin'-somin' (something, something) or give her something on credit, so Olivia gave Girlfriend a ride to cop (score). Knowing how the dope-lady carried on conversations with some of her regular customers, Olivia thought she ought to go in the dope-house with Girlfriend, to try and speed the transaction up so that she wouldn't be hangin' around that type of place too long. She didn't like going to places like that anymore. She really didn't even want to give someone a ride or be in a car with someone or others who were making a drug run (purchase). She was only being a friend because she related to how Girlfriend must have felt sitting at home tweaking (fidgeting), wanting to hit the pipe. After getting to the dope-house, the door person whom Olivia went to school with, let Olivia and Girlfriend in and announced to the dope-lady they were there. The door person then directed Girlfriend towards the stairs and told her to go on up to where the dope-lady had many other times and was at that time, serving her customers. A couple of guys were downstairs where Olivia sat and waited for Girlfriend, but they were leaving right as Girlfriend was going upstairs and they told the girl on the door they would be back. No sooner than the guys went out the door, the door person headed up the stairs. Olivia knew Girlfriend would get engrossed in conversation and smoking a little dope upstairs since the dope-lady got her smoke on (smoked crack) as well, so she spoke out to the door-girl to tell Girlfriend not to leave her downstairs waiting for a long period of time. Olivia didn't want to go upstairs and she didn't want to sit downstairs waiting too long because for some reason, she felt very, very uncomfortable. She was ready to go. Less than five minutes after the door-girl got upstairs, Girlfriend came downstairs with the door-girl behind her, who let her and Olivia out the door. Olivia didn't show it though, but she was very relieved to be out of that house. A car pulled up across the street from the dope-house, which wasn't unusual because there was always someone already there purchasing some crack or smoking it and there was always someone coming in or leaving out of that house. Olivia's car was parked in the driveway. She and Girlfriend were in her car by the time the driver of the car that pulled up, had gotten out of his car, so they were just about on their way. By the time Olivia started her car, the driver of the car that pulled up, was walking up the sidewalk along the driveway. After getting a few steps past Olivia's car, the guy back-tracked, walked over to Olivia's car and looked through the windows while asking at the same time, if the dope-lady was in the car, whom he called by name. Olivia and Girlfriend both replied at the same time, "no, she's not in here". They both thought the guy seemed awful mysterious. Neither one of them had seen the guy before, but he was more than just a stranger. He was very strange. The guy didn't look strange or anything like that. He was just mysterious. As he walked up to the screened-in porch of the dope-house, Girlfriend and Olivia watched him and was checking him out in a sly way. That's when Girlfriend asked Olivia, "is that a gun on his side"? Olivia looked at the man's right hip, which was the only side of the man's body other than his back, she could see. She replied by saying to Girlfriend, "I can't tell if he's carrying a gun". What Olivia saw was just a glare that looked to her like a clip-on key chain or something like that. Olivia didn't want to hang around any longer than she had. She wanted to get the fuck away from there, so if the man did have a gun, she wouldn't be there to witness or be a part of whatever the man came there to do. Not wanting to be too conspicuous, she calmly, but hastily backed out of the driveway, drove down the hill away from the dope-house and took Girlfriend home. She didn't know what the deal was. All she knew was that something wasn't right, so she couldn't get away from the dope-house fast enough. When she got Girlfriend home, Olivia went inside with her and sat there for about fifteen minutes, but she had enough drug action for one night that she never should have been associated with, so she told Girlfriend she was going on in (going home) and would probably talk to her the next day. Everything was all good by then, as far as Olivia knew. Whatever she was feeling while she was at the dope-house, had passed, she made it home and chilled like a villain (figure of speech) the rest of the night. Not giving the night's activities a second thought, she climbed in bed after getting into a nightgown and watched TV until she fell asleep. Olivia watched soap operas in the afternoons, but before the first soap she watched came on, the news aired for thirty minutes, so when she awakened late that following morning, she just laid in bed and took it easy while she waited for the soaps to air. As she stared at the TV with her mind somewhere else, Olivia saw a house she recognized, which interested her to pay attention to what the news reporter was saying. To her surprise and fear, Olivia was overwhelmed to learn that the house shown on the news, was the dope-house she had taken Girlfriend to the night before. She was shocked to hear that two women had each been shot twice, whom were said to be the lady who owned the house (the dope-lady) and a friend (the door-girl Olivia went to high school with). After hearing the full report, Olivia jumped out of bed, grabbed some clothes to put on and got dressed. She even fell to her knees while trying to hurry and get dressed. Olivia was afraid for the dope-lady and her old class-mate, what they were going through and the terror they had to face, but just as well, she was shook up and astonished about knowing that had she not put the rush on Girlfriend to hurry with her drug transaction at the dope-house, had she and Girlfriend been in the dope-house five-to-seven minutes longer, they would have still been in the house when that guy got there. Olivia believes in fait. She believes the danger that was getting near her, was the reason she felt so uncomfortable while sitting in the dope-house that night. She believes that only by the grace of God, did she and Girlfriend get out of that house in time. Because she was very sad and felt the need to be with Girlfriend, after getting dressed, she drove to Girlfriend's house, sat and talked with her who too, was sad and in tears. What happened at the dope-house was unbelievable. The whole ordeal was a real wake-up call for Olivia. It was a really prime and important example of how drugs can and will kill and was also something she had to see and apparently, damn near be a part of to learn why it is essential for one to change all of his or her playmates and playgrounds associated with drugs, when recovering from drug addiction. The dope-lady was shot twice in the head and 'the door-girl was shot once in the back of her neck and once in the head, so the guy who peeped in the window of Olivia's car that night, was no joke. He was on a mission and he would have shot

Olivia and Girlfriend too if they had still been in that house, just as he shot the door-girl. He went there to eliminate the dope-lady, but he wasn't gonna leave any witnesses to his crime, so all Olivia could think about was how it could have been her too, who was shot. While she was at Girlfriend's house the day after the shooting, detectives arrived looking for her and Girlfriend to question them and they took her and Girlfriend to the police station to make formal statements of their knowledge of what went on at the dope-house while they were there. After the questioning, the officers took them back to Girlfriend's house. Olivia hung around there and conversated with Girlfriend for a few minutes and then she went home. She had to work the part-time job she had that evening, so she wanted to get home and unwind before going to work. This was a hell of a day for her to have to go to work. While she sat at home and contemplated whether or not she wanted to call her job to report that she wasn't coming in, the new guy she was dating called on the phone. After telling him what happened and telling him she was debating on taking off work that evening, the brother thought it would be better for Olivia to go on to work. He brought to her attention, that she would only sit at home and trip (think bad thoughts) all evening if she didn't go to work and she didn't need to do that. Olivia agreed with him and went on to work when she was supposed to be there. Actually, the brother's suggestion was good for Olivia because she got busy with her work on the job and hardly had a chance to give a thought to what had happened. About an hour and a half to two hours after her tour at work began, Olivia was interrupted by a manager on the job and was told that someone was there to talk to her. She couldn't even imagine who was there to see her and with all that had gone on, was curious, but a little anxious. After she got to the room she was directed to, two detectives were there waiting. The detectives brought along with them, a couple of mug-shot albums for her to browse through and identify anyone who looked like the guy who peeped through the window of her car the night before when the shooting occurred. At first Olivia picked out mug-shots of three different guys who most looked like the culprit. After narrowing the search down to the three pictures, the detectives asked Olivia to narrow her selection down to one of the three she had already chosen. The culprit didn't have any distinctive features or anything that Olivia noticed the night she saw him, but he had an evil aura about himself that made him unforgettable. "The guy was dressed to kill too. I mean that literally", said Olivia. She said he wore a black cap, he had on dark pants and wore an army fatigue jacket that came just past his waist. When he looked through the window on the driver's side of Olivia's car where she sat, he didn't smile, he had a gloomy tone to his voice and his eyes were devilish. "His presence was very eerie", said Olivia. She says she can still identify the feeling she felt then, when she thinks about it today, as though her encounter with the man had only happened yesterday. That's why she was able to point her finger at him without doubt when the detectives had her choose one of the three men the selection was narrowed down to. Olivia recognized the culprit when she first saw his picture and could have saved the detectives some time in their search, but she didn't point him out right away because she was just following the detective's instructions and going along with their program. When they asked her on a scale of one to ten, how sure she was that the last mug-shot she fingered, was the man she saw last at the dope-house, Olivia told them the guy was number nine on the scale. When they asked her why she was sure, but not one hundred percent certain, Olivia told them it was because the man she saw at the dope-house wore a cap. That's how sure she was that the guy she fingered in the mug-shot album, was the man she saw at the dope-lady's house and even believed he was who did the shooting that went on there. That's all the detectives needed from her at the time, but she volunteered and told them the make, model and color of the car the man was driving that night and she told the detectives what state the license plates on the man's car was from. Oh she was very helpful. She wanted the guy caught and arrested for the dope-lady and the door girl's sake, but also because (even though the man didn't see her face too well since the window on her car was rolled up) he probably remembered her car as well as she remembered his. Anyway, the detectives thanked Olivia for her cooperation and help and told her they would contact her if they had any more questions. The officers then left and Olivia got back to work. When she got off work, she was very suspicious, but careful going home. She made it there safely and was still shook up, but the brother she was dating came to see her and spent the night there with her, so all was well the rest of the night. The brother had to work the following morning, so after Olivia saw him to the door, she climbed back in bed and turned the TV on to catch the morning news and see if the news reporters had an update on the apprehending of the man suspected of the shooting at the dope-house. Sure enough, the reporters did have an update on the attempted homicide, but the shit had gotten even deeper than it already was. After a little investigating, the detectives who were on the case of the shooting, got an address for the man Olivia fingered in the mug-shots she looked at and they went to the man's home on the other side of the bridge to arrest him or take him in for questioning. It seem apparent that Olivia was one hundred percent right in fingering the shooter of the dope-lady and her door-girl since the man barricaded himself in his home when the police arrived. Either he was guilty of the shooting at the dope-house or something. The police even confiscated many weapons and drugs from the man's home after gaining entry. According to the news reporters, detectives and other officers had been at the man's house since two o'clock that morning. It was now five or six hours later and the man had still not surrendered nor had he opened the door for the officers to go in and talk with him. Finally, the stand-off ended around noon when the suspect shot himself in the head, taking his own life. Some more shit Olivia thought she would only see in the movies. She did drugs for years, had seen or heard news reports or had been told about criminal incidences that were drug related, but she had never been caught up in the mix of anything like this and didn't want to ever be again. That is why she didn't see Girlfriend again for a long time. After her close encounter with death once again, Olivia realized that even though she didn't use drugs anymore, being around them or people who used them, was as detrimental to her health as her using them was. Even though she still enjoyed kickin' it with her girlfriend, Girlfriend was one of those playmates Olivia had to stay away from. For the sake of her life and her sobriety, she didn't visit her girlfriend and seldom talked to her on the phone after the gunman committed suicide, she was careful not to be with someone while he or she was making a drug run or drug transaction and she was even skeptical about going to liquor stores. After all, alcohol is a drug, even though most people don't know that, won't admit it or justify the difference between the liquid drug and dry substance drugs. However, the square life was now appealing to Olivia, more than it ever had been. The lifestyle she use to think was boring, was now the lifestyle she wanted to live. The new guy she was dating was the right guy to get that working with too, since he didn't indulge in mind-altering chemicals, he had never been about the pimpin', he had never been arrested except for a minor traffic violation, so he didn't have a criminal record and he attended church every now and again. To boot (as an added bonus or plus), this guy was fine (good-lookin'), intelligent, hard working, humorous, and very talented. For the most part, he was cool.

Olivia had fun times with her new lover. She even fell in love with him, but no matter how much fun the two of them had together, no matter how much sex the two of them had or the fact that the brother practically lived with her, every time she assumed for one minute, hers and his relationship was as deep as she felt it was and wanted it to be, the brother would quickly, but nicely, set her straight. "I don't have a woman, I'm not anyone's man except my own and me and you are just friends", is what he would say. Even though he was nice about telling Olivia the real deal, it hurt her to hear it and she got tired of getting the same response whenever she felt their relationship had advanced. Olivia wanted this guy to move in with her permanently since he had lost his apartment by now. She wanted him to sleep with her every night and the whole nine yards, but that's not what he wanted. At the end of that year, she got her first real job with good pay working for the IRS, so in March of the following year, she moved from the apartment she was in and rented her first house on the other side of the bridge, which was where the brother was from. The brother helped Olivia move her furniture and things and even spent most nights at the house too, but that didn't change the status of his and Olivia's relationship. This guy felt if he didn't commit to a woman or live with her, he could stay away for as long as he wanted (even though he didn't) and wouldn't have to worry about getting put out of the house if things weren't the way a woman wanted them to be. He wanted his own apartment, but for now, he was getting the milk free just like Tony did, so as long as he had it like that, he wasn't going to buy the cow (make a committment) neither. Olivia was on to his game though. She vowed to herself that if he got his own apartment, that was going to be the end of his and her relationship and so it was. She was so sick of giving a guy as much of her as he wanted and her only getting what was given to her, that she said she could scream. She had never been the kind of girl who would pressure a guy to give her what she wanted or else, but she was starting to feel that she needed to be that way. "Nobody is gonna commit to me if I keep giving the milk and the beef away free, so I need to be a little bit more demanding and stronger because my ass had been and is still getting played", is what Olivia thought. She was good at playing for high stakes and not settling for less with the tricks she dated when she worked the stroll, but when it came to affairs of the heart, she was the one who always got the short end of the deal. She was finally starting to care more about what she wanted though. Olivia was tired of getting hoodwinked and bamboozled, so she decided from then on, that she would only give a guy a certain amount of time to show her what she wanted to see and to make a committment to an established relationship with her, that was more than friendship. When that time was up, she would do what she had to do. This brother's time expired about two weeks after he got his own place. Two weeks from then, Olivia moved out of the house she was renting and went to stay with her aunt and uncle. She was tired of moving from place-to-place every year, so her plan now, was to save enough money to pay down on a house she could buy. She was good friends with the brother's sisters who lived in one of the houses their mom owned and she could have stayed in the house with them, but she didn't want to seem as though she was trying to be around or near their brother, so she only stored some of her furniture in the vacant house their mom owned, which was next door to the house the two sisters lived in. She put the rest of her furniture in a small storage room that she paid rent for. Olivia stayed with her aunt and uncle for about a month, but things didn't work out too well, so she ended up doing what she really didn't want to do, renting one of the bedrooms in the house the brother's sisters lived in. She really didn't want to live with anyone except the man she chose to be with, but for what she had planned, she needed to save some money. She had grown really close to the brother's family and relatives during hers and his relationship, so she fitted in with his sisters really well and ended up staying with them for about ten months.

Not long after Olivia moved in with the brother's sisters, she met another brother at a different nightclub. Actually, she was coaxed into meeting Mark. The first time she saw him was at a nightclub, but as she and the girl she was kickin' it with was bar-hopping, they ran into Mark at another club that was only a few blocks away from the one they first saw him at. Still being as proud as she was and the lady she always tried to be, Olivia didn't come on to Mark. If a guy didn't notice and approach her, Olivia figured he wasn't that interested. "Oh well", is what she would say. Just the way her last relationship jumped off, the girl Olivia was clubbing with, introduced her to Mark and all but made them hold hands and kiss one another. She was the one who executed the introduction that turned into a three-year affair. The time Olivia gave Mark, was about as much of a relationship as the one she had with the brother she previously dated. Once again, Olivia fell in love with a man she couldn't be with the way she wanted and needed to be with a man. Mark, along with the last two men she had relationships with, wanted the pussy and whatever else they could get, but all three of them claimed they weren't ready for a serious relationship or they just lead her on for as long as they could. "Oh they loved the pussy, head (blowjobs), ass and all, but I fell so deeply in love with them and gave them what they wanted, that told them I was too weak to leave them alone. I had learned my lesson about giving up the money, so after Tony, I didn't have a dime to give the brother or Mark. Because I gave my heart though and wore it on my sleeve (sorta' speak), I kept getting played into hangin' around, even though I wasn't getting what I wanted. A meaningful relationship. That's when I really got it through my thick skull, that old saying, "just because he wants to make love, doesn't mean he loves you". "Man, that saying is so very true", Olivia admitted. Mark was helpful in moving her furniture when she found another house that she rented, he took her places and spent a lot of nights with her, but she wasn't the one he wanted to live with or marry. Instead, he ended up marrying a woman whom he had been dating the entire time he dated Olivia. The woman even lived two street blocks over from the street Olivia lived on. Three weeks before Mark married this woman, he moved in with Olivia and stayed with her for five days or a week at best. The last day he was there, Mark waited until Olivia got to work that morning and called her three hours later to tell her he was going to be with the other woman. The news he gave Olivia devastated her badly. Between that day and the day she found out he was married, she didn't see or hear from him. Olivia figured he had married the woman during that time because he had mentioned a couple of times before he came to stay with her, that the woman wanted him to marry her, but Olivia didn't think he was gonna do it. She was surprised when her doorbell rang one night and it was Mark at the door who dropped by for a visit. Olivia let him in because it was a habit she had not broken yet, but also because she wanted to find out what was up with him. As he had always done, Mark came in and got right down to business, caressing Olivia's ass and breast as he kissed and held her. Olivia knew something wasn't right, so she had guards up that Mark didn't even know she had, since she had always been so weak for him. Olivia had never resisted Mark when he wanted to make love to her or just visit, so Mark expected her to give up the pussy whenever he wanted it. It wasn't like that this night though. Olivia wanted to conversate with Mark, to find out any major changes he had made, so she wasn't gonna let him go up in her until she knew what they were. Trying to play it cool, she didn't question him with force and he didn't fondle her with force. As Olivia questioned him, Mark was persistently aggressive though, in trying to go up in her, but Olivia kindly kept him from going too far. She didn't mind the kissing, touching, bumping and grinding, but she was determined not to give up the pussy to him again, until she knew what was really going on. Finally, two hours had gone by when Mark had either gotten tired of trying, ran out of time or realized he didn't have nothin' comin'. With his pants still on, he got up from Olivia's bed, put on his shirt and shoes and then told Olivia he did have something to tell her. That's when he confessed that he had gotten married. Olivia had a really strong intuition anyway, that he had. It turned out that she didn't see a ring on the newlywed's finger because he had taken it off in the bathroom when he first arrived and he put it in his pocket. When she asked Mark what he was doing at her house if he loved the woman whom he was now married to, Mark's answer was that he couldn't help it that he enjoyed making love to her and that he just wanted to do it one more time. That didn't make sense to Olivia. She was glad she didn't give up the pussy to him because she would have felt like a fool afterwards and she would have felt more used than she already did. She didn't trip with him though. After his confession and after he and Olivia conversated about him being married, Olivia congratulated Mark and wished him good luck as she saw him to the door. That was the end of the episode of her life with him. For some reason though, she was relieved after she let Mark out the door. She wasn't angry nor was she sad. It was as though she had closed one door so another could be opened and for that, she was glad because she was then able to move on.

Olivia still wanted to have lots of money with or without a man in her life, but just as most women were when they were teenagers, from the time she started fuckin', she dreamed of marrying the guy she loved, buying a nice home, having a couple of children and living happily ever after. Unfortunately, it usually don't work out that way, at least not at first. With all the bullshit games some people play, one finds him or herself having to search long and hard for that special someone. Sometimes it takes half of a person's life to find the right mate. Olivia had consecutively gone from man-to-man as though she were a traveler going from flight-to-flight to get to her destination. It was rough for her, but thank goodness she took the chance and was patient with a beautiful, but somewhat confused man whom she met at the end of hers and Mark's relationship and is now married to. Olivia invested three years in this man before they were married. The first year and a half, the two of them dated one another, but knowing that Olivia had fallen in love with him and him not wanting to lose her, this man moved into her home and stayed the next two years. Even though he was somewhat of a street person, he tried to keep a nine-to-five job. He grew up in church, so he had a good up-bringing with religious beliefs also. Two good and important qualities that Olivia now looked for in a man. Therefore, he understood when Olivia told him that neither of them could get the blessings that may have been in-stored for them, while living together in sin. The two of them had lived together for a year and a half by this time. Being the man he is, this guy knew it was wrong to shack-up, but also knew how tired Olivia was from enduring all the things she had with him, so he felt she deserved more and did right by her in asking her to marry him. Olivia was willing to let him go if he wasn't ready for marriage or didn't want to marry her, but that's not what he wanted. By this time, she had grown up quite a bit and after her relationship with Mark, promised herself that she would not hang on to or try and be with someone who wasn't trying to get with or be about her. This time though, she had something with this man that she couldn't have with the other men she dated. A man who loves her and cares about who she is and what she wants out of life. Now that everyone has grown up, those other men try to steal (get Olivia back), but they had their chances and neither of them saw in her what her new husband sees in her. That is one of the reasons they can't touch what she has with him. Olivia loves her husband, is very much in love with him and believes he is the man whom will finally make her teenage dreams and fantasies come true.

Now that she has the man she hopes to spend the rest of her life with, Olivia is able to focus more on getting financially established. As she once heard a wise man named Ice-T say, "even though one is or was of the pimp and whoe game or whatever his or her hustle is or was, there are other financial levels one can explore". Olivia no longer classifies herself as a whoe. "I used to be a whoe, but not because I just like being a whoe, selling pussy or other sex or that I just like giving a man my money. I was whoeing because of my love for money at first. Then I did it because it had to be that way when I was with Bernard, whether I wanted it to be or not", she explained. She had always been fairly intelligent, book-wise. She just got off track and got caught up in the fast lane and drugs. Since she had come to her senses after she finally left Bernard in Alaska and more so since her second drug treatment program, Olivia utilized her brain and the intelligence she had, in trying to fulfill her desire for money the legit way. After organizing a rental agency in the year nineteen ninety-four, she didn't have the capital she needed nor did she have the help and resources the business needed to expand, so she put the business on hold in the year nineteen ninety-six, organized and operated a cleaning service. While both businesses got off the ground and made her a little money, Olivia still had to survive by working a job for someone elses company too, so she couldn't put all the work and effort she needed to put into her own businesses, to make them as successful as they could have been. That's why she ended up putting the cleaning service on hold as well. She won't let that stop her though. Today, she continues the life-long strive to have those riches and fine things she first dreamed of when she was a child sitting on the porch of her home, counting the coins she was able to collect. Tired of the struggle because she left home sooner than she should have and put herself through all the things she did, Olivia keeps on going, determined to financially get where she wants to be or die trying. For then, she will have succeeded in trying, than to have failed because she gave up.

Written By:

**Jerri L. Smith**

## About the Author

The author of this work is a 42 year old Afro American currently in the telecommunications business in the state of Texas. She is to this day, living a drug-free life, with peace of mine and solitude, which has allowed her to finish this work and pursue her ideas for fictional work that she hopes will be as entertaining as the contents of this novel.

Made in the USA
Las Vegas, NV
10 March 2022

45429596R00121